Sweet Nothings

ALSO BY KIM LAW

Caught on Camera (The Davenports)

Sugar Springs

Ex on the Beach

Sweet Nothings

A Sugar Springs Novel

KIM LAW

Montlake
Romance

Printed in the United States of America.

Published by Montlake Romance, Seattle

www.apub.com

ISBN-13: 9781477809587
ISBN-10: 1477809589
Library of Congress Number: 2013907479

To everyone who has lost loved ones of the furry variety.
We lost one of our dogs during the writing of this book,
and it left a new scar in my heart.
We miss you, Blackjack.

Chapter One

Joanie Bigbee checked the display and the backup stock of the pink- and red-topped cakes one last time to make sure everything was ready to go. Then she stared out at Sugar Springs High School as if the force of her concentration alone would make the doors burst open and the kids flood out. It was Valentine's Day, so what better way to kick off her new business, Cakes-a-GoGo, than by taking advantage of teenage hormones and the need to express their love? Or lust?

"A cupcake for your sweetheart" seemed like the perfect plan to her.

She'd have only fifteen minutes before the break was over and everyone returned to their last class of the day. After that, she'd be off, turning her converted Volkswagen van toward Main Street to catch locals and tourists in their small Tennessee town who might also be in need of a sweet dessert. She ran her hands down the sides of her skirt and sucked in a deep breath.

"What are you so nervous about?" Destinee asked. She was Joanie's only employee so far. The girl worked afternoons as part of the high school's school-to-work program. "You don't get stressed."

"It's my first day. I have a right to be a little nervous."

The girl rolled her eyes and let out a long, dramatic sigh. "It is not your first day. We've been open for two weeks now. If we weren't, I wouldn't be getting outta school early every day."

"Ah, so you're just using me?" Joanie teased as she peered out the open order window. She was ready to kick this party off.

Destinee was right—the actual business had been open for two weeks—but today was the inaugural trip for the cupcake van, thus making the full vision a reality. And yes, Joanie was nervous. It was rare, but for some reason Cakes-a-GoGo seemed to mean more to her than past ventures.

"I thought you were working for me because you're interested in learning about running your own business," Joanie added. "Not simply to get out of school early."

Destinee produced a noncommittal shrug in a way only teenage girls were capable of doing. "Sure. And the fact that you need the help. You couldn't handle everything yourself."

The smile threatening at Joanie's lips remained hidden. Destinee had come into the space she'd rented on the square about a month ago as word had gotten out that Joanie had sold her beauty salon and would soon be opening a cupcake store in the postage stamp–size tourist town.

The girl had done her best—both then and since—to hide her enthusiasm for being a part of seeing a business go from the ground up. Apparently it was *uncool* to be excited about working. But she'd failed in keeping her exuberance under wraps. Joanie had seen it, as well as recognized a bit of herself in the girl.

There were services and shops that needed to exist, and if no one else was going to make it happen, then she would do it. She'd started and sold more local businesses in her thirty-two years than most people ever thought about. All of them thriving under their current ownership today.

"The doors just opened," Destinee squeaked, bouncing up on her toes. Heightened energy vibrated through them both.

With a wide smile and a straightening of her shoulders, Joanie reached to the back of the van and flipped the two switches that would turn on the lighted sign atop the vehicle as well as pump sixties dance music through the outer speakers. Cakes-a-GoGo was open for business.

Fifteen minutes later, Joanie flipped off the lights and music and slumped back against the counter as if her body had been beaten continuously since the school doors had opened. She was so happy not to be a teenager with all those hormones and emotions running rampant through her.

"That was exhausting," she moaned. "I've no idea how you go in there every day around all that."

"Girl," Destinee began, "you ain't that old. You hung in." A gleam sparkled in the teen's dark eyes as she began to wipe down the counter where more than one cake had ended up top down.

"I feel like we did nothing but throw cupcakes out the window for a solid fifteen minutes," Joanie said. "Like we were being attacked and the cakes were our only weapons. Did we actually manage to collect money or was that purely a fight we just lost?"

Laughter rolled from the teen as she flipped open the cash box and waved her hand with a flourish over the mound of bills. "Poor Joanie. If you're thinking of doing this every week, you'd better start eating a heartier breakfast. It won't get any easier."

"I believe that." She picked up one of the few remaining cupcakes and peeled the paper down to take a bite. "Or lay off the sugar. Nothing like a sugar crash when you need the energy to handle a hundred kids."

The two of them chuckled together and celebrated their mini success as they cleaned up the van, then they headed back to the shop to replenish their stock.

As she pulled into the space reserved for her, she noticed a shiny red, *enormous* four-door pickup parked in front of the real estate office a few storefronts down. She'd seen a similar truck in town a few weeks back, right around Christmas, and couldn't help but wonder if this one was driven by the same man.

A man who'd set her engine on purr the instant she'd met him.

Not that she would do anything about it if it was him. He'd practically had "homebody" stamped across his forehead. She didn't get involved with men looking to settle down. Period.

Before she could call around to find out who it was, her cell phone rang. Glancing at the display, she saw the number for the nursing home where her grandmother had been living the last three years.

She tossed Destinee her keys. "Go on in and grab the boxes in the back. I need to take this."

Destinee headed off to refill the van while Joanie slid her finger along the screen to answer. It would be one of two things. Either her ailing grandmother had finally passed, or they were calling about the bill again.

"Hello." Joanie tried to keep a smile on her face, knowing anyone peeking out the surrounding storefronts might be watching her. Any sign of a frown could easily blow up into a rumor that would take on a life of its own. It was part of the fun of living there, seeing what kind of gossip spread on any given day.

"Ms. Bigbee," an efficient, female voice answered. "This is Gloria Williams, billing coordinator at Elm Hill Nursing Community."

Joanie's shoulders sunk. It was about the bill.

The insurance payment along with what she managed to send every month hadn't been covering things for a while now, and she knew it. She'd assured them at the beginning of the year that things would turn around as soon as she had the new business stable. If only they'd give her a little more time.

Ms. Williams explained how the home had to turn a profit or their owners would shut them down, then followed with, "We hate to do this, but we're putting you on notice."

Joanie turned her back to the street and held her breath. She had no other way to take care of GiGi if she got kicked out.

"You have two months, Ms. Bigbee. Get caught up on your bill, or your grandmother will have to find a new place to live."

Joanie's breath whispered out from between tense lips. "I understand, Ms. Williams. I'll take care of it."

Though she wasn't sure she could accomplish it in two months.

Joanie disconnected and pressed the fingertips of one hand to her forehead, feeling a rare headache coming on. She'd been planning to sell GiGi's place for a while now to cover expenses, but the house needed to be remodeled before it could be sold. It was so outdated, she couldn't imagine anyone willing to pay a decent price for it in its current shape.

The funds to improve it were limited, as well.

She let out another tense breath and scrolled through her contacts hoping she'd stored the number of the contractor she'd previously discussed renovations with. Might as well find out how much the work was going to cost her.

Locating the number, she said a silent hooray that she wouldn't have to figure out where she'd stashed the man's business card, and pushed the button to place the call. Only when it started ringing did she remember that he'd left her a message over two weeks ago which she'd forgotten to listen to.

As she waited for the phone to be answered, she tossed one last glance over at the red pickup, then headed into the shop so no one walking by would overhear.

Destinee passed her on her way out, arms loaded with the remainder of the cupcakes.

Three minutes later, Joanie hung up just as Destinee came back into the store. There was no way she could afford the repairs.

Which put her back at square one. Sell the house for little more than nothing, or bring GiGi home.

Neither was a viable solution.

"I swear," Destinee said, her voice low and humming with energy that grabbed Joanie's attention. "That man is *hot*. Ms. Lee Ann did fine when she snagged him." Destinee was facing the window, hands propped on her rounded hips, and Joanie followed her gaze across the street.

The same nervousness she'd felt before the high school doors had burst open fluttered back through her. That was not her best friend's fiancé.

"That isn't Cody, D. That's his brother, Nick."

Wide eyes turned her way. "There are two of them?"

Joanie nodded, not taking her eyes off Nick, and forcing herself not to wipe her palms down the sides of her skirt again. Why the man made her nervous, she had no idea. She'd taken in all six-foot-four of his lean, taut, manual labor–created muscles when they'd met at Christmas, and she hadn't been nervous then.

She'd been turned on, yes. But not nervous.

And yes, it had been unnerving to be turned on by someone who looked identical to her friend's fiancé, even when said fiancé did nothing for her but provide an attractive view. But while unnerving, only a dead person could keep from ogling a hunk of man like that.

Only, along with her appreciation for his very fine form, she felt something new stirring inside her this time.

Something that seemed to wake from a long hibernation and jabbed at her from the inside as if screaming, *Me! Me! Let me have him!*

It disturbed her even more when she had a quick flash of the man her mother had run off with on Joanie's thirteenth birthday. She hadn't thought about him in years. Bill had been an out-of-towner, too. Just like Nick. And also in construction. As well as friendly, what she'd thought of at the time as genuinely nice, and a total cutie.

Strike, strike, strike.

Nick was hot, but he was off-limits.

She wasn't her mother and she would never fall victim to a man, no matter how bad her insides flamed at the sight of one. And she certainly wouldn't fall victim to the Bigbee Curse.

Nick lifted his gaze from the paper he held in his hand and scanned the street before him, then spied her van out front. He swept a hand through his dark hair, pushing it off his forehead, and turned in their direction. The jabbing inside her intensified.

"He's coming over here," Destinee whispered.

Blood rushed through Joanie so rapidly she worried she'd fall over where she stood. Instead, she shook her arms and rolled her shoulders as if getting ready to go into battle. Whatever was going on inside her, she could put a stop to it. She'd seen plenty of good-looking men in her years. She'd even slept with a few of them. There was no reason this particular one was going to get to her.

"He probably wants a cupcake," she stated. "Let's meet him outside since they're all in the van."

Joanie pushed open the door as he reached the sidewalk, and couldn't help but smile as they made eye contact. *Dang*, he was fine.

Too bad she couldn't have just one itsy-bitsy taste to put out the fire he lit.

Nick Dalton paused with one foot on the sidewalk and stared at the woman before him. Joanie Bigbee had pale blond hair in wild ringlets bouncing all around her head . . . with light pink–colored ends. She wore a fuzzy sweater matching the color in her hair, a narrow, *very* short skirt in a similar pink, and completing her outfit were white tights over nicely toned thighs and yellow go-go boots up to her knees.

He scanned her all the way to the bottom of the chunky heels, blinked to make sure he was seeing correctly, then back up to the wide smile beaming at him.

She was a fantasy come to life.

And the smile? It almost made him embarrass himself on the spot.

Hell, she'd looked fairly normal when he'd met her at Cody and Lee Ann's Christmas dinner a couple months ago. Sexy, but normal. She'd been charming and fun and they'd tossed out the innocent flirt or two, but he hadn't had the urge to drag her to the ground and unwrap her like a present.

Today he did.

Today he was pretty sure he would if he could figure out how.

"Joanie?" he finally croaked out. "Umm . . ."

He sounded like an idiot.

Light laughter floated through his foggy brain and he felt himself smile in return. That's all, just standing there like a dolt, smiling for all he was worth.

A movement at her side caught his attention and he forced himself to look away from her. A young, cocoa-skinned girl with hips that would one day drive men wild stood there taking him in with a look on her face that said she knew exactly what he was thinking. She glanced from him to Joanie, then back at him.

"I think he likes the boots, Jo," the girl said.

I think he likes everything, he thought.

He had to get a grip. Forcing himself to glance at anything but Joanie in the hopes that blood would once again make it to his brain, his gaze landed on the van—which was the reason he'd come over in the first place.

It was an old Volkswagen model, and though it'd had extensive work to turn it into what appeared to be a traveling cupcake stand, it still looked like it belonged in the sixties. The aged yellow of the top and bottom panels appeared to be the original color, and the hand-painted flowers and cupcakes dotted all over the outside screamed *groovy*. It was one of the coolest things he'd ever seen.

"Did you come over for a cupcake, Nick?" Joanie's words jerked him back to her, and he gave her another once-over before remembering that yes, in fact, he had come over for a cupcake.

"Looked appealing." He nodded, then noticed the unlit OPEN sign in the store window behind her. The van was also boarded up tight. "Are you not open for business? I could come back."

Escaping might be best. He hadn't come to Sugar Springs to hook up with anyone. He had priorities. Get to know Cody and his girls. Open a new branch of his company. And now, find a place to stay.

When he'd spent a week in town before Christmas, he'd seen a lot of potential for business there. It was a thriving little tourist town, and had some amazing neoclassical architecture details in its historic homes. He wanted to get his hands on a few of those houses.

To add to the charm, Sugar Springs was situated at the base of Great Smoky Mountains National Park. Everything about the town was gorgeous. With the right improvements, traffic would pick up even more as people headed in and out of the park.

He snuck another peek at Joanie's legs and those boots, thinking about the weeks ahead. Focusing on business first didn't necessarily mean he had to be a monk.

A frustrated sigh pulled his attention to the young girl as she held up her hands in a sign of irritation and headed between them to the van. "Yes, we are open," she said, her words drawn out in teenage angst. "You two stand there gawking at each other. I'll get everything set up."

The words jolted Joanie, and Nick realized she'd been staring at him, same as he'd been doing to her. He couldn't help the grin that once again covered his face.

Interesting. Maybe he *would* ask her out. Why not have a little fun while here?

Joanie jumped into action and disappeared into the van behind the girl, taking her legs with her, and his heart gave a momentary protest but then settled down to function as it was supposed to. Slow and steady. A dependable life force. Not the raging bull it had been since she'd walked out the door.

It gave him the chance to remind himself that whether she was cute or not, he was not in the market for a woman. Especially not someone like her. He preferred the more traditional. Not go-go boots, pink hair, and a cupcake van.

He shook his head, hoping to clear the idea from his mind.

His goal here was to further the connection with the brother he'd only recently learned about, and to hopefully find their still-missing third brother. He wanted to get to know them. They were his family now.

Then he could use his company as a reason to come back to visit on a regular basis.

And though he did enjoy a nice date with a fun woman, dating was *not* a priority. He had to remember that.

The order window in front of him popped open and Joanie's smiling face beamed down at him. Her hair bounced around, doing its own thing, and he had the vague thought that if he wasn't careful, his priorities could easily be shot to hell.

"What'll you have?" she asked. Gone was her seeming fixation on him. She was now all about the cupcakes. She flipped out a menu of choices and it hung from a metal arm to the side of the open window. "Our special this week, to celebrate Valentine's Day, is cherry chip. I'm calling it Cupid's Love. You can get it with either pink . . ." one hand flicked the pink tips of her hair, "or red icing. We also have—"

"Pink." The word shot out as if it had been yanked from the back of his throat, and her eyes locked with his for a brief moment. "I want pink," he reiterated.

A slight smile danced across her lips and his blood inched up a degree.

He took in the pink in her hair and the matching sweater hugging her body, and his heart once again lost its rhythm. Yes, he wanted pink. And what the hell was that about?

He dated all the time, enjoyed going out with plenty of women. No one got him so flustered that he practically swallowed his tongue just from talking to her.

"Then pink it shall be." She plucked out a fat cupcake with icing piled high and tiny red hearts sprinkled on top, grabbed a couple napkins, and handed it all to him. "It's on the house, big guy. Now tell me, what brings you back to town so soon?"

He would have thought she'd heard from Lee Ann or Cody that he was coming.

Before he could answer, music blared from the speakers above him, making him take an involuntary step back. When he did, he glanced at the top of the van, the sign now flashing in lights. Apparently the teenager was trying to tell him something. Move on. Quit ogling the owner.

Joanie laughed with honest happiness, the sound warming him deep inside, and he decided that cupcakes were going to be one of his favorite things in the coming weeks.

"I'll come out and we can talk," she said, before turning to the girl. "There are customers heading this way. Can you handle them?"

"Sure thing, boss. Just take it outside."

Another light trill of laughter came from Joanie, and Nick caught himself doing that stupid grin thing again. He really had to stop that.

She bounced out of the van as people trickled over from nearby stores to get their own dessert, and he followed until they stood a few feet to the side of the foot traffic.

"The first day of a new venture is pretty exciting," she said. Her exuberance was contagious.

"So this is day one?" That must explain the outfit. She had to be freezing in that skirt.

"First day for the van, yes. The store's been open for two weeks, though we didn't do a big grand-opening thing." She motioned to the store window behind her that matched the decor of the van. "I wanted to wait until the van was ready. Eat your cupcake, Nick." She eyed the dessert he hadn't yet tasted. "You'll make my customers think it isn't any good."

He did as instructed, biting into the decadent cake, then shot her a look as his taste buds took hold. It was amazing. She laughed out loud again, and he couldn't help but catch sight as several of the men who were in line turned to watch her, as well. That's when he realized that nearly all the customers were men. One guess as to what had pulled them outside.

"So tell me what brings you back so soon," she said. "Visiting Cody, I assume?"

He nodded and took another bite, pretty sure some of the pink icing had landed on his nose. Wiping at himself with a napkin, he swallowed and said, "I'm actually hoping to open a branch of my company here. And yeah, I want to spend time with Cody and the twins. So I took a few weeks—four, maybe six—to come check it out, see what I could get going."

Captivating eyes, the color of storm clouds on a late-summer day, widened. "That's a long visit. You staying with Cody?"

Nick nodded and thought about the cramped one-bedroom that wasn't big enough for one of them, much less two. Wanting to set a good example for their teenagers, Cody and Lee Ann had agreed to maintain separate residences until they married. "Until the real estate agent can find me something else. She'd had a place lined up but I just found out that it fell through."

Joanie gave him a teasing shake of her head. "You're going to be walking all over each other."

"Tell me about it. When Boss is there, we practically have to shuffle to the side just to walk through the same room." His brother had a Great Dane who was as big as them. Boss stayed with Lee Ann and the girls most of the time now, but when Nick had visited before Christmas, it had been the two of them and the dog, all in the five-hundred-square-foot space. Not comfortable.

"So you just up and came here for a few weeks?" she asked. Her features took on an interesting gleam as she studied him. "Feels like a big change for somebody like you."

Nick raised his eyebrows. "People change. Didn't you own a salon two months ago?"

A gorgeous smile stole across her face. "Yes, but that's me. It's who I am. I flip businesses and move on. I never stick to one thing for long." She reached out and swiped a bit of frosting from his cupcake. "I wouldn't think you'd be comfortable not having your routine around. Weeks in a new place without so much as a place to stay?" She shook her head, making *tsking* noises with her teasing. "Seems out of character."

The comment felt insulting, maybe because it was so true. This quick move was very much unlike him. He was used to his life. He liked it. He'd worked hard for it.

But he wanted to get to know his family.

Opening a new office wasn't unheard of. He already had one just outside of Jackson and another in Columbia. But yeah, normally he moved a little slower before hanging a shingle. Took a longer time researching. He made sure he had all the facts, and then he pounced. Then he wouldn't stop until he got what he wanted.

He wasn't about to tell Joanie she'd pegged him so quickly, though. "You've met me for all of one day, sweetness. Not sure you could know from that what does and doesn't fit me."

She snorted then, her glorious laughter once again pulling the other men's attention, and he had the urge to step in between them and her. Before he could, she reached up and wiped at his nose—yes, he'd been wearing pink icing—and he couldn't help but turn a smug look to all eyes watching them. He may be wearing icing, but the hottie in the go-go boots who smelled like cherry pie had just touched *him*.

"I met you for only one day, yes," she began as she wiped her fingers off on one of his napkins, then tossed a wave at the latest arrival to her van. "But you were wearing an apron and baking cookies when I first saw you. That strikes me more as someone who's settled nicely into his life. Has a routine and probably a dog or two. Won't you miss it?"

Joanie grinned again at the giant of a man in front of her who was trying hard to look as if she hadn't nailed him so perfectly. Standing there, pretending he had no issues stepping outside his comfort zone. He was a homebody if ever she'd seen one. A routine, a pattern. He likely took every woman he asked out to the same restaurant for their first dates. The man didn't take weeks-long trips away from his life.

Getting here and realizing his rental plans had been thwarted had to be twisting his stomach into knots. But he did a good job of hiding it.

"I don't have dogs," he finally answered. "And I'm perfectly fine spending a few weeks here. It's a great town."

The cold wind whipped up her skirt and she fought a shiver, but heated up as she watched his long-enough-to-dig-your-fingers-into hair whip in the gust of air. She couldn't help but think he grew cuter the more he denied her charges.

"As long as you can find a place to stay, right? That change in plans must be bugging you."

His dark eyes narrowed slightly, and she almost giggled at the perturbed look. He was fun to tease.

"Wait." She held up a hand, a thought hitting her like a lightning bolt, then glanced down the road at his truck and the magnetic sign she now noticed slapped on the side of the door: DALTON CONSTRUCTION. "You're looking for work here? You don't have anything lined up already?"

He shook his head. "Just got into town last night. Once I get settled I'll begin checking out the potential. We specialize in renovations, but we do new construction and general contractor work, too. The latter, mostly out of our two branch offices. I'm hoping a mix of work might be available here."

Could the solution be that simple? It almost seemed too easy.

But she had to ask.

"How about if I give you a job?" she carefully suggested, mentally crossing her fingers. "*And* a place to live?"

It wouldn't be the best place in the world to live, but it would be free. Surely that would get her a nice discount on the work.

"What . . . exactly did you have in mind?" He spoke the words carefully, and Joanie couldn't help but picture the big man moving into her small space in the house she rented two streets over. That hadn't been the idea, but at his slow-worded question, the picture popped to the forefront. The way he seemed to take in her whole body at once gave her the notion he was thinking the same thing.

She tried to laugh off the thought, but the sound got stuck in her throat. The man was still making her nervous, and the sudden idea of him being so close, even living at her grandmother's house, set her body on edge. Did she really want him underfoot as she cleaned out years' worth of living?

But what other choice did she have?

If she didn't come up with the money, GiGi would move in with her. Then she'd be forced to spend more time taking care of the woman than she did her own business.

As harsh as that felt, Joanie had no apologies for her feelings. Her relationship with GiGi had been cemented years ago. They were family, but pretty much in name only. The two of them simply could not get along.

She pushed the thoughts away, refusing to dwell on the past. She may not want GiGi to move in with her, but she *could* make sure the woman was taken care of.

"My grandmother's house needs some renovations and I can't afford the full cost of the work," she finally said, then shrugged one shoulder and glanced toward the customers waiting in line, shame overtaking her that she was asking a virtual stranger for what felt like a favor. "I can get a loan from the bank, but not for the full amount. I thought . . ."

She paused, grateful when he lessened her embarrassment by finishing her sentence. "You thought I could live there and do the work for you?" he asked.

When she looked back at him and nodded, his solid, brown eyes drilled into hers.

"It's not out of the question," he confirmed. "What terms were you thinking?"

A trade of the occasional roll in the hay came to mind but she quickly pushed the idea away. He might light her fuse, but it stopped there.

"I was thinking . . . rent for labor?" No way would he go for that, his labor alone would be worth far more than the cost of a rental in the small town. But she was a businesswoman if nothing else. Might as well shoot for the moon.

"Congrats on your new business, Jo." Brian Marshall, an old friend who was part owner of the Sugar Springs Diner, stepped over and interrupted the conversation. He held up half of a chocolate cupcake as he scrutinized Nick. "Though with the way these taste, you're going to fatten us all up."

Her laugh came honest and easy, her nerves lifting. She and Brian had hung out together over the years, fun only, and he never made her nervous. He was a good friend. She teasingly ran her gaze over his fine form. "That would be a real shame, Brian." She winked. "I'll be sure to cut you off if I see things getting out of hand."

She caught a glimpse of a woman farther on down the sidewalk, checking Nick out. Gina Gregory. Gina had been a customer of Joanie's when she'd owned the salon. The woman always scouted out any new man potential who showed up in town.

"I guess that's all I can ask," Brian said, pulling Joanie's attention back. A heavy arm came around her and scooped her to his side, and she slid her own around his waist. The tight hold and the way he was staring down Nick made her wonder what was going on inside his head. She had no thoughts that Brian could be jealous. It was more like a big brother checking out the man currently holding her attention captive.

He gave a jerk of his chin in greeting. "Brian Marshall. You must be Dalton's brother."

"Must be." The two eyed each other but Nick didn't bother introducing himself. There was zero chance Brian didn't know his name anyway since the last time Nick had been in town he'd gotten mixed up in gossip involving Brian's sister. The two had apparently hung out at the local honky-tonk, the Bungalow, one night and had gotten *quite* friendly on the dance floor.

"How do you know our Joanie, here?" Brian asked, his arm remaining tight around her shoulders. He was beginning to get on her nerves. She could take care of herself. Always had.

Nick smiled. It was not the friendly look of a man pleased to meet another. "She and I just made a deal." His voice took on a deeper, somewhat challenging tone. "I'll be moving into her house just as soon as we finalize the time."

Chapter Two

Joanie walked through the musty living room of GiGi's house and sneezed as dust wafted up and tickled her nose. She really should have come over and cleaned before Nick moved in, but after the testosterone thumping between Brian and him the afternoon before, he'd convinced her to let him move in this morning, leaving her no time to spruce up the place. Not that she'd wanted to clean anyway.

And certainly not at this ungodly hour.

She smacked a hand against the back of a cushioned chair, then grimaced as a puff of dust rose in the air. She groaned. What kind of person let someone move into a place like this? Not to mention the two of them had yet to discuss the work that needed to be done. Nick would probably take one look and bolt.

At the sound of his truck crunching across the gravel driveway, she headed to the front porch and stepped out. The early-morning sun hit his windshield just perfectly to keep her from being able to see him through the glass, but she could make out something fuzzy and orange filling up the passenger's side dash. What in the world?

He turned the truck off and silence settled over the quiet country setting, putting her in an even worse mood. All this quiet made her remember how much she'd once hated living outside the city limits. There had never been anyone around to play with and nothing to do. She'd lived there with her grandparents and mother. Pepaw had run off when she'd been eight, her mother when she'd been thirteen.

The driver's side door of the truck opened and two booted feet stepped out. Then the orange thing moved and in the next instant a huge cat plopped down on the ground beside him.

The man came with a cat?

She crossed her arms over her chest and scowled. Of course he came with a cat. He was a nester.

Having a cat was even worse than a dog.

He shoved the door closed as she headed off the porch and moved in his direction, fighting the yawn trying to escape. She'd give an arm for a good cup of coffee.

"I see you found the place." She attempted to make her voice polite, but it was barely seven in the morning. She should still be in bed sleeping.

As her feet left the last step, she finally caught full sight of him, and as it had yesterday, her breath stuck in her throat. Geez, the man wasn't subtle in his looks.

A long-sleeved flannel shirt covered his wide chest and shoulders this morning, and his hair looked as if it'd just come from the shower. Her fingers itched to mess it up. After she got more sleep.

In his left hand was a large insulated cup. The kind that routinely held coffee. She might have to beg.

"Your directions were good." His deep voice set her lower stomach on agitation. "Plus, it's not like there's much around here that would be hard to find."

"Isn't that the truth?" she grumbled. She actually loved Sugar Springs, but before ten in the morning, she rarely loved anything. She turned and headed back to the house. "Let me show you the place."

The cat streaked past her and she jumped, then muttered an unlady-like word under her breath. Nick came up behind her and put a hand on her elbow. He leaned in, one side of his mouth lifting slightly. "Not a morning person, Jo?"

She narrowed her eyes at him. "Who wants to move into a place at this ungodly hour?"

His partial smile went to full bloom and her head went a little light. "I've been up since five, darlin'. I drove up into the mountains. It was a beautiful sunrise."

"Oh my God. You're one of those people."

His perkiness, along with the tempting aroma of the coffee, made her head throb. She turned and headed into the house. When she opened the door, the orange fluff shot in before her.

"And I can't believe you come with a cat," she said.

He chuckled behind her. "I can't believe you're the same person who was charming half the town into cupcakes yesterday afternoon."

She turned loose the screen door and it smacked shut behind her, leaving him to find his own way in. Once he did, he stopped in the middle of the dingy-brown carpeted floor and simply stared. She turned from him, not wanting to see the expression on his face. He was going to back out of their deal, she was certain of it. Who could blame him? The place hadn't been livable when GiGi had last been there, and it certainly wasn't now.

Not to mention it looked like a horror story out of the early 1900s.

"I'm sorry—" "Wow." They both spoke at the same time. The shock in his voice managed to pull her back to him. Embarrassment spread over her features that she'd let him see the place like this.

"I should have insisted you not move in until I at least got the place cleaned up."

He waved her words off before moving through the living space into the spacious kitchen. Once there, he turned in a large circle, taking in the room full of plain wood cabinets, the yellowed wallpaper with the burned spot on the wall behind the stove, the equally dated kitchen table, and the many boxes filling the space of the back bay window. The wall adjoining the utility room looked as if it might come crashing down any second.

"You can leave now and I'll call someone to come clean. We can try this another day."

"No," he said. "This is fine. I can clean, no problem."

"You're going to clean the house?"

He shot her an odd look. "A little elbow grease and it'll be good as new. No big deal."

If the man wanted to clean her house, who was she to stop him? She grunted, knowing she was beyond unpleasant, but unable to do more than silently acknowledge the fact.

Then she stood there, taking in the house that had seen only the most rudimentary of renovations—*four decades ago*—as she listened to his footsteps wander throughout the rest of the place. She wished she knew what he saw when he looked at it. As his booted feet sounded up the stairs, she wondered if he could tell she was the one everyone had once felt sorry for.

Poor thing, her own mother left her when she was only a teenager, and she and her grandmother were left to make ends meet in that falling-down place.

"The house is really in great shape," he called down from an upstairs room.

Her jaw fell open. The man was delusional.

She made her way up the stairs, which had more than one "soft spot," avoiding the cat who once again ran between her feet, and crossed to stand at Nick's side. He'd stopped in the room that had once been hers.

"GiGi never put anything into remodeling this heap. What hasn't already fallen down is well on its way."

"There are some issues, yes, but the main structure is good. And it's got such history. It's gorgeous."

"It's a two-story box just waiting for a heavy enough wind to come knock it down." She pointed to a spot in the corner of the room that had water stains all the way down the wall. "The roof has been leaking since I lived here."

"We can fix the roof. We can fix the sheeting that's no doubt weakened from the leak." He walked to the back window and looked out over the yard. "Imagine what that yard will look like filled with the right landscaping."

She stepped to his side, peeked at the cup he was carrying, and wondered if it didn't hold more than coffee, then tried to see the backyard through fresh eyes.

It was large. That could be beneficial. It was flat. There was a scraggly spot that had once been a butterfly garden. Some random large rocks where she'd played as a child, imagining them as a fortress or throne, but more often as a stove and tabletops where she'd cook a meal for her pretend guests. She looked straight down. One side of the back porch roof had totally collapsed into the screened-in room.

"You're out of your mind," she muttered.

Brown eyes cut down at her. He studied her for a long time, long enough to make her twitch and look away, then passed his cup over to her.

The smell of coffee hit her nose and she looked up at him in surprise.

"Clearly you need it more than me," he said. "Take it, and then tell me what you really see when you look at this place. Not what you saw in the past, or what shape it's in now, but close your eyes and tell me what you see."

She shook her head, but did take the coffee. "I see exactly what's here. It's a falling-down mess, out in the middle of nowhere, and no one will ever want it."

"Joanie, it's three miles outside of town. That is not out in the middle of nowhere."

"For a kid it is. It's a lonely place."

"Not if it's filled with siblings," he insisted. "It would be the perfect place to grow up. Ideal for raising a family. Enough space to have friends over on a regular basis, both adults and children, and exquisite views of the mountains from the front porch. You could sit each evening and simply enjoy the ending to a nice day."

"Oh good grief, you're such a romantic." She turned and headed back out of the room, dodging a weak spot that had been in the floor all her life, and turned up the coffee cup.

He followed. "No I'm not, I'm simply able to take something raw and see the possibilities in it. Now tell me what you see."

She turned, halfway down the stairs, and scowled back up at him. "I see nothing but a house falling down, Nick. Honestly. And this isn't lack of coffee talking. It's an old home that is worth pretty much nothing, but if I can't make at least a little out of it then GiGi will be kicked out of the nursing home and she'll have to live with me. In my tiny, two-bedroom rental. And trust me, she and I don't get along well enough for that. Even if she wasn't sick, that arrangement wouldn't be in the best interest of either of us."

Stomping the rest of the way down the stairs, she was relieved that she didn't put a foot through any of the risers. By the time she reached the first floor, the caffeine was beginning to kick in. She faced him as he made his way down behind her, and she tried for an apologetic look.

"Listen, I'm sorry I'm in a mood this morning. You were right, I'm not a morning person, but that isn't hard to figure out, is it?" She laughed a little, then took another long drink of the heaven in her hands, the warm liquid easing her tension all the way down. "The fact is, I really don't see anything when I look at this house. I've no idea where to start, but the last contractor who gave me an estimate quoted a price twice the loan I can get from the bank."

He nodded. "There's a lot of work to be done. I'll need to bring in a few guys to help with different areas. Electricity, roofing, plumbing. I have licenses for all, but I can't handle everything myself."

Worry settled in her and almost brought her to tears. She should just give up and go ahead and bring GiGi home. At least that way she'd save what little money she always managed to send as payment.

"I can spot you for the extra labor."

"What?" She gaped at him. "I can't let you do that. I'm already taking advantage of you by not paying *you* any labor."

The smile at his lips let her know that she was definitely taking advantage of him. "I can spot you. Plus, turning this house into what *I* see will go far toward giving my company a foothold in the town. You'll be doing us both a favor."

Her mouth twisted, but she had to admit he had a point. If he could pull off making this place something other than the shambles that it currently was, it would be a walking advertisement for his business.

"What's your deadline?" he asked.

Now she really was embarrassed. She peered out the front window as if something out there interested her. "I need it sold in two months, so . . . four weeks? Six at most."

And that was pushing it. It would mean it would need to sell pretty much the moment it went on the market.

Nick remained silent for several seconds and then walked over and took the coffee from her. He turned the mug up, his head tilting back at such an angle her vision got caught on the ridge in his throat.

Once the last drop was gone, he lowered his hand and locked his gaze with hers. "I sure hope you know how to wield a hammer."

Joanie's eyes went wide. "That's what I'm hiring you for."

He laughed. "Darlin', I wouldn't call what I'm about to do your hiring me. But that's okay," he held up a hand at her panicked look and hurried to finish, not wanting her to think that he was backing out of their agreement.

The fact was, the whole situation excited him. He could turn this house into a masterpiece and she would bow down at his feet when he was done. The whole town would. And the idea of him doing most of the work himself instead of merely overseeing the details gave him even more of a thrill. It made him realize how much he'd missed being active on the job site. Plus, it would give him a definite extra two weeks with his brother before he headed back home. He couldn't wait to get started.

"To meet your deadline, sweetness, we'll pretty much need to work round the clock." And he couldn't help but want Joanie there for part of it. She was fun to be around, even when she was grumpy. "I can't hire men and expect them to be out here all hours of the night. Maybe hammering isn't your forte, but surely you can pitch in. I could totally see you doing demolition."

He winked at her, picturing her, with her blond and pink curls, wielding a sledgehammer. The idea of her wearing her go-go boots while doing so popped into his brain and he realized that thinking of her helping was bringing on more enjoyment than he needed at the moment.

Pushing the image from his mind, he looked over the dusty room. First things first. It might be February, but they had to let in some fresh air.

"Tell you what," he started as he began opening windows. Most were stuck but came loose with a quick rap of his fist along the sash. "You leave me to it for the day and then come on back after you shut down your store tonight. I'll run into town for supplies and spend the day cleaning. That'll give me time to formulate my ideas for what I see this place becoming." He looked back at her. "Deal?"

The caffeine had brightened her features but she still looked as if she'd rather be in bed. Which brought yet another unneeded thought to mind.

She nodded. "I hate to leave you with all this yourself, though."

"That's okay, I'm a big boy. I've cleaned a house or two before." Far more times than most guys, he imagined. His mother hadn't been big on cleaning up after herself.

"As for me helping . . ."

He lifted his brows when she stopped midsentence.

She finally gave a slight shrug and continued, "I'll do whatever I can, but I also have to sort through the contents in the house. I was hoping to do that after hours."

The thought that she would be there with him in the evenings shot a spurt of adrenaline through him. He'd been teasing about needing her help, mostly just looking for an excuse to get her to come around, but it looked like he didn't have to bother. She would be there anyway.

He couldn't stop the grin, knowing it was similar to the goofy one he'd kept exhibiting every time he'd looked at her the day before. Something about her simply made him happy.

"We'll work it out. You come on back tonight and we'll figure out a plan. Bring dessert. I'll take care of dinner."

With a slight nod and worry lines creasing the space between her eyebrows, she bit her lip and took another long look around the room. "You really think you can turn it into something someone would want?"

His chest expanded at the challenge and he crossed to stand in front of her, finally letting himself touch her as he'd been wanting to since he'd driven up and seen her standing so forlornly on the porch.

He put a hand under her chin and tilted her face up to his. Her skin was soft against the years of calluses built up on his fingers. "I'm positive I can make something of it, sweetness. In fact, I predict it'll be so nice you'll want to keep it for yourself instead of selling it."

"That's not going to happen." She shook her head. "But I will be thrilled to get rid of it."

Chapter Three

Joanie flipped the switch to turn off the OPEN sign and locked the front door. She was wiped. Customers had been nonstop all day— the extra business likely from having the van out the day before—and she was grateful. Really. But she could use a long bath and a relaxing Friday evening off.

Only, she was going to get neither.

Her cell vibrated and she pulled it from the pocket of her jeans. It was Lee Ann.

"Hey," Joanie answered, flipping out the main lights in the store. "I'm just closing up for the day. What's up?"

"You have a date tonight," Lee Ann accused.

Joanie froze. "No I don't."

She hadn't so much as thought about dating for months now. Nick's face came to mind and she grinned, admitting to herself that what she'd thought about doing with him would not be considered a date.

"I beg to differ," Lee Ann started. "I've heard it from three different sources. You and my hunky brother-in-law-to-be are apparently having a date. He's cooking for you. Not to mention living with you."

"He is not living with me. He's at the Barn." GiGi and Pepaw had named the house during the early years of their marriage, though no one knew why it had gotten that name. It had been their little secret.

Joanie could almost see her friend shrugging. "Close enough. He'll be all up in your space, and if he's going to be renovating the house—which I also heard from several sources, none of which were you, by the way—then I assume you'll be constantly in the middle of things, cleaning out Georgia's accumulation of junk from three-quarters of a century of living there."

Not to mention the years GiGi's parents had lived there before her.

"Oh wow." Joanie pulled a red-cushioned chair out from its matching bistro table and sat down. The enormity of what lay ahead was overwhelming. "There's a century's worth of stuff out there, Lee. I'll never get through all that." She shoved the corners of a handful of napkins back in the dispenser. "And you didn't hear about it from me simply because I haven't had time to call you today. This place has been packed. I'd planned to call later and beg an emergency girls' day."

Until Joanie had sold the salon, she and Lee Ann had made Monday afternoons their time for pedicures and much needed girl talk. She'd kept the business closed just for the occasion—along with handling the administrative stuff she hated so much—and though she would be doing the same with Cakes, each Monday so far had been too full with getting the business off the ground.

"Girls' day," Lee Ann said, making the idea sound as appealing as a tropical getaway. "*Yes.* Just name the time and place." Joanie could hear occasional clicking on the other end. Probably Lee Ann was at the computer in her photography studio, touching up some shots. "And of course you'll get through Georgia's stuff," Lee Ann continued. "Cody and I will help. The girls, too. Though they'll probably spend more time bugging Nick than being useful. They're crazy about their uncle."

Forcing her heavy limbs to move, Joanie rose and scooted the chair up under the table, imagining Nick entertaining his nieces. She suspected he would love that. "Tomorrow night?" she suggested. "Ditch Cody and the girls. Let's make it a real girls' night. Want to go to the Bungalow?"

"Perfect."

"And by the way," Joanie added as she continued through the room, "the Barn is a disaster. I'm not sure it can be fixed."

"Nonsense," Lee Ann chided. "Nick's a genius with his hands. You'll be thrilled with the outcome."

The thought of Nick's hands brought to mind other things Joanie bet he could do with them. Which had nothing at all to do with this conversation. She needed to get a grip.

Or get laid, apparently.

She rolled her eyes at the direction her thoughts had taken, and returned her mind to the topic at hand. "I'll be *thrilled* when the nursing home quits calling for money."

"They called again?" Lee Ann asked.

Joanie nodded, even though Lee Ann couldn't see the action. She stepped behind the counter and began pulling out a selection of cupcakes to box up. "That's why I jumped at the chance to get Nick's help," she added. "I have two months to sell the house and settle the charges before they kick her out."

"Oh. Wow. That's fast."

"Yeah. So you really think he can do it? Turn it into something worthwhile?"

"Of course. He's brilliant."

Joanie's mind wandered back to Nick. And his hands. And shoulders. And legs. She really had to stop thinking about him like that. They were working together. That's all. Two people, helping each other out. He was just a nice guy.

And a really good-looking one.

"Uh-oh," Lee Ann said. "You keep going quiet. What am I missing?"

"Nothing," Joanie mumbled, pushing the six-foot-plus vision of lean muscle from her mind. Her friend was too perceptive. She wedged another cupcake into the nearly full box.

"Oh," Lee Ann drew the word out. "I get it. Nick. You like him."

"Of course I don't."

"Come on. I saw the way you looked at him at Christmas, remember?"

She had looked at him at Christmas. She'd shown up at the mountain cabin Lee Ann had rented, and Nick had answered the door, spatula in hand, and smelling like warm chocolate chip cookies. If she'd had a glass of milk at that moment, she would've been tempted to take a big bite.

After watching him throughout the day, though, she'd determined that he was a man who needed a wife and kids. The type of guy who would burrow into a woman's heart until she went dumb for him. The type women would twist themselves inside out for. Just to please him.

Given how her family had a habit of coming out on the wrong end of men's charms, she wanted no part of someone like him.

"What you saw," Joanie explained patiently, "was appreciation for a hot guy. Casual flirting."

She couldn't help it. She was a flirt. Everyone knew that.

A beat of silence passed before Lee Ann asked, "Then what's going on now?"

"Nothing," Joanie answered. She licked icing off her fingers. "Why do you ask?"

"Because you keep going quiet. You're thinking about him."

"I'm not . . . it's just . . ." Joanie sighed. Why was she fighting it? "There's something about him that's bothering me this time, is all. It's not like it was at Christmas. He makes me nervous. Jittery. And I don't like being jittery."

"Okay." Lee Ann turned serious in an instant. "Then let's figure it out."

She loved Lee Ann for this. The problem solver.

"What specifically has bothered you?" Lee Ann asked.

"The way he looks at me," Joanie stated. She pictured Nick standing out front of her shop, smiling at her as if he couldn't remember his name. It had been cute.

"He saw you in your miniskirt, didn't he?"

"Uh-huh." Joanie nodded.

"You know your legs make men go dumb, Jo."

"I have to show them. It goes with the theme."

Lee Ann snorted. "And with making a fortune selling cupcakes."

Joanie giggled and licked her fingertips one more time, catching a spot of blue icing on her tongue before closing the box she'd just packed.

"So Nick ogling your legs bothers you?"

"Not exactly." How did she explain it? "It's just that, every time he'd look at them he'd get this really goofy grin. But something about it kept feeling like . . . I don't know. *More.* Another example was this morning when we were talking at GiGi's," she hurried on to say. "He kept looking at me as if he could see something inside me that isn't there. He kept asking what I saw when I looked at the place. I see a heap that needs to be burned to the ground, yet the way he was looking at me made me want to run to the mirror and check for myself. You know what I mean?"

"Hmmm . . ."

Before Lee Ann could continue, Joanie jumped back in. "And yesterday, yeah, he was hot for my legs. He wanted me. Big deal, I've seen that my whole life. But Lee, I wanted him too. *Bad.*"

There was a tiny pause. "Then go for it, hon. Have some fun."

"He comes with a cat." She enunciated each word carefully.

Laughter rang through the phone. "What does his cat have to do with anything?"

Joanie sighed. "He's a nester. He wants serious. I can't sleep with someone who comes with a cat."

She grabbed her purse out from under the counter and slipped the strap over her shoulder.

"Yeah," Lee Ann admitted, her voice hesitant. "He is the settling-down type."

"My point," Joanie replied. "Let's drop it. It's a ridiculous conversation, anyway. He's working for me. That's all."

"And preparing for a hot date."

"Oh, good grief. It is not a date." It wasn't. It was a business dinner. "How did anyone possibly get that idea?" Joanie flipped off the remaining lights and grabbed her jacket from the coat rack. She headed through the back room.

"Well, let's see," Lee Ann began. "He was picking up supplies at Sam's Foodmart and mentioned that he was cleaning your house before you got back out there tonight. Jean from the store would have told someone else who came in, who carried it from there to who knows where, where it got all around town, so that now everyone thinks there's a hot date going on this evening."

Joanie shook her head, amazed at the path the rumor had taken. "He picked up cleaning supplies and that turned into a hot date?"

"He also picked up two steaks, potatoes, and the fixin's for a salad."

"Oh." Yeah, that could do it. She pushed open the back door. "Well, we're not having a date. Feel free to spread that around. He said he'd provide dinner. I'm taking dessert."

"He also got wine."

Joanie narrowed her eyes. *It was not a date!* And he'd better not be thinking it was. "Maybe wine's just his thing."

She knew she might sound silly, but she wasn't about to so much as hint at a date. It was bad enough the whole town already thought it was one.

Rolling laughter filled Joanie's ear as she stepped into the quiet alley and locked up. Lee Ann was clearly enjoying her discomfort.

"Are you about finished?" Joanie spoke into a pause in the laughter.

"Okay, I'm sorry. I know. It's business, not a date. But I have a word of advice."

Which did not surprise Joanie at all. "What's that?"

"Dalton men have something about them, Jo. Something that's pretty irresistible."

Joanie set her cupcakes and purse on her passenger seat and shrugged into her jacket. "And?"

"And . . . since he's making you nervous already, you need all your wits about you if you plan to make sure it stays only business."

Joanie smirked. *No shit.* "So how do I do that?" she asked.

"My advice? Don't drink the wine."

The sun had just disappeared below the horizon as Joanie's Mini Cooper pulled into the driveway, her lights flashing over the front yard, and

Nick's blood began that double-time thing it liked to do when she was around.

He'd spent the day scrubbing out the grime in enough rooms to make the house livable, but she had never been far from his mind.

He liked her. He liked that she didn't seem to take herself too seriously and that she didn't make excuses for who she was. That she smiled and laughed, and was just generally fun to be around—even when she was in a grumpy mood.

She stepped from the ragtop and he was pleased to see she'd returned pretty much as she'd been that morning. Jeans and a pullover with a light jacket thrown over the top. Not that the jeans weren't flattering, but he wasn't sure he could have taken the boots and skirt tonight.

As she came up the porch steps, she stopped to look him over, crisscrossing shadows from the encroaching darkness keeping him from reading the expression in her eyes.

He lifted his beer in salute. "Have a seat. I bought a couple rockers while I was in town. Needed a place to be able to enjoy the evening since the inside of the house smells like it's been closed up for years."

"It has been closed up for years," she grumbled. She eyed him where he sat. "You do anything without that cat?"

He glanced down where the cat lay contentedly curled up in his lap. "Cat comes and goes as he wants, but he's fond of this spot. Though he'd be more so if we were sitting in front of a big-screen. With cable. And not outside in the cold."

Slim eyebrows, slightly darker than the blond hair on her head, lifted. "I had the cable disconnected a couple years ago. I'll call and get it turned back on."

He watched her. Her mood wasn't as cranky as it had been earlier, but it still wasn't like yesterday afternoon when she'd been selling cupcakes. "And the big-screen?" he prodded.

She shrugged. "Afraid you're stuck with what's in there. Be glad it isn't black and white, is all I can say. GiGi wouldn't upgrade for years." She eyed his cat again, looking at the animal as if he were the reason for the world's problems. "The heat works," she finally added, lifting her gaze to Nick's. "Though I can't help if you prefer it out here."

He grinned at her directness, and reached out with his foot to push the other chair toward her. His movements sent Cat scurrying across the porch.

Instead of sitting, she watched Cat until he leapt off the far end of the porch and then she turned back to him. "You named your cat 'Cat'?" She crossed her arms.

"His full name is Caterpillar." Nick itched to see if he could turn her mood around. "We found him curled up in the machinery on a job one day and he never left. Have a seat, sweetness." He nudged the chair again. "I'm not going to bite."

"*Hmph.*" She finally sat, then reached out and placed a white bakery box on the concrete railing surrounding the porch.

"Are there cupcakes in that box?" His mouth watered at the thought.

"Half a dozen, all for you."

"You are trying to fatten up the men in this town, aren't you?" He couldn't help but picture her looking over Brian Marshall the day before. The back of his neck tingled, wishing she would do the same to him right now.

She leaned back in the rocker and closed her eyes, and instantly seemed to melt into the wood slats of the chair. But she didn't respond to his question.

"Want a beer?" he asked.

She shook her head.

"Wine then?"

One eye popped open. "You get the wine to go with the steaks?"

Ah, small-town gossip at its best. He gave a simple nod. "A couple bottles. Wasn't sure what you preferred, but you struck me as more the wine than beer type."

"*Hmph,*" she reiterated, but he had no clue what it meant.

"Wine then?" He moved to get up, but her words stopped him.

"Don't think I'm drinking tonight."

"Oh?" He sat back down. "Any particular reason?"

She shook her head again, then stood and put a few feet between them. "Just a bad idea. How about we get to your thoughts on the house? I've got a long day tomorrow and need to get home."

Something made him think it was more likely she didn't want to be there alone with him.

Sensible. He would be smart to go along with it.

His previous thoughts of all work and no play had taken a crashing nosedive the instant she'd grilled him for naming his cat "Cat." She was simply too cute.

Joanie stopped as she stepped inside the house, amazed at the difference since she'd been there that morning. It still smelled musty, but the thick layer of dust was gone, and she no longer had the urge to sneeze.

The screen door closed behind her and she looked back over her shoulder. She had to give the guy credit, he was a cleaning machine. "Remind me to have you at my house to clean sometime."

The quick curve of his mouth snagged her attention in record time. Why she'd spent the day thinking about the man was anyone's guess, but she had to get focused on the job ahead and nothing else. Especially not that mouth.

Or the fact that he was already getting to her. And he'd done nothing more than buy rockers for the front porch.

She headed into the kitchen and was equally surprised to find the oven working and the kitchen table cleaned off save for the sketches lying on the stained Formica. Looking at them, she realized they were Nick's plans for the house.

"Wow." The word came out softly as she slid into a chair and pulled them closer. "You came up with these fast."

He headed to the counter and plugged in a portable grill before joining her. "Remodeling is our focus in Nashville. We take plenty of other jobs too, but renovating an existing structure like this one is what I love most."

"Lucky I found you," she murmured. She looked up from the papers and was struck by the naked vulnerability she saw in his eyes. He was nervous to hear her opinion? The thought caused a pang to echo in her chest. Pointing to the last sheet, she asked, "What's that?"

"A third floor."

"Why would I—"

"We're going to have to strip the rafters and shore up the joists anyway. Adding a narrow staircase on the second floor could be done at the door of that back bedroom and not take up too much space. What we lose in storage, we can add on the third floor. All I'm thinking is a single space up there. A bedroom with a sitting area and an overlarge bath. It'll be a guest room, or maybe the hideaway of a teenager who needs more privacy than the rest of the kids."

The type of space she would have loved as a teen. She shook her head. "That'll mean I need more from the bank. I don't think I can get it."

"It'll also bring in double what I put into it in the sale of the house."

"But if I can't get it to begin with?"

Nick returned to the counter to toss the steaks on the grill, then grabbed another beer from the fridge. When he came back, he poured a glass of wine from a bottle he had breathing on the counter. He put it down in front of her. "In case you change your mind," he said.

She looked at the glass, then shifted her gaze to the counter where the steaks were sizzling. Steaks, wine, cooking her dinner. How stupid did he think she was? She couldn't be wooed with food.

And certainly not when he was performing step one of his seduction routine. She'd seen men like him before. They made the same moves for every woman, assuming they were all alike.

Well, they weren't. She wasn't.

And she wouldn't be treated as if she was.

Making an instant decision, she rose from the table and pulled a chair over to the far corner cabinet. If she wasn't mistaken, there would be something more to her liking on the back of that top shelf.

Nick said nothing, but she could feel him watching her as she climbed up, stretched her hand over the plastic cups at the front of the shelf, then wrapped her fingers around the neck of something far more entertaining than wine.

She smiled when she pulled out the dusty bottle of Jack. GiGi always had one around. She'd probably even managed to sneak a bottle into the nursing home with her.

"If I'm going to drink," Joanie started, glancing back over her shoulder to find Nick eyeing her, "it isn't going to be some lame wine you're trying to seduce me with."

His brows went up.

Before she got down, she caught sight of a metal box shoved to the side on the top shelf. She grabbed that, too, along with the bug-eyed owl salt and pepper shakers sitting beside it. They were covered in sticky grime from years of nonuse, but she'd clean them up and take them to GiGi when she visited next week.

"You drink whiskey?" Nick asked as she ran the top of the bottle under the water to clean it of dust.

"Not much of a wine girl," she verified. She pulled down a tumbler. "You want some?"

Nick merely shook his head and held up his beer.

His silence told her that she'd shocked him. Good. She didn't like people pigeonholing her.

Once she poured herself a drink, she returned to the table, where he lined up all the papers and slowly walked her through the full design. The man really did have a vision.

"Prices are best guesses at this point," he said. "You never know until you get into a project what issues you may hit, but upon my initial inspection, I think we'll be pretty close to these figures."

She sipped at her drink, enjoying the burn. It'd been a long time since she'd had whiskey. "Yet it's still thousands more than I can get."

"Right, but that's where I come in. I'd like to bankroll the rest of it for you, free of interest. I get repaid when you sell."

She opened her mouth to protest, but he reached over and captured her hand in his, making her snap her mouth closed. The warmth from his palm oozed through her, tugging gently, and she glanced at the amber liquid in her glass. She hadn't drunk nearly enough to be experiencing the urge to lean closer to him.

"It's a win-win," Nick added. His thumb stroked between two of her knuckles. "It'll be a masterpiece when I'm finished. You'll probably have multiple offers within days of putting it on the market."

"What's in it for you?" Surely he wasn't thinking this would win her over.

"It's simple," he said. "I want my company to succeed here. Your allowing me to do this sets me up for that."

She pulled her hand out from under his and lifted her glass. The liquid burned all the way down, clearing out her sinuses along the way.

The funny thing was, looking at the drawings was making her nostalgic. Which made her uncomfortable. It wasn't as if she'd lived the world's worst life in the house, but she had few good memories to fall back on. Just plenty of crap.

She had her mother constantly morphing herself to chase the dreams of some man. Pepaw leaving, causing GiGi to get stuck in a life with no meaning. Then there had been Adam. Couldn't forget good ol' Adam. She'd been sixteen when that had happened. She'd learned real quick that she'd also inherited the ability to go stupid for a man. Just like every other Bigbee woman.

Nope, nothing good here. There was only heartache and loneliness in this house.

Yet, what Nick saw when he looked at the space made her remember she'd once had similar dreams herself.

As a kid, knowing the house had been in her family for generations, she'd imagined one day growing old with her own family here. Yet over the years, as her relationship with her grandmother deteriorated, the last thing she'd wanted was to live in this house one minute longer than necessary. She'd moved out fifteen years earlier and hadn't looked back since.

The signal on the grill sounded and Nick went to serve up their food. She finished off her whiskey, already feeling the effects, and briefly recalled Lee Ann warning her not to drink tonight. When Nick came back, she looked from the plated food to the strong, solid jaw of the man before her and the nervousness she'd felt the day before returned.

"It's a big decision," she said. She licked her lips. "Putting that much into it, taking your money. I'm going to need some time to think about it."

He nodded. "Of course." He handed her a fork and knife and she took a bite of the crisp salad, noticing he'd even included a small cup of butter for her baked potato. The man had the routine down to an art. He thought of everything. "Just don't wait too long," he added. "I'll start on some of the basic work that has to happen while you think through things, but we're going to need the majority of the six weeks to get all of this done."

And at the end of it, she'd say good-bye to the house that had been in her family for over one hundred years.

Her chest suddenly burned, and it had nothing at all to do with the whiskey.

She forced down a few bites, asking questions as she continued thinking through the drawings in front of her. She really wanted to do it. If for no reason other than to see the house restored to the glory she suspected it had once been.

Yet, something warned her it wouldn't be that simple.

"The food is really good," she stated, when she realized she'd been downing the meal without being gracious enough to thank him for cooking. She pushed the remainder back and stood with her glass in hand. "But if you don't mind, I think I'll sit out on the porch for a bit. I need to think through this some more."

What she needed was to gather up her bag and head home. Sleep on the decision. But she wasn't quite ready to walk away yet. It had turned out to be a very nice evening. Even if he did think they were on a date.

Before going outside she tipped the bottle to pour a couple more fingers, raised her glass to Nick in a silent toast when he chuckled softly under his breath, then grabbed her coat and headed for the front porch and the silence she knew she'd find there.

She wasn't disappointed. The only thing greeting her were the sounds of the few insects out in the late winter night and a lone dog barking from somewhere off down the road.

Within minutes of sitting, Caterpillar came around the side of the house and crawled up into her lap. The big orange fluffball settled down as if he did so every night, and she tilted her head back and took another drink.

What a day. She felt as if her emotions were running as wild as all the teenagers' she'd witnessed the day before—first from Nick and the tension she felt just being in the same room as him, and now as the memories of the past and long-forgotten dreams consumed her. She knew she would sell the house. There was no other option. She didn't want to live there anyway. Yet no matter what renovations they did, selling wasn't going to be as easy as she'd always thought.

The door squeaked and Nick stood in the shadows, with the light from inside the house at his back.

"Come on, I'll take you home," he said. He held a foil-covered plate in his hand—her remaining dinner, she suspected—and motioned with it to the glass she held in hers. "I've plied you with too much alcohol, and wouldn't like myself if I let you drive out of here."

She nodded. That was probably for the best. Though she couldn't blame the drinking on him.

She followed him to his truck and climbed in as he held the door for her. He watched her until she had her seat belt fit snuggly around her, set her dinner on her lap, then slammed the door and headed to the other side of the truck.

After telling him which house she rented, she realized she was still carrying her glass. She drained it, her eyes watering with the quick gulps, as she went back over the pros and cons of letting Nick make all the renovations he'd drawn out.

Pro: The resale value would be higher; the house should sell fast.

Con: Nick would be around even more than she'd anticipated. And being around him made her want to do things that weren't wise.

Pro: It would make the area stunning instead of an eyesore.

Con: It would still be outside of town, so who would see it?

Pro: She would not only be setting her grandmother up in good financial care, but leaving a legacy, as well.

Con: She would have to watch a dream she hadn't even realized existed come to life only to sell it and move on.

A lump settled behind her breastbone and she turned to watch the dark night go by, blinking back hot tears as they drove down the quiet street. Seeing the Barn reinvented would be both exciting and heartbreaking at the same time. Because yeah, she'd once wanted the house and all the assumptions that came with it, even if only in a small child's world.

Before she'd realized how out of her reach dreaming for the world could be.

Nick pulled up at her house and turned off the truck, and she sat quietly taking in the barren front porch with the lone dollar-store lawn chair parked in the corner. She sat out there most nights, if only for a few minutes to unwind from the day, and it had never occurred to her to get anything other than the small, foldout chair. Nick had been in town for all of two days and had already put rockers on GiGi's porch.

"Thanks for bringing me home," she said. She opened the door and by the time she jumped to her feet Nick was there to walk her to the house. She put the empty tumbler on his seat and turned back to him with the covered plate in her hands. She couldn't remember when a man had ever fixed her a to-go plate before.

"You'll make a decision soon?" When she looked at him, he added, "On the renovations?"

"Oh." She nodded, then smiled as she realized how light-headed she was. She had the urge to lean against him as they walked. "Yeah, I'll think about it this weekend."

The streetlight caught the glint from his eye as he took her arm and led her to the porch. "I'm beginning to see why you said you shouldn't drink. You're a lightweight."

She nodded, then laughed softly. "I get relaxed easily."

"I'll have to remember that."

She glanced at his mouth as he led her up the steps. He had the best mouth. "Are you really going to let me help do demolition?"

His bottom lip curved and she smiled along with it. "No, sweetness, I was just teasing. I'm not letting you anywhere near a sledgehammer."

She frowned. "I'm sure I would be good at it."

"No doubt you would." They reached the porch and he slid his hand down the outside of her arm as he released her. "But I think I'll let you stick to packing up the place. You have a lot to take care of there."

She made a face. "I know. My grandmother was a collector of many things. Wait till you see what's stored in the attic."

The thought of everything she had to go through in the coming weeks was overwhelming.

"Joanie." Nick's voice was soft, and she pulled her mind from the masses of junk awaiting her at GiGi's and focused on him. It was harder to do than she'd thought. That had been good whiskey.

"What?" she whispered.

His hand touched her jaw and she tilted her face up, leaning forward at the same time as if he were reeling her in. She glanced at his mouth again. She'd bet he'd be a really good kisser.

A passing car stopped at the corner, its lights landing on Nick's face, highlighting that his gaze was on her mouth, too. Which was no good at all. She couldn't be kissing him.

Their eyes met and time stood still. Then she took a small step back and broke the moment. He exhaled.

"Thanks for bringing me home," she said again, turning her back to him to open the door, only to find it wasn't locked. She'd forgotten to lock her door again. She glanced over her shoulder, unable to walk in without looking at Nick one last time. "I'll uh . . . bring dinner or something next time."

"Sounds good." He looked past her into the dark house. "Was your door unlocked?"

"I forget to lock it sometimes." She could tell he was going to suggest he check to make sure no one was inside, so she turned to him once again and put her hand to his chest and pushed. He didn't budge. "Go home, Nick. It's Sugar Springs. If anyone came in while I was out, they probably just cleaned the house."

His jaw had hardened, and it took several seconds before he shifted his gaze back from the living room to her. "You're an odd one, Joanie."

That was one of the more polite adjectives she'd heard over the years. *Flaky, flighty, unfocused.* "It's one of my biggest charms."

She looked up at him then, liking that he still seemed to want to go inside and check under her bed and in her closets. "I'm safe, Nick. No one is here, and I guarantee no one snuck in to do my dishes while I was out."

At that, he finally took a step back. "Okay, I'll go. I'll get Cody to help in the morning and we'll bring your car back."

She nodded, but didn't move to go in. Instead, she continued watching him as if waiting for something else. Not a kiss, though. Thankfully she'd caught herself before letting *that* happen.

No matter how much she'd wanted it.

"I wasn't trying to seduce you, you know?" Nick's soft words were spoken into the night, his face tilted down to hers. "Back at the house." He propped himself against the door frame and studied her when she didn't reply. "Not that I would have a problem with it."

Or that it would be too difficult, she added silently. If she weren't on guard for such behavior.

With great effort, she stepped back, putting one foot on the threshold of her door, and putting a breath of air between them. "Good night, Nick."

"Lock the door," he said. "So I don't worry about you."

She nodded, oddly charmed that he felt he might need to worry about her. Charmed all the way around, in fact. He had some strange effect on her.

She stepped inside and closed the door, then leaned against it as if her legs were no longer able to support the full weight of her body. He'd almost kissed her.

And she'd almost let him.

Had she learned nothing over the years?

A soft rap against the door had her jumping away from it.

"Lock the door, Joanie," his low voice came through the wood.

Oh, good grief. She threw the deadbolt, fast, as if afraid he would come in if she didn't, and then she caught the sound of his booted feet heading in the other direction. Next, there was his door slamming, then the roar of his truck.

Finally, after he backed out of the driveway, she turned her back to the door and sunk down to the ground, her plate of food still gripped between her hands. She put the plate on the floor and stared into the darkness, terrified she was already in over her head, and knowing she'd gotten there by doing nothing more than thinking about kissing him.

What would happen after spending several weeks in his presence, working side by side?

Chapter Four

H ey, Uncle Nick," Kendra said as she came into the kitchen, holding her arm up in front of him. Cody's black-and-white Great Dane, Boss, trailed her. "Did you see the present my boyfriend got me for Valentine's Day?"

Her boyfriend was thirteen, and if Nick were to guess, on his last week with that moniker. The girl had gotten her first boyfriend only two months before, and already she seemed to go through them as if she had a quota to make.

"Sure didn't," he said. He grabbed Kendra's arm and squinted as if he could barely make out the silver bracelet circling her wrist. "He give you a new freckle or something?"

"Oh, Uncle Nick." She gave him a girl-slap. He loved being called Uncle Nick. "I don't even have freckles. It's the bracelet, goofy." She shook her hand so the jewelry rattled. "Isn't it the greatest? It has a charm with my birthstone, a heart for February since that's when we started going out, and then a panda bear since that's my favorite animal in the world."

Her twin sister entered the kitchen behind her, and mimed shoving her finger down her throat. "All she does is talk about him. And she'll dump him by next week."

Nick was at Lee Ann's house on a Saturday night, making a batch of chili for the girls and his brother, while their mother was out on the town with Joanie.

"At least she kept him long enough to get a gift out of him," he said to Candy. He wondered if they were already learning that trick at thirteen.

Candy wore a horrified expression, but a follow-up one of acceptance, while Kendra merely smiled. The look of knowledge.

"I didn't tell him he had to buy me anything," Kendra pointed out.

"Words every man has heard at least once, but we all know where we'd be if we didn't buy the gift." He patted his leg and Boss came over. Nick took pleasure in rubbing the animal's big head. He was a cat person himself, but if he were to get a dog, he'd want one the size of a horse, too.

Kendra merely shrugged and opened the refrigerator. "It's how it works. I'm hungry."

"Chili will be ready in twenty minutes. Think you can wait?"

She grabbed an apple from the bowl on the center island and tossed one to her sister. "Sure."

They were gone, Boss along with them, as quickly as they'd arrived, and Nick was left standing in the kitchen alone. Cody would be back soon. He'd run up the street to get something from his apartment.

Nick pulled a tape measure from his back pocket and began measuring the length of the counters and jotting down notes, not noticing when he was no longer alone in the room.

"What are you doing?" Cody asked. With his arms folded over his chest, and a scowl on his face, he looked quite formidable.

If Nick wasn't aware he would appear identical in the same stance, he might have been intimidated.

"Working on your wedding gift," he replied, then moved to begin the process on the cabinets.

"What wedding present?"

"The one I'm giving you, idiot."

Cody shot him a curious look. "We aren't getting married for months. Why are you already thinking about a present?"

"So it'll be finished before the wedding." He pulled Corian samples from his front pocket, eager to discuss his plans with his brother. He could get everything ordered, and as soon as he had Joanie's house finished, he could spend a few days here. "I'm giving you and Lee Ann a kitchen makeover. New counters, cabinets, floors. Even new appliances. I'll do the work myself."

Cody gawked at him, his features losing some of their sternness. "Have you lost your mind? You aren't giving us a new kitchen."

"Of course I am," Nick said. "Remodels are what I do."

Cody grabbed an apple from the basket and tossed it back and forth between his hands. "We can't accept something like that."

"We're *family*," Nick stressed. He made plenty of money, and had it to spend. He didn't see what the problem was. "It's what families do for each other."

"A blender, dude. Buy us a blender. We're family with or without a kitchen."

Hell, nothing was going right. First he'd almost gone in for a kiss last night only to have Joanie reject him before he could make a move. And now his brother was being a pain in the ass about a stupid gift.

Not to mention the potential gold mine that was the house renovation—if Joanie would let him do it all. Once finished, all he'd need to do was post his sign out front, and he'd have all the work he wanted.

If she gave him the go-ahead.

Frustrated, he decided not to fight the kitchen battle at the moment. He'd draw up a design, then spring it on Lee Ann. Surely she'd be less inclined to toss his offer back in his face.

Nick let the tape rewind into its case, the thin metal bending and popping, the only sound in the room. When it finished, Cody shot him a hard look. "And if you're thinking of going around me to talk Lee Ann into it, I'll smash your face."

Nick eyed his brother, thinking a good fistfight might be just what he needed at the moment. Something to lessen some of the tension that had been building since Joanie had pulled down a bottle of whiskey and set him back on his ass. She was absolutely not like the women he dated.

Which, he'd discovered, was quite the turn-on.

"Why won't you let me do this?" he snapped, irritation getting the better of him. He held up the counter samples. "Tell me Lee Ann wouldn't like countertops made of this stuff. Or we can go granite."

"She'd love countertops made of that, but you aren't going to give them to her."

"Fine," Nick growled under his breath. He washed the dog off his hands and went to the chili to give it a stir, thinking back over how far he and Cody had come since they'd first met.

It had been less than two months, so he supposed he could accept that they still had some growing closer to do. Bonding and whatnot. Didn't mean the jerk couldn't accept a gift when it was offered to him.

"I'm still going to talk to Lee Ann about it," Nick couldn't resist adding, knowing that if he could get the idea in front of Lee Ann, he'd be golden.

"You do and I'll break your arm."

The tone was hard enough to indicate Cody meant it. Maybe not a full break, but Nick got the impression he'd be crossing some invisible line. Though he still didn't understand why. He popped the cornbread in the oven. "Okay. I'll back off it for now."

"Forever."

"*For now.* I won't say anything to Lee Ann. But I don't see what the big deal is."

Cody tossed the apple back in the basket and grabbed a soda from the fridge. He popped open the top. "The big deal is, it's too much. No one gives that kind of a gift to someone they just met. Even if they do look alike."

"I have it to spend." Nick grabbed his own drink off the counter and turned it up, certain Cody was wrong. If he had it, there was nothing wrong with spending it on those he loved. He'd worked extremely hard over the last ten years to be able to do just that.

"Then spend it on yourself. Or maybe on figuring out how to get Joanie to kiss you."

"What the—" He cut off as Coke splashed up his nose from jerking the can at Cody's words. He wiped the back of his hand across his face. "What are you talking about?"

Cody shrugged, and went into a monotone, "Lee Ann's mother called this morning to make sure she'd heard the news. Linda Sue from the beauty salon had called. Said you got stonewalled on the front porch. Apparently in the middle of Linda Sue's headlights."

Nick could only stare in amazement.

Cody smirked. "Small-town living at its best."

"Wow," Nick finally managed to get out. "Even more impressive than I would have given them credit for." Especially since he hadn't even gone in for the kiss. He'd only planned to. Until she'd stepped back.

"Tell me about it," Cody muttered. He sniffed the chili and made an appreciative noise. "It never stops."

Nick could handle the gossip. He actually thought it was charming. What he couldn't handle was this fixation he had on Joanie. He needed information before deciding what to do next.

"Any idea what the issue is with her?" he finally asked.

Cody raised an eyebrow. "With Joanie?"

Nick nodded. "Would be nice to know where the potholes are so I don't blow out a tire before I get out of the gate."

Cody took another long swallow of his drink, eyeing Nick over the can. Finally he set it down and motioned for Nick to follow him. They crossed the living room, not stopping until they were in Lee Ann's studio.

"What's the deal?" Nick asked, looking around. "The house bugged?"

"No, but the kids are girls, they like to talk. And there's a vent into their room in the kitchen. If they want to, they can hear everything being said in there."

Nick stared, his jaw slack. "So they know I bombed with Joanie?"

"Oh yeah. But they probably already knew that. I am, however, making it so they don't know everything else we're about to say."

He supposed that was something. "So what's the deal with her?" he asked.

"Her mom walked when she was thirteen," Cody started. "Joanie came home, on her birthday no less, and the woman had cleaned out her stuff. Just gone. It apparently wasn't the first time she went with some guy. But unlike the other occasions, this time she didn't come back. Or contact them again, as far as I know. "

"Ouch. But that can't be a secret. Not in this town." Surely Cody wasn't sharing with him something that hadn't been public knowledge for twenty years.

"Sure, everyone knows. But they don't talk about it anymore. I'm not going to be the cause of them bringing it back up. It can be brutal when the past gets roused up. Everyone thinks they know every little detail—whether the 'facts' are based in reality or not—and they're more than happy to share them with anyone who'll listen."

Thinking about Joanie and her issues with her mother made him think about his own mother. She had never left, but he'd often wished she would. In reality, when he'd turned eighteen, he'd been the one to leave her. Only, that hadn't turned out so well, either.

He looked at Cody. "Anything else?"

Cody lifted a shoulder, along with one corner of his mouth. "There's apparently a Bigbee Curse."

"A what?" Nick couldn't believe his brother had said that.

"A Bigbee Curse. Bigbee women have bad luck with men. Her mother dated a string of losers, her grandfather walked after thirty-three years of marriage. Apparently it goes back a few generations."

"Let me guess. Joanie believes in this curse?"

Cody smiled, the action tight and unanimated. "If she doesn't get close, she doesn't get hurt."

"You do know how ridiculous this sounds?"

"I'm just spreading the story, man. And to make it better—"

"Better than the Bigbee Curse?"

Cody smirked. "Shut up, wiseass, or this will be the last thing I ever tell you."

Nick made a motion of snapping his mouth closed.

"To make it better, Joanie's birthday is in a few weeks. She'll be the same age her mother was when she fell for the last guy who pulled her out of here. So getting close to you? Right now?" Cody shook his head. "Don't see it happening."

Which stupidly felt like a challenge.

"Seems a man would be smart to steer clear," Nick said.

"That would be the safe bet."

Nick was tired of playing it safe.

"Thanks for the info." He clapped his brother on the shoulder, unsure how he was going to proceed. The smart thing would be to forget Joanie existed, other than for a job.

Then he pictured her standing in her doorway last night, wanting him to kiss her as badly as he'd wanted to do the same, and he worried it was already too late.

He turned to head back to the kitchen. "Let's eat."

"Hold up."

When Nick glanced back, Cody held a business card between two fingers.

"I got it from a buddy who came into the office this morning." Cody was one of the two local veterinarians, both working out of the same clinic. He could have gotten a card from anyone in town.

"What is it?"

"The name of a PI. I think it's time."

Nick went motionless while his blood slammed through his body. Cody was ready to find their other brother? They'd agreed last month to put it on hold for a while, both wanting to get used to each other first before bringing another into the mix. Nick reached out for the card, reading the name on it. The guy was out of Knoxville.

He looked at Cody. "You're sure?"

Cody nodded. "It's time. Let's go find another brother."

Nick couldn't help but smile. Yes, he very much wanted to go find another brother. He let out a laugh.

"Yes," he agreed. "Let's do."

Late-season snowflakes dusted GiGi's yard as Joanie turned into the drive Sunday after church, making her wish for a heavy snow. It had been a couple of years since they'd had a really good one, and they always reminded her of times long past. Before her mother had left. But more importantly, before Pepaw had left.

She still didn't understand what had happened to make him leave.

One day he'd been around all the time, playing games with her in the afternoons, and the next he'd been gone. As sudden as that.

Pepaw had been the one to stay home with her after school due to the fact he'd lost an arm in Korea. He had his military benefits, and GiGi and her mother had jobs.

Though he'd been a bit of a curmudgeon at times, it had been a plan that worked. Until her mother ran off with a man, or quit her job because the guy she was currently dating "didn't care for it."

Which made Joanie wonder briefly who her father was. Had he been just another deadbeat in a long line of them? She'd always assumed so since she'd never gotten an answer out of her mother.

Not knowing was for the best. She didn't need to know the kind of loser she came from on that side of her family. She'd had enough motivation to be who she was by watching her mother's escapades over the years.

Enough reminiscing. She had a house to empty out.

She turned off her car and opened the door, shocked by the burst of wind hitting her in the face, and silently grateful it wasn't a Thursday when she'd need to be wearing a go-go outfit. Equally thankful she'd run home after church and changed from her dress into jeans and a sweatshirt.

Grabbing the tape dispenser and broken-down boxes from the backseat in one hand, she scooped up the deli-prepared, uncooked pizza from her passenger side with the other. Nick might have already eaten lunch, but this way she could at least feel she'd paid him back for dinner.

Especially since Friday night hadn't been a date.

She thought back—for about the millionth time—to the two of them standing on her front porch.

He wasn't her type. He would want more than she would ever give.

Yet the fact remained, she'd wanted to kiss him.

She had to fix that notion today. There was too much to get done together over the coming weeks. Whatever this attraction was between them, it had to end. Now.

She headed up the sidewalk, noticing the handful of early daffodils sprouting, and found herself surprised that Nick hadn't poked his head out the front door. Surely he'd heard her car turn in. She glanced back at the driveway. Yep. Big, giant red truck, sitting right there. Though she wasn't sure how she hadn't paid attention to it when she'd pulled up. Too busy thinking about the past, she supposed.

When she got to the door and Nick still hadn't shown, she pursed her lips, trying to decide what to do next. It didn't feel right to just walk in. He was living there now. Plus, she didn't have a free hand to open the door with anyway. What was he doing that he hadn't heard her?

Or maybe he had, and he was playing nonchalant. Just as she intended to do.

Irritation had her kicking the door several times with the toe of her sneaker. The aluminum of the screen door rattled on its hinges, and finally she heard life from inside the house. Heavy footsteps headed her way.

It was about time.

The door swung open, and Joanie's mouth dropped open.

The goggles on Nick's face, along with the bits of dust and dirt covering his hair and the rest of his face, would have been funny, if not for the way his dark eyes stared out at her through the thin layer of dust. And the way his gray T-shirt was plastered to his chest.

He was drenched with sweat, looking like a crazed person, and she was suddenly ready to toss the idea of keeping it friendly, and help him with a shower instead.

She held up the hand with the pizza riding on her palm. "I owed you food."

He blinked, glanced at the pizza in her hand, then stepped back and let her in.

"I'm sorry," she started, passing by him and ignoring the dirt clinging to his extra-wide shoulders. Looked like demolition had started. She headed to the kitchen. "I should have called and let you know I'd be coming by today. I thought I'd empty out the kitchen cabinets so they'd be ready to rip out when you got to them."

When she turned after unloading her hands, he'd removed the goggles and had the bottom of his shirt lifted, wiping off his face. His abs looked delicious. Her mouth went dry.

"No problem," he finally said. He dropped his shirt, but her memory hadn't forgotten the show. "But you didn't owe me food."

She reached out for the knob on the oven and turned it on, then forced herself to quit gawking at his torso. "I told you I'd bring food next time."

"Or something," he said.

"What?" She couldn't stop herself from peeking back at him, wishing he needed to wipe off his face again.

"You said you'd bring dinner, or *something*, next time." Was his voice deeper than usual? Or maybe it was just scratchy. Kind of like an animal's low growl. "I was wondering what the something might be."

Brown eyes, now free of goggles and dust, swept over her as if implying the something he wanted had nothing to do with the pizza she'd brought. She glanced down the hall, momentarily letting a very naughty thought run through her head. The pizza *would* take twenty minutes to cook.

As if using it as a shield, she picked up the box and held it out in front of her. "I brought pizza."

He gave her a quick smile. "So I see."

"Are you hungry?" She faced the stove, forcing her breathing to be calm and steady, and tried to wipe the memory of his ripped abs from her mind. She was going for nonchalant, she reminded herself. Calm. Cool.

He was just a man. A man with a cat.

Who'd put rocking chairs on GiGi's porch.

She pulled in a deep breath, feeling her insides calm. That last thought had done the trick. He was a nester, looking to settle down, and she would not fall victim to a man. She was there for pizza and to work. Only.

And maybe to clear up any misunderstandings left from Friday night.

Nick stepped to her side and pulled down a glass as she stooped and put the pizza in the still-heating oven. He poured himself lemonade from a pitcher in the fridge, then after downing half the glass, rested his hips against the counter and eyed her.

"Yes," he stated matter-of-factly, and she realized he was replying to her question. "I'm starving, actually. I hadn't realized it was already going on one."

She glanced at his sweaty T-shirt. "You've been working a while, then?"

"Since sunrise. Though I did run into town for donuts after the diner opened." He reached for another glass. "Want some lemonade?"

"We can't kiss, Nick," she blurted out, wanting to jab a finger in her eye over the way she'd brought it up.

He slowly pulled his arm back down, an empty glass in his hand. "So . . . no to lemonade?"

"No to kissing," she reiterated.

"I got that." He tilted the pitcher and poured her a glassful. He handed her the glass and she turned it up, furious with herself for letting him make her nervous. She felt just like her mother had always acted around men. Swooning and silly.

And it pissed her off.

Once she'd finished off the tart drink, she set the glass in the sink, ignored the pointed stare Nick was leveling at her, and bent over to assemble and tape up a box.

"I figured emptying out the cabinets would be a good place to start," she rattled. "You go on back to whatever you were working on. I'll be fine in here."

"Joanie." Nick's voice was steady and solid. She ignored him.

The sound of the tape ripping from the roll as she bound up the bottom flaps broke the silence.

When she still didn't pay attention to Nick, he reached out and stopped her by putting his hand over hers, and then pulling her up and around until she stood facing him, feeling like a fool. He had done nothing to her, yet she was running around, acting as if he'd tried to get her naked on her front porch.

He hadn't even leaned in for the kiss.

She'd just known he wanted one.

Because she'd wanted it, too.

"Nick," she whispered. "I'm serious."

"I can see that."

"We're just working together. I don't . . ." She lifted a hand in the space between them, then let it flutter back to her side. "I don't do this . . . really. It's just best not to."

Nick wanted to ask if the problem was because she worried she'd fall victim to the *Bigbee Curse*—which was a ridiculous load of crap—or if it had something specifically to do with him, but figured the best thing was to drop it. If she didn't want anything to do with him in that way, he wouldn't push the issue.

No matter how much he suspected she was lying to herself.

There were reasons she didn't get close, just as there were reasons he tread carefully with dating, as well. He could respect that.

He'd been let down one too many times in the past himself. He still wanted the kind of love that lasted forever, but he was cautious about going for it. He just hoped time didn't completely pass him by before he found it.

"How about I take a quick shower while the pizza is cooking," he suggested. "Then I'll help you out in here? I'm tired of smashing things anyway."

He'd spent the morning ripping down the back porch, rejoicing in the use of his muscles and the time spent clearing his head. Joanie was intoxicating. He didn't know what it was about her, but he'd thought about her nonstop since he'd arrived in town.

That needed to stop.

Of course, it hadn't helped, her showing up on his doorstep, looking cute and perky in her skinny jeans and oversize Nashville Predators sweatshirt. He'd wanted to peel the sweatshirt off her so he could once again see her curves.

"You don't have to help," she pointed out. "I can do it."

"It'll go faster this way." And it wasn't simply that he wanted to be in the same room as her. Surely. "Then I can spend tomorrow morning playing caveman in this kitchen."

Swinging a sledgehammer was rejuvenating. He was anxious to take out these cabinets. They might have a seventies kind of "charm," but that wouldn't go far in getting this house sold.

"You given any more thought to my suggestions?" he asked.

"To taking your money?"

He angled his head at her. "How about becoming temporary business partners?"

Gray eyes met his and his chest swelled as if he were that caveman and had just dragged a dead animal in to feed his woman.

"I like that," she said. She nodded, then dropped her gaze once more to his stomach. His muscles clenched involuntarily when the tip of her tongue peeked between her teeth. A man could get used to a woman looking at him like that.

He needed to get out of there before she realized how much he was enjoying it. "So . . ." he started. "Yes? Business partners?"

"Yes," she breathed out the word. She seemed to realize she'd been staring at him and looked away, picking up the metal box that she'd pulled from the top shelf of the cabinets Friday night. He'd left it on the counter for her. "The bank is closed tomorrow for Presidents' Day, but I'll go by Tuesday. If I can still get the amount they promised me, I'll let you handle the rest."

A rush of excitement shot through him, giving him the urge to pick her up and swing her around in a circle. Likely, she wouldn't appreciate the act. Blood surged low in his body, and he knew that every part of him would appreciate it.

"Sounds like a plan," he muttered. "I'll be back in ten."

He headed to the bedroom before he did anything stupid. Like kiss her sweet face.

Chapter Five

Joanie was at the fold-up desk in the living room when she heard the bedroom door open and Nick's feet hit the bare hallway. She held her breath, imagining what he'd look like right after a shower.

Damp hair, no shirt, jeans riding low.

Her fingers curled against the papers that were wedged into the open drawer as she thought about what it would be like to take her time and roam over all that muscle.

Nick stepped around the corner and she almost moaned.

She let out a breath instead. At least his hair was damp. Everything else was covered up. His shirt was even buttoned up to his throat. Why not at least a tight T-shirt?

She looked back to the papers beneath her hand and uncoiled her fist. He was behaving and *not* taunting her by letting her see his recently sweaty flesh.

Which she did appreciate.

Even if the view wasn't quite as nice.

"What are you doing?" he asked, heading in her direction. His long legs made fast work of the distance.

The smell of sausage and mushrooms was beginning to permeate the air, and as she glanced up at him, she watched him draw a deep breath in through his nose, and could see that he enjoyed the scent, same as her.

"I'm trying to find a key to open this box." She had the box she'd pulled out Friday night on the desk in front of her, and had gone through every drawer she could think of, looking for a matching key.

"I have a cutter in the truck. I can cut it open for you."

She shot him a look. "There's no need to damage it. I just wanted to see what was inside."

Without having to ask GiGi for the key.

When Joanie had first seen the box shoved away on the shelf, she'd had an instant memory of GiGi treating the small blue-and-black metal container special. It had actually surprised her to find it here. GiGi had taken several things with her to the nursing home when they'd checked her in, and given how she'd protected this box over the years, Joanie had expected it to be with her.

Nick leaned in and the scent of soap and man hit her in overload. She fought the urge to shove her nose against his neck and breathe him in.

His finger flipped up the small lock. "I can cut just the lock. It won't damage the box."

She pulled the box away from him and scowled. "You aren't cutting anything." You didn't just rip into things without trying to find the key first. Maybe she'd come across it somewhere else in the house. "I'll just take it home."

And if she didn't find a key before the day came that GiGi passed away, she'd cut it open then. She shook her head at Nick and tucked the box into the larger cardboard one at her feet. In it she'd added several things she'd found as she'd searched for the key.

Nick followed her movements with his gaze. "Are you taking all that stuff home?"

"Yes."

He grabbed the stack of old *TV Guides* she'd uncovered in the back of a kitchen drawer. "You have some need for these?"

"Did you see the celebrities on the front of them? There are some big stars there. GiGi was keeping them for a reason. They're collector's items."

"And the old Coca-Cola cans?"

His tone irritated her. "Collector's items," she muttered. "They're over twenty years old."

Nick stood straight and she watched him scan the two connecting rooms, his eyes taking in the many boxes and stacks of papers that GiGi had accumulated over the years. They were shoved into corners and up against the walls. Then he landed on the three empty boxes she'd left on the kitchen floor—still waiting for her to get to work cleaning out the cabinets. Finally he returned to the box at her feet.

"You claim your grandmother is the one who's a hoarder?"

Joanie bristled. "I never said *hoarder.*" She narrowed her gaze at him. "Are you implying I am?"

He shrugged. "If the shoe fits."

"Nick Dalton," she took on a tone of outrage, and stood, feeling inferior sitting there with him towering over her. "You just don't understand that some things need to be kept."

He lifted a brow. "And some things need to be tossed."

She breathed slowly through her nose, knowing he was right, but as she'd started uncovering the items, she'd kept remembering how much they'd meant to either GiGi or Pepaw. She and her grandmother may have grown distant over the years, but Joanie wasn't simply able to toss everything out so callously.

Nick went to the kitchen when she didn't immediately reply and pulled open the ancient oven door. The smell of gooey cheese and spicy meat wafted into the room.

"They'll probably hit the trash eventually anyway," she grumbled, following him into the kitchen. "I just hated to get rid of them without making sure they didn't have some value."

"I know," he said. "I'm sorry I teased you. It isn't easy going through your family's things."

His serious tone hinted that he did understand, and then she remembered that he'd recently gone through his mother's things himself. She'd passed away right before he'd come to find Cody.

So he did get it.

He just probably wouldn't choose to keep *TV Guides* and old Coke cans. Or small, secretive boxes.

"I'm sorry you lost your mother recently," she said softly.

Nick put the pizza on the countertop and scrounged around in a couple drawers until he found an old pizza cutter. He glanced at Joanie. "Thank you, sweetness. But it wasn't a big loss."

His words broke her heart. He was such a caring guy—anyone who met him could tell that. She couldn't imagine him losing his mother and it not meaning much.

"I'll get us plates," she said.

They each got pizza, Nick grabbed more lemonade from the fridge, and Joanie found the two of them sharing stories over the next thirty minutes. Nothing huge, just talking and laughing together. It was enjoyable.

When she got up to pour herself more lemonade, Nick scooted his chair back and rose to follow her.

"You know what I think?" he asked.

"What's that?" she buried her face in her glass when he stepped beside her at the sink to rinse off his plate. She'd enjoyed sharing the meal with him, more than she would have thought, but hoped he didn't ruin the moment by saying something lame like, "I want to kiss you with the passion of a hundred men."

She snorted at the thought, sending lemonade burning up her nose.

Her sudden coughing fit made Nick look at her curiously, and she ended up with his strong hand patting her on the back.

"You okay?" he asked as she finally calmed down. "What happened?"

She shook her head. "Just had a funny thought as I was drinking."

He studied her under hooded lids as if trying to decide if the funny thought involved him, then shook his head as if the answer didn't matter.

"What were you going to say before?" She found she really wanted to know. Even if he was harboring the passion of a hundred men. She grinned again, this time pulling his narrowed gaze to her mouth.

She dropped the smile.

"That I think we could be more than temporary business partners," he said.

Oh, crap.

"I think we could also be friends," he finished.

Joanie looked up into his strong, competent face. Shocked. She gave a little smile and a smaller nod. Yes, she thought. Maybe they could be friends. "You're a good guy, Nick."

"So I've been told." He didn't sound as if he appreciated the compliment, but held out a hand to shake. "Friends?"

She found she very much wanted to be his friend. She nodded and clasped his hand. "Friends."

And now she wouldn't even feel bad about letting him help her empty out the kitchen cabinets. She hated doing stuff like that.

The cloying smell of old people assaulted Joanie the instant she entered Elm Hill. Then came the misery lurking from the eyes of every inhabitant she passed in the common room.

GiGi would look the same, misery and defeat written across every feature, but chances were good she wasn't even out of her room. The last couple of weeks when Joanie had called to check on her, she'd been informed that GiGi hadn't left her room voluntarily in days. She was wheeled out for meals, parked in the sunshine by a window for an hour a day, and the rest of the time, she sat in her room alone.

It hadn't been much better when the woman had lived at home. She hadn't stayed in her bedroom then, but she'd rarely ventured from her house in years. Of course, she also had a bad heart and was likely heading toward crazy. She'd had to depend on Joanie to take her wherever she needed to go. Joanie had offered regularly, but she also had never begged when the woman said no.

"Good afternoon, Ms. Bigbee," the receptionist said. "Your grandmother hasn't had the best day today. I'm sure she'll be thrilled to see you."

Joanie glanced at the woman's name tag. Helen. Helen didn't have a clue of which she spoke. "I'm sure she will, Helen." Joanie forced a polite smile. "Thank you."

Three minutes later, Joanie stood before her grandmother's private room, but stopped to take a fortifying breath before entering. Then she took another.

She made monthly visits, just as she'd promised when she'd signed the nursing home papers, but wondered every time who she thought she was fooling. Her grandmother didn't want her there any more than she wanted to be there. She made that clear every time Joanie came in. Rarely did they do anything but argue or get on each other's nerves. Exactly as it had been for years.

Too bad. It was her duty as the only remaining family member to visit, and that's what she was going to do. Whether either of them liked it or not.

She'd drive the forty-five minutes into Knoxville—there was a closer home she could have put GiGi in, but they didn't have as good a reputation—spend a good hour chatting the old woman up, pay the charge each month as best she could, then do it again on the same Tuesday of the next month.

And if she didn't get Nick to get the house fixed up and get it sold . . . soon! . . . the place would kick GiGi out and Joanie would have to figure out how to take care of both of them under the same roof, plus the cupcake store, all without going completely insane.

The thought of Nick made her think of the last couple of days. With the store closed yesterday, she'd ended up at the house again, going through years of Bigbee history from the kitchen and living room. Though he'd been working hard himself, he kept taking breaks and coming over to help her out.

He'd been more than willing to haul the piles of trash out to the Dumpster he'd rented. His willingness gave her the impression he was trying to make sure she didn't drag too much of it home with her. Which she appreciated. It was cute, him watching over her like that.

She'd still snuck out a few boxes he hadn't seen, though.

The thing she'd enjoyed the most about the last two days was that she'd laughed with him. A lot. And he hadn't tried to kiss her again. At all.

She'd caught him checking her out a couple times. But then, she'd checked him out, too. Other than that, all had remained friendly. Just as she'd asked.

Which wasn't nearly as fun as she knew something else could be, but it was definitely safer.

She shoved Nick from her mind. She'd gotten the bank loan secured today, and she still needed to tell him it was a go, but other than that, she didn't need to be thinking about him. What she needed was to go inside GiGi's room, and pretend she wanted to be there.

She sighed.

The door squeaked with her light push, and she stepped inside the darkened room.

GiGi wasn't sitting in her chair as Joanie had expected. Instead, she was lying in her bed, the covers pulled up to her chin, and Joanie could hear her struggled breathing from the door.

Oh my goodness. What's wrong?

Joanie edged across the room in the shadows cast from the corner lamp, trying not to wake her grandmother, but wanting to get a good look. Was she okay? From the breathing, GiGi sounded as if she might be on her deathbed. The sudden thought of losing her grandmother, no matter how little they'd gotten along over the years, settled a pain in her chest she hadn't been expecting. She hadn't felt anything more than annoyance toward this woman in so long, it caught her off guard.

"GiGi?" she whispered, panicked when she saw the paper-thin, yellowed skin stretched across her gaunt face. She looked years older than she had only a month ago.

Slits opened in the wrinkled face, and eyes appearing almost black in the shadowed room stared up at her. "Morning, girlie."

Relief rained over Joanie, traveling down her shoulders. At least GiGi sounded normal. "It's evening, GiGi. Tuesday night. I'm later than usual."

When Joanie had had the salon, she'd visited every third Tuesday before she went in to work. It was a schedule that allowed for some exercise with her grandmother once a month. The time walking in the courtyard had used up part of the hour so they didn't have to sit staring at each other for sixty long minutes as they both tried to figure out what to say.

As GiGi's eyelids fluttered closed, a thin hand snaked out from under the covers and patted the mattress beside her. "Have a seat. Tell me what you've been doing."

Joanie put the white bakery box she carried on the bedside table, scooting over three small ceramic owls, two of them with chips on their ears, and pulled the single guest chair over to the bed. She lowered herself to the seat. Her face drew tight as she struggled to accept her grandmother in this condition. The thought of sitting on the mattress was actually one she considered, but given the frailness of the woman, she was afraid to jostle the bed.

The realization of someday no longer coming for visits put a cold fear inside Joanie that she hadn't known she was capable of. Her fingers turned to ice.

She couldn't get over how bad GiGi looked. Only a month ago, she'd been sitting up when Joanie had visited, complaining that Joanie had fixed her hair in a way that didn't suit her face, and that her clothes weren't "proper" for a decent young lady.

Joanie glanced down at the dark-washed jeans tucked into the knee-high lace-up boots and the bright green sweater that fit tighter than GiGi would probably approve of, and hunched her shoulders to take attention away from the tightness across her chest.

"Can I get you something, GiGi?" she asked softly. "Some water maybe? Did you eat dinner?"

Worry filled Joanie. Something she wasn't used to. She couldn't help it when the woman lay prone before her looking as she did. She'd have to call the doctor to find out what was wrong with her.

"I don't need anything, girlie. Just sit down. You apparently haven't been doing much of that lately."

Joanie briefly closed her eyes, feeling the normal irritation creeping in. Her grandmother always thought she knew best, and made no bones about letting her opinion be known. "You don't know what I've been doing lately, GiGi. I'm fine."

Gray eyes that matched her own stared back at her. "You opened a cupcake store."

Shock kept Joanie quiet for long seconds as she wondered how GiGi knew anything about Cakes. And what she thought about it. Finally she forced herself to relax back into the chair. She pressed her shoulder blades against the vinyl-covered cushion and nodded. "How did you know that?"

"I still keep tabs on you, girlie. I have ever since you put me in here. I know all about the cupcakes and the van. Even about that short skirt you had on last week." Blue-veined lids once again covered her eyes as if the words had been almost too exhausting to get out. "Wonder you didn't catch your death of cold out in that skirt," she continued in a soft grump.

Joanie smoothed her hands down her now-covered legs, reminding herself that the woman was old and didn't need an argument, even if she was looking for one. "I had on tights, GiGi. And I wasn't out in the weather for long. Plus, the day wasn't that cold."

"It's February. You should have been in a skirt down to your ankles. Knowing you, you had to show off those legs, no matter the weather."

And knowing GiGi, she would think her a tramp. "It's part of the brand. I wear it to go with the name."

One eye peeked at her. "And you chose 'Cakes-a-GoGo' for the name?"

Joanie bristled. Yes she'd chosen the name, and she loved it. "It's a good name. And I'm doing a good business. It'll only get better when tourist season starts."

"You'd think you'd settle down and keep one of these businesses you start. Why do you always have to start all over with something new? Just like your mother, always bouncing around to different jobs."

"I don't want to argue with you today, GiGi," Joanie spoke before her grandmother could say more, her voice slightly elevated. She didn't need

GiGi pointing out her faults, or how much she was like her mother. "I'm here to visit. To see how you've been, what you've done this last month. Not talk about all the ways I've done wrong. Can we please just do that?"

GiGi pressed her lips together and turned her head to look away and Joanie took a quick breath. She hadn't meant to burst out like that. She hated when she did that. But GiGi had been nagging at her for as long as she could remember about one thing or another.

Either she was going out with the wrong boys, or she was wearing the wrong clothes, had her hair done wrong, or she was just plain unreliable. Just like her mother.

She didn't want to hear any of it today.

But she also didn't want to hurt GiGi's feelings, no matter how annoying the woman could be.

Grasping for topics, Joanie decided to mention the work she was having done on the house. Which made her think of Nick. And the almost kiss. And then the not kissing. She silently moaned. They were just friends. It was a good thing.

"I have to sell your house to pay the bill here," she blurted out.

That got GiGi's attention. She turned back. "Or I could just go home," she said.

Not this again. "You can't, GiGi. We've talked about this. You can't handle the stairs, and . . . well . . ." She shrugged. "You can't be left alone in the house either. You caught the kitchen on fire three times the last month you lived there."

"I didn't burn nothing down."

"Yes, I know. But you did start fires."

"Little ones." Her grandmother wore a mutinous expression that reminded Joanie of a small kid.

"You just as easily could have killed yourself."

Dark eyes silently stared back at her and Joanie wondered if her grandmother would voice the thought she knew was running through both their heads. *If I died, then you could quit worrying about me. Quit pretending to care.*

That's what it felt like most of the time. Pretending to care. Then a memory from when she was eight rushed through Joanie and she almost gasped. She and GiGi had been standing at the stove. GiGi had been teaching her to make cupcakes from a recipe she'd come up with, and Joanie had spilled a huge glob of batter on the floor. GiGi's dachshund had quickly run into the mix to lap it up, but hadn't stopped soon enough and had slipped, sliding across the floor, coming up with pink cake batter smeared all across one side of his head.

She and GiGi had burst out laughing together, and Pepaw had promptly declared the cupcakes would be called Lucky's Charm, named after the dog and his ever-present "charm." They had always named the cupcakes GiGi had come up with. She'd forgotten how often they used to bake together. Up until Pepaw left.

Just as she'd mostly forgotten how she and GiGi had once liked each other.

"I hired a guy named Nick for the job. I'll take pictures as the work progresses and bring them here to show you. He has brilliant ideas, GiGi. It's going to be incredible when he's finished." She needed to get her mind back from the past before she slipped into too many memories from before her grandfather had left. She would have sworn everyone had been happy then. Possibly even her mother. At least a little.

Snippets of her grandparents holding hands and laughing together flashed through her mind, confusing her like it always had. She'd wished so many times that nothing had changed, and that he hadn't left.

That he'd loved *her* enough to stay.

Her grandmother studied her quietly, but said nothing. Joanie assumed it was anger over the fact the house would be sold instead of Joanie not letting her go home, but something about the sadness in her eyes made Joanie wonder if it was more.

"I found your old recipes a few months back." She changed the subject. "The cupcake ones. That's what I'm using at the store. Everyone loves them."

"I wondered if any of them were mine."

A small smile flittered across Joanie's face. "All of them are yours actually. You may have taught me to mix the recipes and bake them, but your talent for coming up with the creations to begin with never did rub off on me."

"That's too bad." Her voice came out so quietly that Joanie caught herself leaning forward to catch it. "I had hoped it would. That talent came from my mother."

Nope. Joanie shook her head, wishing she had some gene from her grandmother that didn't end in her making a fool of herself over a man.

She glanced at the clock, thinking to get through the hour and then get out of there. Only, for the first time in years, Joanie looked her grandmother up and down and realized she didn't want to leave so soon. She wanted to tell GiGi all about the store and the van, and just how much she was enjoying this new venture. It was different than the others. This one felt more right, though she couldn't quite put her finger on why.

It wasn't as if Sugar Springs hadn't needed all the other services she'd begun. They'd been good ones, good for the community.

But they didn't necessarily *need* a cupcake store. This one just felt good.

And for some reason, she wanted to share it with her grandmother.

She forced herself to relax back into her seat once again, and began talking about the recipes she'd used so far, and which ones were coming up in the near future. GiGi focused her full attention on Joanie, seeming to be completely engaged in the story.

"I do a special cupcake of the week, and this week's is the one you once called Orange Bite after we discovered that putting a peppermint cream in it gives it a nice pop. I'm calling it Orange Paparazzi."

GiGi smiled, and her face brightened. "I always loved that one. It tastes like orange sherbet."

"Until you get to the middle." Joanie laughed, tension easing from her shoulders. GiGi was going to be all right. She was just having a rough day. Joanie pointed to the small box she'd set on the bedside table. "I brought you a couple so you can see if mine are as good as yours."

They continued talking about cupcakes and the people who'd come into the store until Joanie looked up at the clock and realized she'd been in her grandmother's room for almost two hours. She really needed to get back.

She reached for her purse, where she saw the small owl faces of the salt and pepper shakers she'd found at the house. Instead of pulling them out and giving them to GiGi, though, she glanced around at the different owl figurines lining the window shelf and the top of her grandmother's dresser, and decided to take this pair home with her.

Having something at her house that she knew GiGi held dear suddenly seemed important.

GiGi reached out a hand and Joanie slid hers around it as if grasping for a lifeline. Seeing GiGi in this state had loosened something inside her and she realized she was going to miss the woman when the day came that she passed. Joanie should have done more to keep them closer over the years.

"This man you've got taking care of the house. He's a good one?"

Joanie nodded, refusing to give credence to the fleeting sadness that drifted through her every time she thought of selling GiGi's home. "He came with great recommendations, and I've seen some of his work. He's terrific."

"I mean, he's a good guy? A nice man?"

Joanie blinked, then shrugged. "He seems to be one of the good ones."

"That's what I thought."

Joanie needed to find out where GiGi was getting her information.

"Don't push him away too easily, girlie. You're growing up. He might be just what you need."

"I don't need anyone, GiGi. He's just fixing the house. He's going to make it as good as new. That's all."

Paper-thin eyelids dipped low and her grandmother sucked in a ragged breath, then let out a wheezing cough. "Help him, Joanie. Help him see the beauty it can be. Put yourself in it. I wanted you to have the house after me."

A lump tightened Joanie's throat at the same time the words rooted her to her seat. GiGi had wanted her to have the house? She'd never known that. "I can't live there, GiGi. I have to sell it for the money. I need to make sure you're taken care of."

I could take care of her myself. The words popped in and out of her mind. She couldn't take care of her. She didn't have the time. She had to work. Plus, her rental had stairs. GiGi wouldn't even be able to make it to the bedroom every night.

GiGi said nothing for a bit, then brought her hand up to pat Joanie's cheek. The touch felt fragile, like a bird's wing. "Take me home, girlie. I don't want to die here."

Panic flared. "You aren't dying anytime soon, GiGi. You're too stubborn for that."

She knew a better person would consider the plea, but she couldn't bring herself to do it. GiGi was well taken care of there. Better than Joanie would ever be able to do for her. The woman was going to live for years to come, anyway.

Gray eyes dulled in front of her and her grandmother dropped her hand back to the bed. She nodded, a small movement of her pale face and thinning gray hair.

Joanie rose before she did something stupid like cry over the fact she and her grandmother had had such a crappy relationship. She leaned over to give her a kiss on the forehead, and felt a rush of emotion that hadn't been there in years. She'd enjoyed her time with GiGi this evening. If things had been different, she would have liked to take her home. The woman may live for years, but that didn't mean GiGi would be around forever. Joanie closed her eyes. This was for the best.

As she stepped back, she couldn't help but wonder if they could take steps to close the huge crater that had opened up between them over the years. A truce of sorts had seemed to start tonight, though she didn't quite know what had been the cause of it. Things had just been less dramatic than she could remember them being in years.

Maybe if she came to visit more often, she could build on it. She rolled her lips together as she thought through the idea. Yes, that might work.

She would start coming to visit more often. But not too often. She didn't want to push too hard.

"I'll see you soon, GiGi," she whispered. "I'll come back sooner next time."

The woman's eyes were closed now and her breathing had slowed. She didn't reply. She'd fallen asleep.

Joanie let out a breath and tiptoed from the room, wishing that their relationship hadn't taken such a downward turn, and admitting for the first time that it might have been as much her fault as it had been GiGi's. Joanie was certain she hadn't been easy to live with after her mother had left.

She glanced back at the door as she closed it softly behind her. She would fix this before it was too late. She may not be able to bring GiGi home, but she would make sure the house made enough money to keep her comfortable.

And Joanie was definitely going to start visiting more often.

Chapter Six

N ick turned off the sander and shook sawdust from his hair, then
stood still as he listened for sounds in the night. He'd thought he'd
heard a noise outside the house. The distinctive thud of a door closing
came next, confirming that yes, someone had pulled into the driveway.

His heart took off, ignoring his command to remain calm, as he
glanced at his watch and hurried to the door. It was after ten and he could
think of only one person who would swing by unannounced this late on
a Tuesday night.

Well, two people. It could be his brother. But he hoped it wasn't.

Even though he'd spent a large part of the last two days with Joanie—
doing his best *not* to flirt or do anything overt—he wanted her around
again. She made him smile.

And he liked making her smile.

He opened the storm door just as she hit the top step of the porch and
a calmness washed through him. It felt right having her there. She looked
across the porch at him, a lost look on her face, and his barely-hidden-
under-the-surface desires vanished.

"What's wrong?" he asked.

She shook her head, her eyes a bit too wide. "Nothing. I just wanted to
stop by. To, uh . . ." She glanced back out at the driveway as if the answer
lay hidden behind the yellow doors of her compact car, then sucked in

a deep breath and faced him again. She ducked her head slightly and he could no longer get a full view of her in the light spilling out from behind him. "To tell you that I got the loan taken care of at the bank earlier. So if you still want to cover the rest, we can work that out between us. If not—"

"I do," he jumped in. "I'll get papers drawn up so it'll be official." He eased the rest of the way out of the door, having the feeling that if he moved too fast he would spook her away. Excitement at the idea of turning his plans into reality warred with him to get out, but he could tell something was eating at her. Knowing that put a damper on anything else he was feeling at the moment. It worried him. "Want to come in and tell me what's wrong?"

She stared through the open door behind him before heading across the porch. "Can we just hang out here a minute? I'm not ready to go home yet."

"Sure." He motioned to the door. The switch for the porch light was on the inside wall. "Want some light?"

"No," she answered quickly. She paced in the shadows. "I prefer the dark."

"Okay." He moved to perch on the concrete railing, but stopped halfway down. "Want a beer? Whiskey?"

A ghost of a smile curved her lips. "No, thanks."

He finished lowering himself but remained quiet, hoping she'd fill him in on the problem. She didn't. Finally, her melancholy mood getting to him, he decided to start the conversation with something that should lighten her spirit.

"How about you tell me why your hair is now orange?"

"What?" She stopped in front of him and lifted her hands to her hair. "My hair is not orange. It's blond."

He grabbed a curl and slid the end between his fingers. "The tips, blondie. Why are the tips orange?"

"Oh." She smiled and his pulse informed him it was no longer just about kissing; he wanted her in his bed. "It matches Orange Paparazzi." At the blank look he gave her, she added, "The cupcake of the week."

He cleared his throat. "You change your hair color to match your cupcakes?"

"Only the cupcake of the week. And only the tips." She pulled one of the orange locks in question in front of her face and held it up for him to see. "It's a temporary wash, so it won't damage my hair by changing it so often. I have boots to match, too."

There went all the blood that had been in his brain. "More go-go boots?" he croaked out.

"Yep." Her smile flashed, showing him a hint of the carefree woman he liked so much, and not the sad one who'd shown up at his door. He almost leaned in and kissed her.

He needed to get away from her before he did something stupid, but couldn't bring himself to move her aside. Or to walk away himself. Instead, he glanced down at the brown boots she wore. "When do you plan to wear these orange boots? Or did I miss them already?"

Please, he silently pleaded, *please don't let me have missed them.*

The thought that she might have been prancing around town in the orange boots, and if he was guessing correctly, an orange miniskirt, had him more than ready to go.

She stepped back from him, and moved to rest her rear on the railing to his side. "I've designated Thursdays as the day I take out the van. At least until tourist season starts. I'll take it out more then and on Saturdays when the local soccer and baseball games kick off."

"So that's when you'll wear your boots?"

"And the matching outfits, yes."

He gulped. "Do you need any help on those days?" The thought of leaving her alone for all those men to ogle irritated him.

She laughed, a clear sound ringing out in the dark night that made him feel good inside. "Thanks, but I have Destinee for that. I suspect she'll be far more help than you would be. You'd probably try to eat all the cupcakes."

"Yeah," he said. "Cupcakes. That's what I was thinking about."

The woman was going to be the death of him before he got this project over with. But then, he could choose to stay out of town on Thursdays and avoid temptation. He almost laughed. *Not likely.*

She shivered at his side and he realized she was freezing in the cold night air.

Without thinking, he wrapped an arm around her shoulders and pulled her close. "Do you want to come in? I have the heat going."

"No thanks," she murmured as she glanced toward the door, looking as lost as she had when she'd arrived. It was almost as if something inside the house was what made her sad.

"What's the matter, Jo?" He squeezed her shoulders. "Tell me. Let me help."

She shook her head. "It's nothing."

Since she was pressed against his side, he could feel the tension coming back. Something had happened, and he wanted to fix it. "Do I need to go beat someone up for you?"

"No!" But the question had the desired effect and her body softened again, easing into him along with her light laughter. Her head tilted in line with his body and pressed into the curve of his arm.

They sat there like that for several moments and he gave up on her sharing with him. He wouldn't push it. Cat leaped up onto the railing and Joanie reached out and scratched him behind the ears. Cat seemed to be more interested in Joanie than in Nick, but who could blame him? Nick would be too if their situations were reversed.

"I think my grandmother might be dying," her soft voice spoke as if to the cat, but Nick knew it was for him.

A pain settled in his chest. "Oh sweetness, I'm so sorry."

Cat purred and pushed up closer to Joanie as if sensing her hurt.

"We're not close anyway. And she's been sick for a long time."

"Still, she's your family." He wanted to put both arms around her, but was afraid doing so would send her running. "Is that where you've been tonight?"

She nodded, still focused on the cat.

"Joanie?" He wanted her to look at him. She'd mentioned before that her relationship with her grandmother wasn't the best, but clearly seeing her sick had upset her.

"What?"

"Are you okay? What can I do to help?"

"Nothing. I'm fine. It's probably still months away, anyway." She leaned down to the cat, breaking contact with Nick's arm, and rubbed a cheek against the side of Cat's head. "Maybe years."

She stepped away from the railing and away from him, then glanced around as if trying to figure out the best escape route, managing not to make eye contact while doing so.

Seeing the Dumpster at the end of the porch, she turned and headed in the other direction, passing in front of him, face averted. "I'll see you again Friday night," she mumbled. "I'll be back to start on the bedrooms."

Before she could get past him, he snagged her by the arm and stopped her. "Look at me."

She didn't, instead tilting her chin up in the air, her face pointed away from him as if letting him know she was tough and didn't need his comfort. He lightly squeezed her arm.

"Look at me, sweetness. I want to help."

With terrible slowness, he watched her chest move up and down with a deep gulp of air. She finally turned to him. Tears had streaked down both cheeks and more filled her eyes, waiting for their turn to run free.

"Come here," he said, a second before he pulled her to him.

Once snuggled up against him, he wrapped his arms around her and held her tight while she turned loose and cried. When her own arms snaked around his waist, he almost cried with her. It was not easy watching this woman hurt.

"I'm sorry I'm getting your shirt wet," she muttered into his chest.

Instead of worrying about that, he squeezed her closer, slipping a hand around the back of her head to hold her in place. "That's what friends are for, isn't it? To be here when you need us?"

She nodded against him, and he could tell the tears were already beginning to slow. It hadn't lasted long, but it had been pretty powerful stuff. "I should be crying to Lee Ann. She's always been the one I go to when . . ."

Her words trailed off, but he knew what she was about to say. "When I need someone." And tonight she'd come to him.

The enormity of that action filled him. Joanie may not want them to be anything to each other, but he wasn't sure either of them could stop whatever was happening.

When the tears dried, she remained tucked in tight, and he sensed her embarrassment now overshadowing her pain. Both at letting him see her cry, and also at knowing she must look a mess and that he would witness the damage when she stepped away.

Instead of waiting for her to work up the courage to raise her head, he did it for her. Holding her steady between his hands, he lifted her face to his. Mercifully, it was a clear night, and the moon glowed down on her, highlighting her tear-stained face. She was beautiful.

He used his thumbs to swipe over both cheeks, then leaned in and pressed kisses along the paths of her tears. She closed her eyes as he did, and he fought the urge to kiss her properly.

"Would you like me to drive you home?" he whispered.

She merely shook her head, her lashes resting against her pinkened cheeks, her lips turned down at the corners.

"Then let me take you inside and tuck you into my bed. I'll sleep on the couch. I don't want you to have to go home alone."

Spiky eyelashes fluttered, then lifted, leaving dark eyes staring up at him. "You really are a good guy, Nick. I like that."

He typically hated being called a good guy. It had landed him with too many of the wrong women over the years. And this was the second time she'd done it. "I'm here for you whenever you need me, sweetness."

"I know." Her lips curved a little and she nodded. "I appreciate it."

He wondered if she'd appreciate it if she knew how much he enjoyed her being pressed up against him.

"So . . ." He cleared his throat and forced himself to lower his hands. "Bed?" He had no idea how he would get any sleep with her in the same house, but was determined to stand by his words.

"No." Her voice was small, yet there was strength behind it. She may falter, but she stood back up. "I don't need to stay at the Barn tonight."

He stared at her. "The Barn?"

A sad smile touched her mouth. "That's what GiGi calls this house. The Barn. She and Pepaw named it."

Seemed Joanie inherited her oddities honestly.

"I'm fine, Nick," she added, giving him another of those sad smiles that lasted only a second. "Really. I just needed to let that out, and I guess I didn't want to go home and do it alone."

Yeah. He knew about needs. He had some of his own. And sometimes they outweighed good judgment.

Ignoring his better sense, he lowered his head before he could change his mind, and pressed his closed mouth to hers.

Joanie's eyes opened wide the instant Nick touched his lips to hers, then warmth moved through her and she let her lashes drift closed. His lips were firm, yet had just the perfect amount of softness, and were so toasty warm that she wanted to curl up with them so she'd never be cold again.

She let out a little noise and edged forward, wanting more.

He complied.

He angled his head and when she parted her lips, he slid his fingers into her hair and quietly slipped inside her mouth. Normally she wanted a harder kiss, something faster and more to the point, but she had to admit, he was making quite a point just the way he was.

Kind of a . . . *wow* kind of point.

His hands gripped her face and tilted her up the slightest bit more, taking the kiss even deeper, and she became a puddle below the waist. Parts of her came alive that had almost forgotten how to work.

Then it hit her . . . Nick was kissing her!

He wasn't supposed to kiss her. Business, not pleasure.

She wouldn't fall for him.

But oh God, it was a nice kiss.

A groaning sound came from him, reengaging her and making her grip his waist and pull her body against his. When her breasts brushed over the planes of his hard chest, she moaned and pushed even closer. She wanted to touch him, to feel what he wore under those flannel shirts.

And she wanted him to return the favor.

She forgot all about how kissing him was not in the plan, and got lost in his expert movements.

A girl could spend hours letting this man make love to her mouth.

Too soon, he pulled back, his breathing as ragged as hers, and peered down into her face. It was so dark with his shoulders and head blocking out the moon that she could barely make out his features, but she knew the look that was in his eyes. It was the same one in hers.

He wanted more.

Then she remembered his cat, and the rocking chairs, and the fact that he was the type that could sweep her off her feet.

And leave her broken.

Damn it.

"Let me take you out, Joanie," he said, his voice as uneven as she suspected hers would be if she tried to talk. "I want to show you a good time, buy you really excellent whiskey, and make you smile. And I want to kiss you again. A lot. Can we do that? Will you let me?"

Oh, crap. She blinked and took a quick step back, lowering her gaze as she did. She could not go out with him. Had she learned nothing in the past thirty-two years? Bigbee women could not do relationships.

And he was definitely looking for a relationship.

"Ummm . . ." she said. She peeked back up at him, cringing slightly, knowing he wasn't going to be happy with her answer. "No."

Nick stood dumbfounded, his arms dropping to his sides.

She shook her head. "I'm sorry, Nick. I just can't. I don't date."

What in the world had she been thinking kissing him like that? Without another word, she hurried off the porch and to her car, refusing to look back, and certainly not answering when he called her name. She slid behind the wheel and started her car.

She'd known what it would be like if she let that man kiss her. It would be freaking awesome.

Exactly as it had been.

Of course it would be, because he had that incredible mouth.

And now she had to live with knowing what it tasted like. And felt like. And what it made her feel like.

A tingle slid down her spine, and she thumped the base of her palm against her steering wheel as she spun gravel pulling out of the driveway. She had to forget what that man could do with his mouth.

Because if he could make her feel like this without using his hands?

Crap!

Chapter Seven

Nick stepped from the empty storefront into the cold sunshine of the day and clipped his cell phone to his belt. It was Thursday. He'd come to town to check on potential office space to house his company. His trip had nothing to do with it being cupcake van day.

He'd hired a handful of guys throughout the week to help with the work at the house . . . the *Barn*, he corrected himself, shaking his head at the name, though accepting that something about it fit. Not that the house looked like a barn, but the uniqueness of it fit with what he'd already figured out about Joanie.

The workers were temporary until he knew for certain he could get more jobs. He also had a good selection of résumés from prospective office managers. Now all he needed were contracts.

And a cupcake.

He glanced across the street to the empty parking spot in front of Joanie's shop, wishing she were back. The van had headed out fifteen minutes earlier as he'd been talking to Jane, the Realtor. Then his phone had rung, and she'd given him the key and asked him to lock up when he left, leaving him with privacy.

The call had been the private investigator. They'd been trying to find more than five minutes to talk since Nick had first called him Monday morning. Nick had wanted to fill him in on what he'd been able to learn about his brother up to that point—which was sorely little. Adopted, one year older than Cody and him, likely moved out of the state with the adoption. That pretty much summed it up.

They'd hung up today with an agreement to do business, and the promise of a contract to be e-mailed later that night.

A thrill of adrenaline shot through him at the thought of finding the third Dalton brother. Could it be as easy as it had been with Cody? Finding him wouldn't be, but maybe they could have the same seamless connection when they did meet up. He hoped so. It may be thirty years in the making, but hopefully it wasn't too late.

He made a quick stop by the veterinarian's office to catch Cody up with the situation, then popped into the diner for a cup of coffee.

"Hey sugar," Holly Marshall greeted him as he stepped to the counter. She struck him as a young Dolly Parton with big hair, tight jeans, and purple cowboy boots. All she needed was a guitar.

She was part owner of the diner, and a fond memory of his first night in town. The day he'd met Cody.

After getting over the shock of discovering a twin, then coming face-to-face with the man himself, he and Cody had done the male bonding thing by drinking until the wee hours of the morning.

Holly had been at the Bungalow that night, her high-heeled silver-and-pink shoes—that had seemingly matched nothing about the dress she'd had on—catching his attention, and had been more than happy to dance the hours away with him as he'd silently railed over the shitstorm his life had been. A worthless mother, a twin she'd given away, and another brother he had yet to find.

All he'd wanted as a kid had been a brother. Someone who'd understood what it was like living with his mother. Then he'd found out he had two and they'd been given away before he could remember them.

He'd been angry. So he'd tossed back the alcohol and he and Holly had danced . . . and then some. But they'd done nothing that needed to be taken behind closed doors. Everything had been purely innocent fun, him blowing off steam, her simply having a good time.

They'd made out, they'd danced, and then she'd taken him and Cody home and dumped their drunk asses in Cody's apartment.

"Hey cutie," he replied. He tapped one of the long blue earrings she wore and gave her a wink. "Give me a large coffee to go, will you?"

Joanie was out in the cold, and he happened to know she liked coffee.

Holly set down an insulated cup in front of him. "Going for a cupcake?" she asked.

As if there were any other option.

He merely shrugged, then took a sip of the hot liquid. He intended to give it to Joanie, but liked knowing that they were sharing it. Just as they'd shared a smoking-hot kiss a couple days before.

"Van's back," Holly said.

Nick spun on the stool and looked out the window to where he could see the van, lights flashing, parked right out front of Joanie's store. There was a line of men already, twenty deep.

He sighed.

Slapping down enough bills to cover the coffee and a healthy tip, he smirked at Joanie's grin, then headed out into the cold to be as pitiful as every other male standing out there.

As he went, he wondered if Joanie had been thinking about that kiss at all. He had been. Pretty much nonstop for the last forty hours.

Now all he had to do was figure out if he wanted to push for another one, or if he was going to back off. An intelligent person would choose door number two. She didn't want to go out with him.

He should drop it.

But he at least wanted to know what had been behind that no. Didn't he deserve that much? She'd kissed him as if she'd found water in the desert, then run when he asked her out. The least she could do was explain herself.

Spotting her orange-tipped hair as she leaned out the window of the van, his feet picked up speed. He was anxious to see this week's outfit up close. He could already make out an orange sweater, and there was no doubt a matching skirt was beneath. Probably a very short skirt. He didn't know how the woman didn't freeze her sweet cheeks off.

He stopped by his truck to grab the contract for financing the renovation, and headed across the street. He wanted a cupcake.

He also wanted a sweet thing in an orange miniskirt for dessert.

Before he made it to the van, a call came in about a potential job and he stepped to the side to take it. He'd been working the streets all morning, letting it be known he was setting up shop. Everything was rolling along, just as he wanted.

He got in line with the other men and began waiting his turn, turning the collar of his coat up to keep the wind from going down his neck. The third time he saw Joanie rub her hands up and down her arms, he left the line and headed to the back door of the van.

"Nick?" Joanie looked up in surprise as he opened the door and reached inside for her.

"Come with me," he said. He had hold of her forearm and was dragging her out.

"I can't just come with you. I have customers."

He shot Destinee a look asking if she could handle it and she nodded. "I got it, boss. You go talk to Hottie there. He looks like he needs you more than I do."

Destinee smirked and Nick narrowed his eyes. The teenager was too knowledgeable for her own good. No, he didn't *need* Joanie. He merely wanted her to take a minute and warm up. If he was using that as an excuse so he could have her all to himself, well, he saw nothing wrong with that either.

"What are you doing?" Joanie's voice rose as he tugged her away from the van. He met her gaze, then pointedly turned back to the crowd. Every pair of eyes was focused in their direction. Speculation was already running rampant, what with him living out at the Barn. Did they need to know more?

"You're freezing," he said patiently. "I'm merely helping you to step inside for a few minutes so you can warm up."

"There's a heater in the van. I'm perfectly fine."

He grabbed her hand, finding it ice-cold, and held it up between them. "Then maybe you should have been using it."

He glanced at the van, having the momentary concern that the teen might be just as cold, but she was bundled up properly and even wore gloves. When Destinee saw him watching her, she pointed at the store.

"I'm not going to let you drag me out of my own business," Joanie protested, but he noticed she left her hand in his warmer one.

"Sweetness, two minutes, that's all I ask. Come inside, warm up, and don't make me have the conversation we're about to have out here in front of everyone."

That got her attention, which made him feel a little guilty. He had a contract for her to sign, and they didn't need privacy for a contract.

The kiss on his porch, though—and him asking her out . . .

He hadn't yet decided if he'd bring that up or not.

She looked at the crowd, smiled one of those electrifying smiles, then turned to him and frowned.

"Fine." She blew out a breath, the bangs of her blond hair puffing up in the air as she did, and snatched his coffee out of his hands. She then turned for the store, tilting the cup up as she went. He followed, keeping enough distance to enjoy the view. The go-go boots were the previously mentioned orange today, paired with white tights. He liked the look.

As he made his way into the building, he caught sight of Lee Ann's mother, Reba London, watching from the back of the cupcake line. He would bet a hundred dollars that woman wasn't standing out in the cold just because she was looking for a treat.

The door closed behind them, and he grabbed Joanie's free hand to keep her from running away. He then took the coffee and set it on the nearest table, and clasped that hand in his, too. Using the excuse that he wanted to warm them, he held her hands together inside his.

"You're freezing out there," he said.

"I'm fine."

"You're a freaking Popsicle. Did no one ever teach you to wear clothes in the winter?"

He was rubbing his palms against the backs of her hands, feeling some life come back into them, and couldn't help but want to pull her closer. With her pink cheeks and ever pinker nose, he wanted to do more than warm up her hands.

"I have a contract for you to sign." Best to take his mind off what he wanted when they were standing in front of glass windows with half the town watching. He turned her loose and reached into the inside pocket of his coat.

"Is that why you pulled me in here?"

"I pulled you in here because you needed to warm up. Why don't you put a coat on before you go back out? Or better yet, pants." Then all the other men out there couldn't drool over her as if she were a piece of meat.

He removed the paper from his pocket and they moved to the counter so she could read and sign it. She brought the coffee with her and sipped it as she read.

"It's pretty straightforward," he said. "Leaves it with the max we talked about that I can put into the house, all of it to be payable upon close of the sale."

She nodded and grabbed a pen, then signed with a few quick strokes.

"Thanks for doing this, Nick." Her gray eyes peered up at him as she folded the paper into thirds, eyeing him as if he held a secret. "I appreciate it."

"Like I said, it'll help me out as much as you." And if he was doing it just a little because he liked her so much, that was his own business.

He tucked the paper inside his jacket and knew he should let her go back out to the street, but found he wanted a few more minutes alone with her. "You coming to the house tonight?" he asked. She hadn't been there since Tuesday night. "We need some of the bedrooms emptied before we can go much further."

"Is it okay if I wait until tomorrow night? I sort of want to go home and take a long, *hot* bath tonight." She smiled, her nose crinkling with the action. "I'll admit that I'm freezing my rear off out there if you'll let me have tonight to do that."

"Sure." He would've admitted he wanted to help her out with that bath if he thought it would get him anywhere. He kept his mouth shut.

"Thanks." She picked up the coffee, holding it up between them. "Can I keep this?"

He gave her a small smile. "I bought it for you."

Her lips tilted up. "You're a sweetheart." She reached out to pat him on the arm, but before she could head back outside, he caught her hand in his.

"About that kiss," he said.

She froze. She looked out the window as if seeking someone who could help her escape before carefully facing him once again. There was apology in her eyes. "It was a mistake, Nick."

"Was it the kiss itself that was the problem?" He was a glutton for punishment. "Or did it just not do it for you?"

Joanie eyed him from between narrowed lids. "Do you really need someone to tell you that you're a great kisser? Is that what you're looking for?"

It didn't hurt. "What I'm looking for is an answer. Why not go out with me? We could have a good time."

"I told you, I don't date."

"Never?"

"Not . . ." She motioned her hand back and forth between them. ". . . real dating. Not with someone like you."

"So there are men you *have* said yes to?" Why was he pushing this line of questioning?

She gave him a yes-dumbass-I-have-said-yes-before look. "A few times," she admitted slowly. "Yeah."

He couldn't help but laugh, though there was no joy in the sound. Not sure his battered ego could take any more, he kept plugging ahead anyway. "Then what's wrong with me?"

He counted the number of times she blinked. The number was not a good sign.

"Dammit, Joanie." He didn't let her answer, his temper suddenly firing. He dropped her hand and paced across the room. "It was just an invitation to dinner. What was the big deal?"

She followed behind him. "That's the thing. It wasn't just an offer for dinner."

"Sure it was."

She stopped in front of him, standing too close, and he could smell a mix of fresh air and—he leaned a fraction closer and sniffed—oranges. She smelled like oranges.

"No it wasn't," she answered. "You come with a cat, Nick."

He rolled his eyes heavenward. "What in the world does my cat have to do with me asking you out, Jo?"

She lifted one shoulder. "It wouldn't stop with dinner."

"You mean sex?"

Her cheeks were still pink from the cold, but he would swear they turned a shade deeper. She turned so that she once again faced the windows. "No," she answered. "I'm not talking about sex."

"Because I'll have to admit, I wouldn't have complained if it had turned into dinner *and* sex. But that wasn't what I was asking for."

"And it's not what you're asking for now either. I know that."

"I'm not asking for anything now. Other than an explanation. Forget going out. That's off the table. But will you tell me, at least, why you *don't* want to go out with me?"

She whirled around to face him, her eyes glinting with irritation. "Because you would want more *after* the sex."

"What are you talking about? I want a nice evening with a beautiful woman, and if it ends with us in bed, then I'd be happy. And whether it did or not, I'm not looking for more." Liar. He wanted everything. He just didn't think he was ever going to find it. "I've got too much going on to think of anything past one night."

That wasn't entirely true, because he'd already thought about having many nights with her. And not all the fantasies involved the two of them ending up in bed together. Which just proved her point. *Dammit.*

Her head tilted to the side. "You'd be perfectly happy to roll around with me for the night, then be nothing but friends the next morning?" she asked. "Because I have to tell you, that might be something I could get behind."

The idea of having her naked in his hands and then maintaining a nothing-but-friends relationship didn't exactly sit well with him. Other women maybe. But with her? It sounded good in theory, but something told him it would be harder to pull off than it seemed.

"See!" she raised her voice, pointing at him. "That's what I'm talking about."

"I didn't say anything." His own voice rose to match hers, his hands going up in the air.

"You didn't have to. I read it on your face. You would definitely want more."

This was the weirdest conversation he'd ever had. Frustrated, he began pacing again, then stopped in front of her. He grabbed her hand and held it down by his side. "The pause was because yes, I might want more. In all honesty, I *do* want more. *Someday*. But that's not what my asking you out was about. It's not what I'm looking for right now. I just thought we could have a good time."

"But that's why I said no. Because you do want more. Someday."

"So you won't even give us a chance? Maybe we wouldn't be good together and this whole conversation is a moot point."

Her eyebrows raised, and he had to give her credit. Based on their kiss, he suspected boredom in the bedroom would not be a problem between them.

"I know better than to risk it, Nick." Her voice lowered and she squeezed his hand in hers. "I'm not the relationship kind of girl. I actually *only* do the sex."

"I do that too," he insisted. He said the words, but acknowledged that hearing them from her caused a stutter in his heart. They sounded so callous.

He had the thought to ask why she was that way, but suspected it had to do with her mother. Bad experiences. The Bigbee Curse. He wanted to growl at the mere idea of it.

She shook her head. "You need more. I can't give it to you."

He hated when people thought they knew what he needed. "Fine," he snapped out, releasing her. "You win. We won't go out."

"It's for the best," she started, but he stopped her with a look.

She tilted her face up to his. "I'm sorry," she whispered. "Go find your-self a girl who does want more. No matter how hot our kiss, you and I just don't make sense."

He lifted his hand to rub the backs of his fingers over her cheeks be-fore realizing what he'd done. The softness reminded him she was right. He'd want more from her. If he couldn't have it, better to know it now. He lowered his hand.

"Nothing to be sorry about, sweetness. You're right." Though it felt like acid burning his stomach as she said the words. "You and I weren't meant to be. We'll just continue being friends. How about that?"

A sweet smile curved her mouth and his blood rushed south, belying his words. "I'd like that very much," she said.

Perfect. Just what he needed. A *friend* who kissed like a sex goddess and dressed like a wet dream. This was going to be a breeze.

Chapter Eight

Joanie picked her way across the uneven gravel, lamenting the fact her grandmother had never seen fit to pave the driveway. It was one more expense she would have to come up with the money for since she'd forgotten to make sure it was in the estimate for the work Nick was doing. She couldn't very well turn a house into a jewel when the first thing buyers saw was a ratty old driveway.

But she'd worry about that some other day. Tonight she had other things on her mind. Dealing with Nick and not thinking about having sex with him, for one. Ever since that had been tossed out the day before, that's *all* she'd been thinking about.

A single kiss with the man had left her panties wet and her tongue twisted in knots. She couldn't imagine what naked, head-to-toe contact would do to her. And it didn't help any that it had been months since she'd gone out with a man.

"Ouch." She gritted her teeth as she stepped on the gravel wrong and twisted her ankle in her high-heeled boots. Why she'd come over directly from work instead of running home to change clothes, she had no idea. It wasn't as if she was trying to impress Nick.

She had a job to do, and it was going to be a dirty one. Showing up in a dress was ridiculous. Especially coupled with the boots. Just because

Nick didn't seem to be able to take his eyes off her legs when she wore boots didn't mean she needed to taunt him with them.

Or taunt herself with silly ideas.

They weren't going to date, for crying out loud. Heck, she'd told him to go find someone else. It would be silly to try to impress a man she had no intentions of getting involved with.

She climbed the steps, doing her best to shove away the anxiety she'd felt since their conversation the day before, and went to the door. Since he knew she was coming over this afternoon, she didn't knock, just reached for the knob instead. She found the door locked.

Taking a step back, she stared up at it as if doing so would explain the situation. There was a light glowing through the bare living-room window. Yet as she looked at it, she realized the single bulb seemed to be the only one on in the house. She tilted her head back to stare at the porch fixture above her. It was on.

Was he out?

Maybe he'd run out for dinner and would be back soon?

Swirling around to look at the driveway, she noticed his truck wasn't there. How did she keep missing something so large?

"Stupid men," she muttered. "Never can do what is expected of them."

What was she supposed to do now? Go back home? Wait around on the porch for him to return?

She rolled her eyes. No. She was neither going to go home nor wait. He had been fully aware she was coming over tonight. She'd told him only yesterday afternoon. That meant she could go on in and there would be nothing wrong with it.

Returning to the car for her purse, she dug around inside until she found her spare key, then unlocked the front door. Though she wasn't in the mood to wait on Nick, she also wasn't thrilled to paw through GiGi's bedroom alone. The idea of it just felt too personal. Vulnerable.

GiGi was going to die someday, and close relationship or not, that was going to be rough.

She thought about the call she'd made to GiGi's doctor the other day. He'd confirmed she had gotten worse—her heart was steadily declining—but had said she potentially had weeks, even months, left. The nurses had told her just that morning that, though GiGi was continuing to keep to her room, she had looked a little brighter when she got up today.

Joanie took that and went with the more positive. It wouldn't be weeks, but months. It had to. They needed more time.

She still would have preferred Nick be there tonight, though. Knowing he was in the house made going through everything easier.

She pushed the door open and the first thing she noticed when she stepped inside was how much had been done since she'd been there Monday. It was even beginning to smell like new construction instead of old person.

The living room carpet was gone, and only a single recliner and the TV remained in the room. Nick had moved some of the larger items into the garage, waiting for her to either dump them or take them somewhere else, so she assumed the couch and end tables had seen the same fate.

Walking through the rooms, she set the box of cupcakes down and dropped her purse on the rickety kitchen table. He'd really made a lot of changes this week. She pulled out a slim camera and began taking pictures to show GiGi the next time she went to see her.

The wall connecting the utility room was new, the built-in corner cabinet had been stripped down to bare wood, and the cabinets had been ripped out and replaced with lots and lots of gorgeous, glossy cream-colored wood. Suddenly the room hinted that it might belong in the twenty-first century. It looked like what a farmhouse should look like. She turned a circle in the middle of the space, taking in the rest of the room.

The browning linoleum had been ripped up and remained in a heap on the kitchen floor, with the dusty curtains that had once hung on every window now draped over the top of the pile. She picked her way down the bare hallway to the back of the house, poking her head into rooms as she went, finding boxes and piles of GiGi's belongings shoved to the middle of the rooms.

A toothbrush in a glass cup caught her attention in the bathroom and she stepped inside the room and looked around. Pieces of Nick dotted the place.

She turned and left. She wasn't there to dig through the man's stuff. She had work to do. Might as well get to it and enjoy the quiet evening alone.

She reached down and unzipped her boots, then tugged them off. No need to prance around in hot shoes if there was no one around to appreciate them. She then headed into the master bedroom to work.

This was the space Nick had claimed as his, and she could swear she smelled him the instant she stepped through the door. Hot maleness assaulted her senses, and she *knew* that was the imprint of his head in the pillow of the unmade bed.

Nerves twisted inside her. The sight of the tangled sheets did nothing to help her peace of mind, as all she could do was imagine Nick lying there asleep. Or not asleep.

She fanned her face. She had to stop thinking of him like that.

Turning right, she opened the closet door and frowned at the mess stacked from floor to ceiling. *Sigh.* She wished Nick was there with her.

A thigh-high pile of trash, four bags of clothes for Goodwill, and three boxes of fabric for the quilting ladies later, she sat back on her heels and eyed her work. She was only a third of the way through the small closet. And she'd thought this would be an easy place to start.

She stood and pulled two boxes down from the top, discovering part of GiGi's collection of spoons, and decided she would take those home and sort through them later. Next was a cigar box crammed full of envelopes.

As she flipped through them, she found they were all addressed to GiGi, with postmarks dating back to the fifties. She pulled out the wad of pages from one of the envelopes, and flipped through them, only to find Pepaw's scrawled signature at the bottom of the last page. She flipped the envelope over in her hand and squinted at the return address, then her eyes grew wide.

Korea?

She once again scoured the letter, skimming over the words, then slowed and read more carefully. It was a love letter.

They hadn't gotten married until he'd returned from the war, but he'd been sweet on her before he left. This one was dated 1951. Pepaw would have been eighteen, and GiGi fifteen.

How precious.

Her insides went warm and melty at the thought of him wooing her from all the way on the other side of the world, and she sat on the floor to begin sorting through them, peeking inside each to read the handwritten dates so she could put them in chronological order.

Before she got through more than a handful, she heard a noise outside and scrambled to her feet.

Slamming car doors kicked her into a faster speed until she realized it had been more than one door closing. Who was here? When she got to the living room, instead of stepping over and looking out the main window, she peeked out the narrow window framing the door to find Nick escorting a buxom, overdressed, over-made-up woman to the front porch.

Joanie recognized her instantly.

Gina Gregory.

Everyone knew Gina was not only on the hunt for a husband, but she would stoop to any level to get one. Do *anything* to get one.

Irritation tightened Joanie's shoulders. Gina probably thought she'd already found one.

Before Joanie could do more than straighten and step back behind the door, Nick opened it and motioned Gina in, giggles, wiggles, strong perfume, and all.

The woman made Joanie's teeth hurt.

"So this is where you're staying?" Gina's slightly slurred comment kept Joanie from speaking, but the familiar way Gina ran her hand up Nick's arm literally brought bile to Joanie's throat. There was no way he could miss the signals Gina was lobbing. If the body language didn't do it, the massive expanse of boobage muffin-topping out of her shirt would.

Joanie's stomach rolled. She caught a reflection of herself in the darkened side window and wanted the floor to open up and swallow her whole. Her hair was a mess with curls sticking out in every direction and a nice dust bunny riding high on the crown of her head.

She swatted at her hair while at the same time swiping at the streak of dust across her chest with the other hand. Nick caught her in the act, looking like she was playing the game where kids try to pat their heads and rub their tummies at the same time. Only she wasn't rubbing her tummy.

"Joanie?" Nick stopped. "I thought you'd be gone already."

She narrowed her eyes at him. "You parked beside my car."

"Hmmm," he said. "I guess I did."

Did he think his going out with Gina was going to make her jealous?

"Oh, Nicky." Vomit-inducing sweetness oozed from Gina's mouth. "Let's not interrupt her. You can show me your place another night."

"It's my place." The words barely whispered out of Joanie's mouth. How dare he bring this woman to GiGi's house.

Nicky patted the hand clenching his forearm and eyed Joanie, his expression strangely blank. "You're right, Gina. Let's head out. We'll leave Joanie to finish up here."

They left in the same flurry of perfume and wiggling hips in which they'd arrived, and Joanie closed the door behind them. The nerve of the man. Bringing Gina Gregory into this house.

The fact that Joanie had not only turned him down, but suggested he go find another woman wasn't lost on her. But seriously, *Gina Gregory*? He was going out with her for one reason only. Which, of course, he'd said yesterday he'd be perfectly happy with. A good-looking woman, a good time, and a hop in the sack after.

The definition of a man's ideal night.

Her skin crawled. Had he planned to sleep with Gina at the house?

Disgust rolled through her. She shouldn't care who he dated or what he did with them. She and Nick were only friends.

Then, why did she feel such jealousy?

She shoved a newspaper off the recliner and plopped down with the remote. The cable had been restored, so she curled her legs up under her, patted Cat when he jumped up to sit in her lap, and flipped through the stations until she tired out her thumb. Then she watched whatever was on the screen. Or more aptly, stared.

It didn't matter if Nick was out with Gina, or if he was sleeping with her right at that moment. He was a red-blooded man. That's what he should be doing.

Because Joanie was standing by her guns. She wouldn't go out with him. He was the type of man who'd want more. He was the type to get inside her head and then the next thing she knew she'd be alone and broken. She'd be just another in a string of bad Bigbee relationships.

She closed her eyes, refusing to feel anything. It was for the best. It wasn't as if she and Nick had anything more between them than the one kiss, anyway. Thank goodness.

When Joanie woke later, a crick in her neck and her back cramped, Nick was coming in through the front door. She glanced at the face of her cell phone. Three hours had passed since he'd last been there. He really had done it. He'd slept with Gina Gregory.

The rotten jerk.

Nick stopped in the doorway and stared at her, no expression on his face.

Her vision suddenly blurred and her throat burned. She stood without speaking—couldn't if she'd wanted to. She didn't see her boots, so she grabbed only her purse and left without a word.

As Joanie passed, Nick inhaled the dust that still clung to her, as well as the underlying scent of oranges. He wished he hadn't been such an idiot.

Why had he brought Gina back to the house? Was he really so petty that he'd wanted Joanie to see he was not sitting around waiting for her? That he *was* the type who could sleep with a woman one night and move on the next?

Though he'd proved that not to be true tonight.

The idea of sleeping with Gina had quickly been tossed out the window. Not only because he'd kept thinking about Joanie, but because it had become very clear that if Gina was given even the tiniest hint of suggestion, she would dig in and wouldn't let go. The woman may be willing to sleep with him on a first date, but that was not her ulterior motive. She wanted a husband.

And he didn't want her.

He slammed the door as Joanie got into her car without so much as a backward glance, and then stormed across the room, yanking off his jacket as he went. The damned fabric smelled of strong perfume and a woman that wasn't Joanie.

After he'd dropped Gina off, he'd driven around for hours, waiting for Joanie to leave, refusing to let her see him come home early. He couldn't let her know she'd been right. He wasn't the type of man to take a sure thing and move on to the next. At least, not when someone else clouded his mind.

He did not want to fall for Joanie. She was not what he was looking for. Yet stupidly, she was all he seemed to think about.

And now he owed her an apology.

Whether she wanted a relationship or not, they'd had a connection. He shouldn't have tried to make her jealous. But dammit, she got under his skin. One damned date. That's all he'd asked.

He threw his coat on the bed and stomped into the bathroom. Who was he kidding? One date wouldn't crack the surface of what he wanted with Joanie. Maybe it wouldn't go more than a few weeks, who knew? But what was so wrong with wanting the opportunity to explore the option?

She was fun. They could have a good time together.

When he returned to the bedroom, he took in the mess scattered outside the closet door and shook his head. Joanie had great intentions, but she stunk at follow-through.

He spent the next few minutes dragging what he was fairly certain was trash out to the Dumpster, then loaded up the bags of clothes into the back of his truck. Since they were of the fashion of a woman much older than Joanie, he suspected they were meant to be donated. He'd check with her later and drop them off wherever she needed them to go.

Next he opened the three boxes pushed haphazardly to the middle of the floor and stared down at the mounds of colors and fabrics, unsure what she intended to do with those. Surely not keep them. Though given the amount of junk he'd watched her load in her car to take home with her so far, it wouldn't surprise him.

He checked the two smaller boxes next. Spoons?

He nodded. *These* she intended to take home. Junk.

The fabric went into his truck, spoons were stacked beside the front door so she could easily sneak them out when he wasn't looking, then he returned to the bedroom and stared down at the piles of letters spread out in a half-circle. She'd clearly been sitting in the middle of the pile. He stooped to study them more closely.

They were yellowed and crinkled with age, and all appeared to be addressed to her grandmother. He pulled one out and saw that it was signed by Gus Bigbee. Joanie's grandfather.

Scanning over several lines of the block penmanship, it hit him like a brick to the side of the head that they were love letters. From the man who'd left his wife after thirty-three years of marriage.

What history he held in his hands. He couldn't help but wonder if Joanie could get any answers about her grandparents' lives from these letters. Or if she already had.

While he'd been out with Gina.

He growled under his breath at his stupidity, then carefully gathered the envelopes back into the cigar box that sat empty in the floor. When he stood, he looked around, trying to decide what to do with them. He could add the box to the spoons by the door, but his gut told him it would be better if Joanie wasn't alone when she went through them.

They were personal. He couldn't let her read those alone. So far, anything she'd come across that had been the slightest bit personal had caused her to go quiet, while at the same time get a faraway look on her face.

She was fighting through the past, as well as her feelings about her grandparents.

And he didn't want her to have to do that by herself.

He'd been the only one around to dig through his mother's things after she'd passed, so he understood how it felt. Losing her may have only hurt from the loss of the idea of a mother, but reliving her life through her personal effects had not been easy.

He made a decision and took the letters into the kitchen, placing the box inside one of the new cabinets. He would offer to read them with her. After she calmed down from tonight.

When he once again returned to the bedroom, ready to shuck his clothes and crawl under the covers—where he knew he would only dream about Joanie, because that's all he'd dreamt about for days—he pushed the closet door closed, but opened it again when something caught his eye. A small black square in the back corner. He stooped to look closer and as he picked it up, realized it was an old Polaroid.

The cute girl on the swing had to be Joanie. It was her smile. He could practically hear her happy laugh just looking at it. Which made him smile, too.

Oh geez, he had it bad.

He opened the drawer beside the bed and dropped the photo in, then turned out the light. Joanie was supposed to be over this weekend to continue cleaning out the house. Maybe he could use the picture as an opening to an apology.

"Three hours. Can you believe that?" Joanie dragged a fry through her chocolate shake and popped it in her mouth as she sat across from her friend the following Monday afternoon. The salty, chocolate treat did little to help her remaining irritation over Nick. "There's no doubt in my mind what he was doing for those three hours."

Lee Ann did what good friends were supposed to do and grunted her disgust, as she'd done with everything else Joanie had ranted about for the last forty minutes. They'd spent the weekend together working side by side at GiGi's, but since they'd been alongside Cody and the girls, Joanie had held off on sharing the full details of Friday night's disaster. She hadn't wanted to risk anyone getting the idea she was jealous.

She'd dragged her friend over to the Barn so she wouldn't have to be alone in the house with Nick, but needn't have worried. There had been a houseful of workers around all weekend. It was astonishing what had gotten accomplished. She was already starting to see Nick's plans coming to fruition. Even more unbelievable, she'd managed to spend hours there without once having to make more than the barest hint of conversation with him.

She was skipping out on going back tonight, but she couldn't do that much longer. There was too much to get done. She would eventually have to talk to him again, she knew, but not yet. Right now, she was still too annoyed at his veiled attempt to rub Gina in her face.

This afternoon she and Lee Ann had decided to do their normal Monday girls' day, so they'd ended up at the diner. They were currently on a milkshake kick, and the diner made the best.

"I just don't get it," Joanie continued. "Why'd he ask me out one day and then sleep with her the next?" *And why did I end up in tears about it?*

Two French fries and a gulp of chocolate shake later, Lee Ann pierced Joanie with a questioning look. "If it's bugging you so much, why did you refuse to go out with him in the first place?"

"Are you listening to anything I've been saying? I can't go out with him because he's a long-term guy. You know I don't do that."

"I know you haven't in the past. But I don't see why you can't."

Joanie gave her friend a long-suffering stare. "Because I won't be like my mother when it comes to men. *Or* my grandmother. Or any other number of Bigbee women. Did you forget about that? We're losers in love, Lee. The whole town knows that. They've written newspaper articles about it." She shook her head and shoved another milkshake-covered fry into her mouth. "I'd rather be without than be a broken shell of myself," she said around the food. "Or be pathetically chasing one after another my whole life."

Lee Ann just stared at her and then dipped her own fry in her shake. "Your mother was a loser. If a deadbeat walked in the room, she was on him like white on rice. But she bent over backward to morph herself into what she thought they wanted. No wonder she never kept any of them. She didn't know how to love. You're nothing like that, Jo. Everyone in town loves you because you are so genuine. You're always you."

Joanie glanced down at her plate. Lee Ann must have forgotten what had happened when Joanie was sixteen and her grandmother had gone out of town.

GiGi had discovered Pepaw had died and was being buried at Arlington, but Joanie had refused to go. He'd left them. She didn't see why they needed to be there for him. So GiGi had left, and Joanie had invited her boyfriend, Adam Langston, over to keep her company. She'd thought it would be romantic.

She'd thought they were in love.

And she'd stupidly thought the curse didn't apply to her.

It was amazing how quickly she'd learned that not to be the case. Seemed she hadn't missed out on that trait after all. She could pick losers just like the rest of her female relatives.

She'd lost her virginity and her self-respect all in one fell swoop.

The guy hadn't even talked to her again after conning her out of her panties.

Joanie buried the past back where it belonged and lifted her gaze to her friend. Lesson learned. She would not repeat.

"Then how do you explain GiGi?" she asked. "She and Pepaw were married for thirty-three years and he just up and left. Not only did he break her heart, but did you ever see her get over it?"

That had been one of the main issues impacting GiGi's and her relationship. Joanie couldn't understand why GiGi had never moved on. It was pathetic. Just like her mother. Just like Joanie—if she wasn't careful.

But she was careful now. She wouldn't fall for someone just so he could break her in the end.

"I have no idea what happened to make your grandfather leave, but I wish you'd open your eyes and see who you really are," Lee Ann said. "You aren't your mother and never have been." She sounded as if she felt sorry for Joanie. Which ticked Joanie off.

"I never said I was," Joanie's tone was heated. In fact, she'd constantly pointed out that she *wasn't* like her mother.

Lee Ann ignored Joanie's interruption. "You're a gorgeous, stable woman who loves her community and loves being a part of it. You deserve love, and you would be really darned good at it if you'd only give yourself a chance. Businesses can't make you happy forever."

"It's worked for me so far," Joanie muttered.

But she would silently admit that some nights she wanted more. She had male friends who she occasionally hooked up with, but those were getting far more occasional and far less what she wanted.

Yet she had no idea how to do anything else. Fear that she would become her mother paralyzed her.

She didn't want to change for a man. And she certainly didn't want her whole life crushed because of one, either.

"I'm fine the way I am," she insisted. "Plus, Nick's already moved on. He has Gina now. They're probably planning the wedding already."

Lee Ann shoved the fries back and leaned forward. She lowered her voice. "He likes you, Jo. Can you not see that? I watched him all weekend and that man is disgustingly crazy about you. And I think you like him, too. Give it a shot. You might find you like it."

"I might find I end up begging for scraps just like my mother," Joanie said.

Lee Ann shook her head, looking at her as if she were a pathetic child. "Grow up."

Hot anger shot through Joanie in an instant, but she tamped it down when Holly approached their table. The bracelets on her wrists announced her arrival before she got there.

With her blond hair pulled back in a knot at the base of her head and a sharp look in her green eyes, Holly peered down at them. "You two about finished?"

"What?" Joanie asked, looking around at the mostly empty diner. "Are you needing this booth?"

"I just need you to *not* raise your voices any further. I suspect whatever you're talking about—since I heard the word *love*, mention of your mother, and the phrase 'grow up'—you don't want my customers knowing about."

"Oh geez," Joanie moaned. "Thanks, Holly. And no, I don't need anyone hearing what we're talking about."

"Okay," Holly nodded. She nudged Lee Ann to scoot over so she could sit. "So . . . someone's in love? Surely not your mother?"

Holly was several years younger than them, so likely the only things she knew about Joanie's mother came from years of gossip.

"I wouldn't have a clue about my mother or her love life, Holly. For all I know, she's still with the man she ran out of town with."

Bill. Though Joanie had serious doubts her mother had managed to keep him, either. He had actually been a good one. He'd liked Joanie. Had taken her to the movies and to football games in Knoxville along with him and her mother.

And then he'd run off with her mother without so much as a backward glance.

Just like all the others.

"Who's in love, then?" Holly asked, her smile looking a little too innocent.

At Joanie and Lee Ann's silence, Holly waved her hand. "Okay, fine. Then can I at least tell you what I came over to share? You won't believe it."

"As long as it doesn't involve Gina Gregory," Lee Ann groaned.

Joanie kicked her under the table.

"Hmmm. Interesting." Holly looked from one woman to the other. "That's exactly who I came over to talk about. Have you already heard?"

Frustration whipped through Joanie. She did not want to sit there and listen to tales of Nick and Gina. "Tell it to Lee Ann," she muttered. She grabbed her purse. "I'm out of here."

"Stop." Lee Ann shoved her foot onto the booth beside Joanie, preventing her escape, then jabbed her in the side with the toe of her shoe when Joanie tried to shove it out of the way.

"Let me go." Joanie's hissed words barely made it across the table.

"I'm clearly missing something." Holly narrowed her gaze as she took in the two women.

Joanie just shook her head. "Nothing."

"Uh-huh," Holly said with a hum. "Then sit there and listen. I've got the best gossip I've had in years, and I want to share it."

"I do not want to hear details about Gina sleeping with Nick." Joanie managed to free herself from Lee Ann's foot and slid to the outside of the seat.

"That's just it. She didn't."

Joanie had half her rear off the seat before Holly's words penetrated. "What?"

An ear-to-ear smile split Holly's face.

"What are you talking about?" Joanie didn't move from her half-on, half-off the seat position. "He was with her for hours the other night."

Holly's brow creased. "You mean at dinner?" She shrugged. "They were there probably an hour and a half, nothing out of the ordinary, but it's what happened afterward that's the best. And she's telling the story herself."

"Wait," Lee Ann said. She reached over and captured Joanie's forearm as if thinking that would hold her there if Joanie wanted to leave. "Start from the beginning. Nick took Gina to Talbot's, right?"

Talbot's was the "good" restaurant in town.

Holly nodded. "Right. Then they went to his place afterward."

Pain pricked Joanie in the temple. She didn't understand why hearing GiGi's house referred to as anything but her own bothered her. She hadn't lived there in years. "But when they got there I was there. Cramping their style."

"Right." Holly nodded. "Only, according to her, nothing ever happened. She's been over at the salon for the last hour, ranting to Linda Sue about the fiasco. That's what she's calling it. A fiasco. Saying all night Nick was coming on to her. Fawning all over her."

Joanie met Lee Ann's eyes across the table, where a sympathetic look greeted her.

"After they left your grandmother's place, they headed to her house. Just where she wanted him, if you know what I mean."

"We know." Joanie and Lee Ann spoke in unison.

"When they got there, Nick continued being the perfect date. Helped her out of the truck, walked her to the door, and then pecked her on the cheek." Holly giggled and clapped her hands like a schoolgirl. "Pecked her on the cheek. She didn't even get a kiss on the lips."

Joanie and Lee Ann stared at each other again, Joanie realizing the more Holly talked, just how much she'd been played. The man had intentionally tried to make her jealous. Just as she'd thought when he'd shown up at the house with Gina.

Relief coursed through her that he was gentleman enough not to go all the way just to prove a point. And the point had been proven, though she had no idea what to do with it.

"I'll tell you," Holly continued, "according to Linda Sue, Gina is fit to be tied. Pacing back and forth, ranting about the indecency of the man to get her worked up all night and then not so much as lay a kiss on her. It couldn't have happened to a better person."

Holly finally ran out of steam. She eyed Joanie. "That was bugging you, wasn't it? Thinking he'd slept with her. And only a day after you two were seen in your shop talking about sex."

Joanie blinked, her eyes going wide. "What?"

"Oops." Holly rose from the booth and smiled so big a dimple popped into one cheek. "I see orders that need to be delivered. I'd better go."

Before she could run off, Joanie clamped a hand down on Holly's arm. "What are you talking about? Who said we were in Cakes talking about sex?"

Holly merely smiled again, then pointed her chin in Lee Ann's direction. "Ask this one. It's her mother who's doing the telling. The church crowd in here heard all about it yesterday."

Silence settled over the table as Holly left and Joanie turned to Lee Ann. A blush was coloring both cheeks, letting Joanie know that yes, Reba London was indeed spreading rumors that Joanie and Nick had been talking about sex.

Of course, they had been. But no one had heard them!

"How could your mother possibly know what we'd talked about in the store last week? I know you didn't tell her." Joanie had called Lee Ann from the tub that night after she'd gotten home to share details of her and Nick's conversation.

"Apparently Mom was in line to get a cupcake when you and Nick went inside."

"And what? She snuck in the back to eavesdrop?"

Lee Ann shook her head. "She didn't have to. You faced the window during part of the conversation."

At Joanie's blatantly confused stare, Lee Ann finally added, "She knows how to read lips. She took a course on it."

"Oh. My. God. What is wrong with your mother?"

Lee Ann gave a noncommittal shrug. "It's her hobby. She's trying to top Ms. Grayson for most number of scoops."

"So she stands around reading private conversations?"

"You know the rules. You guys had this big conversation in front of the glass windows while there was a line of people right outside your door. What's wrong with you? Of course there are going to be rumors about that, even if they aren't true."

Joanie dropped her head to the table and considered pounding on it while she was down there. Yes, she knew how it worked. Of course there would be rumors. If she'd done nothing but sign the contract he'd brought her, there would have been rumors. He did drag her out of her van right in front of everyone. And she'd let him hold her hands more than once while they'd been inside.

She peeked up. "What else is she saying?"

"Sure you want to hear it?"

Ugh. "Yes, tell me." Another one of those rare headaches was finding its way to her again.

"That you guys were in there talking about sex, and you were clearly arguing. There's speculation that maybe you'd already had sex and something wasn't good about it. The bet is currently leaning toward you being the issue."

Joanie just stared.

Lee Ann smiled. "But good news, with this new turn concerning Nick and Gina, they might start thinking that Nick is the one with the problem."

"One can only hope."

If this were anyone but her, Joanie would love it. The people of this town always made things interesting. Then she caught sight of Brian grinning wickedly at her from the grill line as Holly talked his ear off— no doubt Nick and Joanie sex rumors—and an idea bloomed as to how she could both use the hobbies of the townspeople, and get back at Nick at the same time. "I've got it," she said.

"Got what?" Lee Ann looked genuinely puzzled.

"How I can get back at Nick. I need a date."

"A date? You won't go out with Nick, but you want a date with someone else?"

"Well no, there's no one I'm *wanting* to go out with, but I can't just sit back and let Nick get away with what he did."

"What did he do? Talk about sex in your store?"

"Geez, Lee Ann. No. He took Gina out to mess with me."

"O . . . kay." Lee Ann nodded slowly, and Joanie could tell she wasn't yet buying it. "But just because he didn't sleep with her doesn't mean he did it to mess with you."

"Then he didn't come home for three hours?"

Lee Ann grew pensive for a few seconds, and then a curve flitted across her lips. "He didn't come home for three hours."

"Right," Joanie stressed. "Messing with me. And I'm going to get him back."

"You know you're asking for trouble, hon. Maybe you should let this one go."

"I can't." She didn't want to examine why not. "He deserves to think I'm doing the same thing he made me think he was doing with Gina."

"Yet you still don't want to go out with him?"

Joanie didn't answer her. She didn't actually know what she wanted at the moment. "Will you help me or not?"

They were best friends. Of course Lee Ann was going to help her. "Tell me what I can do."

Chapter Nine

As Joanie and Brian turned onto her street, she jerked up straight at the sight of Nick's pickup lurking in the driveway of her rental house.

"Looks like it worked," Brian spoke from the driver's seat. "Dalton is waiting."

"Yeah," she murmured, her pulse climbing to a run. "I see that." That meant Lee Ann had done as planned and dropped just enough info to her mother so it had gotten back to Nick that Joanie was on a date.

And it had bothered him so much he'd actually shown up?

Excitement flooded her. This couldn't have worked out any better.

So now he not only knew that she and Brian had gone out, but that they'd stayed out hours later, too. He had to assume she'd been at Brian's house all this time.

She grinned across the dark interior of the car, suddenly anxious to wrap up the date part of her night. "Thanks for helping me out."

"No problem."

Since they'd been friends for years, Brian had been more than happy to be a part of her plan. He was the love-'em-and-leave-'em type when it came to the women he dated. Called himself a confirmed bachelor. And he wasn't shy about sharing the pleasure around.

But he was one hundred percent committed to his friends.

The rare times she needed help, he was one of the few she'd call. When she'd told him yesterday that she needed him, he'd canceled his previous plans with no hesitation.

That was Brian.

She'd met him at Talbot's tonight, but they'd purposefully left her car at his house after watching two Mel Brooks movies. Nick had stayed out three hours after dinner—Joanie made sure to stay out four.

"Prepare yourself." Joanie squirmed in the seat. "You'll have to kiss me when we stop."

He shot her a lecherous look. "Darlin', kissing you is no hardship."

She shook her head. He was so full of himself.

He'd kissed her once years ago when they'd briefly considered hooking up, but it had fallen a little flat and she'd decided he was better as a friend, instead of her being one of his playthings.

"Don't pull into the driveway." She reached out and put a hand on his arm as if to stop him. "Stop on the road, back a little so you're not directly under the streetlight, but enough to be able to see what's going on in the car."

"Don't want to be too obvious?" Brian snickered.

"Don't be a smart-ass." She swatted at him as she scanned the area to make sure Nick was watching. She couldn't find him in the shadows of her porch at first, but then made out a figure in the chair in the corner. She had to assume that was him. "I've got to teach him a lesson," she added. "He took Gina out the other night just to irritate me."

"Hold out and don't give him any. That'll teach him."

Good idea in theory. But after acknowledging to herself the past few days that she couldn't sit by and watch Nick be with someone else in that way, she was now rethinking her plan. Maybe they could have a little fling. They could keep it casual. If they both knew the rules going into it, what would be the harm?

Brian stopped on the street and put the car into park. He drove a sporty two-door, fitting perfectly with the "date" she'd been going for. "I heard he didn't put out for Gina. What's wrong with the guy? She's a sure thing. Is he gay?"

"Definitely not gay." Joanie turned in her seat to face Brian so they appeared more intimate, and leaned her head on his shoulder. "Put your arm around me."

Brian complied. "Then what's wrong with him?"

Joanie raised her hand to Brian's shoulder and caressed. "Nothing. Do I look okay? Do we look natural?"

He flicked his eyes down the front of her shirt and grinned. "They look pretty natural to me."

"Not those, smart-ass." She smirked. "But thanks. Now get ready to kiss me. It'll have to be a long one."

He shook his head. "You do realize that man has it bad for you, right?"

"You've barely met him. How would you know?"

"Darlin'." He cupped her cheek and angled his head to hers. She watched his gaze stray to her front porch before returning. "I don't have to have another conversation with him to know he's crazy about you." He dipped his head and almost touched her lips. "He's about five seconds away from snapping your porch railing with his bare hands."

Brian latched his lips onto hers and she kissed him back with everything she had. All in all it was a very nice kiss, but there simply was no spark. Nothing like when Nick kissed her.

She pulled back enough to speak, but not enough to be obvious. "You've got good technique. Is he still watching?"

"Yeah." Brian dropped his mouth to her neck. "You sure you don't want to change your mind and become more than friends?"

He nipped her neck and she laughed. He was funny.

"I'm not joking," Brian said. "I know my way around a woman's body. Many more compliments than complaints. If that's all you're needing, and Romeo up there wants more than you're willing to give . . ." He let his words trail off as he peered down at her.

They got each other. She didn't know exactly what made him the way he was, and he didn't know everything about her, but they understood marriage and romance were not something either considered.

She patted him on the cheek as she pulled away. "You're a sweetheart. But you know it's best to keep it as we are. We're better as friends."

With the door open, light from inside the car highlighted Brian's face. She reached across and used her thumb to wipe lipstick from his lips. "Thanks again for changing your plans for me," she whispered. "I'll pick up my car tomorrow."

"No problem, darlin'. Good luck with Romeo."

She waved as Brian roared off, then she headed across the yard for her house. Nerves quivered through her entire body. Nick was waiting for her. Her feet slowed as she pictured him coming in on Friday night. He'd looked at her with a blank face, like he hadn't wanted her to know what he'd been doing.

Now she saw it for what it really was. He'd wanted her to think he'd been all up in Gina for the last three hours. He'd wanted her jealous.

Well, he got it. She hadn't liked it one bit, but he wasn't the only one who could play games. If he thought he wanted sex and friendship after, she would give it to him. After she pissed him off with Brian.

Her feet hurried forward, nearing the steps. Tonight had been fun. She hadn't hung out with Brian like that in years. But she'd constantly found herself wishing the hours would go by so she could come home and see if Nick would be here waiting.

She'd desperately wanted him to be, and that had worried her. This was only going to be about sex. Sex shouldn't make her desperate. It was a good time, nothing more.

So why did seeing him on her porch, knowing she might have pushed him too far, make her nervous?

No better time than the present to find out. She sucked in a deep gulp of cool night air and headed up the steps.

Nick could not believe what he'd just witnessed. After hearing from five different people about the date, he would have bet money it was purely for show. She must've figured out he hadn't really been interested in Gina. He'd even expected Joanie to stay out a while after dinner, just as he had.

But after sitting on her cold porch for close to three hours—waiting to make her admit she'd been as jealous as he was—and then watching the molestation going on by both of them in Hot Rod's car, Nick's temper was out of control.

When her foot hit the top step, he couldn't keep quiet any longer. "It's two o'clock in the morning."

"Oh!" Her hand fluttered to her chest. "Nicky, I didn't see you."

"Stop it with the 'Nicky.' You knew full well I was here."

"No, I was—"

He stepped forward and clamped a hand around her elbow. "I know exactly what you were doing."

He grabbed the door, which he'd already discovered hadn't been locked, and shoved it open. He dragged her inside. Once there, he slammed it and pulled her to his chest. The heat from her body immediately warmed him.

"If all you want is sex, baby, let's go for it. I guarantee I can keep it simple." He mashed his mouth to hers.

She stiffened in his grip before softening, then reached up and twined her arms around his neck. Her moan pulsed through him, the faint bite of alcohol on her tongue spiking his anger.

He clamped both arms around her, his nostrils flaring, taking in her scent. Hot and sexy. He squeezed her closer until he flattened their bodies together, aligning them perfectly. She was for him. Not that asshole Brian Marshall.

Her fingers tunneled through his hair as her lean body quivered against his. He couldn't believe she would be this responsive if she'd just spent hours in another man's bed. But he'd seen that kiss. It had not looked like an innocent good-night kiss.

Wrenching his mouth from hers, he tugged the edge of her top to the side and fastened his lips to her skin. It tasted slightly salty, musky. He clamped his teeth on her shoulder.

"Ahhh . . ." Her chest pushed forward.

He slid his hands down her sides and over her rear until he gripped the bottom of her skirt. Yanking it up, he cupped her butt in his hands, then reared back as he realized he held bare flesh. He squinted through the darkness. "Where is your underwear?"

"Thong." She stretched toward his lips. "Take me to bed, Nick. Please."

"Tell me you didn't just sleep with Marshall."

Holding his lips away, he lifted her body against his and squeezed both hands. He loved the feel of her butt cheeks in his palms. She wrapped both legs around him.

"I didn't just sleep with Marshall," she whispered, pressing soft kisses to his throat.

He growled. "Never?"

"Never."

It would have to be good enough. "Don't let me catch you kissing him again."

She smiled up at him. Too sweet this time. "Okay, Nicky."

Crap.

Joanie barely got one foot down before she slipped and ended up on the ground, her bare rear splatting against the tiled entryway. Dang. Why had she teased him one last time? She'd already won.

From her position on the floor, with her skirt riding her waist, she scowled up at Nick only to be taken aback by the dark fury directed her way. His hands clenched at his sides. "Is that all this is to you? A game?"

She stood and straightened her skirt without answering. Was it? Yes, she realized, she supposed it had been. She hadn't liked seeing him with Gina, so she'd made sure he hadn't liked seeing her with Brian more. She put some space between them and flipped on a lamp, spilling pale light across the room to highlight the mess that she was. There were scattered books and magazines. A pile of unopened mail on the end table.

Seeing the TV remote on the floor, she kicked it out of the way and picked up a throw pillow. She faced Nick, the pillow in front of her, her arms crossed over it. "I'm sorry."

He stared at her, jaw set. "For?"

"For taking it too far." She licked her swollen lips. She hadn't meant to hurt his feelings. "For . . ." She shrugged. "Making it a game." She shook her head, not wanting to admit the truth, but not liking when people refused to do so, either. "I was jealous of Gina. Happy? I didn't like you taking her out. Not one bit. But you already knew that. You planned it that way."

Nick took a step toward her. He stopped in the middle of the room and watched her, and she suddenly felt more awkward than she had in years. He studied her as if he could see inside her.

"What?" She pulled the pillow tighter against her.

"So you decided the best thing to do was to get back at me?"

She tilted her chin in the air. "You know I did."

"Why?"

Her mouth hung open. "I just told you. I was jealous."

"Yet you don't want to go out with me."

"I still don't."

How stupid did she sound right now?

He laughed at her. Honest to God laughed out loud in her face. "You do know how ridiculous you sound?"

"*Yes*," she stressed. "I'm very well aware of how ridiculous I sound, but it's the facts. I don't want to go out. I don't want to get involved." She paused, trying to decide whether to throw it all out there or not, then decided to go for it. What would it hurt at this point? "But you mentioned sex the other day. Maybe I wouldn't be opposed to a sex-only kind of thing. If you really thought you could keep your emotions out of it."

His face was as hard as granite. She wasn't sure if that was because he was angry, or if he was merely thinking about her proposition.

"Can I ask what your problem is with getting involved?"

The question caught her off guard. It was one she rarely got asked. Most men were more than happy to keep it light. She bit down against her bottom lip as she thought through how she wanted to answer him, then decided to go for the truth. At least part of it. She wasn't about to tell him she had an overriding fear that she'd fall over backward for some man only to have him trample on her heart.

"I've seen too many examples of relationships ending badly. I don't intend to be one of them."

He stared at her, his eyes giving nothing away. Finally, he asked, "The Bigbee Curse?"

The fact that he said it with a straight face and didn't make fun of her kept him from getting kicked in the nuts. It was a joke around town, and too many people had teased her about it over the years. That didn't keep it from being fact.

"I won't get hurt," was all she replied.

Nick gave a single nod. "So, sex only? That's all it can be for you?"

"Yes," she said. "Sex. Friends. Nothing personal."

"And if I can't promise that?" he asked. "If I can't promise to keep my heart out of it?"

Damn, maybe just this once she would have been okay without total honesty. She couldn't make herself not want him, yet she wanted desperately to believe that neither one of them would make it more than it was.

"Then you'll know going into it that *I* will keep my emotions out of it. If you don't, you'll get hurt."

He studied her again, just as intently as before, and she found herself wishing she hadn't turned the light on. He was making her nervous again.

"Okay," he said, giving a little nod. "Sex only. But if I decide to care, you can't run away. It'll be my choice if I get hurt. Deal?"

She nodded. She wasn't sure she had a choice in the matter.

He nudged his chin toward the pillow. "Put that down and come here."

"You come get it."

He shook his head.

What was wrong with this man? She had already caved and admitted she'd been jealous. Did she have to go crawling over to him, too? She shook her head in return.

A shadow passed over his features. "Okay," he said. "We'll meet in the middle."

He took a step toward her.

She loosened her grip a little.

He took another step and angled his head, giving her a steady look, letting her know she had to do more than turn loose of the death grip she had on the pillow.

"Are you sorry you took her out?" Joanie asked, knowing she didn't have to say Gina's name.

He nodded. "Very."

"At least you didn't kiss the floozy," she mumbled and lowered the pillow a fraction.

His eyes narrowed. "But you obviously *did* kiss Marshall."

She smirked. "He's a friend."

"He's a guy."

"Well, yes." She remembered Brian's offer before she'd gotten out of the car. She wouldn't take Brian up on it, of course. Even if she wasn't about to sleep with Nick.

At the thought of what she was about to do, parts of her began to stir to life.

"I didn't like it," Nick grunted out.

She smiled at his emphatic statement. "I didn't really either."

"Joanie." His tone suggested she back off the teasing.

"Okay." Frustration bounced between them. He wanted her to meet him halfway, and she wanted . . . She concentrated on the man in front of her and gave a mental shrug. She wanted Nick. She just wanted him.

Tossing the pillow behind her, she mentally crossed her fingers that she was doing the right thing and waited.

He didn't move.

She clamped her lips together and stuck her nose in the air. "It's your turn to take a step forward."

He narrowed his eyes. "You can be so annoying."

"It's my number one talent."

When he didn't move any farther, she threw up her hands. "Fine." She stomped the remaining foot to stand directly in front of him. "Here I am. Joanie Bigbee, cupcake baker extraordinaire. Either take me to bed or get the hell out of my house because I can't take any more tonight."

The corners of his mouth quirked. She wanted to kick him in the shin. But more importantly, she wanted to wrap her arms around him and hold on until morning.

He lifted a finger and traced her lips, the roughness of his skin from working in construction pinging sparks throughout her body. "Hello, Joanie Bigbee. I'm Nicholas William Dalton. House remodeler and general Mr. Fix-it."

She wanted him to fix her.

He trailed his fingers down her throat, stopping at the base of her neck. She could feel her own pulse thumping against his skin.

"Thank you for coming to me," he whispered.

Her heart raced. He was already making this more than it was. "Will you take me to bed now?" she asked.

If she hadn't been staring at him so intently, she would have missed the tiny flash of disappointment in his eyes. He grabbed her hand and pulled her to the couch. "How about we stay out here for a bit? Take it slow."

She groaned. "What is it with you? Do you not get this whole sex thing?"

Nick settled them on the cushions and pulled her to his side. The hand he curved around her shoulder slipped just inside the opening of her shirt and his fingers feathered over her neck. Heat bounced from her shoulder to her nipples and then straight between her legs.

On the other side of her, Nick touched his mouth to the side of her neck. Goose bumps lit over her body. He was trying to seduce her. That wasn't needed.

She turned her face to his, determined to find his lips. "You're a romantic, Nick. Quit trying to make this more. It's chemistry. Sex."

Without giving him a chance to argue, she flipped herself over and straddled him. His arms came up to grip her hips, knocking a plastic grocery bag off the couch in the process. She leaned in for a kiss but missed as he looked toward the sound.

"Dang, Joanie. What's with the clutter?"

She shrugged. "I sometimes don't put stuff away immediately. It's no big deal. Can we get back to kissing now?"

"We weren't kiss—"

He shut up when she put her mouth to his.

Heat flared between them and both of them groaned. He brought his hands up to grip her head, and plundered her mouth with his tongue, reminding her very quickly how much she'd enjoyed this the last time, and making her very thankful that Gina had not gotten to experience this heaven for herself.

She slipped her hands lower, shoving them under the untucked tail of his shirt until she reached hard, hot, male flesh. His abs were off the charts.

"Oh, *Mama*," she whispered. She wanted to lick every inch of him.

Continuing to straddle him, she sent her hands on an exploration of his chest as he nibbled down her throat and turned his own hands loose over her back. He was hard everywhere she could find. She wiggled closer on his lap and confirmed that, yes, he was hard there, too.

Large hands headed under her skirt as they'd done when the two of them had first come into the house, and she whimpered when he got a good, firm hold. From what she could tell, her butt fit perfectly in his palms.

She shivered when his lips dipped below her collarbone. It took barely more than a touch and she was a drooling fool for this man.

"Can we go upstairs now?" she whispered. Straddling him on the couch was one thing, but she wanted them prone. She wanted to see what she was touching. And she wanted to watch him do the same. "If we don't go now, I'm not sure my legs will hold me to climb the stairs later."

He brought her face back to his, his hand holding her chin captive. Brown eyes focused on hers. "Then I'll carry you."

He kissed her, and she once again lost her breath.

His grip didn't allow her to turn away—not that she wanted to—and the hand on her butt started a rhythmic squeezing thing, making her thrust into him in time to his pumps.

Oh God, she was riding the seam of his jeans and she could feel herself already nearing an orgasm.

"Please, Nick," she whispered against his mouth. "Take me upstairs."

He didn't change course. One hand kept her face held in place, and the other kept her grinding into him. It didn't seem right—her getting all the attention—but she was helpless to stop it. Widening her legs, she bore down on him and her eyes rolled to the back of her head.

"Oh God, Nick. I'm going to come."

"I know." His voice was low and rough. "That's my plan, sweetness."

She couldn't help it. She ground down on him with one last push and threw her head back, fighting for breath as the orgasm engulfed her. Circling her hips over and over, she worked to get it all out, but it kept coming, it kept rolling through her, and she wasn't certain she would keep breathing long enough to finish.

When her body finally calmed, thankfully without her passing out, she sat panting, her elbows locked and her shaking fists gripping his shoulders. Her hips were thrust as tight into him as she could get. She slowly came to the realization that she was staring at the ceiling and forced herself to ease the stiffness of her spine and return to a more natural, upright position.

The smugness covering Nick's face was almost as hot as what he'd just done to her.

"That was pretty good," she said, her breath still not quite back to normal.

The corners of his mouth inched up. "Wait till you see what I can do with my clothes off."

"Upstairs," she said. "I want you on my bed."

His eyes went dark again and his arms clamped around her. He stood. "Tell me where."

Before she could point him to the stairs leading up from the back corner of the room, the bag he'd knocked off the couch earlier crinkled at her feet. The strange thing was, neither of them was touching it.

"What in the world?" she asked, staring down at the floor. The bag was moving as if something were inside it.

At her question, he followed her gaze. They stood there, her wrapped around him, high up in his arms, and watched as something inside the bag continued to move. Finally, he let out a little laugh.

"I forgot," he said. He put her down and she practically whimpered at the loss of connection. "I brought you a present."

"You brought me a present? And what? You put it in the bag I'd left on the couch?"

"No." He stooped down and reached a hand inside and pulled out something black. "I brought you a cat. I'd put him in the kitchen."

Joanie took a fast step back, her hands up as if to ward both Nick and the cat off. "Why would you bring me a cat?"

"Because you needed one." He held the small animal up and she felt her heart give a little tug. "His name is Bobcat."

The small black cat watched her from Nick's palm, its ears twitching, its tail missing.

"I got him from the clinic. Cody said a basket of them were dropped off a couple days ago. Bobcat, here, looked like he'd be able to keep up with you."

Cute as he was, she did not want a cat. She shook her head as if to clear the picture, then shifted her gaze to the man.

"I don't do animals, Nick."

Animals were kind of like men who wanted to settle down. They were step one in getting too attached.

"It's just a little cat. You like mine; I've seen you play with him. I thought you'd like your own."

"You thought wrong." She took another step back as if getting too close would make her catch something she couldn't give back. "Take him home with you. I don't want him."

"Come on, Jo. Look at this thing. How can you not want him?"

A tiny black paw reached out toward her as if asking her to take him. She shook her head.

"You keep him."

A look of disappointment settled over Nick, making her feel as if she'd done something wrong, but she wasn't the one who'd brought a cat to someone without knowing if it was a good idea or not.

"Not everyone wants pets, Nick. Sorry. I don't want one." She shook her head again and moved to the door. "You take him."

She felt the tiniest bit bad that she'd had a chance to get off tonight and he hadn't, but she blamed this one on him. She couldn't continue enjoying herself knowing there was a cat down here making himself at home.

Nick stepped into the adjoining kitchen and picked up a carrier she hadn't noticed, then came back with the cat in one hand and the carrier in another. "I'll take him for now, but he's still yours. Whenever you get ready for him."

"I don't want him," she repeated. She opened the door, keeping her eyes on the cat and not on Nick. "I'll see you tomorrow night at the house."

After Nick was gone, she leaned back against the door and let out a heavy breath. Who brought someone a cat?

A nester. That was who. Not someone who did casual sex.

A knock sounded on the door.

"What?" she yelled without opening it.

"Lock your door, sweetness."

Crap. Did the man never ease up?

She locked the door and sank to the ground. She'd just had the hottest orgasm of her life, only to find out the man who'd given it to her thought she would want a cat.

No.

No, she did not want a cat.

She didn't want anything from him.

Chapter Ten

C at raised his head from where he lay in the patch of sunlight in the second-floor bedroom, looking around as if he'd heard a noise. It had to be Joanie. Nick's heart thumped hard inside his chest. She was bringing dinner. And hopefully an amiable mood.

Two nights ago he'd been at her place, had her coming apart in his hands. Since then, he'd had forty-eight long hours to think about what he was doing and if he really wanted to do it. He'd come to a decision.

When he'd agreed to a sex-only relationship with her, he'd known there was no way he could stick to it, not completely. It was Joanie. She was sweet. Fun. Sexy. And she brightened a room just by walking into it. How was he not supposed to fall for that?

Plus, in the back of his mind he'd told himself she couldn't stick to not caring for him either. She was too open and honest to be able to keep such a distance.

But at her blatant rejection of Bobcat, he'd had to question his initial thoughts. The way she'd backed away from them, one would think he'd been holding out a snake instead of an eight-week-old kitten. What had she said?

She didn't do pets?

That was bull. She'd played with Cat every time she'd been over here. There had been evidence she'd done the same the night before while he'd been out, too. He'd left before she'd arrived, heading to the Bungalow for dinner to try to figure out how he wanted to proceed. When he'd returned, he'd found the feather toy he'd picked up for Bob lying on the floor as if she'd been sitting there playing with him.

But the way she'd backed away from the two of them at her place had indicated that whether she liked animals or not, she had no intention of getting attached to one. Fine. He liked cats. He could always use another. He wasn't afraid of getting attached to them at all.

It had just been a small gift, for heaven's sake. Cats weren't even hard to take care of. It had seemed the thing to do, both as an apology for his behavior with Gina, and as a . . . well, just as a gift. He liked giving people things. Especially people he cared about.

He caught sight of her climbing from her small car and his breath hitched in his throat. She was dressed in all yellow today. It was Thursday, cupcake van day, and apparently she'd decided not to change before coming over. He smiled, appreciating the thought, and hurried down the stairs. He opened the front door before she hit the porch.

"I'm guessing you smell like lemons today." God, she looked good.

She stopped, glanced down at herself and then back up at him, and gave him a slow, appreciative smile. "You noticed."

He'd noticed everything about her.

"You always smell like your theme. What's the flavor of the week? Lemon pie?"

"Lemon tart." She grinned and held the bakery box up, and began climbing the steps toward him. "I brought you some."

"I see that." He hoped she'd brought him some more of what he'd gotten a taste of the other night, too. Even if she was able to keep her emotions out of it, he couldn't say no if the offer was still on the table. He guessed he was an idiot like that.

He took the bag of food from her when she passed in front of him, and he breathed in her scent. It was so intoxicating it almost made him dizzy. "Too big a hurry to change before coming over?" he teased.

Not that he was complaining. She could wear those go-go outfits every day of the week and he'd be a happy man. Except for knowing that the rest of the town's population of men would be just as happy.

That dimmed his ardor.

He closed the door and followed her in, watching her walk in front of him and smiling when Bob and Cat both came over and wound themselves welcomingly through her ankles. She squatted in the middle of the room and scratched each of them behind the ears until they purred. She was *so* a pet person. He'd known he hadn't imagined that.

"I have a change of clothes in the car," she said. "You didn't come to the shop today."

Laughter burst from him. He loved her lack of subtlety. "You wanted to make sure I didn't miss the show? Not that I'm saying you should have changed, mind you. I'm quite enjoying the view."

She peered up at him over her shoulder, her lids heavy, and flicked her gaze quickly over his body before returning her attention to the animals. "Maybe I'm just making sure you see what you missed."

He crossed to stand behind her, purposely getting into her space. "Does that mean I've missed my chance?"

Getting entangled with her was not a good idea. He knew he couldn't keep it light. Just as he knew she had every intention of making it nothing but.

She finally finished with the cats and stood facing him, not bothering to put distance between them. Though she was still a good six inches shorter in her boots, it felt as if she was right in his face. He wanted her closer.

"I guess that depends on you." Her tone was telling. She moved away before he could either say anything or reach out and grab her, and set the box of cupcakes down on the seat of the recliner. Then she peeled off yellow gloves he hadn't even noticed. It was darned near the sexiest move he'd ever seen. He was in way too deep with this woman, but he was fine with it. He wanted to drown in her.

Once she had the gloves off, he grabbed her hand and dragged her away from the front windows toward the kitchen. He was tired of the dance. He wanted her. Now.

"What are you doing?" she asked when he set the food down on the table and continued pulling her across the room. "I thought we were going to eat."

She'd called earlier to make sure he would be home, offering to pick up dinner and bring it over since she would be working tonight. It had made him wonder if she'd been annoyed when she'd shown up last night and hadn't found him at the house. Had she wanted to make sure he stayed in?

He hoped so. He liked the idea that she was thinking about him when he wasn't around.

When he had her in front of the kitchen counter, the new stainless steel stove top to one side and the built-in oven to the other, he finally answered her. "I wanted to show you something."

She looked around and her eyes lit up. "You got the new appliances put in."

He gripped her by the waist and hoisted her, plopping her on the top of the granite. She let out a breathy "oh" as he stepped between her legs.

"I installed the new counters, too," he said. "Do you like them?"

She wiggled her rear back and forth. "I do. They're very . . . " She lowered her gaze to his crotch. "Hard."

"You're evil." His hands found her thighs. He'd been itching to touch them since he'd walked out of her house the other night carrying her cat. He rubbed his thumbs back where they lay against her legs and she slowly lifted her gaze to his. "We could still change our minds," he said.

The gray of her eyes deepened. "I think I owe you one."

"You don't owe me anything, sweetness." He gripped her behind the knees and tugged her closer, hitching her skirt up and spreading her legs wide around his hips. The tops of white stockings showed beneath the hem of her skirt and his heart skipped a beat.

Her smile made his jeans completely uncomfortable.

He grasped the bottom of her pale yellow sweater and slowly began to lift it over her head, the blood roaring in his ears as he did. She locked her gaze to his and raised her arms, letting him do as he pleased. When he had the top off, he tossed it behind him. Her small, firm breasts were now displayed, plumped up in a pretty half-cup yellow bra, and he couldn't care less about whether her sweater picked up sawdust from the floor where it fell or not.

"I'm kind of small," her voice was soft. He lifted his gaze, finding hers not quite meeting his, and he believed it was the first time he'd seen her exhibit any amount of shyness.

He reached out and cupped a breast in his hand. "You're amazing," he said. He gave a small squeeze, enjoying it when her breathing picked up and her top teeth clamped down on her lip. "I've been dreaming of touching you like this."

She wiggled forward another inch and slipped her fingers inside the waistband of his jeans. He sucked in a breath when she grazed over the top of him. "I can say the same thing about you," she whispered.

Ignoring her wandering fingers as best he could, he focused back on his task. Her skin was a smooth, light cream, and he wanted to taste every square inch of it. He reached behind her and unhooked her bra and let out a low growl as the straps slid slowly off her shoulders. She put both palms over her to keep the garment from falling to her lap.

The mischievousness he liked so much looked up at him then and he felt another kink in his armor go. He was screwed.

"I think you should take your shirt off before I let this fall."

"You do, huh?" He grabbed the bottom of his T-shirt and ripped it over his head. "No problem."

He tossed the shirt in the same general vicinity as hers, feeling his chest expand as she took him in with her eyes. There was nothing to compare with a hot woman looking at him the way she was. As if she wanted to have him for dinner *and* breakfast, and then do it all over again.

He focused on her hands. "Your turn."

The bra fell to her lap and he lost all ability to think.

They reached for each other simultaneously. Him capturing a breast in each palm, and her running the tips of her fingers over the terrain of his chest. He scraped the pad of a thumb over one nipple and her spine arched.

"I like that," she breathed out the words. "I'm pretty sensitive there."

He flicked over her again and she moaned. It was a soft "oh" sound that came with a hot breath. "That's going to make this a whole lot of fun, because I happen to be a fan of this spot."

He leaned in and closed over one nipple, sucking it deep into his mouth, and she pushed out further toward him. His hand worked her other breast, alternating between gentle squeezes and tweaks, as her body practically vibrated against his.

Her hands fell to his waistband, where she gripped the denim, and he stroked his tongue against her, noticing that she somehow managed to taste like lemons as well as smell like them. He gave a moan of his own when she lifted her legs to clamp around his waist. The movement put her flush against him.

"Oh shit, Jo." His words didn't sound like his own. "I'm trying to do this right, but you're so . . ." He trailed off as she dug her heels into his ass and ground herself hard against his jeans. She'd come the other night by doing exactly that, and though it had been the hottest thing he'd ever seen, he wanted a piece of that action tonight.

Lowering his hands, he went for the waistband of her skirt, searching around until he found a zipper, then jerked at it until it would go no farther. He pushed the material off her hips, grateful as she lifted herself up so he could tug it below her butt, and equally happy when his hand slid over bare cheeks while doing so.

"Another thong?" he guessed.

She nodded. "Always."

Hell. Her underwear was going to kill him.

"We're leaving it on," he said.

She lowered her legs and helped him get the skirt past her feet, then went to work on his zipper while he fumbled in his back pocket for his wallet.

"There's a condom in here somewhere," he muttered, trying to keep focused long enough to complete the act before he looked back at the woman sitting practically naked in front of him.

"Hurry," she whispered. She had his jeans open and was pulling him out into her soft, seeking hands.

When he got the packet freed, she threw the wallet to the floor and took over.

"Hurry," she whispered again, almost as if she were telling herself this time since she was the one now in control.

His breath hissed as she finished the act, her hand fitting snugly over him for brief seconds, and only then did he let himself fully take her in.

She was gloriously naked from the waist up. Her breasts flushed, dark nipples perky and begging for his touch, and blond curls wild around her face. Her gray eyes were slits as she seemed to be studying him just as intently. Her lips were plump and slightly parted, little pants bursting rhythmically from them.

Below the waist, she was a dream come true.

A small triangle of lemon-colored silk covered her where she met the counter, then white lace started the stockings on those long, long legs, disappearing behind the boots on their way down.

He couldn't think of anything else in the world he would rather be doing.

When her gaze traveled back up his body, going slowly over his chest, with her fingers following reverently in their path, he couldn't imagine wanting a woman more.

"You're built like a freaking god," she said, licking her lips. Her gaze finally locked on his and she wrapped those legs around him again. "Take me, Nick. Now."

Yes. That was exactly what he was going to do. He gave her one long kiss, wanting to taste that mouth before he forgot all about it, and then he shoved the material of her panties aside and positioned his head just between her lips.

"Oh, God," she whispered. "Crap, that already feels good."

"You're good for a man's ego, sweetness." He put his hands to her rear, gripped and lifted her just the tiniest amount, and then he plunged. He buried himself. And he almost died with the sensations that ripped through him.

They both gasped and froze, then he pulled out and did it again. She felt insanely good.

Again, he thrust, wanting all of her. Wanting to make sure she wanted him in return.

"Nick," she whispered. She had her arms wrapped around his neck, her head thrown back in pleasure. Her eyes were closed. "Nick," she whispered again, not seeming to expect him to answer. "Yes. Oh, God. Yes. Nick. That feels so good."

Shit. He wasn't going to last a minute with the noises she was making.

He brought a hand around to touch her, determined to make sure she came before he did, and almost lost his bet when her inner muscles contracted around him. "Hurry, babe," he whispered. "I can't...I...*hurry*," he growled out the last word.

He couldn't stop pumping.

They were both wild, thrusting and grinding. He had one hand clutching the cheek of her ass, the other working furiously around front, and he could feel sweat rolling between his shoulder blades as he fought against his orgasm.

"I can't wait." Damn, she was too hot. "You've got to—"

His words were cut off by her scream and the way she stiffened in his arms. Then he quit worrying about anything else, and let go with her.

Joanie was still wearing her boots, but both of them had moved to the bed and were now eating the chicken strips and macaroni and cheese she'd brought from the grocery store deli. Nick had grabbed the food on the way through the house as if he'd needed sustenance to keep going. She would bring him chicken every day if it got her another round like they'd had in the kitchen.

"Don't let me forget to take pictures before I leave tonight," she said. She'd forgotten to bring her camera with her the night before.

"Are we taking pictures of us doing naughty things?"

She laughed. "No! I'm taking pictures of the house as it's being worked on. To show them to GiGi during my visits."

"*Hmph.* Not nearly as much fun. Which reminds me." He pushed up and reached over to the small table she remembered having once been in her bedroom. He'd apparently dragged it in to be used as a bedside table. "I found something the other day I wanted to ask you about."

He pulled a small piece of paper from the drawer.

No, not paper, but a picture. An old one.

"That's you, isn't it? You're not blond in it, but you're not really blond anyway." He wiggled his eyebrows at her, implying he'd gotten a good look at the fact she was naturally a brunette.

She took the small square from him and studied it, her heart squeezing a little. It was her and GiGi. She'd been six and had just finished the piece of birthday cake GiGi had made for her. They were sitting in the swing that had once hung on the front porch, both smiling, her missing front tooth obvious, and Lucky's head lolling on her lap. She remembered how happy she and GiGi used to be.

"Yeah." She nodded. "That's me and GiGi. Pepaw took that picture."

"I wondered if that was her." He put the picture back in the drawer and gave her a quick, hot kiss on the mouth, effectively erasing the melancholy mood that had threatened to creep in with the picture. "You were cute back then."

"You saying I'm not cute now?"

He roamed his gaze down over her, making appreciative noises as he went. "There are other words I'd use these days."

Good answer.

Rising up on her elbows, she took a sip of the soda they were sharing, handed it back to him, then looked down at herself to see what he saw. "Hey, my panties are still on."

She turned to him. She'd forgotten they hadn't removed them. "Why are my panties still on?"

Dark eyes traveled over her body again, slowly and with more intent, before landing right smack in the middle of her crotch. He licked the chicken crumbs off his fingers.

"Nick?" If he was suggesting he would like to lick something else, she could get down with that. "My panties?" She wiggled her hips and watched his gaze grow warmer. "Why did you want them on earlier?"

A calloused hand stretched out and she began quivering even before he touched her. When his fingers did land, she lit on fire. He traced the triangle of her underwear as if in deep concentration, then gave her a fast, hot smile.

"Because I wanted to see you walk away from me in them." He handed her the Coke and rose to a sitting position. "Did you know you have the best-looking butt I've ever seen?"

"Is that because you haven't seen many butts or . . . oof!" She reached out her other hand to steady the drink as she found herself being flipped over onto her stomach. Nick threw one heavy leg across hers, straddling her thighs, and trapping her beneath him.

"The best ass," he said, patting said body part. "Period."

She smiled. He was fun.

She lifted her rear and wagged it at him and then squealed when she felt his teeth sink into her.

"You bit my butt," she complained, looking back over her shoulder at him.

What she got in return was a wicked smile and a lecherous wink. "Hang on, babe. I'm about to bite it again."

He did, instantly making her wet and wanting. The man knew what he was doing with a woman.

As he continued to gently tease at the flesh of her rear, she rested her head on her folded arms, over the lumpy mattress that should have been thrown out years ago, and enjoyed his ministrations. She'd come over the night before, fully expecting to find him there, maybe upset because she'd refused his "gift" of the cat, but also ready to put it behind them and move on. Or maybe she'd been projecting what she'd wanted to find.

Instead she'd found an empty house, *two* cats who'd wanted someone to play with, and the knowledge that his absence was making her jealous yet again as she wondered if he was out with Gina. Or maybe someone worthwhile this time.

Not that she had a right to be jealous. Sex only didn't necessarily mean exclusive. Still, it had bothered her. A lot.

She'd called Lee Ann, who'd called her mother, who'd told her immediately that Nick was at the Bungalow having dinner. Alone. After he also hadn't shown up for cupcakes today, Joanie had confirmed he'd gone home alone last night, too. Which meant what? He'd gone out for dinner simply because he'd been hungry, and then he'd been too busy for dessert today? Or he'd needed time away from her to think?

Probably it had been the latter. Especially since she'd been at the house until late and he hadn't come home before she'd left. He'd been avoiding her.

After the small taste of being with him that she'd gotten at her house, she'd decided she would make it clear she was serious. She wanted a "relationship" with him. And she had come over tonight with the intention of pushing one. Thankfully, he'd already come to that same conclusion all on his own.

And she'd ended up riding high on a new kitchen counter.

She smiled as she felt his palms slide down her legs. She liked the way the rough spots on his fingers lightly scratched at her skin.

"I hadn't realized until I saw it earlier that these things didn't go all the way up," he murmured, popping the elastic at the top of her thighs.

She peeked at him, glad she'd exchanged tights for stockings today. "They aren't nearly as hot if they go all the way up."

"I agree." He inched farther down her legs and nipped on the inside of one thigh. She squirmed.

"Hold still before I have to spank you." His low voice made her nipples hard.

She gulped. "You wouldn't spank me." Oh geez, would he spank her? One could only hope. She put the drink on the side table just in case this was about to get interesting.

Instead he began tugging on the zippers of her boots. When he got one loose, he yanked at it from the heel. As it came off, he leaned forward and nipped at her bottom again. This time she groaned.

"You're teasing me, Nick." Her breath was definitely not steady. "Do you think that's fair?"

"Who said anything about fair?" He pulled off the other boot, and gave her a playful swat.

"Oh crap." Her butt poked up in the air as if asking for more and she heard him chuckle.

In the next instant he began peeling down her stockings. He moved off her legs, but when she rolled to her side to help, he put a hand on her rear and held her down.

"I'm doing this, woman," he said. "Stay put."

No problem. She went back to her position on her stomach and enjoyed the feel of his hands slowly inching down her thighs.

"We're going to be exclusive, right?" She mentally thumped herself on the head. She hadn't meant to ask that. It made her sound so . . . needy.

His hands paused for a brief moment before he said, "We'd better be," and then he continued moving on down her leg. When he got to her feet, his hands stilled and she smiled into the sheets.

"You've got socks on over your hose."

"To keep me from getting so cold when I'm outside."

"Hmmm." He bent her leg at the knee and she could picture him craning his neck to look around to the other side. "They look like peeled bananas."

"Yep." She could tell from his tone that he didn't get her style. "Aren't they cute?"

He pulled them off. "Anyone ever told you you're odd, sweetness?"

She slumped into the bed. "Plenty of times."

She was on her back the second the words were out of her mouth, staring up at the giant of a man who'd just been worshipping her body with his hands.

"It's a good odd," he said. His look indicated that she needed to be sure she heard him.

"Okay." She nodded. "Sure."

He pressed a hard kiss to her mouth. "Good," he stressed. "The kind that makes a room glow just because you walked into it. Everybody wishes they had some of that."

Why was this turning serious? "Okay," she said. "I get it. It's good to be me."

"It is," he insisted. "And don't you forget it."

He kissed her again and then he was on her, touching her, and letting her touch him. When he finally pulled off her thong, she just smiled. She liked the idea of them being together in this way. It was a good one.

And if she had the occasional thought that it was also good to be him, she gave herself permission to have it. He was a really good guy. She even thought she might try to remember to lock her door that night just because of him.

Chapter Eleven

D on't burn yourself."

Joanie smirked over her shoulder, about to point out she could handle a simple task, but instead simply paused. Nick was standing at the stove with his back to her, a dish towel draped over one shoulder, no shirt, and well-worn jeans riding low on his hips, and she wasn't sure she didn't whimper out loud at the sight. She also happened to know the jeans were not buttoned. She'd seen to that herself.

He was so insanely sexy.

Especially when he cooked for her. As he'd been doing all week.

She'd helped, of course, and one evening had even brought over a slow cooker full of stew she'd had simmering all day. But Joanie would give Nick credit. His meals were far superior to hers. And he seemed to like cooking. So she let him.

They'd developed a routine of sorts, with both of them working at the house after business hours, then dinner and a movie or maybe a televised hockey game, then whatever extracurricular activities came to mind. Unless one of them mixed things up and those extracurriculars came early. Like tonight.

"I'm sure I can grab rolls out of the oven without burning my fingers." She finally pulled herself away from staring at him to reply to his comment. They'd gotten waylaid earlier when he'd gone to take a quick shower to clean up from the day, so dinner was running later than usual.

"I don't know." He turned to her and leaned back against the counter, crossing his arms over his chest, and she started the staring thing again. She would have gotten stuck eyeing his pectorals if he hadn't given her the kind of smile that perked her girl parts right up. "Your fingers tend to dawdle when they touch things," he said.

If she were easy to blush, she'd be doing it right now. Because he had an excellent point. Her fingers did like to dawdle. All over his shoulders, and his chest . . . her gaze dipped . . . and his abs and his butt and those seriously well-sculpted thighs.

She bit her lip as she lifted her gaze back to his. He seemed to be thinking along the same lines.

"Dinner first," he croaked. "I'm starved."

A smile slid across her face. "Dinner." She nodded. "First."

She'd come over every night since they'd christened the new kitchen. Instead of her cleaning out the house while Nick continued with the renovations though, he'd ended up helping her out more nights than not. Because, he claimed, she wasn't tossing enough in the trash.

Already her second bedroom was filling up with boxes of papers and documents she'd found, as well as collectibles. Who knew? Maybe when she had time to go through it all, she'd find some clue as to where her mother had been all this time. Possibly she'd corresponded with GiGi at some point. It *had* been twenty years. Hard to imagine anyone not making contact in that amount of time.

Joanie caught her breath at the thoughts rolling through her head. She'd never cared to know anything about her mother. Not since those first years when she'd stupidly thought her mother would return as she had all the other times. Her leaving had simply become a part of Joanie's life.

"What's wrong?" Nick asked. He came over to her, ducking down to try to catch her eyes. "You're upset."

"No." She shook her head, failing when she tried for a smile. "Just thinking about everything I still have to get through before we're done."

She quickly faced the oven and opened it, reaching in to grab the rolls, but jerked back when she accidentally touched the cookie sheet with her fingers.

"*Damn*," she muttered.

Nick grabbed her hand and held it under water. "I told you to be careful," he chastised.

"I was being careful."

"No, you weren't. You weren't paying attention because you were trying to avoid telling me something." He made her look at him while still holding her hand under the cold water. "You do that a lot, but then always end up telling me anyway. Might as well go ahead and spill it. You know you want to."

At her mulish look, he returned one of his own.

"Come on, sweetness." He leaned down and nuzzled her neck. "What was it? You know you'll feel better getting it out."

She kind of hated that he read her so well, and hated just as much that he was constantly there to "fix" it. But she also kind of liked it. It was nice. She'd discovered she liked sharing things with him, even if she pretended she didn't want to. Something about the two of them talking in the evenings made sense.

It was because she hated stressing over things, she decided. Telling Nick her issues allowed her to get them out of her head and move on. It made the days end better.

But this time she wasn't sure she wanted to go there. She hadn't talked with him about her mother yet.

She pulled her hand from his and dried it on the towel across his shoulder, accidentally-on-purpose letting the tips of her fingers trail over his skin. "It's your turn to talk tonight. Tell me about that space I heard you checked out on the square. It's been a couple weeks but you haven't mentioned signing a lease yet."

"Haven't managed to get any clients yet."

He returned to the stove to turn the chicken and she saved the rolls from burning. He was making a paprika chicken dish with rice and garlic-pepper broccoli on the side. Her mouth was watering just thinking about it. It sure beat her frozen dinners. Cooking for one was no fun.

"No need for an office if I have no clients," he finished.

"I'm sure they're just waiting for you to get done with this place. Wanting to see how it turns out." The food wasn't the only thing that smelled good. She rose up on her tiptoes behind him, steadying herself with her palms on his back, and pressed her nose to the base of his neck. He smelled like soap and man. "Mmm, you smell good."

He reached around and patted her on the behind. "You feel good. And you're likely right. That's what I keep telling myself, anyway. They trust me because I'm Cody's brother, but not enough to go into a contract with me just yet. Also, I'm not sure I need an office at this point. Life is pretty laid-back here. I'll be in Nashville so I will definitely need an office manager here, but I suspect the calls could simply be handled by cell. At least for a while."

Joanie dropped back to her heels and ignored the little voice screaming at the thought of him leaving. She'd known this was temporary. Heck, *they* were temporary.

She scooted around beside him so she could get a good look at his face, and leaned one elbow on the counter. "Is that okay with you?" she asked. "Your other locations are bigger. Are you really prepared for a smaller operation here?"

"Sure. As long as there is *some* operation, I'm good. I just want the work. I want a reason to come see my brother and nieces more than the occasional weekend."

He was such a family man in the making. She couldn't imagine how he'd managed to turn into that when he'd come from an alcoholic mother and a bad home life. Joanie had learned those facts from Lee Ann after she and Cody had almost split up back in December.

Nick had come to town to find his brother, shocking Cody not only with the fact that he had not one, but two brothers, but also surprising him to learn that the woman who'd given birth to him had recently died from liver disease. She'd apparently been a drunk for at least Nick's whole life.

She'd sold Cody to some adoption agency, though somehow he'd ended up in the system. But she had apparently succeeded in her other attempt at selling a kid. That would be their older brother. Joanie had no idea why she'd kept Nick.

Nick worked in silence for a few minutes while Joanie moved around the kitchen, pulling out plates and silverware—they'd loaded a handful of dishes back into the kitchen after he'd finished with the cabinets. When she glanced his way, she caught his dark eyes watching her.

"Want to tell me what was bugging you a few minutes ago?" he asked.

She shook her head. He could be so pushy. "Nope." She needed to keep the focus on him. "But you can tell me about your other brother. You hired a PI to find him, right? Any news there?"

A wry smile settled over his mouth. "Okay, sweetness, we'll play this your way. But you know you're going to tell me before the night's over. And not just because I want you to."

No, not just because he wanted her to. Which bothered her even more. She wanted to share her worries with him. She really did. She wanted to spend evenings like this, cooking and talking together. She wanted it so bad she almost cried every night when she crawled from his bed and went back to her own.

They were not in a relationship. Not a real one. They were merely sleeping together. She'd had the same arrangement with men before.

Yet not one of them had she wanted to hang around and cook dinner with.

Also, not a one of them had ever looked at her beyond the sex. None had worried what bothered her, or whether she locked her door when she went home at night.

"Your brother?" she asked, all smiles and innocence, determined to quit thinking about how nice this week had been.

Nick chuckled and leaned over to kiss her. "No news yet, but we knew the guy was backed up for a few weeks when we hired him. He came recommended, though, and given it's been thirty years, Cody and I figured a few more weeks wouldn't hurt." His hand snuck under her top and stroked her stomach. "What's your next question? I can play this game with you all night."

She eyed him, wanting to be frustrated, but knowing he had a point. She was going to tell him what had been on her mind, but it drove her crazy to know that. Before Nick, she'd only shared those things with Lee Ann. What was so darned special about him?

He pressed one more kiss to her mouth and this time she parted her lips and he slipped inside. They got carried away for a couple minutes before he remembered he was cooking, and she remembered she was hungry.

When he turned to the stove, she thought back over what she'd been contemplating before. Would she find anything about her mother in the boxes she'd hauled home?

Though she didn't want to get into her whole "past," she knew he had to already know about her mother leaving. He was living at the Barn, for heaven's sake. He'd also known about the Bigbee Curse. He had to know about Grace.

"You know my mother left when I was young, right?"

He glanced at her and simply nodded.

"Earlier . . . I was just wondering . . . why she never came back." Geez, did that sound pathetic. "I mean, I don't dwell on it or anything, but the thought crossed my mind that she might have contacted GiGi in the past that I didn't know about. Then I wonder . . . is she still with the guy she ran off with?" Joanie shrugged. "Things like that. So it occurred to me that some of the stuff I've taken home with me could potentially hold answers. Or . . . not," she finished lamely.

Steady brown eyes watched her carefully as he stirred the dish without looking. "You've heard nothing from her since she left?"

Joanie shook her head. "Not a word."

"That had to be rough." His understanding tone made her want to lean into him. "You were what, thirteen?"

"Somebody's been busy," she said, raising her eyebrows. "Who filled you in?"

"Cody." He pulled her to him and kissed the top of her head. "Only because I asked. I wanted to know what I was up against."

She decided not to remind him he wasn't up against anything. Just because he rocked her world every night didn't mean her path could so easily be changed.

He kept her against him but reached out and pulled the skillet from the burner, then he put his arms around her and began to sway back and forth as if they were slow dancing at a junior high dance. Finally, he asked, "Have you ever talked with your grandmother about it?"

"No." She burrowed her cheek against his warm chest. "It wasn't the first time my mother had left, so I think we both expected her to get dumped and come running back home. Like she always did. Only, this time, she didn't come back."

And now that Joanie thought about it, her grandmother had not seemed surprised that she hadn't returned. GiGi had even acted from day one as if Grace's leaving with Bill had been different. Almost immediately, she'd switched to longer hours to account for the loss of income into the household. As if she'd known Joanie's mother wouldn't be returning.

"Maybe you should," Nick said. He brushed his lips across her temple. Joanie looked up.

"Go see her," he urged. "Ask her about it."

"I will go see her. I'm going Tuesday. But I'm not going to ask her if she knows why her daughter left us and never came back. If we haven't talked about it in all this time, there's no need to now."

"Now is the perfect time," he urged softly. "Before it's too late."

His words were an unneeded reminder that she and GiGi were running out of time for a number of things.

Though Joanie hadn't been back for another visit yet, she had continued calling to check on her grandmother. Seemed GiGi hadn't improved much. The doctor hadn't had anything more to report than he had the last time.

Joanie had the sudden thought that she didn't want to wait until next Tuesday to visit. She could take an evening off from packing—and from Nick. That would probably be good for both of them.

Maybe she'd go tomorrow night. She could take the pictures of the house she'd already made. And maybe stick around a little longer, too. Last time hadn't been so bad.

At her continued silence, Nick pulled them apart, and peered down at her. "Why not ask? You need answers."

"And you think she has them?" Joanie stared up at him, wishing she believed that he was right. "You think she's been sitting on reasons for two decades but for some reason she'll come off them now?" She shook her head. "Even if she did know, she wouldn't tell me. We don't have that kind of relationship."

She paused, then pulled out of his arms and muttered "anymore" as she turned away. They hadn't had that kind of relationship for years. It had all begun going terribly wrong within the years following her mother's exit from their lives. GiGi had become hateful and distant. Joanie had rebelled.

It had not been a good time.

And it had never improved.

Lately she'd found the distance between them bothering her. GiGi had doted on her at one point.

Joanie picked up the plates and began dishing up their meal.

"Joanie—"

"Let's drop it, okay? She doesn't know any more than I do. My mother left, chasing after yet one more man, and this time maybe she kept him. Apparently I wasn't worth sticking around for, and neither was GiGi. We don't need to bring it up again."

"I'll go with you if you want."

Joanie had taken her plate and was headed to the couch they'd dragged back in from the garage earlier in the week, but stopped in the middle of the room. She faced him. "No. I just need to forget it. It's been twenty years, and I got over it a long time ago. Had a weak moment tonight, but I won't again. Now let's just eat."

Nick watched Joanie turn away and continue to the couch, ignoring him as if he wasn't there. He grabbed his plate and two beers and at the last minute pulled the cigar box of letters from the cabinet. He kept forgetting to bring them up to her, but tonight seemed a good time for it.

Walking into the living room, he stopped dead in his tracks.

Joanie was half sitting, half lying on the couch, legs stretched out to her side, and uncomfortably propping herself up on her elbow, waiting for him to take his spot. Once he sat, she would lean into him, which matched how they'd spent the past few evenings.

Both cats were snuggled against her. Cat at her feet, not wanting to show his love too much since he was still a little irked that the new, cuter cat had invaded his territory. But Bob was wound into a compact ball in front of her stomach. It's exactly as it had been every other night that week, but Nick realized for the first time how normal it looked. And felt.

They were spending every evening together, doing normal things. Talking, laughing, making love. Playing with their pets. But they weren't "dating" because she didn't date. They were just having sex. Then she was going home.

Only it was more. He knew it was.

And that surprised him as much as it would her if she paid attention to the facts.

His rib cage suddenly felt as if it were going to collapse in on his organs. And he didn't know if that would be a good or a bad thing. Because he was falling for her. Hard.

It was going to destroy him when she dumped him.

None of the other women he'd dated had he ever felt this close to. He'd tried to make relationships last. He'd even thought he had one or two that were going somewhere. Especially when he'd dated Angela. She'd even come with a ready-made family.

But in the end, it was the idea of what they could have had together that he missed as opposed to the women.

It might just be different with Joanie, though. He was pretty damned sure of it, actually.

He shoved the thought to the back of his mind, unsure how else to play things, and eased into his spot on the couch, eyeing the blue curl that settled down on his shoulder. He was even starting to get used to her ever-changing hair. "What are we watching tonight?"

A quick smile turned his direction and his body sang hallelujah that he had her in his life for as long as he could have her. She made him happy.

"The Predators are playing Detroit," she said.

He had learned over the last week that she not only preferred hard liquor and beer over wine, but she was a rabid hockey fan. This had first come to light when he'd suggested a movie. Stupidly, he'd picked up a handful of what he would refer to as "girl" movies. They had worked well for dates in the past.

But as Joanie had done that first night, she'd given him one of her what-do-you-take-me-for looks, tossed the movies to the side, and tuned the TV to a sports channel.

She always managed to surprise him. And he loved it.

He hadn't told her yet that he had season tickets to the Predators back in Nashville, but wondered if offering to take her to a game would get him the chance for a real date.

"Sounds perfect," he said, deciding not to toss the carrot out just yet. Surely in another week or so he could talk her out of the house. If not, then he would offer the tickets. The regular season would be ending soon, but they had a few games left they could catch. Maybe for her birthday at the end of the month.

Which reminded him, he had to come up with something really great as a gift.

He'd been fighting the urge to buy her things all week, assuming she'd refuse them since they weren't really "dating," so he'd concentrated his attention on doing things for her instead. Such as dinner and helping her out at the house. He liked taking care of her. He'd do more if she'd let him.

She grinned at him again and wiggled down deeper into his side, disturbing Bob, but he soon came back. Nick couldn't blame the cat. Her lap was a nice place to be.

"You had good ideas, Nick."

"Huh?" Had she read his mind? Knew he would rather it were him in her lap instead of Bob?

"The house." One arm motioned to the redone living room that was missing new paint and floors due to dust and dirt still being a part of the rest of the house. "I love what you're doing with the place. It feels right. It matches what I would want if it were my home."

The bite of chicken he'd just taken grew dry in his mouth as he suddenly had a picture of the two of them and a handful of kids running around the place. That was no way to be thinking. He may not get everything about her, but he got enough to know she wouldn't go for something like that. She was terrified of commitment. Even if it did come with season tickets to the Predators.

Plus, he lived in Nashville. He had his whole life set up there. He'd even built a five-bedroom house in the perfect neighborhood for raising kids for the day he *did* find the woman he could spend the rest of his life with.

It broke his heart to admit that he couldn't see Joanie in that neighborhood. Nor did he think she'd ever want to be there. He could only imagine the horrified looks she'd get if she drove up in her cupcake van and climbed out in a go-go outfit.

The men would like it, though.

Setting his plate on the floor, his appetite failing him, he lifted the cigar box to his lap. He needed to focus his mind somewhere other than the thought of the two of them *not* fitting together in his life. It was depressing.

"I found these the other night," he said. "Thought it might be fun to go through them together."

Joanie smiled over at him, but when her gaze landed on the box her lips fell flat. Vertical lines formed between her eyes. "Did you get those from the bedroom?"

"Yeah." He opened the lid and pulled out the top envelope.

"They're letters from Pepaw to GiGi. When he was in Korea."

Nick nodded. "I peeked at one. Looked like love letters."

Warm gray eyes studied the envelope in his hands as if trying to decide whether it was a good idea to pull the papers out or not. Nick held his breath. He could see the tension in her. The nerves. He really believed that if she read these, they would help her in some way, but he knew he couldn't force it.

Finally, her eyes lifted to his and she gave a tiny nod. "I was trying to order them the other night. I wanted to read them in chronological order."

Nick grinned at her. She was tough. He'd known she would have the guts to read them.

He also knew he could order them way faster than she could. She'd get sidetracked on something and end up having to start all over. "You finish your dinner while I sort them. Then you can read them out loud while I eat."

Her lids lowered again to stare at the letters, and he watched her take in a deep breath. Her guts made him want to toss the letters aside and kiss her.

"That sounds like a good plan," she finally said.

She sat up straighter on the couch, upsetting both cats with her movements, while Nick quickly flipped through the envelopes, organizing the letters. They started in July of 1951 and went through February of 1953.

"He was over there a while," Nick murmured as he concentrated on his task.

"Until he lost his arm."

He jerked his head up. "I didn't know that. How sad."

Joanie nodded. "From the elbow down. He and GiGi's brother went in together. They were best friends. Then they re-upped together.

Neither would leave the other over there alone. Only, Pepaw was the only one to come home."

Pain thumped in Nick's chest.

"Both their names are on the plaque at the base of the statue on the square," she added. Nick could see a faraway sadness in her eyes, but her voice didn't falter. She was merely stating the facts. "Pepaw earned a Purple Heart trying to save GiGi's brother, and then came home and married the girl he'd loved for years."

She shrugged and glanced up. "At least, that's the way the story goes."

Pushing her plate to the side, she muted the television, and took the first letter.

Chapter Twelve

J oanie lifted the vase of fresh flowers from the seat of her car, as well as the tote bag with the packet of pictures she'd printed out at the pharmacy down the street. Also in the bag was the locked metal box she'd found in GiGi's kitchen. It had occurred to her that morning that the box had not shown up until after Pepaw had left. Which made her more than curious about its contents.

Therefore, she'd brought it with her. She planned to ask GiGi about it if she seemed up to the conversation today. Then hopefully she'd find out where the blasted key was.

The white bakery box was the last item she grabbed, and then she marched, focused on her mission, into the nursing home.

It was Saturday afternoon. She'd spent the morning working at Cakes, had run home and changed, then headed into Knoxville to visit GiGi. She'd found herself more than excited about the trip.

Especially after all the letters she and Nick had read the night before.

She didn't understand what had gone wrong with GiGi and Pepaw after so many years, but that had been a lot of love packed into a small amount of space. It had surprised her by how it had lightened her heart.

GiGi may have been stuck in her life for the past twenty-five years, but for the first time, Joanie truly believed that at one point she'd been really happy. And that made Joanie happy.

"Good afternoon, Helen," she spoke to the receptionist as she breezed into the building, noting the surprised look on the woman's face. Joanie had never visited on a weekend, and other than GiGi's first few months of residence there, she hadn't visited but once a month since. And always on a Tuesday—as if that were her "assigned" day.

Today was different. Today she actually *wanted* to be there. She wanted to see her grandmother. The thought of waiting until Tuesday had suddenly seemed ridiculous. It was her grandmother. She should come see her anytime she wanted.

She was aware of the difference in her attitude. Only, she wasn't exactly sure what had caused it. She wondered if it had anything to do with Nick.

He had pushed her to read the letters last night. He'd made going through GiGi's stuff these last few weeks far easier to take, and had even made her laugh many times as she'd come across items she'd at first been certain were going to make her sad.

Of course, he'd also suggested she discuss her mother with GiGi today.

That wasn't going to happen. There could be no good from bringing up Grace to her grandmother.

As she approached GiGi's room, Joanie didn't hesitate entering this time. She placed her hand on the door, and smiled wide as it opened and she caught sight of GiGi inside the room.

She was awake, propped up in bed, and had the small television on the other side of the room turned on. The volume was down, but at least she wasn't just lying there staring at the ceiling as she had been the last time Joanie had visited.

GiGi still didn't look healthy, but there was more color in her skin today. It gave Joanie hope.

"Hi, GiGi," Joanie said, entering the room.

The older lady's thin eyebrows lifted, no doubt surprised at the sight of her granddaughter standing inside her room on a weekend day. The smile on Joanie's face probably added to the confusion. She didn't remember when she'd last entered any room her grandmother was in with a smile.

She should have done so much better over the years.

"Is it Tuesday, and I missed some days?" GiGi asked. Her tone was neither hard nor hateful, as Joanie had grown accustomed to over the years. In fact, it was pleasant. Happy. "I know my days are numbered, but I didn't think I'd lost my mind just yet."

Joanie laughed out loud. She'd just made her grandmother happy, possibly for the first time in years, and the feeling inside her was like the petals of a giant sunflower spontaneously bursting open in the sunshine.

"It's Saturday," Joanie announced. She held out the flowers. Miniature roses in reds, oranges, and yellows. "Special delivery. Thought these could brighten both you and your room." She set them down on the small bedside table, opened the blinds on the window to let more sunlight into the room, then pulled out the packet of pictures and waved them in the air. "I brought pictures of the house renovation. It's gorgeous, GiGi. You're going to love it."

GiGi's gaze settled on the flowers before coming back to the pictures in Joanie's hand and then lifting to her face. Her lips turned up in a gentle smile. "He's good for you," she said.

Joanie paused. "Who's good for me?"

"This man. Nick. He makes you happy."

Fighting a scowl, Joanie propped her hands on her hips. How could her grandmother know there was more going on between her and Nick than simple renovation? "Are you still spying on me?"

A thin, frail shoulder lifted under the light-green polyester top. "Someone has to take care of you."

Joanie started to roll her eyes at the words, feeling the usual irritation that the woman was butting into her life where she wasn't needed, but then stopped. She just looked at her grandmother, realizing for the first time that she was lucky to have had her grandmother *in* her life. Someone had needed to take care of her. Her mother certainly hadn't done it. Not even when she had been around.

It had always been GiGi and Pepaw. Making sure she got to school, shaping her life, giving her memories to store up for later years. After Pepaw left, it had just been GiGi. They'd all pretended Grace had something to do with her upbringing, but that was a lie. Her mother had never wanted her. She'd never had anything to do with her.

But GiGi had never turned her back.

Joanie stepped to the bed, a heavy lump filling up the space from her heart up to her throat, and gently scooted GiGi's legs over on the mattress a few inches. She sat on the bed with her grandmother and reached out to touch the too-frail hand. "Thank you for taking care of me over the years, GiGi," she said. "I don't think I've ever said that to you, but thank you. Life certainly would have been harder without you in it."

The recognition in her grandmother's eyes that Joanie had just had a growing-up, mature moment added to that national-park-size lump in her throat, and Joanie was suddenly terrified. GiGi was very sick. She didn't have too much longer to live.

And then Joanie was going to be alone.

"I'm sorry Grace never came back." The words rushed out of GiGi's mouth, her voice a soft rasp as if she were fighting back tears. "It was my fault. You would have had your mother back if not for me."

Shock had Joanie rooted to her seat. "What are you talking about?"

GiGi shook her head back and forth and tears began to slowly drip from her eyes. "I told her not to come back. I caught her packing up her clothes to leave with Bill. She'd told you for weeks that you three were going to be a family. She'd made you believe. You were so hopeful. He was so nice to you. And then I caught her packing up her clothes with no intention of taking you with her. I told her she was done hurting you that way. That if she left that time, she was not welcome back in my house." Silence pulsed through the room before GiGi quietly finished with, "I didn't think she'd leave."

"GiGi," Joanie whispered, unsure what else to say.

"I'm so sorry." GiGi shook her head again. "I'm so sorry."

Her grandmother had told her mother not to come back?

Joanie's first thought was to be mad. Furious. How dare she? But then all of GiGi's words penetrated. She'd been trying to protect Joanie. She'd tried to keep her mother from hurting her anymore.

That was way more than her mother had ever done.

With tears in her own eyes, Joanie leaned forward and pulled her grandmother into an embrace, both of them holding each other in a way she couldn't remember them ever doing.

"It's okay, GiGi," she whispered.

"I'm so sorry," her grandmother repeated again. "I didn't think she'd leave. I shouldn't have done that."

Joanie pulled back and wiped at the tears streaking GiGi's face. "I suspect it was for the best." And she honestly did. Her mother hadn't cared for her. At least someone had cared enough to see that as a problem.

"I should have told you about it a long time ago." GiGi's words were almost too soft to hear. "I wanted to. But I didn't know how."

Joanie closed her eyes as if that would hide the pain. She suspected GiGi was only telling her now because she knew her days were numbered. The thought made Joanie replay her and Nick's conversation from the night before. The one about her mother. Should she ask GiGi about Grace? She didn't want to upset her more than she already was. But then she felt Nick's strength as if he were right there beside her, holding her hand.

She opened her eyes. She needed to do this.

"Have you heard from her at all since she left?" Joanie asked. "Anything?"

A sad look came over her grandmother, dulling her eyes and making her seem even more fragile than she was. "Never one word," she whispered. "It was as if she was glad I'd given her the ultimatum."

Grace's leaving hadn't just hurt Joanie, it had broken GiGi's heart.

That had to destroy a person in a way Joanie couldn't even imagine.

In a vivid moment of clarity, Joanie realized she had to do better for her grandmother. She had to bring her home.

She didn't know how, but she'd figure it out.

"I'm going to bring you home with me, GiGi. As soon as I can make arrangements so I can take good care of you."

Only . . . *how*?

When GiGi's house sold, she could use the money to hire a nurse. They could put a bed in the living room of Joanie's rental.

It wouldn't be ideal, but it would work.

Or she could find a different place to rent with a bedroom on the first floor.

"I can't do it today." She squeezed her grandmother's hand. "I wish I could. But I'll come visit more often. I'll be back Monday. How's that? I can stay longer on Mondays. And then again next Saturday. I'll come twice a week. After the house sells we'll make it work. You'll live with me."

Again, the thought of getting rid of the Barn caused Joanie a moment of pain. She didn't want to sell the house. But she had no choice. It wasn't as if she could give up her rental and move her and GiGi there. She owed too much on the upgrades.

But she would do something. She'd figure it out. And she would not let GiGi die here alone. Maybe being back in Sugar Springs would even extend the time she had left.

Thin, wispy gray hair moved slowly up and down as her grandmother nodded. Her eyes were watery again, but no more tears fell. She gave a hesitant smile. "You're a good granddaughter," GiGi said, which felt like a lie. She wasn't. She hadn't been in years.

Better late than never, she thought. She *would* be a good granddaughter.

"I'm going to take all these pictures and make a scrapbook for you." The idea popped into her head from nowhere. "I've found so many things in the house that I know you love. I want to take some of them, as well as these pictures and the rest I'll make as we finish up, and create a scrapbook. We'll call it 'The Barn Book.'"

The smile on GiGi's face wavered, and two narrow lines of tears once again slipped over her bottom lids. "I like that," she admitted. "'The Barn Book.' Your grandfather would have loved it."

Silence fell over the room at the mention of Pepaw, and Joanie caught herself thinking back over the letters she'd read the night before.

She wanted to understand what had gone wrong.

It wasn't as if she *needed* the knowledge. But she wanted desperately to know what had happened between her grandparents. Nothing about his leaving had ever made sense.

Why had Pepaw left not only GiGi, but her, as well?

Squeezing GiGi's hand, she took a deep breath and silently prayed she wasn't making a mistake by bringing it up. It had already been an emotional day. "Why did Pepaw leave, GiGi?" she finally asked.

Her grandmother looked at her with wide eyes, and then lowered her gaze and shook her head. "He didn't leave, hon."

Joanie blinked. "Yes, he did. Twenty-five years ago. Then you went to DC and buried him eight years later."

Had her grandmother blocked it? Forgotten?

Was she finally losing her mind?

GiGi shook her head, but kept her eyes downcast. "He couldn't help it. He didn't leave us."

"Of course he did," Joanie insisted, fighting the small flame of anger. She remembered it with clarity. "He told me good-bye before I went to school that morning. He *told* me he was leaving. I cried at school all day. And then when I came home, he was gone. And he never came back."

It occurred to her that his not coming back hurt more than her mother not coming back. That seemed like an odd thing, but given he'd been the more stable one in her life, she supposed that made sense.

Her grandmother just shook her head. "He didn't leave. He was a good man. A proud man."

Well, he may not have left GiGi, but he'd certainly left Joanie.

GiGi reached for the pictures in Joanie's hand. "Show me what you brought." Her tone was back to being tight and hard. She'd closed off.

Joanie stared at her for several seconds, wanting to push for more, but she knew her grandmother well. That stubborn tilt to her jaw was in place. She was not talking about Pepaw any more today.

Joanie let out a frustrated sigh and opened the pictures.

They spent the next thirty minutes with somewhat stilted conversation, going through photos that Joanie had taken from every angle of the house. There were even a few shots of Nick in there. She flipped through those quickly, but her grandmother stopped her on one.

It was of Nick from the night before. She'd taken the picture when she'd first gotten there, right before he'd gone off to shower. He'd been standing in the new third-floor room—which was nothing but studs and framing at this point—sawdust and sweat covering him, his eyes glowing as he'd explained every detail the room was going to have. He'd followed up the description by telling her what he wanted to do with her in that room once it was finished.

She gulped, seeing the ardor in Nick's eyes, and hoping her grandmother didn't.

"He's good-looking," GiGi said. "He and you would make pretty babies."

This brought Joanie to her feet, spilling the pictures onto the floor.

"We're not having babies, GiGi. He's working on the house. That's all."

"Okay," GiGi whispered. "I'm just saying he's a pretty boy. He'd make pretty babies."

Joanie realized her grandmother had grown tired. She was struggling just to keep her eyes open, and her shoulders had slumped down farther on the bed.

They'd been talking for well over an hour, and GiGi had been sitting up that whole time. Plus, she'd gotten upset. Twice. Joanie needed to go and let her rest. She rose and gathered the pictures, then set the packet on the bedside table. She'd get more printed out for the scrapbook, and leave these here for GiGi.

"I'm going to let you sleep now, GiGi."

Her grandmother nodded and Joanie helped her down to a prone position. Joanie hovered another minute as if unsure what to do next, then leaned in and kissed her on the cheek, fighting her own tears at the feel of the paper-thin skin beneath her lips.

"I'll be back Monday, GiGi. I'll bring the scrapbook." She pulled the cupcakes from her bag and set them on the bedside table, then turned to go, but stopped at GiGi's next words.

"I had a pretty boy once."

Joanie eyed her grandmother whose eyes were now closed. Was she talking about Pepaw?

She must be. There had been no other boy in her life, as far as Joanie knew.

Heck, maybe her grandmother really was losing her mind. Joanie just hoped it hadn't been exacerbated by bringing up Pepaw.

Before she could come up with a response, she heard soft snoring from the bed.

With one last glance at her grandmother, Joanie stepped quietly from the room, holding a love in her heart she'd never realized was there. It felt right. They were going to fix this thing that had been between them for so long.

She was going to do right by GiGi.

Chapter Thirteen

L ed Zeppelin pumped from the speaker of Nick's docked iPod as he worked at loosening a board inside the shed. It was Saturday afternoon, and he was at the house alone. The guys he'd hired had been working ten-hour days for over two weeks, so he'd given them the day off. That didn't mean he got one. Instead of working in the house, though, he'd decided to spend the early-spring day cleaning out the sheds in the backyard. Doing so would allow him to dump the junk before letting Joanie have a look, risking her dragging the majority of the contents home with her.

The woman had issues. She was as much of a pack rat as her relatives, but every time he tried to talk her out of something, she was so darn cute for her reasons for wanting to keep it that he caved. In the end, she *was* getting rid of most of the junk in the house. He'd just been surprised at how much she'd kept.

There were two sheds in the yard, and he'd already emptied the majority of the first one into the Dumpster. What he hadn't been sure about, he'd piled up for Joanie to decide. This building, however, was proving more difficult. He'd uncovered a few pieces of furniture that looked as if they could be of value, several boxes of Christmas ornaments that seemed unique enough he couldn't bring himself to toss them, and now was working his way through a haphazard stack of lumber, trying to get at what lay beneath.

He wasn't sure what he'd find at the bottom, but the chains he'd caught sight of had given him a suggestion. If it turned out to be what he thought, it would be the perfect birthday present for Joanie.

The board came loose with a strong, two-handed yank, and he lost his footing, nearly catching himself as he stumbled backward, but ending up in the dust on the floor. Luckily, the board hadn't released any of the other random pieces, and nothing rained down on his head.

He shoved himself up, exhausted, but knowing there was little time to spare. He'd already spent too many hours during the week with Joanie when he should have been putting in work on the house, not to mention that he needed to make a quick run to Nashville the next day. There were a few details at the office he needed to handle, and he should check in on his house. He lived in a good neighborhood, but a house sitting for weeks unattended could attract any kind of trouble.

His mind went to Joanie again, and of how every night with her he felt as if a clock were ticking down. It would be nice if she'd stay over once in a while, or invite him to her place. But he supposed her actions fit within the definition of what they were doing. Though he did have to admit the definition was starting to get to him.

He hauled a few more pieces out of the building, then came up short when he realized he had company. A black, overcompensating-for-something sports car sat parked beside his truck. One he'd seen before when it had held Joanie and Brian, kissing as if the world were coming to an end and they didn't want to go out breathing.

"Seems you've made progress out here." Brian stood under the new roof of the back porch, the door to the house open behind him. "Looks good."

Nick tossed his load into the Dumpster before turning to the other man. Did people just show up and walk through houses unannounced in Sugar Springs? He'd liked the place until now.

"I have. What are you doing here, Marshall?" He could be more polite, but the sight of him and Joanie kissing had left an impact.

Brian pushed off the support post, and headed toward Nick. "Pop sent me over to check out your work. Said you were looking to build some cabins on our property."

The Marshalls had a six-room bed-and-breakfast, offered several year-round tourist activities, and had seventy-five acres backing up to the river that edged the county. They were looking to expand.

"That's right." Guess this meant he was going to have to be civil to the guy. He jerked his chin at the house. "Want a look around or did you already see everything?"

"I only walked straight through. You didn't answer so I figured you were working. Heard the music out here and came on back." Brian went silent while Nick bent to the speaker and shut off the song. "Also wanted to ask what your deal was with Joanie."

Ah. The real reason for the visit.

"I'm pretty sure that's none of your business." He stared the man in the eyes, jealousy eating him up inside. This person had known Joanie a long time, and whether Brian wanted her in his bed or not, they had a closeness she and Nick didn't share. That bothered him. "Did you want to see the house, or were you just stopping by to piss me off?"

A small smile graced Brian's face. "That answers one question."

"What's that?"

"You don't simply take people's bullshit." He headed for the still-open back door. "Good deal. That's what Joanie needs. And yes, I want to see the house. Got a beer? I'll take one of those, too."

Nick scowled at the man as he walked away, trying to figure out if the comment meant that he was *for* Nick and Joanie being together, or against. Or maybe he was just screwing with him. Didn't matter, anyway. He followed and got out that beer.

"You think you know what Joanie needs, do you?" Nick asked.

Cat jumped up on the counter and Brian scratched him behind the ears. When Bob, who couldn't yet master the height, purred at his feet, Brian leaned down and scooped him up, too. "Nice cats."

How could Nick hate a cat guy?

"What do you want, Brian? You want to know about me and Joanie? Yes, I'm seeing her. I'm crazy about her. I wouldn't do a thing in the world to hurt her. Is that what you want to hear? Tell that to her and I'll punch you in the throat."

He began leading the way through the house.

"And if I were to ask her the status between you two?" Brian asked. "Would she say the same thing? Because I have to tell you, no one has seen you *out* with her. Other than drooling over her at Cakes. You're there on Thursdays as if it's your business to protect her and her legs from every other man in the county."

"I'm there on Thursdays because I want a cupcake."

Nick was impressed he got that out with a straight face. Marshall had it right; he was there, ready to go Rambo on any guy who got too close. Not that it mattered. All Nick could do was sit back and watch. Joanie would do exactly as she wanted to do, and he could either get with the program or stay away.

They headed up the stairs, Nick answering questions about the house as they went. When they reached the third floor, Brian checked out the space in detail.

"You do nice work," he finally declared. "Good eye. Doesn't look like you skimp on quality. I'm impressed."

"What'd you think I was doing out here? Building a pup tent?"

Brian gave him his smile again and it pissed Nick off. The man was a good friend of Joanie's, he was what most women would refer to as "hot," and he would clearly do favors for Joanie whenever she asked—such as keep her out all hours of the night just to piss Nick off. Did that mean Brian had once had one of her sex-only relationships?

He knew people had pasts. Hell, he had a past. But he didn't like the idea of this man discovering which thong Joanie wore each day. Or peeling them off her.

"Take it easy, Dalton." They headed back downstairs, Brian leading the way. "I'm not your enemy here."

"You're not anything to me."

Brian stopped on the stairs and gave him a measured look. "Hurt Joanie and I will be."

Terrific. An ex-lover who had her back. Exactly what he needed. Then he wondered if that would be him some day.

Most likely. At least he wouldn't have to be a year-round fixture protecting her.

"I won't hurt her," Nick confirmed. "It'll be the other way around if it's anything."

What a pansy-ass thing to say.

Calm blue eyes watched him for another ten seconds before Brian's face shifted and the pleasant demeanor was back. He laughed out loud and continued downstairs. "I suspect you might be right. She's not one to get caught."

"No one said I was looking to catch."

Marshall laughed even louder, a sound which only irritated Nick more. Because he knew Brian was right, even if he hadn't voiced his thoughts.

Nick wanted to catch her.

Wasn't he already well on his way to falling in love with her?

Joanie passed a couple twenties across the counter and waited for her change. It was just after lunch on Monday and she and Lee Ann were having their usual girls' day. Only instead of milkshakes or pedicures, Lee Ann would be helping her make the scrapbook for GiGi.

"These are some impressive photos you got here," said Bert Wheeler, the photo technician at the local pharmacy. Joanie had brought in her memory card that morning, and of course Bert would have checked out every photo as they'd printed.

Bert was nearing retirement age and was what some would call the "curious sort." Joanie would call it nosy. But then, if she really hadn't wanted her pictures to be seen, she would have printed them herself. If she had any idea if her printer worked. Or had ink.

It was easiest just to bring them in. Plus, she didn't mind him looking. It was simply part of life in Sugar Springs.

"Nick does good work, doesn't he?" Joanie pulled the photos from the pack and leaned on the counter in front of Bert, flipping through them as she'd done with GiGi two days before.

After her and Nick's conversation Friday night where she'd learned he had yet to secure a contract for another job, she felt inclined to point out the good work he was doing to anyone who would listen. Bert talked to most of the people in town in any given week, so he was a good one for Joanie to preach to about the value of the job Nick was doing.

"You should drive by there, Bert," Joanie urged. "It's not just the inside that looks different." In fact, the whole thing was starting to look pretty stunning. She wished she could keep it. For her and for GiGi.

It was way too big for the two of them, but she loved what Nick had done to the kitchen with the slightly rustic look that fed into the living room and the walnut flooring he'd picked out to go down. She would have never guessed she would like the rustic look, but it fit when she looked out the windows and saw the mountains in the distance.

Then there was the back porch. With its electricity and three walls of insulated windows, it was now more like an extension of the house instead of an afterthought. The right furniture could provide a comfortable year-round escape. And of course, the room on the third floor would be a dream come true.

She could go on and on. The front porch. Who could resist those rockers? As the temperature had begun to inch steadily up over the last few days, she'd found herself spending several evenings out there, doing nothing more than relaxing and enjoying the ending of the day.

The fact that Nick had been by her side hadn't gone unnoticed by her either. She liked being with him.

But she hated how much she was liking it.

"I drove out that way last night," Bert was saying. "Me and my Betty." He whistled then. "Mighty fine-looking house. We ain't looking to move, but I'll sure be interested in seeing the inside once it's finished."

This pleased Joanie and made her want to run to tell Nick. "It'll be going on the market by the end of the month, and Jane plans to do an open house that first weekend." Jane was the Realtor they were working with. She'd been out to the house the other night to take a quick look around, and was thrilled to get the listing. Joanie was both happy to list it with her, and sad at the same time. She would hate to see it go.

She flipped to another picture as Bert leaned in closer, his head right next to hers, studying each one as if he hadn't already seen them all. She glanced up at Lee Ann, who stood a few feet away, watching her.

What? Joanie mouthed.

Lee Ann merely gave a shake of her head. *Nothing,* she mouthed back.

"I found this one interesting," Bert commented as Joanie flipped to the next photo without looking. "In fact, I called Reba when I saw it. Told her I believed she might be wrong."

"Which one?" Joanie looked back down. What would Lee Ann's mother have to do with one of her pictures?

Then she saw what Bert was talking about.

It was of Nick. One she'd forgotten about taking Saturday night after she'd returned from Knoxville. He'd just come from the shower, a white towel slung around his hips, his very fine chest in all its naked glory, and one of those grins that melted her insides in place on his strong jaw. The smile was so good, that her body got a little revved just looking at it now. While at the same time, her brain screamed at her to ditch the picture.

"Yep," Bert continued. "Told her I didn't believe you two had an issue in the bedroom at all. That is not the look of an unsatisfied man. Trust me. I've worn that look a time or two, myself."

Joanie cringed at the image his words conjured.

She turned the photo face down and frowned at Bert. "Of course we don't have issues in the bedroom. Who's . . ." She stopped, remembering what Lee Ann had told her about the rumors after her and Nick's "sex" conversation at Cakes. The bet had been that she wasn't doing something right in that department. She narrowed her eyes. "People are still talking about that?"

"Yeah. Especially seeing that you're out there so late every night."

"I have work to do out there," she explained. "That doesn't mean we're running around doing . . . *things* . . . every night."

He picked up the picture and waved it at her. "That ain't all you're doing, sweetheart."

Lee Ann moved to her side and took the photo from Bert. Joanie was just about to thank her for stepping in to help when Lee Ann murmured, "Oh yeah. I've seen this look before. You're right, Bert. This is one happy man."

Joanie snatched the picture from her. She then realized that with Cody and Nick being twins, Lee Ann probably had seen that exact look. That didn't mean she needed to agree with Bert.

Joanie gathered up the now scattered photos and shot her friend a dirty look. "Are you about finished?"

Lee Ann shrugged. "Just about." She handed over a ten-dollar bill. "Put me down for April fourth."

With that, Lee Ann left the store without another word, leaving Joanie to gawk back and forth between the door her friend had vanished beyond, and Bert. Bert opened the cash drawer and stashed the bill inside.

"What did she just bet on?"

Guilt passed across Bert's face. "I uh . . . believe I'm supposed to keep this one quiet."

Joanie shook her finger at him. "You're betting on me, in *front* of me, and you won't tell me what it's about?"

Bert shook his head.

"Can I get in on the bet?"

He looked out the window as if seeking help, his mouth puckered in thought, then back to her. "You'd want to bet without knowing what you were betting on?"

"No, Bert! I want you to tell me what I'd be betting on. Come on, let me in on it."

He scratched his jaw as he thought through his options. As a general rule, part of the game of the money bets was to try to up the ante. If he let her contribute, that would be ten dollars more they didn't already have.

Finally, he frowned and shook his head. "Sorry, Ms. Joanie. Can't do it."

"Fine." She gave him a growling kind of sigh and scooped up her packet of photos. "But this is not funny. You all really should find better ways to amuse yourself."

She left the store, knowing her words were hypocritical. If the tables were turned, she might very well be in on the bet. It was one of the town's favorite pastimes.

A slight breeze hit her as she stepped out on the sidewalk. She swiped the hair back out of her face and saw Lee Ann already heading down the street, almost to the library. That's where they planned to work on the scrapbook. There was a little table out on the back patio that would afford enough privacy that they could talk, while still having plenty of space to get the job done.

Clearly, Lee Ann knew she had some explaining to do, so she was putting distance between them as fast as possible. Joanie took off after her.

When the townspeople had been guessing on where the trouble lay with sex between her and Nick—as if there were any trouble in that department—she didn't think there had been any money put down. Money bets signified something serious like when someone would be delivering a baby, or how long a person would last at a job. There had been bets in the past on how soon Joanie would sell whatever business she'd owned at the time. In fact, there was likely one out now.

Was that what Lee Ann had bet on? Normally she didn't get involved in those as she often felt like she had insider information.

Joanie entered the library—Lee Ann having disappeared before she got there—and headed across the lobby of the small, four-room building. It wasn't huge, but Larissa Bailey, who'd moved to town three years ago when Sugar Springs had gotten a library grant, did an excellent job of stocking both popular and educational treasures.

"Afternoon, Joanie."

Joanie took her sights off the back door and swiveled around to find Larissa standing at a shelf over to the side of the room. Her white-blond hair and soft, shy smile always made Joanie think that if they had an angel in town, she would be it.

"Hey Larissa." Joanie looked around and realized there was no one else in the room. "You alone today?"

"I just finished story time about an hour ago and it's been pretty quiet since."

Larissa never said she was lonely, but no one saw her out much, and her demeanor pretty much shouted meek and mild. Joanie peered through the large windows overlooking the sunny patio, saw Lee Ann sitting at the table, ignoring her, and made an executive girls' day decision. She knew Lee Ann wanted to hear how things were going between her and Nick, and Joanie wanted to know about the bet, but she felt the need to invite Larissa to join them instead. There would be plenty of other Mondays in which she and Lee Ann could play catch up.

"Larissa." Joanie paused until the woman looked up from where she was now shelving books. "Are you any good at scrapbooking?"

"That's one of the classes I teach here. Did you want to come to one?"

"Oh, no. I hate scrapbooking." Which was very odd given she had every intention of getting a really good start on one today. "But Lee Ann is going to help me work on one for GiGi. It's pictures of the house renovation, as well as a few other odds and ends."

She patted the bag she had slung over her shoulder where she held miscellaneous pieces of GiGi's collections from the house, along with the last letter Pepaw had mailed from Korea.

Larissa nodded. "I've heard it's turning into quite the showplace."

"It is," Joanie agreed. "Nick is doing a fantastic job."

Larissa lowered her gaze as if embarrassed. "My brother is helping out there."

"I've seen him. He does great work himself."

Joanie thought about Nick and how he'd not only had the foresight to create what the house was becoming, but how he was training some of the younger men as they worked alongside him.

"I was wondering if you might want to join us out back while you have no one in here, Larissa?" Joanie asked her. "Unless you have something else you need to do?"

"Oh." A slight blush colored Larissa's pale cheeks. Joanie suspected she didn't get invited to a lot, and that included just hanging with the girls. "I don't know." She looked around at the rows of books. "I probably should do some straightening or something."

From what Joanie could see, nothing was out of place in the whole building.

"Okay." She wouldn't push. "But if you change your mind, we'd love for you to join us. It's girls' day." She gave Larissa a quick grin. "No boys allowed."

She headed toward Lee Ann but stopped at the sound of a book being slapped down on one of the shelves. She looked over her shoulder and found Larissa standing tall.

"Yes," Larissa said with timid authority. She wore a smile and gave a simple nod. "I could use a girls' day. Heck, I could use two of them. I think I will join you."

Joanie gave the other woman a wide grin, and they walked out to the patio together.

Lee Ann looked up at the change in plans, and then gave Larissa a welcoming smile. "Please tell me you're here to help. Joanie might be able to decorate a cupcake, but that's only because she simply has to squirt a glob of icing on top. When it comes to really making something unique, she's a dud."

All three women laughed and got to work. They talked about mundane things, about the St. Patrick's Day parade coming up that Sunday, and did their own amount of gossiping.

"I heard Holly say she's thinking about moving to Chicago," Larissa supplied.

Joanie snorted. "She won't go."

"You don't think so?" Behind the purple-rimmed glasses, Larissa's wide eyes were green trimmed in gray. They were simply gorgeous. "She seemed enamored with the idea," Larissa added.

"She's been saying for years that she's going to leave. Thinks she's big city," Joanie explained. "She isn't going anywhere."

Lee Ann pasted a picture of the new third-floor room in the book and nodded. "She loves working in the diner. Loves being in the middle of everything. She'd get lost in a big city."

"She'll still be here saying the same thing next month," Joanie predicted. She looked up at Lee Ann. "I think we should start a bet."

Lee Ann's blue gaze blinked before refocusing on the book she and Larissa were doing most of the work on.

"I think it's funny all the bets I hear about around here," Larissa chimed in. "There's one going on right now—"

"That she doesn't need to know about," Lee Ann finished.

"Oh." Larissa looked between both women, then nodded. "Yeah."

"Lee Ann," Joanie tried hard for a tone to indicate she meant business, but that wasn't something she'd ever mastered. "Tell me what's going on."

"Oh look." Larissa rose from her seat. "Someone just came in. I'll leave you two girls to it."

She was gone in the blink of an eye, and Joanie turned to her friend. "Spill it."

"It's no concern of yours."

"It's about me. How can that be of no concern?"

"Because it's not something you need to know about. I'll tell you after it's over. After we see how it comes out."

Joanie flipped to a new page in the book and began trying to work the pictures into a pleasing pattern, adding some ribbon she'd found in one of the envelopes of GiGi's letters. "I think it's crap you won't tell me. You're supposed to be my friend."

"I am, sweetheart." Lee Ann took the photos from Joanie and smacked her hand away. "That's why I'm doing this instead of you. It should be something Georgia will enjoy looking at, not something that makes her flinch."

Joanie grew silent as she thought through possibilities for whatever bet was going on, but also about going to see GiGi today. Just as she had

Saturday, she was looking forward to the visit. She'd decided to work on the scrapbook for a while today, and then take whatever they had done when she went. By the following Saturday, she should have even more to show her. GiGi would enjoy seeing the bits and pieces of her past come together.

"Can I ask what day Holly has her money on with this bet you won't tell me about?" Joanie asked. Holly held the record for winning the most bets, so maybe her guess would give Joanie a clue.

Lee Ann looked up, her face pinched even though Joanie could tell she was going for relaxed. "She chose your birthday, in fact."

Less than three weeks away. Eighteen days.

Something big was supposed to happen then, huh? She and Nick were shooting on having the house on the market by then. Was everybody betting on when someone would make an offer?

That could be it, but it felt more personal.

Her birthday . . . Her mother had left on that day. At the same age Joanie was about to be. Did that have anything to do with the bet?

And then her heart sank as it occurred to her. The Bigbee Curse.

All Bigbee women fell to it. Now that she had Nick in her life, everyone must assume she was going to go the same route.

Get dumped. Have her heart broken.

Have him leave her.

Well she had news for them. She wasn't in a relationship. She couldn't get her heart broken.

Only, she worried that wasn't exactly true. The mere idea of Nick returning to Nashville gave her palpitations when she thought about it. That's why she didn't think about it.

They were having fun, having a good time.

And every single one of the people placing money on her was going to lose it.

"Do I win the money if it doesn't happen?" she asked.

Before Lee Ann could answer, Lee Ann's cell rang. She jumped on the call as quickly as if discovering a life raft in the middle of an ocean. Then her face tightened.

"I'll be right there." She finished the call and slipped the phone back into her purse. "I'm sorry, Jo. I've got to go. Candy got sick at practice. I need to go home."

"No problem." Joanie started gathering the materials, shoving them into her tote bag. "I need to head on to Knoxville, anyway."

Lee Ann handed her the scrapbook. "You're visiting more often."

"Yeah." Joanie held up the book. "I told her we were going to work on this. I want to show it to her."

"Good for you, hon." Lee Ann patted her hand and then rose. "It's good to see you two working things out."

It was good to be working things out, Joanie thought. It just felt right.

She grabbed the rest of her things and headed back through the library, tossing out a quick good-bye to Larissa, then climbed into her car with a smile on her face. GiGi was going to love what they'd already gotten done.

Twenty-five minutes down the road, her cell phone rang. She glanced at the screen and her stomach sank. It was the nursing home. She'd sent a payment last week, but it hadn't fully covered the bill. She'd been hoping it would keep them quiet until next month.

At least with them calling, she could get the conversation out of the way and they wouldn't have to have it face-to-face when she got there.

She answered.

"Ms. Bigbee?"

The voice on the other end was tight and strained. And male. It wasn't the normal lady from billing. She had the sudden, overwhelming feeling that she needed to drive faster. "Yes?" she asked hesitantly.

"This is Sam Wilpot, director of Elm Hill Nursing Home."

Joanie felt her shoulders sag. GiGi was worse. She knew it without having to hear it. "I'm sorry, Ms. Bigbee, but your grandmother took a turn for the worse this afternoon. We called her doctor in—"

"I'm heading there right now," Joanie interrupted. "I'll be there in twenty minutes." Ten if she blew out the speed limit.

She glanced down. She'd pulled her foot off the accelerator without realizing it and was now barely going twenty miles an hour. She forced herself to press down harder.

"Ms. Bigbee." The man's steady, quiet tone stopped her.

She held her breath. "What?"

"I'm sorry, Ms. Bigbee. We did everything we could. Her doctor arrived within minutes and CPR was performed for half an hour, but your grandmother's heart simply stopped beating. We couldn't revive it. She was pronounced dead at three thirty-five this afternoon."

The phone slipped from Joanie's hand as tears poured down her face.

Chapter Fourteen

N ick jumped from his truck and slammed the door, hurrying around to Joanie's side. It had been forty minutes since he'd first gotten the call from her. She'd been on the side of the road, about halfway between Sugar Springs and Knoxville, crying so much he'd barely been able to get out of her where she was or what was going on.

To say he'd broken a speed limit or two getting to her wouldn't be a lie.

He'd called Lee Ann on the way to let her know that Georgia had passed. She had assured him she would call the funeral home to alert them of the situation, and she and Cody would retrieve Joanie's car later that night. All he needed to do was take care of her.

Which was exactly what he intended to do.

He made it to the passenger-side door and reached inside, scooping her up against his chest, shuddering when she wrapped her arms around his neck and clung to him like a hurting child.

"Don't let me go," she whispered.

He shook his head. He'd hold on as long as she'd let him.

"Never, baby." He pressed a kiss to her forehead and then headed for her house.

Expecting to find the door unlocked, he reached for the knob. But when he pushed, he was stopped. Her house was locked up tight.

"I need your key," he coaxed her.

She lowered one arm from around his neck and dug in her purse, finally pulling out a key, and he took it. He clicked open both the deadbolt and the lock on the knob, then pushed inward to the late-afternoon shadows slanting across the room.

He'd only been in the house the one time, and they hadn't gotten out of the living room, but she'd mentioned that her bedroom was on the second floor.

As he cleared the top step, he turned and headed down the small hallway, peeking in rooms as he went. A bathroom was first. He could see the counter covered with products, and a couple pair of white stockings hanging over the shower rail. The next room, he hoped, was her spare bedroom. The bed and every space but a small pathway around it was covered in stacked boxes. He hadn't realized she'd brought that much stuff home.

He moved down the hallway to the quiet, peaceful room decorated in a light purple with butterflies dotting the edges of the walls. The bedspread had lace and looked frilly and girly. Everything about the room felt like Joanie.

"I'm going to put you in bed, baby," he told her when he started to lean over the mattress but found her tightening her grip. He kissed the outside edge of one wet eye. "Let me tuck you in, sweetness."

"You won't leave?"

He shook his head. "I won't leave."

"Okay." The word was said as if she'd already forgotten what she was agreeing to, and Nick hurriedly ripped the covers back and deposited her inside. He went to the bathroom, where he found a washcloth and wet it and was back in less than thirty seconds.

"My GiGi died, Nick." Joanie peered up at him as he sat beside her, her gray eyes swimming in tears, but at least the tears were finally slowing. "I was making her a scrapbook."

"I know, baby." It tore him up to see her like this. He wiped her face and leaned over to press a kiss to catch some of the fresh tears. "She would have loved it," he whispered.

"I should have made her a scrapbook before."

What did he say to that? She also should have visited more often? That would make him a hypocrite, wouldn't it?

He tugged off her shoes, then did the same with her jeans. Once he had her comfortable and mostly calm, he went for a glass of water and brought it into the room, suspecting she would eventually realize she'd dried herself out with the crying. He stood looking down at her, wanting to crawl in beside her, but worried she'd get the wrong impression.

She'd been careful to keep it sex only between them when they were in bed together. The evening hours before they got naked was another story, but he didn't think she realized they were more than bed buddies at this point. He wanted to hold her, to comfort her, and to do anything in the world he could to ease her grief. Because he knew exactly what she was going through. It hadn't been that long since he'd experienced the same thing himself.

"Will you lie down with me, Nick?" Exhausted eyes steadily watched him. "Just to talk," she added. "And maybe . . . to hold me."

Oh God, yes. That was all he had to offer anyway, and he was more than glad to give it. He had his work boots off in record time and was slipping between the sheets before she could change her mind.

Once comfortable, he wrapped her in his arms and held on. He breathed in her scent, noting the same peach smell he'd picked up on when he'd seen her the day before. It matched the mixture of pinks and oranges in her hair.

Joanie lay there in the growing darkness for several minutes, both of them listening to nothing but the other breathe, before she shifted to look at him. Her face was a mix of sadness and something else he couldn't quite name. But when she spoke, he recognized it for what it was.

"Did I tell you GiGi begged me to bring her home? She didn't want to die there."

It was guilt. He ached for her.

"I failed her, Nick. I failed and she died hating me."

"Shhh," he soothed. He stroked his palm over her silky hair. "She did not hate you, baby. No way anyone has ever hated you."

"My mom hated me." The words pierced him.

"No," he said. He made sure she was looking at him when he spoke. "Your mother had other issues. I've no idea what they were. Who knows if anyone does, but her leaving had nothing to do with you."

"How could you know that? You weren't even here."

He didn't. But there was no way the selfish woman's actions were because of a teenage Joanie. "Because you're what makes people want to get up in the morning, babe. Someone like that could never be the cause of another person leaving."

Did she realize what he'd just admitted? She was his world.

He was in trouble.

"But I did let GiGi down." She pulled her chin from his hand and focused on his chest. "She wanted to come home. She wanted to never go there in the first place."

That one stung. But he had one, too. He found he wanted to share it with her. Not only because it might make her feel better, but he had the thought that telling her just might make him feel better, too. He hadn't shared it with anybody.

"We all make mistakes, sweetness. You put her in a place where she could get the care she needed. You were working hard to sell the house you love just so you could provide for her."

"I never said I love the house."

"But you do." He put a finger over her mouth when she started to argue. "I see it every time you walk in the front door. It's your home, baby. It's where your memories are. Your hopes and dreams that once got crushed . . . they're still in that house, waiting for you. You were doing all of this for GiGi because you wanted to give her as much as you could, even though selling the house was going to hurt."

"I could have brought her home and moved in with her when she first asked me."

He took a deep breath. "Or you could have walked out when you turned eighteen and did everything you could to forget about her."

Gray eyes peeked up at him. "Is that what you did? Did you leave home at eighteen?"

He nodded. "And I didn't go back until after she died."

"You hadn't seen her in fourteen years?"

He shook his head. He hadn't meant for this to become about him, but if it helped her to see she could have done so much worse, he'd gladly share it. "I was so lonely with her—no siblings, no other family, feeling like the only reason for my existence was to take care of her. So I left. I was determined to find more."

Her eyes questioned him as to whether he'd found that "more" he was looking for and he gave a quick negative shake. He'd found guilt, several relationships that went nowhere. But he hadn't found more. Unless he could convince Joanie she was his more.

"I did check in on her a few times a year. I called her occasionally. Called the neighbors to see if she was causing them trouble, mostly."

The words paused, but he knew he had to go on. Joanie was watching him, her own grief forgotten for the moment.

"She had my number in her phone. Five days after she died, the landlord found her and called me."

Joanie sucked in a breath. "No one knew until then?"

He shook his head. "I'd been so desperate to not be like her. To get away from her and find whatever I thought was missing from my life. In the end I'd put her in a position where she lay dead, alone for days, before she was found."

"Nick." Joanie pressed a cool hand to his cheek. "I'm so sorry." She wrapped both arms tight around him and held on, burying her face in his neck. "We're a couple of really terrific kids, aren't we? What a pair."

Yeah, what a pair. And he could see himself with her forever.

Damn.

If only she wanted him the same way.

He pushed the thought from his mind. He wanted her, yes. But he was not going to beg. He would, however, be pathetic and take whatever she offered for as long as she offered it. Then he would deal with what came next.

When she started to lean back, he cupped her head and kept her against his neck. He liked the feel of her breath against his skin.

"You didn't do anything wrong, Nick." Joanie escaped his hold and propped herself up to peer down at him. He was glad to see that her eyes were dry. "You were trying to protect yourself from the pain of growing up with her. Lee Ann told me all about it when you first came to town. Your childhood *stunk*. You couldn't help what it did to you. She should have done better. Should have taken care of *you* instead of the other way around. She should have made sure you didn't feel so alone all those years."

He shook his head. He needed to get this conversation off of him, but turning it back around on her wasn't a good plan either.

"That's why I brought you Bob," he said. Middle ground. Talk about the cat.

Confusion crossed her face. "Why?"

He rubbed a thumb over her check and admitted that it was one hundred percent love he felt for her. If she would have him, he'd spend the rest of his life showing her how much.

"I didn't want you to feel as alone as I once did," he answered. "Cat showed up in my life and it lit something in me. He might wander off occasionally, but he always comes back. He comes back for me." He chuckled. "Maybe it's just because I'll feed him, but it feels like more. I wanted you to have that, too. I wanted to make sure you were never alone."

Her solemn expression twisted his gut and he had to wonder if he'd just admitted too much. Was she not ready to face facts and see she was just as lonely as him?

After what seemed an eternity, she finally nodded and gave him a tiny smile. "He's already done that."

Joanie woke sometime after midnight and stretched, her body coming into contact with Nick's. She opened her eyes and looked around. She didn't remember going to the house. And she never stayed all night.

But it wasn't GiGi's house she was at tonight. Then she remembered everything that had happened that afternoon. The way she'd fallen apart over a woman she would have recently sworn she didn't even love. The way Nick had come to her rescue and had hustled her home

He'd been the kind of rock she often wished she had in her life. The kind she could consistently rely upon.

She rolled to her side in the iron-railed, full-size bed she'd grown up in and watched him as he slept. He looked so peaceful with his too-long hair swooped down over one eye. And sexy. And so incredibly sweet.

He moaned and shifted an arm, flinging it above his head, and she wanted to snuggle in close and bury her face into his warm skin.

She wanted to be by his side every night.

The thought terrified her, causing her to catch her breath. But then she peered closer and wondered if she could see herself by his side forever.

She rolled to her back and stared up at the dark ceiling, wishing she were different. But she couldn't fight the hand that fate had dealt.

Could she?

She reached across Nick to get the glass she saw there, hoping it contained water, and knowing Nick, she assumed it did. He always thought of everything. She brushed his chest with her forearm when she set the glass back down, and his eyelashes flickered in the darkened room. Leaning over him, she stared down, realizing that it really was more than lust that she felt. He meant something to her. A lot.

When she'd been able to think of nothing but how bad her pain was over the loss of her grandmother, this man had shared a part of himself that she'd known had hurt him to voice. She wanted to share something in return.

Slipping a leg over his torso, she rose up, silent, pulling off her shirt as she did. Next was her bra. She tossed it over her shoulder and watched his gaze come out of slumber and focus on her. She met his hands half way, cupping them and guiding him to her. Then she closed her eyes in pleasure as he slowly explored her.

It wasn't as if he hadn't touched her before. But those times had been more about fun. They'd usually come together with the lights on, sometimes seeing who could one-up the other. But tonight wasn't about who had more tricks up their sleeve. It was about her making sure he understood she felt more than she would ever admit out loud.

She leaned down and put her mouth to his and kissed him as if she needed his touch to breathe. Tonight she had the thought she just might.

"Jo?" He asked when she pulled away, clearly sensing a change in her.

She held his face in her hands, hoping he could understand what she couldn't say. "Make love to me, Nick," she whispered. "Show me."

She wanted his hands on her body. She wanted to forget she'd sent her grandmother to a lonely death, and she wanted to never have known that her mother and grandfather had left her.

It would be so nice to not be scared for once. To be free to love Nick.

Yet the thought froze her cold.

Nick rose up, wrapping his arms around her and gently rolling them both until he was on top. Then he took off his clothes and peeled off her panties, and touched her deeper than she'd ever been touched in her life.

When they finished, she cried for the second time that day.

Sunlight hit Joanie when she rolled over, and she shoved the pillow over her face. It felt as if she'd stayed up way too late and drank way too much. She paused. Or maybe it felt as if she'd had really good sex in the middle of the night. With a really hot guy.

Yeah. She stretched, wearing a smile. That was it.

She was purposefully ignoring the puffy feeling around her eyes and the fact that it reminded her of all the crying she'd done, as well. She would focus on the sex. If she wanted to be honest, she'd focus on the lovemaking. Because that was definitely what had happened in her room the night before.

Nick had been so gentle and loving, worshipping her in a way she had never felt before, and as soon as they'd finished, she'd wanted to beg him to do it again. She'd been terrified it would be the only time in her life she would feel that special to another human being.

She became aware of a warm sensation settling against her side and opened her eyes, expecting to find Nick. Instead, it was a little black ball of fur. Bob was curled next to her and her heart fluttered at the sight. She loved that he seemed to like sleeping beside her. But how had he gotten there?

Her sense of smell was the next thing to come to life and she discovered there was a giant insulated mug of coffee sitting where she'd found the glass of water the night before. She reached for it, being careful not to disturb Bob, and almost ran him off with her moan. She wasn't sure where Nick had picked up the coffee, but she was certain it was the best thing she'd ever tasted.

When Bob wiggled around at her side, she took the opportunity to roll over to face him. That way she could drink without risking pouring it all over herself, while at the same time looking a bit more presentable if Nick was still in the house. She hoped he was.

The silence implied that might not be the case, though, so she focused on pouring life back into her veins and petting the soft fur on the bed in front of her. He really was a good cat. She'd hate to take him away from Caterpillar at this point since the two of them seemed to have bonded, but she found she was growing fond of the idea of keeping him around.

Like Nick had hoped, something about Bob made her feel not quite so alone.

Her eyes finally opened wide enough that she saw her cell phone on the nightstand, lying on top of a folded piece of paper. She reached for both.

The paper held Nick's bold scrawl . . .

Call me when you get up. I want to know how you're doing. I'll come back and get Bob, if you want. He missed his mama last night.

I miss you this morning.

—N

Oh geez. That was dangerous stuff.

She flopped over on her back, shouting an apology as Bob raced off the bed, and covered her eyes with her arm. Last night had been nice. Very nice. But she had to be careful.

Instead of calling him immediately, she glanced at her phone to find it nearing nine and decided to check in with the nursing home first. She'd have to get GiGi's belongings, and make arrangements for the funeral. She vaguely recalled Nick telling her that Lee Ann had called the Sugar Springs Funeral Home the day before. The owner, Cheater Thompson, was also the justice of the peace and owned a small wedding chapel. He rearranged his court schedule around whatever came up.

She spoke with the nursing home and found out that GiGi's room had already been emptied the night before. Joanie could sign for the belongings anytime within the next two weeks. After that, the home would dispose of everything that couldn't go to charity. Joanie's throat grew tight at the coldness of it, as she faced reality. It was an empty room now, nothing else. There was probably someone previously on a waiting list already moving in.

Next up was Cheater, over at the funeral home. It always struck her as odd that the justice of the peace was named Cheater. And it was a nickname for good reason. He'd had three wives and several girlfriends over the years, but women still flocked to him. They didn't seem to mind his reputation, nor the inevitable fact that they would be next on the chopping block.

"Joanie," Cheater greeted her. "I've been expecting your call. How are you, dear? I was so sorry to hear about your grandmother. Anything I can do for you before we get down to business?"

Joanie shook her head, realizing she wasn't ready for this. She didn't want to do it alone. Nick's face popped to mind, but she shoved it away. Things like this were what Lee Ann was for. Her friend would hold her hand and help her through it, and not make anything too big of a deal.

Nick would give her that look like he wanted to fix her whole life, and she would just about die wanting to let him.

She would go with Lee Ann.

Once she made arrangements with Cheater to come in later that day, then texted Lee Ann to see if she would go with her, she had nothing left to do but call Nick.

Bob had returned to the bedroom and currently lay on top of her, smack dab in the middle of Joanie's stomach. It was comforting. She decided right then that no, Nick was not going to take Bob back. Cat could deal, and if he needed time to adjust, maybe they could have a cat play date.

Oh good grief. She'd lost her mind if she was thinking of cat play dates.

She held the phone up over her head where she could see it without disturbing Bob again, and found Nick's number. He answered immediately.

"You okay?" he asked, and her heart melted. He was seriously the sweetest.

"I am. Thanks for the coffee." She glanced down at her stomach. "And for Bob."

She pictured Nick at the house with a sexy little smile, propped back against whatever he'd been working on as he stopped to talk to her, and her pulse woke up with a vengeance. If only he were there right now.

"What time did you leave this morning?" she asked, realizing it didn't bother her like it should that he'd stayed over.

"Six. The guys were showing up at seven so I had to get here and shower and get the day's schedule figured out. And I wanted to bring you Bob." He paused. "I had a hell of a time not waking you up when I came back."

"So I could have my coffee?" she teased. After their middle-of-the-night session, something between them had changed, was more comfortable, closer. It'd happened the instant they'd finished and he'd tucked her protectively against his side.

"No." He chuckled. "Not so you could have your coffee. For some reason, I woke up with something else on my mind."

She realized she was smiling up at the ceiling as if she were a teen in the middle of her first serious crush. "You've met me before my coffee. Think that would be advisable?"

He laughed again, this time loud enough she was sure some of the guys had to wonder what was so darned funny. "You have an excellent point, sweetness. Maybe that's why you found your coffee waiting for you and me nowhere in sight."

"Not that brave?"

"Smart is what I am. I could stop what I'm doing and come back now. If you wanted," he said, his tone dropping to a heated, sexy low. "We could have round two."

Although she wanted to say yes, more than anything else she wanted to say yes, the idea of him coming back when she was still so raw worried her. Plus, she had a lot of things to do today. To start, she had to run by the shop and put a sign in the window announcing she was closed for a few days. With the tourist traffic beginning to pick up, she didn't want to leave any confusion. And then she'd meet up with Lee Ann to discuss funeral arrangements with Cheater.

"Sounds fun," she said. "But I . . . uh . . ." She closed her eyes tight and grimaced. "I have a funeral to plan."

"Ah, babe." The simple words almost brought her to tears. "What time? I'll go with you."

She shook her head and surprised herself with the need to sniffle. She'd have thought she was all cried out by now. "Lee Ann is going. But thanks for the offer."

He didn't say anything and she once again tried to picture what he was doing. Probably rubbing his temples with his thumb and middle finger. She'd caught him doing that several times when she knew he was worrying.

"You'll call if you need me?" he finally asked.

She needed him right then. "Sure."

"Joanie, I mean it. I'll be there the instant you need me. Just let me know, okay?"

"I know. And I really do appreciate it, but I'm fine. I just fell apart a little yesterday. I'm okay today." She wanted to ask him to go get GiGi's things, but that wasn't a good idea. The thought left her too vulnerable. "Thank you for coming over yesterday. It . . . helped. A lot."

"I'll tell you what," he started in a casual tone that had her on instant alert. "How about dinner tonight? You could use a night out."

"Nick, no. I'm good. I can just come by there when I'm finished."

"You don't need to work tonight, sweetness. Take the night off. Let me take care of you." He paused before urging, "Let me take you out."

He was definitely trying to turn last night into something more. She'd known he would. And it had been. But it terrified her to death.

"I'll take the night off," she promised. "But no going out. We don't do that, remember? It's just . . . casual." And she was just a liar. "Right?"

"Casual." His voice was tight. "Right. How could I forget?"

"Nick," she hesitated. What could she say? Forget last night? I didn't mean it when I let you get that close? Tears leaked from the corners of her eyes. She was not supposed to care this much.

"Yes?" he asked. The calmness in his voice caused her to shiver.

"I . . . ummm—"

"I need to get back to work," he cut her off as if refusing to hear what she had to say. "Want me to cook dinner tonight?"

She wanted him to cook dinner every night. "Maybe we should play it by ear. I have a lot to take care of today. Now that I think about it, I'm not positive I'll have time to come over."

The silence across the connection was palpable. It made the hair on the back of her neck rise.

"Nick?" Her tone was pleading, though she really didn't know if she wanted him to accept her words at face value or tell her she was full of crap.

"I get it," he said. "I'll wait for your call. Talk to you later."

His tone caught her off guard, along with the abrupt disconnection. He was hurt. Who could blame him? She'd opened herself to him in a way she never had, and though she hadn't spoken the words, he'd have to be blind to have missed how much she cared.

Just as she'd have to be blind to not get that he returned the feelings. And she wasn't blind.

Before she could call him back and do something stupid, she tossed the phone to the foot of the bed. She had to forget about Nick for the day and somehow find the energy to face her final act for the woman she'd so terribly let down.

GiGi had deserved better than her for a granddaughter. But then, Joanie had often felt she deserved better than what she'd been dealt, too. Life sucked sometimes.

Then you met a man like Nick.

Whom she didn't know what to do with.

With a groan, she sat up and swung her legs off the bed, and watched Bob take off at a run. At least she had her cat.

Chapter Fifteen

The day shone bright and clear, the sky blue, birds chirping. And Joanie's grandmother was being lowered into the ground.

She closed her eyes, not wanting to watch, yet unable to walk away. Lee Ann had left with the twins a few minutes ago, as had pretty much everyone else. Except Nick. He stood behind her several feet, silently watching. She could feel him as if he were right beside her, touching her. It was a good feeling. One she wanted to lean into.

Even if she had avoided him for the last two days.

She hadn't been able to deal with him along with everything else. And though she'd told herself time and again that she needed to end it with him, just nip it in the bud, she didn't know how she could.

There was something too strong about him that called out to her. She wanted to answer, while at the same time wanting to cover her ears so she couldn't hear the call.

"Your grandmother was a special woman. She loved you very much."

Joanie opened her eyes to find Beatrice Grayson standing at her side. The woman was in her early seventies, was the other town busybody, and got around as if she were only fifty. She had a head full of tight gray curls, and wore a long black dress and black shoes with a wide, low heel. Joanie could see her hose gathering into wrinkles at her ankles as if they'd lost the elasticity in them years ago.

"Thanks, Ms. Grayson," Joanie replied. She gave Nick a quick glance and a half smile, assuming he'd follow, and reached out and hooked her arm through the older woman's. They both turned from the grave site. She didn't want to watch anymore. "I don't think I really realized that until just recently."

She wanted to say she had been planning to bring GiGi home, but knew the words would have been spoken only to make Ms. Grayson think better of her. It was too late. She should have never put GiGi in Elm Hill in the first place. Therefore, she didn't deserve to try to make herself look better now.

"She sure loved your grandfather, too," Ms. Grayson murmured, almost to herself, as she shook her round head of curls. "I still don't understand what happened with those two. That man doted on her. And she was so proud of him. She thought he could walk on water. I've never seen two people more in love. It's just not right for him not to be here buried with her."

He'd been buried in Arlington. Though GiGi was the only one who'd attended his funeral, the whole town knew he was there and still respected the time he had served in the military. Even if they did falter in their belief in him, given how he'd up and left GiGi.

They stepped around a small, flat tombstone and Joanie almost tripped when she looked down and read it.

ANTHONY WILLIAM BIGBEE
BORN/DIED MAY 26, 1956
OUR PRETTY BOY

Joanie stopped and stared down, the back of her neck tingling at the sight, her throat opening as if she were going to vomit. She had never seen that.

Not that she spent a lot of time at the Sugar Springs Memorial Grounds. But who in the world was Anthony William Bigbee?

She looked at Ms. Grayson as if she had the answer. Beatrice took in the look on Joanie's face then glanced down at the small rectangular stone. When she looked up, she had a torn look on her face.

She patted Joanie's hand. "You didn't know they'd had a baby boy before your mother was born?"

Joanie's skin erupted in tingles from the chest out, and for several seconds, she wasn't sure she could pull in enough air to breathe. GiGi and Pepaw had borne a son? A pretty boy?

That's what GiGi had said at the nursing home Saturday afternoon. She'd had a pretty boy once.

Oh my God. How had she never known she'd had an uncle who'd been stillborn?

She shook her head, blinking back tears. "I had no idea."

Ms. Grayson patted her hand again, then glanced back at GiGi's grave. When she returned her gaze to Joanie's, she gave her an accepting little nod. "You know I like to gossip, but I'm going to tell you this not to spread rumors, dear, but because I loved your grandmother like a sister once. She and my older sister were great friends. When we lost Marjorie in an accident when I was only a kid, Georgia made sure I didn't get forgotten by the other girls. She took me under her wing. I've never forgotten that. So with that said, I feel she'd want you to know a few more things she probably never told you."

Joanie wanted to sit down, having no idea what was coming next. Her head swam with dizziness. Before she could put out her free arm to catch her balance, Nick took it in his, holding her so that she stood with Ms. Grayson on one side, and Nick on the other.

She looked back at Beatrice. "What else?" she asked, scared to find out, but knowing the fear wasn't about her. It was about what she'd learn GiGi had been through.

"They were each other's rock through everything," Ms. Grayson started. "Her and Gus. He came home from the war, wounded, and she was there. She took care of him. Then they married, with barely any money to their name, but they were happy. I have never seen two people more so. Especially when they got pregnant within months of getting married."

Joanie looked back at the small stone at her feet. It read 1956. Her grandparents had gotten married in late 1953. Dread filled her. "He wasn't the only one they lost?" she asked, peering back at Beatrice. Her heart broke for GiGi.

Ms. Grayson shook her head. "Two miscarriages before this one was born."

"Oh." Joanie expelled the word. She pulled her arm free of Nick and pressed a hand to her mouth. Tears burned the back of her nose as she fought not to release them. "I never knew," she whispered. How had they been able to stand so much pain?

They'd had two miscarriages, then a stillborn baby boy.

And then Grace.

Who'd been selfish her whole life, only to eventually turn her back on all of them.

What a rough life.

And in the middle of it, Pepaw had left, too.

Suddenly, nothing seemed as black and white as it always had. There had to be more to the story of why her grandfather had left. Yet she had no way of knowing how to find the answers. If anyone in town knew, she had no doubt she would have heard about it years ago.

She grabbed the older lady's hand with her free one and squeezed. "Thank you for telling me this, Ms. Grayson. It means a lot."

"She loved you, dear. She loved you as much as that tiny baby under your feet."

Joanie nodded. For once, she believed her grandmother just might have. But at the same time, maybe she'd been as afraid as Joanie of losing those she loved.

Talk about a curse.

Nothing was easy for a Bigbee, apparently.

Nick gripped Joanie's elbow as they made their way across the grass to his truck. Ms. Grayson had climbed into a car with an older gentleman, and he and Joanie were now the only two left at the grave site save for the lone person who would soon close the grave. If not for being stranded there by Lee Ann, Joanie likely wouldn't be heading anywhere with him.

Since he'd left her place early Tuesday morning, she'd avoided him at all costs. That night she'd been too tired to come out and she didn't want to bother him by asking him to come to her. She was just going to go to bed early and get some sleep.

Wednesday, she hadn't answered her phone all day. She'd finally texted him late in the afternoon to let him know she was fine and that the funeral was the next morning, but thought she'd stay in for the evening. She'd be back out to the house later in the week to wrap up the few remaining items she needed to go through.

Nothing about them.

Nothing about Monday night.

He was guessing she'd caught herself caring and that had scared her, but he had no idea how to show her it was okay. That *they* could be okay. If only she'd let them be.

Right now he was more concerned with finding out if there even was a "them." Then he'd figure out a way to make her see it wouldn't hurt to care.

"Thanks for taking me home," she murmured as they neared the truck.

"My pleasure."

He'd begged Lee Ann to leave her. And begged was exactly what he'd done. Her friend was protective, but she also knew he cared for her. Lee Ann had finally agreed, and had come up with an excuse about needing to get the girls back to school. Joanie hadn't been thrilled, but since she'd ridden with Lee Ann, she'd suddenly found herself needing a ride.

Nick had guessed correctly that she wouldn't want to be obvious about avoiding him in front of the other funeral attendees, so he'd stepped in to offer a ride.

"You okay?" he asked as they walked. "Ms. Grayson . . ." He trailed off. Ms. Grayson had said a lot. He could tell Joanie was still soaking it in.

"Yeah," she murmured. "Thanks. I just need to think about all that. I never knew GiGi had been through so much."

"I'm here if you need to talk."

She nodded. He took that as a positive, but at the same time wondered if she'd turn to him if she needed to.

They made it to the truck and he opened the door to help her up. The skirt she wore was black and straight, and hung just past her knees. It was the most sedate thing he'd ever seen her wear, and appropriate or not, he couldn't help but wonder if she had a matching thong on underneath.

Once buckled in, he slammed the door and headed around the front of the truck.

It may not be the most fitting move to question their status right after she put her grandmother in the ground, but it was his plan. He had to know where they stood.

Maybe what had happened Monday night had been nothing but her overload of emotions, but damned if it hadn't felt like more than sex in her bedroom that night. He'd woken ready to tackle the world for his woman.

Then she'd reminded him they were only casual.

He had been pissed.

Sure, that's what he'd agreed to, but both of them knew they were more. He had no idea what was so wrong with having a real relationship.

After he buckled himself in, he glanced at Joanie and almost crumpled at the lost look on her face. She sat staring out the window where she could see the worker on his compact front loader, coming out of the shed and heading toward Georgia's grave. Nick wanted to wrap his arms around her and offer what comfort he could, but wasn't sure that wouldn't make things worse. At least he could get her out of there.

He started the engine. "Where to?"

At his words, she jerked a little and looked around, almost as if she'd forgotten where she was. She lifted a shoulder. "My house, I guess."

She may not like it, but when he got her home, he was going in with her.

Five minutes later he pulled into the small drive and cut the engine.

"You don't have to come in." Her voice was small, and he sensed a total lack of conviction.

He didn't respond, just exited the truck and went around to help her down. When they got to her door, he found it locked. She pulled her keys out of the small black purse she carried and handed them over.

"You've started locking your door?" It had also been locked when he'd rushed over Monday afternoon.

She glanced away and muttered. "I've been remembering more often."

He wanted to think that had something to do with him. Granted, she'd been correct that there was little need to lock her house when, as far as he could see, everyone in town loved her and would never think of doing her any harm, but they did get plenty of tourists around. Living only a couple blocks from the square, anyone could wander around and happen upon an unlocked house.

Either way, he felt better knowing she was locked up tight, safe and sound.

She may not like him taking care of her, but that didn't mean he didn't want to do it.

He got the door open and pushed it wide, grinning at the sight of Bob greeting them. Nick had been surprised she hadn't insisted he come back and get the cat, and then he'd missed them both like crazy. If he wasn't mistaken, Cat missed them, too.

The next thing he noticed were the three boxes stacked haphazardly in the middle of the room. Amid the rest of the scatter. If she wasn't careful, she was going to have as much junk in her house as she'd been cleaning out of GiGi's place.

Joanie entered in front of him and tossed her purse to the couch. "Thanks again for—"

"I'm not leaving," he said, stepping inside and closing the door.

She nodded and then shocked him by turning and wrapping her arms tight around him. She didn't cry, but she held on as if she were wailing inside. He returned the hold.

After several minutes, her grip loosened slightly and he pressed a kiss to her temple.

"You okay?" he whispered the words.

She shook her head and burrowed back into his neck.

Damn, she was breaking his heart. He spent several minutes stroking the back of her head and whispering words in her ear. They didn't all make sense, but he couldn't think of anything else to do. At one point, he thought she might be crying, but when she finally lifted her face, her eyes were dry.

"Thank you," she said. The words were brief, but she looked at him with sincerity.

"For the hug?" There was so much more he'd do if she'd let him.

She stepped out of his arms, but gave him a wobbly little smile. "For doing whatever you did to send Lee Ann away so you could bring me home. For holding me just now. For being you." She paused, and then reached forward and caressed his jaw. "For not pushing for more."

Did this mean she was finished avoiding him? He caught her hand and squeezed. "You may take that back in a few minutes."

Gray eyes questioned him, and he weaved his fingers through hers.

"I'm going to push today," he stated.

She nodded as if she'd known he would, but didn't take her hand back. "I just needed a few days. If you want to . . ."—she paused as if searching for the right word—"continue with our arrangement, I'd like that. I've missed you."

The last words seemed to pop out unintentionally, as her eyes widened after she said them. She dropped her gaze from his, but he tilted her face back up. He leaned in and pressed a soft kiss to her mouth, not letting himself get sucked in when her lips parted, but he did allow himself a few seconds to graze.

When he lifted away from her, he tightened his grip on her hand. "I don't want to continue our arrangement, sweetness. I want more."

She began shaking her head, but he jumped back in before she could say anything. "We already *are* more, Joanie. You know it as well as I do."

"No, it was just . . . I was hurting Monday. I wasn't myself."

"You were more yourself than I've ever seen you. We are terrific together. What's so wrong with seeing where it could go?"

She glanced at the boxes in the middle of the floor before bouncing her sight around the room, finally landing back on him. "I'm not the relationship type, Nick. I told you that from the beginning."

He couldn't believe she was sticking to that story. "Look at the last couple of weeks, babe. We're already in a relationship."

"No." She shook her head, then paused, tiny lines forming between her brows. "We aren't dating."

"We're doing everything *but* dating."

"I don't date."

"Why?" His tone was harsh, but he couldn't help it. He intended to push until he got answers.

A single tear suddenly appeared and rolled down her cheek and he ached to pull her to him. He wanted to tell her that whatever she needed, he'd give it to her. He would be everything for her. If only she'd let him.

But she had to figure this one out on her own. He needed her commitment to a relationship or they would never stand a chance.

"It won't work," she stated, her words coming out almost as a plea. "Haven't you figured that out about me? No one in my family has had a relationship work."

"There's no such thing as a Bigbee Curse, Joanie."

Round eyes looked at him with no emotion in them whatsoever, but he caught a hardness in her jaw that hadn't been there before. He'd pissed her off.

"Maybe not," she said. "But Bigbee women can't make it work. It's been going on for generations. My grandfather left GiGi after thirty-three years. My mother did everything she could to win a man over, going so far as to chase after them when they left town. But they always dumped her and she always came back, her tail between her legs."

Except the last time. He didn't add the words because they would add nothing to the conversation. Her mother was simply a small-minded person. She shouldn't even factor into this conversation.

"Hell," Joanie muttered, then blew out a breath. "The whole town already thinks I'm just like them."

He looked down at her in confusion. "What are you talking about?"

She looked up at him, a pain in her gray eyes that stabbed him low in the gut. "There's a bet going around about when I'll fall victim to the curse. They probably think I'll follow you, beg for your love. As if I'm no better than my mother," she mumbled the last words.

He gaped at her. First, she would never have to beg for his love. But second . . .

"No." He shook his head. "They wouldn't bet on that." The town might be eccentric, but they wouldn't bet on him breaking her heart.

"They are," she insisted. "And it looks like the good money is on my birthday."

"Baby." He grabbed her by the shoulders, wanting to shake her. "It would be a ridiculous bet. You would never have to beg me to love you. I already lo—"

"Don't you dare say it," she whispered harshly. "Don't you dare."

He wanted to shout from the rooftops that he loved her, but the fear staring back at him was real. Their feelings terrified her. He kept the words inside.

"Okay." He nodded. "I won't say it. But you know it."

She shook her head, trying to look away from him. He forced her back.

"You're scared, sweetness. And that's okay. I'm scared, too. What we have between us is strong stuff."

Gray eyes looked at him then, uncertain. He had no idea if pushing her was the right thing to do. He might cause her to slam the door in his face so hard he'd never get it open again, but he knew they were more. He had to make her see it, too.

"Let's try it, babe," he pleaded. "Let me show you what a real relationship can be. No one begging anybody for anything. If it doesn't work, I'll back off. I promise. But if it does . . ."

He stopped talking and held his breath. He didn't have to say what it would be like if it did work between them. They both felt enough to understand.

She blinked and he was reminded of the first time he'd asked her out. It had been a quick no that time, but she'd had the same look she wore on her face now. He couldn't believe he was going to lose her without even getting the chance to try.

She blinked again and this time shifted her gaze to the side. He turned loose of her and simply watched. She didn't walk away, just sort of rotated in place. When she got to the boxes in the middle of the floor, she stopped.

Her arms lifted to cross over her chest, as if holding herself away from some invisible pain. That's when he got it. It was Georgia's stuff in the boxes. He wanted to reach for her, to comfort her, but it was up to her now. She had to make the choice to try.

Chapter Sixteen

Joanie stared at the boxes and thought about what Nick was asking of her. Could she really do this? Could she see where they could go?

It was probably a mistake, but she didn't know if she had a choice.

The pain over losing GiGi had floored her. The idea of walking away from Nick . . . she couldn't fathom. She didn't know how she'd be able to breathe without him, much less get up and function every day.

Which meant what? That the bet was already accurate? She'd chase after him if he left today?

She blinked back tears, terrified she just might. After all the years of being strong, she was petrified at the thought she might do the exact same thing her mother had done. With the potential same results.

But what if he was right? What if they could make it work?

She turned back to him and studied his hard jaw and the hopeful look in his eye. He was so much more than she'd thought when she'd first met him. He seemed to want to give everything he had to her. That astounded her.

What if it was for real?

How could she not at least try to find out?

She chewed on her lip, now almost shy at the thought of agreeing to what Nick was asking. Things were about to change. Hopefully in a good way, but a relationship was such a foreign concept to her. She didn't know what to expect.

Sucking in a bracing breath, she looked up at Nick and cringed, but gave a quick nod.

He went still. Then he let out a breath with a whoosh and asked, "You're sure?"

She nodded again, stronger this time. "Let's try it. But you can't push me for things before I'm ready. You have to take it slow."

He nodded in agreement, yet she somehow doubted he knew how to take it slow. Hadn't he pushed with everything?

"I'm making no promises about how long it'll last," she continued. She wanted that out there in the open so he wouldn't be surprised if she couldn't handle it. "And one last thing . . ." She paused, almost embarrassed at what she was about to admit. "I have no idea how to have a real relationship, Nick. You're going to have to show me."

"Baby." He laughed and smacked her on the mouth with a loud kiss. "All you have to do is exactly what you've been doing. We've been having one, you just didn't notice. With the exception of not being seen in public together," he quickly tacked on.

"No." She shook her head, but questioned his words. Had they been? At times it had definitely been different than anything she'd experienced before. She constantly had the urge to be with him. Far more than she'd ever had with anyone else. She *had* been with him more, actually. All those nights hanging out at his place. Cooking together.

She tilted her head and thought through the past weeks, and then she got it. Yeah, maybe she had been having a relationship after all. How odd.

She laughed then, all the emotion of the last few days seeming to come out that way instead of via more tears. Then she reached for him and laughed again when he scooped her up to his chest.

They kissed for several long minutes before Nick pulled away. He tenderly brushed her bangs back from her forehead before touching his lips to each of her eyelids and then to her nose. When finished, he leaned back and asked, "Do you want me to help you go through GiGi's things?"

Very much she wanted him to help her. She hadn't been able to touch the boxes since she'd brought them home, but suspected with him by her side she could make it through. She nodded. "I think so. But not tonight. I'm not ready."

He touched a light kiss to her mouth. "Okay, babe. Not until you're ready."

She smiled, appreciating his sweetness. "I had something else I wanted to do tonight, anyway."

"Yeah?" Then he seemed to get her meaning and the concerned look in his eyes changed to one of passion. "Anything I can help you with?"

She nodded.

He gave a little growl before he kissed her again, and she went willingly into his arms, laughing freely when he picked her up and carried her up the stairs.

Joanie paced her living room, skirting around the boxes in the middle of the floor, and looked at the clock on the DVR for the tenth time in the last few minutes. She was waiting for Nick to pick her up. They were going on a date.

A real date.

She still couldn't believe she'd let him talk her into it. But as they'd been standing in that very spot the afternoon before, as she'd been faced with her grandmother's mortality, as well as learning that GiGi had suffered additional losses that Joanie had never even known about, she had been unable to imagine her and Nick's relationship going any other way but forward.

It might be the most ridiculous notion, but she wanted to see where they could go. *If* they could go.

Because wasn't she already falling in love with him?

She knew she was. And she didn't know how to stop it.

But she would, if she could only figure out how. She was pretty sure she would. Stopping seemed a whole lot safer than continuing.

Especially given her family history.

Yet going forward was what she wanted. And she wanted it with Nick.

A knock sounded on the door and she jumped, her nerves stretched tight.

"Nick?" she breathed as she pulled open the door. She hadn't heard his truck pull up.

But it was him. He stood on her front porch, a bouquet of tulips in his hand, and wearing a suit as if he'd just walked off a modeling gig for a magazine spread.

He. Was. Hot.

She gulped, then forced herself to smile. "Hi," she said.

Had she gone stupid at the mere thought of going out with the guy? Could she not form coherent sentences any longer?

"Hi," he returned.

The corners of his mouth turned up slowly as his gaze scanned her from head to toe. She'd pulled out her favorite black ankle boots—they were four-inch-high lace-ups—along with her black miniskirt cocktail dress that had the scoop-neck lace top. It was hot.

And she knew she was, too.

They made one really good-looking couple.

They stood there smiling at each other as if they were kids going to their first prom. Finally, Nick broke the silence.

He thrust his arm forward. "I brought you flowers."

The ice was broken and she burst out laughing. "Yes," she said. "You did."

He laughed with her then, before sobering, his eyes going dark and burning steady as he focused on her face. "You're beautiful, Joanie."

Score one point for Nick.

"Thank you," she whispered. She took the tulips and motioned him inside. Bob greeted him as they made their way to the small kitchen so she could find a vase. "So you bring all your first dates flowers, huh?" she couldn't help but ask as she peeked back over her shoulder.

The expression on his face was priceless, and she laughed some more.

His expression leery, he gave a half shrug. "I do, actually."

"I know." She patted him on the cheek as if to let him know that he wasn't in trouble. "It's one of your less obvious charms. But I have to admit, I'm surprised with the tulips. They're gorgeous. I would have pegged you for a roses man all the way."

She pulled out a vase and filled it with water before turning back to him. When she did, she was struck again by the beauty of the man. There was almost nothing at all wrong with him.

Other than he kept thinking she was exactly like everyone else he went out with.

"I am typically a roses man," he admitted. "Red, to be exact." He stepped close and pulled an orange tulip from the vase then touched its petals to her cheek. "But when I went to the florist, I saw these and knew they were more you." He leaned in and kissed the shocked look off her face. "You never struck me as a roses type," he whispered against her lips.

Well, damn. He might just be figuring her out.

Score two for Nick.

She put the flowers down in the middle of the table and picked up her clutch, then smiled sweetly at him. "Where are you taking me tonight?"

Unless he surprised her by suggesting a long drive into Knoxville for a more upscale establishment, he was going to get this one wrong. Talbot's was the only fancy restaurant in town. That would be where they were going.

They stepped out onto the porch and he waited while she threw her deadbolt, then he took her hand in his and grinned down at her. "I'm taking my girl to the Bungalow."

Sonofabitch.

Score three.

Music blared from inside the building as Nick escorted Joanie across the parking lot to the awning covering the front door of the Bungalow. It was the last place he would normally take a date—especially a first date—

but as he'd made the drive to Nashville and back today to pick up a suit, he'd had time to reflect.

He was taking Joanie out. Not any other woman.

And that meant he couldn't do things the normal way. Not only because Joanie was different than any other woman he'd ever dated, but because she was Joanie. She was special. She'd put her trust in him by going against everything she believed in and agreeing to this date, and he wanted to make sure she was aware that he knew what a big deal that was.

He had to show her that he got it. That he got her. And that he got them.

They were unique. He would do everything in his power to keep them that way.

The door swung open as they approached and he slipped his hand from the middle of her back to the side of her waist. Every man in the building was going to be jealous of him. Every man in this building was going to take one look at her, and want her.

But he had her. And he intended to keep her.

As they walked in, they both greeted people on either side of them. Most everyone they passed were residents, but there was the occasional tourist among the faces. No one did much more than offer a quick hello, but he noticed something odd happening after each initial contact. Whoever they spoke to stopped dancing. Or they stopped talking. And they just watched.

Wow. They really never had seen Joanie out with someone, had they?

His chest swelled at the thought that he was the one she'd chosen.

He caught the bartender's eye and the man motioned with his chin to an empty two-seater in the far corner. Nick would owe him a heavy tip for keeping the table clear for them. He might be changing up his normal routine and bringing Joanie to a club instead of a nice restaurant for their first date, but he wasn't about to have them standing at the bar to eat.

When he pulled out the chair for her, she gave him a knowing smile. "You bribed Brandon?"

Brandon was the bartender.

Nick gave an acknowledging tilt of his head. "Whatever it takes, right?"

She laughed and they both settled into the evening.

They enjoyed tasty—if not especially great—food, dirty dancing on the dance floor, and then witnessed something Nick found highly disturbing. Money changing hands.

All night, people would spend a bit of time watching them, then they would head over to one of the servers and slip her a bill. The server would nod, jot something down, and go on about her business.

Then it would happen all over again. All night long.

"They're betting on me," Joanie said.

Nick looked at her. "What?"

They'd just returned to their table for another drink and a breather. He'd discovered Joanie may not be able to outdrink him, but she certainly could outdance him.

"The money exchanging hands." She motioned with her head and he turned to catch yet another person slipping the server a bill. "The bet I told you about. The curse."

The idea made him angry, but that's exactly what he'd determined was going on, too. These people were seriously betting on her. But for what? That was the real question. And was it upsetting Joanie?

"You want to get out of here?" he asked her.

She lifted a shot of whiskey. "Because they think I'm going to fall victim to some curse?" She blew him a kiss, then tossed down the shot. "Not on your life."

But he caught the look in her eye. She sounded all brave, but she was scared. She feared what was between them. And she was certain it was going to end badly.

He would simply prove otherwise.

Two days later, Nick stood at the St. Patrick's Day parade in the midst of Joanie, Cody, Lee Ann, and the rest of Sugar Springs. Everyone was out and about today. Even a good-size number of tourists. If someone wasn't watching or cheering from the streets, they were participating in the parade.

The last few days had been really good. Aside from the damper the obvious collection of the bet had put on their first date, they'd had a good time and it had ended with him at her place overnight. The next night they'd gone into Knoxville for a movie, then grabbed Cat and they'd all once again gone back to her place.

This morning they'd both slept in. When they'd woken, it had taken a long time before either of them were ready to get out of bed. Pretty much a perfect way to start a Sunday morning.

Joanie had also finished clearing out everything at the house over the last couple of days, and the work on the remodel was almost done.

They were targeting having everything ready in another twelve days, and it looked as if he and his crew were going to make it. That would put the house on the market the last weekend of the month, though now that Georgia was gone, the urgency had lessened.

Similar to the urgency for Joanie to go through Georgia's things. Apparently she was content to continue holding off. They'd spent each night since the funeral at her house, but she had yet to tackle that job; the boxes remained smack in the middle of the living room floor, almost as if she didn't even notice they were there. He couldn't blame her for not wanting to go through them. It had taken him a couple weeks to ready himself to dig into his mother's affairs after she'd passed.

The high school band turned the far corner down West Main, heading toward the square. According to everyone around him, the band signified the end of the parade.

"I'll be right back," he said to the group. Joanie shot him a questioning look and he added, "Need to speak to Holly."

With that, he jumped out into the street. He crossed in front of several dancing leprechauns, trying to stay out of the way, but going fast enough that he hoped no one would follow him. He wanted to talk to Holly alone. She'd become a good friend, and he had a question he needed an answer to.

"Nice shoes," he said as he found her in the crowd and sidled in beside her.

She laughed and held up one green, sequined Chuck Taylor. "Thanks. Seemed the day for them."

"Saw you dancing at the Bungalow Friday night," he said. They'd seen her come in before they left, but it had gotten so crowded they hadn't worked their way over.

"Did you now?" She shot him a wide grin. "Saw you, too. And Joanie. That was new." She waved to someone in the parade. In return, handfuls of candy were tossed her way.

He followed the direction of her next wave and saw Kendra in her cheerleading costume, grinning at him from ear to ear. She bombarded him with candy. The junior high cheer squad was out in full regalia and he couldn't be more proud.

Candy had passed earlier as part of the basketball team. Both girls had sought him out in the crowd as if he mattered to them. His chest expanded, feeling like he'd found the answer to his prayers.

He nodded. "Yeah, finally talked her out of the house."

"Good for you." Holly laughed and gave him a one-armed squeeze. "About time someone toppled her world."

He agreed.

He kept Holly against his side and spoke into her ear, "What's the bet, Holly?"

She pulled back. "You aren't supposed to know about that."

He arched his brows. Clearly he did.

"Are you all seriously laying down money on me breaking her heart?" he asked. That had bugged him as much as the thought of them betting that she was going to get hurt. He knew he wasn't one of "them," but he'd thought he was *kind of* one of them.

With a sigh, Holly tugged him away from the group. As he followed, he caught sight of a very tight, very low-cut green shirt out of the corner of his eye and glanced up to find Gina watching him. The line of her mouth turned into a smirk. She hadn't spoken to him since their date, and he'd heard through the grapevine that she had not been a happy camper about how it had ended.

He gave her a friendly smile, hoping she'd forgive him at some point, but knowing there was little he could do about it if she didn't. She'd wanted one thing from that night, and he'd given her something entirely different. She apparently held grudges.

When Holly had them standing behind the main part of the crowd, she tugged his head down to hers.

"It's not a bet about the curse, dummy. No one believes in the curse even though we've teased her about it for years. It's about when she'll realize she's head over heels for you. When she's ready to commit. We all know you two belong together." Holly punched him in the ribs. "It's just a matter of when *she* figures it out."

His pulse raced at the words. He'd known they couldn't be betting on Joanie being hurt, but it had never occurred to him they might be betting on *them*. And they thought it would happen in the coming weeks? It was hard not to grin like a loon.

"She says the good money is on her birthday," he told her. "Who has that day?"

Holly gave him a droll look. "I have her birthday, sweetie. Make sure it's a good one, will you?"

Oh yeah, he definitely would. He already had plans in the works.

"And don't you dare tell her about the bet. It'll skew the results. I could lose my winnings just for talking to you."

With more happiness than he thought possible, he leaned in and laid a big one right on Holly's mouth. She giggled, then wrapped her arms around his neck and gave him a kiss in return.

"For old times' sake," she said. She patted him on the cheek and winked. "You're a good guy."

Yeah, he was. And he was okay with that.

He laughed out loud at the pure pleasure of the day, and smiled all the way back across the street. He made it to Joanie's side just in time to watch the band pass.

"What was that about?" she asked.

Like he was going to tell her that the whole town was betting on them. He shrugged. "Just wanted to tell her hello."

"With a kiss?"

He took his eyes off the parade and looked down at her. "You wear jealousy well, babe. You picked a fine day for it, too. Green goes with the holiday." He winked. "And your hair."

"I am not jealous."

"Right," he said, nodding. "But not to worry, she's just a friend. Kind of like her brother is to you."

At the mention of Brian, Joanie's eyes narrowed. "You're using her to try to make me jealous?"

"Nope." But it didn't hurt. He was still annoyed with the thought that she and Brian had probably once hooked up. Not that it mattered if they had. He had her now. And he didn't intend to let her go.

She huffed out a cute little sigh when he said no more. "Then what was it? I know it's not the first time you've kissed her. Maybe you liked it so much you want more."

He winked at a couple tourists who were avidly watching the two of them, then leaned down and kissed Joanie, catching her off guard, and lingering just long enough to make it interesting. When he pulled away, he smiled at the fact that she was out of breath.

"Does that feel like someone who'd rather be kissing Holly?" he murmured in her ear.

He watched her throat rise with a gulp before she slowly shook her head.

"Then deal with it," he whispered. "It's you I want. Not anyone else."

When she looked up at him, her eyes more serious than they'd been only moments before, he blew her another kiss and had a very dirty thought. He guessed from the way her gaze dipped to his mouth, she had a dirty thought of her own.

He was suddenly ready to head back to her place.

Chapter Seventeen

L et's go through GiGi's boxes tonight."

Joanie looked up from where she lay snuggled against Nick's side, her legs spanning the length of the couch, with both cats lying by her feet, and raised her brows. "What brought that on?"

He shrugged. "It feels like it's time."

"Shouldn't I be the one to decide that?" She straightened but caught the cats before they could get away, repositioning them once she was sitting up. They still ran as soon as she turned them loose.

It was midweek and she and Nick had been back at the Barn the last few days. She'd brought Bob with her, along with a handful of clothes and necessities, so she didn't have to run home before work each morning. It was fine staying at her place, but there was so much more room here. The cats seemed to like it better, too.

The only problem was that the workers showed up too early. The bedroom she and Nick were sleeping in was finished except for the paint and the floors, so she could remain hidden until she felt like coming out, but it wasn't like she could sleep through a houseful of men in work boots clomping all over the place.

"You should have the final say," Nick answered, flipping through channels until he found a hockey game. "But since you've been avoiding the task for a week, I figured I'd nudge you along."

"Well, thanks." Her tone was sarcastic. He did have a point, though. She was avoiding the inevitable. But she wasn't ready to dig into her grandmother's memories. She worried it would bring out too many more of her own, she supposed. "How about we give it a few more days?" she asked. "Maybe a week?"

He reached over and snagged her hand before pressing a warm kiss on her palm. It amazed her how fast her body went from zero to sixty.

"If you do it before your birthday, I'll take you somewhere really fun as part of your present," he teased.

"Oh great, bribery. Is that what this relationship has come down to?"

She liked teasing him, he was so much fun. And she'd found she liked saying "relationship." Almost as much as she liked being in one.

"I'll do whatever it takes to get my way, sweetness."

His words were true. Not that he'd had to try too hard, but every time over the last week she'd thought about saying no to something, he'd figured out a way to talk her into it. She'd been thankful he had. There was something to dating someone that just made her happy. It had been the best week of her life.

But at the same time, she realized she was changing. And that worried her.

"What's wrong?" he asked. "You tensed up."

"Nothing," she shook her head. He wouldn't understand her worry. He thought the curse was silly.

"We don't have to go through the boxes until you're ready," he soothed. "I'm sorry. I'll quit pushing."

"It's not that," she said. "And actually, I'm almost ready to go through them. I want to see what's in there almost as much as I want to avoid it, so that's got to be a good sign, right?"

"Very good," he agreed. He slid a hand up and down her arm. "So what's bugging you?"

She sighed. Might as well tell him. He'd keep pushing until she did. "Just thinking about the curse. And everybody betting on it."

Nick went very still. When he didn't say anything, she blurted out, "What?"

"Can't say." He gave her a slow, very hot smile and she almost forgot what they were talking about.

"You're keeping something from me."

He nodded. "Yep."

"About the bet?"

The blank expression that crossed his face was a dead giveaway.

"What do you know?" she demanded.

He shook his head, his mouth sealed.

So she decided not to play fair.

She rose from the couch to face him and began unbuttoning her sweater. It was a three-quarter-length sleeve, mint-green cashmere that she'd gotten for Christmas a couple years ago that had tiny buttons all the way down the front. It had sold her many a cupcake earlier in the day. Now it had Nick's attention.

He reached for her but she stepped back.

"Uh-uh-uh," she said. "I'll just enjoy this all myself." She slid her hands up over her chest, moaning as she touched herself. "Tell me what you know or I won't let you play."

Nick grinned as only a man could do. "Go ahead, babe. I can do this all night."

She shrugged completely out of her top and watched him swallow his tongue. He hadn't seen the lacy green number she had on before.

Nick couldn't take his eyes off her. He'd seen Joanie in plenty of racy lingerie, but the light green lace she had on under this week's outfit, with the lace just barely covering her nipples, had him forgetting his name.

She stepped another foot away from him and dropped her skirt to the floor, then stood before him in a matching thong and garter belt, and all the blood left his brain. She *was* playing dirty.

They had the lights off in the house, but there was still the fact that she was standing directly in front of the uncovered window, practically naked. He had a feeling that if any man drove by when a bright enough picture flashed on the television screen, he'd run into a tree trying to peek through the window.

He should probably point that out to her, but was having a hard time staying focused long enough to get words to form complete sentences.

She bent down to look directly into his eyes, going for a serious look. "Tell me what I want to know," she directed.

He couldn't think straight enough to remember what she wanted to know. But her ass was now pointing to the window where he could see it reflected in the dark pane.

He gulped and shook his head. She really needed to play a different game if she wanted to get information out of someone.

She scowled at him but forgot to step back out of his reach, so he snagged her and pulled her onto his lap. He had her arms trapped low behind her back and her legs straddled on either side of his within seconds.

"No fair," she muttered, but the words barely left her mouth as he unhooked the front clasp of her bra.

Joanie watched the heat rise in Nick's eyes as he devoured her by sight, then shook in his hold as he closed the distance with his mouth. Instead of claiming her breast, he merely skimmed over it and headed up to her throat. Once there, he nibbled on her, right below and behind her ear. Right where she liked it most.

The touch of his lips sent quivers through her body as if she were experiencing mini earthquakes, one after the other.

"You're not proving anything with this behavior." Her words sounded lame to her own ears. He was proving everything.

Proving that she was ready to go the instant he touched her. That she absolutely could resist him nothing. And proving for the hundredth time that she was glad she hadn't called a halt to things after GiGi had died.

She still didn't completely trust this could go anywhere lasting, but she sure was having a good time seeing where it did go.

As he made his way to the other side of her neck, she wiggled on his lap, and he brought one hand around to skim down her stomach until it reached the top edge of her panties. His fingertips dipped just inside the elastic, making her stomach muscles clench at his touch.

"Nick," she begged. She thrust her hips forward, wanting him to touch her.

"Yes, baby?" he asked.

Darned man. He knew exactly what she wanted.

"Will you please quit teasing me?"

He lifted his head and slid his fingers another half inch inside her panties. "Nope."

"You're a nasty person."

One finger slipped low enough to make her jerk. "I know," he said. He closed his mouth over one breast then, scraping his teeth down over her tender flesh as she strained forward against the lock he had her in behind her back. "But you've got to remember that you started it by stripping in front of me."

When he touched her between her legs this time, the noise that came from her throat did not sound human.

"Please?" she begged, now grinding against his hand.

He lifted his head and covered her mouth with his, curling his finger below and flicking it back and forth over her as she moved. She was already over the line and heading for home when he pulled his hand away and removed his mouth from hers.

Gasping, Joanie struggled not to topple over in her confusion.

"What are you doing?" she breathed out the words.

Before the sentence was finished, he had her down on the couch and was peeling her underclothes off her. He got everything past her feet, then brought his mouth to her tingly parts and started up where his fingers had left off. She lifted her arms, holding his head to her and begging for her release.

Again, right when she was on the edge, he stopped.

"Nick!" she shrieked. "Stop it!"

She reached toward herself, thinking she had to finish, but he caught her hand and shoved her away. "Put your arms above your head, babe."

His words were hoarse and unsteady as he positioned her how he wanted her and then stood and shrugged out of his jeans.

"I just want to . . ." She couldn't help it, one hand came back down toward the juncture at her thighs. "Nick, please. I need—"

"You're about to, babe. I promise."

He had on a condom now, his clothes strewn about the room, and positioned himself on his knees between her legs. Still, he didn't enter her. Instead, he captured the hand that had been creeping closer, and guiding it with his, slid their joined fingers between her wet folds.

She almost came off the couch.

Then he bent, pulling her hand away and opening her, flicked his tongue over her most sensitive spot.

This time she let out a scream.

Again, he guided her fingers.

Then his mouth.

Until she was too buzzed to even know what was touching her.

Her entire body vibrated from head to toe, and she was pretty sure she'd gone blind several minutes ago. She was a strung-out mess.

Just when she was certain she couldn't take it one second longer, he cupped both hands under her rear and slid himself deeply home.

He bumped against her clit and she exploded, her thighs squeezing against his as he continued gliding himself in and out.

She saw stars for a good fifteen seconds before finally drifting back to earth, only to open her eyes to watch the man she'd somehow managed to fall so deeply in love with she didn't know if she'd ever recover from it. He was gorgeous as he continued driving himself higher, a lock of his hair flopped in his face, his dark eyes focused on her, and she knew that somehow, she wanted a world with him in it.

At the very moment she could see he was about to have his own release, she pushed herself up, her palms on the couch behind her, and met him halfway for a kiss that burned all the way to her toes.

They kissed and he shook, groaning into her mouth with his final thrusts. She gloried in the fact that she'd somehow managed to find him, sending up a silent little prayer that she could figure out how to keep him.

Chapter Eighteen

The bell on the door of Cakes-a-GoGo tinkled as Joanie came out of the back room carrying yet another tray of cupcakes. Business had certainly picked up over the last week. So much so, she'd had to skip her afternoon with Lee Ann the day before just to get a jump start on the week ahead.

"I've got to hire more help," she grumbled to herself.

Lee Ann, who'd unexpectedly shown up to spend lunchtime with her, jumped from the seat where she'd been studiously working on the scrapbook Joanie had decided needed to be finished after all, and moved to the counter. "I'll get them."

Waiting on customers wasn't why Lee Ann was there, but Joanie had no problem letting her help since she herself was exhausted. She'd worked all weekend at the house, sweeping, cleaning, and wiping down what seemed to be reproducing mounds of dust. They'd been preparing the walls for painting. The paint had gone on yesterday, and the flooring was being laid today.

Nick wasn't allowing her back out there until it was finished, wanting to surprise her with the final result. Which was fine, as it looked as if she'd be working around the clock herself to keep up with demand.

She hadn't even managed to make it over to the diner or anywhere else in the last few days, but she wasn't complaining. She was happy. A deep-down, full kind of happy.

The thought of the house being finished this week, though, brought mixed emotions.

It would go on the market on Friday. Her birthday.

She hadn't decided how she felt about that.

Other than having the random, unwise thought. The kind where the two of them moved into the house together, she kept running her cupcake business, and Nick saved all of Sugar Springs from ugly houses, and then—maybe after a few years—they made little Daltons of their own.

She could already picture the backyard with a swing set and a soccer goal. She wanted a girl and a boy. At least.

But they *were* putting it on the market, it *would* sell, and Nick would go home. The thought almost stole her breath. He'd probably return to Nashville within days, actually. He'd already hired an office manager to handle any calls here.

The bell tinkled again, and this time a family of six walked in, none of whom looked familiar, but the steady stream of tourists had been picking up all week thanks to the warmer weather and school breaks in many surrounding states. Joanie went around the counter to greet them and left Lee Ann waiting on a couple of regulars at the register.

"Good morning," Joanie enthused, noting the mother's widened eyes as she took in the University of Tennessee orange on the tips of Joanie's hair. "Welcome to Cakes-a-GoGo. Where are y'all from?"

"Iowa," the mother said, introducing themselves as the Fosters. "We drove down last night to spend the week hiking and driving through the park. We're hoping to see a bear."

The kids all agreed, though the smallest one seemed most interested in the cupcakes.

Joanie laughed. She always enjoyed chatting with out-of-towners. "They are starting to come out. There have been a couple sightings reported this week. Be careful, though. They're going to be hungry. Make sure you don't leave any food out if you're picnicking, or you might have uninvited guests."

Joanie and the Fosters continued talking, chatting about what there was to do in Sugar Springs as well as up in the park, about cupcakes, and about UT football since the cupcake of the week was Rocky Top Explosion. It was a white cake with sugared pecans and toffee, covered with a pile of orange icing. UT was her favorite football team, of course, so she'd saved this cupcake for her birthday week. The name had come from UT's unofficial theme song, "Rocky Top."

After they shuffled over to be waited on by Lee Ann, another family came in, this one from Kentucky, along with Brian Marshall, Gina Gregory, and Bert Wheeler from the pharmacy bringing up the rear. The place was packed. Joanie couldn't be happier.

As she continued talking with her customers, she caught Brian's eye. "Stick around if you have a minute. I wanted to talk to you about something."

He nodded and Gina mumbled something about Joanie wanting all the men to herself, then declared she didn't need a cupcake after all. She turned and left the store in a huff, leaving Bert and the family from Kentucky staring after her.

"Guess she decided not to share the gossip herself, after all," Bert said.

The Kentucky family left with their desserts, and as Joanie closed the door behind them, she turned to Bert. "What gossip?"

She'd swear the man turned red from his neck up.

Brian merely snickered.

Joanie glared at all of them, Lee Ann included. "What now? It's about me again, isn't it?"

"Oh yeah," Brian said. "And it's a good one." He had a chocolate cupcake in his hand—chocolate was his favorite—and gave her a sexy wink as he peeled the paper from the sides. "Seems you got Dalton eating out of the . . ." he paused and pursed his lips, his blue eyes just on this side of evil. "Well, I'll just say it's *not* the palm of your hand."

Bert guffawed and Lee Ann lowered her head, covering her mouth to keep in her laughter.

"What are you talking about? Lee Ann." Joanie turned to her friend. "What is it?"

Lee Ann shook her head, tears welling in her eyes. "I'm sorry, hon. I haven't had time to talk to you alone since I got here."

Joanie thought back over the last couple of days and couldn't come up with anything that would have the town going. She lifted her hands, palms up. "What?"

Brian stepped forward and put a comforting arm around her. He gave her a wide grin. "Seems you might want to look into curtains for your living-room window, babe."

"I have curtains on my living room window."

Lee Ann shook her head, her eyes drying and now looking apologetic. "GiGi's living room window."

"I haven't even been out there in days. What have people seen?" The worst she could imagine was a houseful of hot men, working shirtless laying her floors. Now that was a fantasy. Though it would be a nice view for anyone, she couldn't imagine the snickers going on that she was witnessing.

Bert cleared his throat. "Apparently you were there last Thursday night. Gina was driving by and saw . . ."

Joanie looked from one to the other. None of them were looking at her anymore.

What had she been doing Thursday night? They'd watched a hockey game, she'd figured out he knew something about the bet. . . and Nick had driven her out of her mind with his mouth.

"Oh. My. God." She blushed clear to her toes. So much for not being one to get embarrassed. And she'd never even gotten the information out of Nick. That man was like Fort Knox. "Gina saw us?" she asked. "Did anybody else?"

Bert shook his head. "I think it was only her. She told Linda Sue about it yesterday."

Joanie couldn't believe Gina had managed to hold it in that long. But then, talking about Joanie and Nick like that, when not too long ago she'd complained about Nick not putting out for her, might make her look bad.

"At least no one believes any longer that there's anything wrong in that department between you two." This came from Lee Ann, and when Joanie turned to her, Lee Ann held her hands up. "Just trying to find the good in it."

"*Ohmygod*," Joanie mumbled, collapsing into one of the bistro chairs in the dining area. "I'm going to have to leave town over embarrassment."

"Nah," Brian said. "You're tough enough to stick it out. But you might manage to hold the record for the most money collected on a bet."

Joanie gritted her teeth. "What exactly *is* the bet?" she asked.

"Bert," Lee Ann interrupted before he or Brian could say anything else. "What kind of cupcake did you want today? It's on the house."

Lee Ann practically threw a Rocky Top at him and ushered him out the door, trying to shoo Brian with him, but he stuck around. Two more families came in as Joanie eyed her friends. She was missing something. Why would her and Nick being seen *like that* make people toss down more money on when it would end?

Something wasn't right.

When the last of the customers left, Brian came over to her. "What did you want to talk about?"

She sighed. "What's with the bet?"

"That's your question?"

"No." She shook her head. "But I want to know that, too."

"I can't tell you that one. I'm sworn to secrecy."

"Come on, Brian. Be a friend."

He chucked her under the chin and gave her a wink. "I am, babe. I have my money on Monday."

She growled as both Brian and Lee Ann laughed. Lee Ann came over with three more cupcakes and sat down with them. They each took one.

If they weren't going to talk about the bet, she might as well toss her proposal out there.

"I was thinking about this place," she said to Brian. "I'm looking for a buyer and wondered if you or your parents might want to make me an offer."

The Marshalls had a thriving tourist business, and she could see them incorporating cupcakes into their packages. Brian merely raised an eyebrow while Lee Ann threw up her hands.

"Why do you want to sell?" Lee Ann asked. "You love this place."

Joanie gave her a puzzled look. "I always sell."

That was the way it worked. She opened businesses, she sold them, she moved on.

"You've only had it open for a couple months."

Not even that, actually.

"It's already making money," Joanie pointed out. "It's going to be a gold mine. A manager could easily be hired to run it. It would be a great investment."

Brian licked orange icing off his fingers, his attitude laid-back, as always. "If you don't want to run it, why not hire a manager and keep it as your own investment?"

"That's not how I do things."

"Doesn't mean you can't start," Lee Ann grumbled.

Before Joanie could reply, Lee Ann rose from her chair, the metal legs scraping noisily against the floor as she stood. "I've got a photo appointment to get to." She scowled at Joanie. "But I've already told you what I think recently. Grow up. Quit running for once."

"I'm not . . ." But she was talking to air. Lee Ann was already on the other side of the door.

Joanie turned to Brian. "What is she talking about? I always sell the businesses."

He merely shrugged. "Maybe she's thinking you should stop running from that, too."

"Too? What are *you* talking about?"

Brian gave her a hard look, then simply said, "Dalton." Joanie assumed he didn't mean Cody.

She eyed her friend. "What about him?"

"You're running from him." He picked up the cupcake Lee Ann hadn't finished and started on it. "From whatever you have with him."

"No I'm not." Joanie shook her head. "I'm dating him. That's more than you've seen me do before."

"But you're sitting around waiting for it to end," he said. "Right?"

She didn't answer. She couldn't help it. She didn't know how to believe in it.

"I went to see him," Brian said. "Did he tell you that?"

"No!" Joanie sat up straight, her cupcake now forgotten. "Why would you do that?"

His big shoulders moved under the navy T-shirt he wore. "Someone has to watch after you."

She gave him a frustrated sigh and punched him in the arm. "When did you go?"

"Couple weeks ago." He said nothing else, clearly intending to make her beg for information.

"And?" she prompted. "What did you find out?"

He smiled then, a look many women had appreciated over the years, and she had to wonder why she hadn't just taken him up on his offer and kept things simple. Then she wouldn't be in the middle of "a relationship," and she wouldn't be fighting the urge to tell a man she loved him every time she saw him.

"Come on, Brian," she pleaded. "Tell me."

He angled his head at her and gave her a droll look. "He's over the moon for you, babe. You could do no wrong." He picked up her hand and kissed the back of it. "You might want to think about hanging on to this one."

She sat quiet for a minute, letting Brian's words soak in. She was aware Nick was crazy about her. Heck, he'd been about to tell her he loved her a couple weeks ago, but she'd stopped him. But yeah, she knew how he felt. She felt it, too.

Yet something still held her back.

Something terrified her about them.

It was frustrating, because she *did* want to believe in them. She *did* want them to last.

She wanted a life with Nick.

But she was scared out of her mind at the thought of it.

"I can't believe this is coming from you." She said the words expected of her, even if she couldn't quite believe in them anymore either. "Aren't you the one who proclaims himself to be a confirmed bachelor? What do you call yourself? 'Sugar Springs's George Clooney.'"

Long dimples appeared in his cheeks. "Every town needs one."

"Then why can't I be the female version of that?" The words didn't even sound believable to her own ears.

Brian rose then, and she felt tiny sitting there looking up at him. She liked knowing he had her back.

"Because you aren't." He looked around the room, taking in the display counters and the work station on the back wall, the small tables in the sitting area and the van parked out front. Everything she'd worked so hard to set up just the way she wanted it. Then he looked back at her. "This is you, babe. I think you finally found the one that fits. Don't sell it. And Nick? He's yours, too, if you'll let him be."

"Nick lives in Nashville."

"Yeah well, I suppose that's what compromise was made for."

With his words, Brian gave her a wink and walked out the door, and she was left sitting there wondering where her friend had gone who understood she was just like him. She wasn't meant for permanence. Why had he changed?

Or had she?

Chapter Nineteen

The truck turned to the right, and where Joanie expected to feel the crunch of gravel, she instead felt the smoothness of asphalt. Or maybe concrete. Or maybe they hadn't turned into GiGi's driveway at all.

"Where are we?" she asked. She was sitting in Nick's truck, blindfolded with a tie that belonged to him, as he took her to GiGi's to show her the finished result. The truck rumbled to a stop and she felt him shift into park.

"We're here."

A breath caught in her throat. "The drive?"

"Yep." He chuckled. "Paved. A freebie present, just for you."

She couldn't hold back the smile. It was a combination of excitement and nerves. The last time she'd been this nervous had been when she'd seen Nick's truck parked across the square six weeks ago. She practically bounced on the seat. "Then get me out of here. I want to see it. I want to see everything."

"In a minute." He laughed again, the sound low and close and making the hairs on her arms stand up.

Before she realized what he was doing, his lips touched hers and she responded by opening her mouth and inviting him in. It was a good kiss, a hot one, and exactly the kind a girl should get on her birthday.

He broke contact and whispered, "Happy birthday, sweetness."

She surprised both of them by gripping his head and kissing him again, this time in a way that had her ready to rid both of them of their clothes. She was continually shocked by how badly she wanted him. They'd been sleeping together for almost a month now, dating for two weeks of that, and she was still as needy for him as she had been that first night.

When she ran out of air, she pulled back. She was breathing hard.

"You know," he said, giving her another tiny peck. "If someone were to drive by and see us like this, you with that blindfold on, there's no telling what would get back about what was going on out here."

Her shoulders slumped. "Don't I know it? I still can't believe Gina saw us going at it on the couch. I thought the room was dark that night."

"The TV was on."

She lowered her hands and clasped them in her lap. She was far from a prude, but it had been in GiGi's house, for crying out loud. "I suppose it could have been worse, but I'm having a hard time picturing what that would have been like."

His teeth nibbled at her neck. "You could have been doing naughty things to me in front of the window instead of the other way around."

Her breasts responded to the suggestion by getting all buzzed, her nipples tugging across the lace of her bra with each breath she took. If it wasn't two in the afternoon, she'd seriously consider not worrying about what the neighbors might think and doing just what Nick was suggesting right there in the truck. *With* her blindfold on.

She licked her lips. "You'd better get me out of this truck, Nick."

"Oh, baby." He pulled her mouth to his again and gave her a hot, open-mouthed kiss. "Do not have those thoughts out here," he whispered against her lips. "We have a big night ahead of us. I didn't schedule time for something like that until later."

She laughed, loving how she got to him.

"Hell," he said, still sounding as if he wanted to do far more than show her a house. "You're sexy sitting there like that. I've got to get that blindfold off you. Sit tight."

She heard his door open and slam shut, and then her door was opening at her side. He pulled her down as she laughed, and practically dragged her to what seemed like the middle of the front yard. As promised, she'd stayed away the whole week, and she was so ready to see the finished result. He and the guys had wrapped everything up the afternoon before, but instead of letting her come out then, Nick had made her hold off until today. The whole thing was apparently part of her birthday surprise.

After they toured the house, Jane would come out for them to sign the agreement to list it, with the open house scheduled for the next day. Nick apparently had the second part of her present scheduled for later that night, but had yet to tell her what it was.

He stepped behind her and worked at the knot of the tie.

"I hope you like it," he said. She sensed nervousness in his voice.

"I saw practically everything already," she said. "Didn't you just do the floors and walls this week?"

He pressed a quick kiss to her cheek and pulled the material away. "Pretty much."

Her eyes blinked open and she stood in the middle of the yard, taking in the full view of the freshly painted white house and the new landscaping. There were now red shutters around all the windows, a matching front door, and the two dormers on the third floor looked cozy, and totally made the house.

The landscaping was top class as well, with green shrubbery and what looked to be azaleas winding around the front of the house. A tree on the corner of each end.

It was so perfect, she never wanted to leave.

"What are those trees?" she asked. They were small, but pink blooms covered each. She felt her throat grow tight with the emotion of how perfect everything was.

"Dogwoods."

"They're gorgeous." She looked up at him. Scary or not, she could see them both living there. Raising a family there. "Can we go in?"

"Absolutely."

Before moving toward the house, she pulled her camera out of the back pocket of her jeans and made a picture. The house felt inviting. She could no longer envision what it had been like before, and wondered how she'd ever thought she didn't like the place.

As she stepped up on the porch, she stalled. There were the two rockers that he'd already put there, but also an old, large milk can sitting between them. It was black, but appeared to be the original paint. With the lid on, it made a flat surface across the top.

"Did that . . ." She paused and looked back at Nick, wracking her brain for a memory. "Did you find that here somewhere?"

She thought maybe it had been Pepaw's, but wasn't sure.

He nodded. "In one of the sheds out back. This looked like a good place for it. It'll make a nice spot to set down a drink."

He took her hand and threaded his fingers through hers. She gripped his in return. She had the strongest feeling that GiGi would have liked the new look. She moved her sights on around the porch, noticing the scrubbed concrete they stood on, but it was what hung at the end of the space that caused her to lose her breath.

"GiGi's swing," she murmured. Her chest ached when she looked at it. It was the one from the picture Nick had asked her about that first night they'd been together. Her eyes teared up as she remembered all the times she used to sit on this porch rocking with her grandmother. "Where did you find it?"

"In the same shed."

She turned loose of his hand and went over to it, pushing it lightly, then closed her eyes at the sound of the familiar squeak where the chain rubbed against the hook at the top. Seeing it hurt her even more, knowing how she and GiGi had grown so far apart.

"Do you like it? It's part one of your birthday present."

She opened her eyes and looked at Nick. She nodded. How could she not? This was what belonged in this spot.

"Let's go see the inside," she said, suddenly eager to see what else he'd done.

They went through the house, checking out every nook and cranny, and she couldn't help but be all smiles. It was more than she'd ever imagined, but at the same time, it was exactly what she'd imagined. She glanced at Nick. How had he known what was in her heart?

The wood floors were rich and homey, the matte, cream walls were empty canvases, just waiting for a family to fill them with life, and the staircase literally glistened with polish as she made her way up. Nick had done well. It was a showplace.

She stopped in the room that had once been hers and looked out the back window, her heart swelling at the additional landscaping he'd planted in the yard. He had envisioned something spectacular, all right. Nick stepped up behind her, the heat from his body drawing her to him. He put an arm around her waist.

"Close your eyes and tell me what you see," he whispered. It was the same words he'd said to her that first day. She'd seen nothing then. But today . . .

She closed her eyes. "I see life. I see happiness." She swallowed past a lump. "I see hope."

He kissed her temple and she wished GiGi had gotten the chance to see the house. She would have loved it.

When she opened her eyes, she was still looking out over the yard. He'd even created a little oasis in the back corner with a hammock and a water feature. She could picture the two of them lying there talking, relaxing after a long day at work.

"You did a lot this week," she said.

"I called in some favors from guys back home or there was no way this would've all gotten finished in time."

"It's beautiful," she whispered. Whoever bought this house would love it.

Her eyes backed up with tears eager to come out. She wanted to live there.

She didn't want to sell it.

"Wait'll you see the third floor," Nick announced. He grabbed her hand and led her to the small staircase that wound up one floor as she worked to put her emotions about the house back where they belonged. Out of sight.

When they reached the top, she stood in the middle of the room, unsure what to check out first. There were the two small nooks in the dormer windows. Nick had put navy throw pillows and small reading lights in each, with a long bookshelf running underneath. The slant of the roof took space away from the room, but gave it an intimate feel at the same time, while the darker walls, more of a warm caramel color, added to the feel. She could imagine escaping up here with a husband when they needed a few moments alone from the kids.

She looked at Nick, picturing him escaping with her.

Then she turned to the bed he'd put in the room. It sat in the middle of the floor, and wasn't the lumpy mattress, cheap headboard piece of furniture that had been in the room he'd been using downstairs. This was a rustic-looking, carved wooden bed with thick spindles in a light-honey color. There was a navy-and-green quilt smoothed over it as a bedspread. She sat down and gave a little bounce.

"Is this a new mattress?" She ran her palm over the cool wood of the footboard. "And bed?"

Nick lowered beside her, picking up her hand and holding it in his. "I found the bed in the garage and cleaned it up, but the mattress, yes. I bought that new."

"Why?" she asked. "For staging for the open house?"

The other rooms hadn't had furniture in them. He'd even moved his stuff out of the bedroom he'd been using. She supposed it was hidden away up here now.

"For sleeping in tonight." He cupped her cheek and kissed her so tenderly that she whimpered when he pulled away. "I want to spend the night in this room with you. I want to spend many nights in this room with you." He whispered the last sentence and she had the thought that he was saying more than "until the house is sold."

Until then . . . she nodded, already picturing the candles she had that she could bring over. And some big fluffy towels to go in the connected bathroom. There was a giant tub she'd spotted in there that she wanted to try out with Nick.

"That sounds like a lovely way to spend my birthday."

He laughed, the sound so warm she caught herself leaning into him to soak it up. "Oh sweetness," he said. "Spending the night in this room is not your birthday present. It's simply a bonus for me."

With that, he pulled a box out from under the bed. It was wrapped in a pretty pink paper.

"You got me a present? A real present?" She couldn't remember the last time anyone other than Lee Ann had gotten her a gift for her birthday.

"Of course I did." He set it on her lap. "Open it."

Childlike anticipation flooded her as she forgot about being an adult and ripped into the paper. Once she had the ribbon and wrapping tossed to the floor, she sat staring at the white box, so excited she almost didn't want to open it. Just getting something was enough.

"Open. It." He enunciated carefully.

She did.

Inside was an authentic Nashville Predators jersey with her favorite player's name and autograph on it. Alongside it were two tickets for seats on the glass. For tonight's game. Her eyes went round.

"You have got to be kidding me!" she practically shouted. "On the glass?" She shoved everything off her lap and attacked the man sitting beside her, knocking him to the bed as she crawled on top of him, planting kisses everywhere she could reach. Straddling him, she pushed up off his chest and smiled. "Now that's a birthday present."

Nick put the truck into park for the second time that day with Joanie sitting on the seat beside him, and prepared to show her a house. Only this time, they were in Nashville, and the house was his. They'd wrapped up at the Barn earlier, signed the papers with Jane—even though he'd almost suggested they hold off—then Joanie had changed into her jersey and they'd headed to Nashville.

"Wow," Joanie said. She leaned forward on her seat and peered up at the two-story brick.

"You like it?" He pulled the keys from the ignition but didn't make a move to get out yet. When they'd left Sugar Springs, he'd been on the fence about whether to show it to her or not.

In his mind, it didn't really matter at this point. He couldn't see her living there with him.

But he could see himself living at the Barn with her. He just had to hold that one close to the vest until she was ready to hear it. And hope like hell it didn't sell before he could talk her into it.

In the end, simple pride had driven him to his decision. He'd wanted to show Joanie the house he'd built. The one he'd once pictured bringing a wife home to and filling with kids. Now it was not much more than a place to go to bed at night. That's all it had been for years.

But he was still proud of it.

"I love the natural colors in the brick," she said. "Far better than a boring red brick. And the front porch is so cozy." She looked at him with a grin in her eyes. "You going to show me the inside or is this all I get?"

He laughed and opened his door. "Mess with me, woman, and I'll show you my bedroom first."

She shot him a wicked grin that made him consider his threat, then met him at the front of the truck. They walked hand in hand to the front door. It felt good having her with him like that. It felt right.

"Yoo-hoo," a singsong voice rang out from the street. "Hello, Nick."

He and Joanie turned at the same time to find his neighbor, Nancy Porter, standing at the end of his driveway. She had on black yoga pants, some sort of light-blue exercise top, and bright white tennis shoes that had probably never done a day's honest exercise in their life. Also outfitting her was an iPod strapped around her bicep, earbuds wrapped around her neck—but not in her ears—and the various diamond rings she'd convinced her husband to buy her, all circling her fingers.

"Hi Nancy. How are you today? I'd like you to meet my friend Joanie." He nodded his head to Joanie, but kept a firm grip on her, wanting to make sure she didn't get some crazy notion to turn him loose and reel the other woman in. Nancy was like a vampire. If you invited her across the driveway threshold, she suddenly felt free to pop in all the time.

Yet if he didn't go to the trouble to introduce the two women—which was the only reason Nancy would have come over the instant he'd arrived home—she wouldn't go away.

"Nice to meet you," Nancy said in her southern drawl. Her smile was friendly, but Nick didn't miss how her gaze lingered over the orange tips of Joanie's hair. They did things traditionally in this neighborhood. Bright orange hair stood out. "Looks like you're going to a game," she said.

Joanie's hockey jersey must have been a dead giveaway.

The three of them had a moment of chitchat before Nancy smiled and took in Joanie's hair one more time, then she was on her way back to the house across the street. Nick was certain she would be on the phone to several other neighborhood wives within minutes. She was his very own Mrs. Kravitz from that old show *Bewitched.*

Joanie glanced at him as he unlocked his front door, a laugh in her eyes.

He just shook his head. "Nancy is Winding River's Beatrice Grayson and Reba London all rolled into one."

"Ah."

He could see her processing that though he lived in a bigger city, small-town gossip still ran rampant.

He pushed open the door, holding it wide for her to step through. The alarm was beeping so he followed her in and turned it off.

"You built this?" she asked as she wandered through the rooms.

"I did. About seven years ago."

When she got to the kitchen with the oversize gas stovetop and the copper hood, she took it all in and then glanced at him. She ran a hand lightly over the thick slab of granite covering the square island. "Did you build this kitchen for you to cook in, Nick? Or for a woman?"

Heat touched his cheeks. She had such a way of pegging him. "I guess I'd have to say both."

"So you were serious about someone?"

He tossed his keys on the counter, somewhat embarrassed to tell her that when he'd started building the house, he'd thought he'd found the one. "It was years ago. After she dumped me, I realized it had been more about her two kids than her," he said. "I was crazy about them."

"So what happened?" Beautiful, understanding eyes peered up at him. He shrugged. "Said I was a nice guy, but not the guy for her."

She said nothing to that, only lifted her eyebrows in question. The movement produced a very thin horizontal line high on her forehead.

"It was a running theme for a while," he admitted. "You're such a good guy, Nick, but . . . Hell, I brought one girl here after we'd gone out a few times. She took one look, told me I was a good guy, then shook her head and slowly backed away." He chuckled, shaking his head at the thought. "The allure of the 'bad boy' is strong for some women. I guess seeing my house drove the point home that I was never going to be that guy."

He grabbed Joanie's hand and led her out of the room. Enough sounding like a schmuck. He'd figured out over the last few weeks what the problem had been. None of those women had been his type either.

But Joanie was.

"I think you're a good guy," she said. She peeked into the oversize den and he could see she was impressed at the sunken, comfortable room. This was where he spent most of his time. Other than in his bedroom, sleeping. "I've even told you that a time or two," she added.

"You have," he agreed. "I cringed at first."

They stopped in the guest bath and she looked up and met his eyes in the mirror. "You don't cringe now?"

She looked so cute in her Preds jersey and tight jeans. She'd added a blue and gold scarf headband to her blond and orange hair. He had never seen a more perfect woman.

He shook his head. "Now I hope you think I'm a good guy. You see it as something different than all those other women."

A half smile curved her mouth and he turned her to him and kissed her. He wanted to make love to her in his house—though there was no time for that at all. They had a game to get to and he was not going to let her be late.

"I want to be a good guy for you," he whispered when they came up for air. "Because you haven't had those in your life."

She'd told him about her first boyfriend as they'd shared stories late one night. About how he'd talked her out of her panties and then forgot to talk to her the next day. Or the next.

When Nick had learned the guy still lived in Sugar Springs, he'd had the urge to pay him a visit. Joanie had convinced him that it had been a long time, and she had gotten over it years ago. Maybe she had, but it had left a lasting impact.

It had added to her belief that she was on her own in the happiness department.

"I want to make you happy," he told her as he looked down at her. He almost added the word "forever," but wasn't sure she was ready to hear it yet. They were getting closer, though. Before the night was over, he was going to make sure she understood that the love he felt was real. It wasn't going anywhere. And neither was he.

She gave him a slight nod. "You do make me happy." Then she peeked around his shoulder, back out into the hall. "You have a bedroom around here, somewhere?"

"Oh no," he said. "There's no time for that tonight, babe." He grabbed her hand in his and continued the tour. "Another time, though. Definitely."

She laughed. "Maybe I'll visit you here someday. I'll show up in my van to see what Nancy thinks about that."

Her tone was light, but he knew the way the other woman had looked at her had bothered her.

"When are you coming home, anyway?" Joanie glanced casually at him as they took the stairs to the second floor, but he sensed the tension in her. Her house remodel was done. He'd already spent six weeks away from here. It only made sense he return. And he did need to. He'd talked to his partner earlier that day and confirmed he'd be at the office sometime next week.

Though he had yet to figure out how to make a Sugar Springs to Nashville commute a reality. Until he convinced Joanie they were meant for each other.

"Supposed to be back in a few days," he finally admitted. He didn't want to come back at all. "Probably Wednesday. Maybe Thursday."

Her face lost a bit of its glow. Which was good. He thought.

Meant she wasn't ready for him to leave.

"So . . ." she said, seemingly at a loss for words.

"You're not dumping me just because I have to come back for a bit," he told her. He gave her another hard kiss. "We'll figure it out."

He had it figured out already, though the solution had come as both a shock and a seemingly easy answer. But when something was right, he knew it.

He'd sell his house. He'd move to Sugar Springs. It had everything he wanted. Joanie. A brother. Nieces.

Family.

He could make anything else work. He might even sell off his half of the business here. That was something he intended to talk to his partner about. Because the picture of him growing the business in Sugar Springs while Joanie baked cupcakes every day and came home to him at night was the right one. He wanted to make that happen.

Joanie didn't reply.

When she came out of one of his five bedrooms, her words made his heart stop. "I tried to sell Cakes this week."

"Why would you do that?"

She shrugged, not looking at him. "It's what I do."

He had to wonder if her not tying herself to businesses had anything to do with her not tying herself to relationships. It was interesting that she seemed to have the same hang-ups with both facets of her life.

Of course, the "curse" didn't extend to her business, but he had the suspicion that her problem was more fear of commitment. To anything. She was used to constantly changing, all the way down to her hair. Probably it was easier never to admit how badly she wanted something than to risk going for it and it potentially turning out badly.

But she was perfect for that store. He couldn't let her sell it. "Are you sure you want to sell?"

She studied him silently before answering. "I always do."

"That's not what I asked." He pulled her into the master suite and settled them both on his bed so that they could focus on the conversation and nothing else. "Are you sure you want to sell this one? Don't you enjoy it?"

He couldn't quite read the expression on her face. It was part sad, maybe a little hesitant. But definitely withdrawn.

"I do enjoy it," she finally admitted. "A lot. And it means more to me than the others have. It's kind of like it's a part of me and a part of GiGi, all rolled into one. I just figure I should sell. Like I always do."

That's why it worked for her. It so perfectly represented who she was. "Maybe give it some time, sweetness. There's no hurry, right?"

"I suppose not." She lifted a shoulder, then looked around at his room. It made him nervous for her to see this piece of him.

He hadn't changed the space too much from the original neutral he'd built it as, but he had added a dark brown accent wall and the bed was a heavy, block-wood rustic king-size he'd fallen in love with the minute he'd found it two years before. It would fit nicely in the master bedroom at the Barn.

And he couldn't say that hadn't crossed his mind a time or two as he'd done the renovations.

"Who'd you try to sell Cakes to, anyway?" Given the whole town was betting on her settling down with him, he figured they might be betting on her keeping Cakes, as well. The thought being, commit to one, might as well to the other. Might make for a hard sell to a local if that was the mind frame. They tended to look after her.

"Brian Marshall," she answered. "He owns a few businesses. Thought he might like to add this to his list."

Irritation flared at the mention of the other man's name. "I take it he said no?"

"Suggested I keep it as an investment if I didn't want to run it."

"Good idea." Jealousy was an ugly thing. "So there is something the guy won't do for you, huh?"

She'd moved to check out the connecting bathroom, but came back with his words. "What do you mean by that?"

"Come on, babe. The man watches you like a hawk. Maybe you're only friends *now*, but I can see there's more between you."

"He's my friend," she stated.

"I know."

"You don't sound like you know. What do you think? That I have something going on with him?"

"No," Nick stressed. "Really, I don't. I just think you *once* had something going on with him. I know we all have pasts, but this one bugs me." He moved to stand by her, catching her hand in his. "You two are close. I want to be the one close to you."

The stiffness in her fingers relaxed with his words. "You and I are close," she said. Her voice took on an air of awe, as if she might not have realized that before she spoke the words. "I've shared more with you than I ever have with Brian."

He nodded. He knew he was being ridiculous.

"Nick?"

He glanced away from her. "What?"

"There's no need to be jealous."

"I know. You're with me now." He just hoped he could keep her.

"I was never *with* him. He and I are just friends. That's all we've ever been."

He turned back to her. She seemed sincere, and the fact was, she had no reason to lie to him about this. God, he was an idiot. "I'm sorry, babe. I believe you. Just . . . ignore me, okay? I have a lot on my mind tonight."

Like telling her he loved her more than the world. He would do that when they got home tonight. After he made love to her in the third-floor room.

"What could possibly be on your mind?" she asked in a teasing voice. "We're going to a hockey game, and then we're going to end the night with me showing you the new underwear I bought for my birthday."

Ah, hell. *That* pushed Marshall from his mind.

He leaned in and kissed her. "Good idea," her murmured. "Now let's get you to that game so we can get home and get me to that underwear."

Chapter Twenty

M usic blared from the overhead speakers as the hockey game went to a commercial break and the players skated to the bench. Joanie stepped back from the glass—where she'd been standing for the entire last period—and dropped into her seat with an exhausted sigh. Adrenaline rushes were good things, and this had been an awesome game.

She slipped her arm through Nick's in the seat beside her and grinned up at him, snuggling into his side. "Thank you for my present," she said.

His eyes were warm as he returned her smile. "You've had a good birthday then?"

"The best."

It had been. GiGi had made her birthday cakes and let her invite her friends over when she'd been young, and then she'd spent her birthdays over the last decade or so either working or hanging out with Lee Ann. To have an honest-to-goodness date with someone as hot as Nick—and to have glass seats at a hockey game!—was priceless.

She leaned closer, using the excuse of the roar of the crowd to put her mouth next to Nick's ear. "I hope my new panties will explain my appreciation later."

He laughed as she'd meant him to do, then reached down and patted her on the thigh, his fingers slipping to the inside curve of her leg. "If they don't," he promised, "I'm sure we'll figure something out."

Oh yeah. And she already had a few ideas.

She looked at him then, at the love shining from his eyes, and knew she had to do whatever she could to see if this could last. He was good for her. Everything about her had been better since he'd come into her life. Surely she wasn't being as stupid as her mother had been all her life. Joanie wanted to believe that what she had with Nick was so much more than anything her mother had ever experienced with any of the men she'd chased.

Which made her think of Nick and his house. He'd been so proud as he'd showed it to her that afternoon. She'd been just as proud that he had wanted her to see it. Aside from the fact it was Nashville and not Sugar Springs, and the fact that his neighbor was a nosy, judgmental, *bi*—a word that GiGi wouldn't approve of her using—she had really liked it.

He'd built it to house a family. That had been clear from all the details. Large rooms for plenty of places for kids to play. Built-in bookshelves in the "kids'" rooms. An enormous family room. A huge dining room. What did he want with a room that big? A dozen kids?

She blinked, pushing the thought from her mind. She wasn't sure about kids yet, but had the idea that if done with Nick, she just might like it.

But first, she had to figure out if she could give up her life and move there with him. Assuming he asked her to. He had suggested she not sell Cakes. That had at first shocked her. Made her have the fleeting thought to wonder if he was thinking he'd keep her as a monthly booty call when he came to visit Cody. But she'd quickly pushed that from her mind. He wasn't that kind of guy. That was more who she was.

Or who she had once been.

She'd changed. And it was because of Nick.

But could she change enough to move into a neighborhood where she might have to tone back her ways? Keep her hair to only one color?

The game resumed and she squeaked with excitement and jumped from her seat to once again stand against the glass. The guys were so huge when they passed right in front of her. She'd already caught herself on the Megatron more than once, banging on the glass with her palm. She'd even been in the running for fan of the game, but she'd lost out to some woman with a cute kid.

Nick joined her as the entire arena was now on their feet. They were down to twenty seconds in the game, the other team had the puck, and the Preds were up by one. All they had to do was hold out for twenty seconds.

The puck dropped and Nick's hand slipped lightly around her waist. She glanced at him, but he was watching the game, seemingly as into it as she was. Yet she couldn't miss the love in that small touch. And she knew right then that yes, she could move to Nashville if he asked her to. She loved him that much.

Maybe she would keep Cakes as an investment, though. Just in case the two of them didn't work out. That way she wouldn't be left out in the cold with nothing.

But she was bringing her van to Nashville with her.

Nosy Nancy was just going to have to deal. Heck, maybe Joanie would spend her days fattening up the snooty stay-at-home wives who were no doubt running the neighborhood.

Shea Weber, captain of the Preds and a giant of a man, slammed an opposing player into the glass right in front of her. The poor guy's face was smashed into a cartoonish expression. She screamed, pounded on the glass, and the buzzer sounded. They'd won.

She smiled at Nick as they made their way out of the arena. She thought she might have won, too.

"Babe."

The word penetrated Joanie's consciousness, just as the light shaking of her shoulder did. She squinted open her eyes to see darkness and faint lights from the dashboard. She was tipped over on the front seat of Nick's truck, asleep with her head cushioned in his lap.

Her seat belt was still wrapped around her waist, but had tightened so that she would need to unhook and refasten it to keep it from cutting her more tightly across the middle.

"What?" she mumbled. She sat up and adjusted the belt.

"We're still going back to GiGi's, right?" he asked.

She nodded, her eyes drooping again. "I want to spend the night in that third-floor room. We might get a buyer this weekend, so we shouldn't wait."

"Okay," he said.

She dropped her head back against the seat, letting several miles pass. They were back in Sugar Springs. She'd seen the welcome sign on the edge of town when she'd sat up.

"We need to run by my place before we head out to the Barn," she said. "To get the cats."

She nodded. "Yeah, but I want to get something else, too."

She felt him glance her way, but she didn't meet his gaze.

"I want to get GiGi's boxes," she said. "I want to go through them." She looked at him then. "Will you go through them with me?"

He nodded, the expression on his face telling her that he realized she was ready to move on. Both beyond the issues between her and GiGi, and to take a giant step forward in her life. She hoped he knew she wanted that step to be with him.

"Absolutely," he finally said. He reached out and squeezed her thigh. "We'll get them and the cats and take everything home with us."

She liked the way he said that. She liked the idea of going home with him. Wherever that may be.

His cell phone went off, signaling a text message.

"It's almost midnight," Joanie murmured. "Who would be texting you at this hour?"

"I've no idea." He handed the phone to her. "Will you check it? I can't imagine it's anything important."

She took the phone from his hand and the screen lit up in the dark cab. She pulled down the message, then her jaw fell open in shock.

"What is it?"

"It's from your brother."

"Is something wrong?" His voice went to immediate panic. "Is it the girls? Do I need to head over there?"

"No." She shook her head, turning to him with a smile. Everything was working out for both of them. "The PI who you hired left a message that Cody just now heard. He found him, Nick. He found your other brother."

Nick went silent.

"Want me to text something back?" she prodded. The phone beeped again. "Oh wait, here's another. He's in Atlanta," she read. "Let's drive down tomorrow."

She turned to Nick. "Your other brother. Oh my goodness. Aren't you excited?"

He'd grown too quiet.

"Nick?"

Finally he nodded and cleared his throat. His voice came out tight. "Text him back that yes, we'll leave tomorrow. Hell, I'd leave tonight if I didn't want to see your underwear so bad."

She laughed and keyed in the message.

"I'm going to find my brother, babe."

She grinned widely at him. "You're going to find your brother."

They drove through town and he turned onto the street leading to hers.

"Can I ask you to think about something?" he said.

"Sure."

"Will you consider *not* selling the house just yet?"

She shot him a quick look. What was that about? "I have to. I owe the bank, and I owe you. I can't just not make those payments."

"You don't have to worry about me right now." His face went blank and she wondered what else he was thinking. "And I could help you with the bank. If you needed."

She started to shake her head but he added, "Just for a while."

"This has been the plan all along. We just signed with Jane today." She noticed that her breaths had grown shallow. She didn't want to think about the fact she'd actually prefer to keep the house. It wasn't an option. She couldn't afford it.

He turned onto her street. "It's your home, sweetness. I don't think you're ready to get rid of it yet. Maybe at some point, we might . . ."

His words cut off.

"What?" They might what? Was he thinking they might live *there* together at some point?

But he wasn't looking at her anymore. He was looking past her. Toward her house.

"Did you leave a light on when we left?"

"No," she said. She turned on the seat to face her little two-story rental and was shocked to see lights on in both the living room and the kitchen. "That's weird," she muttered.

He stopped on the road instead of pulling into her driveway, and cut his lights and engine. He clicked off his seat belt. "Did you lock your door?"

"Probably." But she couldn't remember doing it. She'd been excited about the game and had quickly changed clothes while he'd gone to put gas in the truck. She'd been on the porch waiting for him when he'd pulled back up. No, she couldn't remember locking the door.

She turned to him. "I don't think I did."

"Stay here."

Nick stepped from the truck, pulling a dangerous-looking black rod from somewhere in the vicinity of his seat, and though she knew the smart thing to do was wait there, she could not imagine anyone in her house wanting to do her harm. At the worst, someone was hurt and had found a place to sit down. She opened the door and hurried across the grass behind him.

"I told you to stay," he whispered.

She blew out a breath. "I told you people don't break into homes around here."

"Someone is in there. So are Bob and Cat."

At the mention of their cats, a rare fury started boiling inside her. "Whoever it is had better not hurt our boys."

There was no way she wasn't going in now. She had to get to their babies.

She let Nick go up on the porch first. She wasn't a total fool.

He reached the door and brought the stick up, readying to swing if need be. It was a thin baton like a police officer might carry. Who in their right mind would think they would need one of those here?

But then, there *was* someone in her house.

The knob turned freely in his hand and he pushed. Not making a big scene, but not hesitating either. As he stepped inside, Joanie bent down and peeked under his arm, looking for the cats.

Instead, she found the intruder. She straightened where she stood.

"Mom?"

Chapter Twenty-One

N ick stared at the woman sitting cross-legged on the living-room floor, her hair a dull brown, her clothes clean but cheap knockoffs. She had a cell phone stuck to her ear and a contemplative look on her face as she stared straight at Joanie.

He looked behind him, took in Joanie's shocked features, color beginning to bloom high on her cheeks, and her gaze locked just as tight with the other woman's. He wanted to refuse to see the resemblance, but it was there. Same bone structure, same build, same eyes. If the woman had blond hair and a little more meat on her bones, they could be twins.

"This is your mother?"

Shock turned to anger in front of him. "Yes," Joanie bit out. She cut her eyes at him. "Nick. Grace Bigbee."

After twenty years, the missing piece just drops back in uninvited? This did not feel like a good thing.

Grace held up a hand as if asking them to wait, then glanced down, concentrating on whatever was being said from the phone at her ear. She nodded slightly.

"Of course, baby," she murmured into the phone. "It's worth plenty of money." She nodded again, smiled a faint smile that looked similar to Joanie's, but wasn't pretty at all, then finished with, "Just a few days and I'll be back. Then we'll go wherever you want."

Joanie shoved him aside and stepped inside the house. "What are you doing here? And why are you going through my things?"

She yanked papers from her mother's hands and that's when Nick realized the woman had GiGi's boxes open and was digging through them. Oh, hell.

"Joanie," he started, unsure what he needed to say, but terrified for both women at the moment.

She ignored him. Grace lowered the cell phone, but didn't move from her spot on the floor.

"I had to do something while I waited for you," she said, her tone indicating Joanie had been out participating in unscrupulous behavior. Grace then, amazingly, grabbed another handful of papers from a box. The woman had some nerve.

Joanie ripped the papers out of her hand.

Nick stepped forward. Joanie was furious, a state he'd never seen her in. Her eyes were wild, her jaw hard. Grace seemed unaffected. Both cats stood on the bottom step of the stairs, watching.

First things first. He needed to get Joanie's mother out of GiGi's belongings, and out of the house.

"Grace," he said, pulling both women's attention. He walked over and closed the flaps on all three boxes. "Maybe you could take a seat on the couch, where we could all talk."

He reached for her hand to help her up, but she only looked at it, her nose wrinkling. She sent a scathing look toward Joanie. "Really? This is who you date?"

"Who I do or do not date is none of your business." Joanie's nostrils flared. He did not like seeing anyone affect her this way.

"I suppose you can't expect much more here in this rattrap of a town, anyway," her mother added. When Nick moved to pull Grace to her feet, she smacked his hand away and rose on her own. She then turned her nose up at the couch and pulled over a chair from the kitchen table. She plopped down in it and crossed bony legs over each other.

Joanie's chest rose and fell with her breaths, but she remained silent. Nick was out of ideas. What did he say when the mother she hadn't seen for twenty years popped back into her life? Especially when he could see what a cold-hearted bitch Grace was.

"How about this?" he said, still standing, a woman on either side of him. "How about I help Grace get settled in at the hotel, and we all three meet up for breakfast in the morning? We can talk then."

Neither said anything, only stared at each other, and he was beginning to wonder if they even realized he was still there. Cat came over and rubbed at his legs. At least Cat knew he was in the building.

"You'd better go, Nick." That wasn't what he'd expected Joanie to say.

"I don't want to leave you here. Let's take your mother to the hotel, and then you and I can take the cats to the house, and—"

"*Cats*," Grace sneered. "That sounds about right. They're probably as horrible as that dog your grandmother had."

So the woman wasn't a pet person. That he could believe. Unlike her daughter.

"Just take Cat and go," Joanie said. "Leave Bob here."

She still wasn't looking at him. "Babe," he said, stepping over and getting in her face so she would have to see him. "This isn't good for you. Let me take you—"

"No," she said. "I'll stay here. I need to deal with this."

He needed to not let her out of his sight. He didn't know why, but he had the worst feeling that if he walked out that door without her, she wouldn't be coming back to him anytime soon. He could feel a wall going up between them as he stood there watching her.

"Come on, Joanie. I'm not leaving you here with her."

Hard, gray eyes turned on him, and he had to wonder if he knew her at all. "You don't have a choice. Take Cat and go."

"Fine." Anger sliced through him, but pushing the issue would only make it worse. He nodded and pressed a quick kiss to her cheek. "Call me later."

She didn't confirm, and he suspected she wouldn't. She was standing right there, pulling away from him in front of his eyes—because of a woman who didn't deserve two minutes of her time—and he couldn't figure out a thing in the world to do about it.

Nick put the baton he carried on her couch in case she found she needed it, then picked up Cat. He considered taking Bob, too, just to force her to come looking for him later, but didn't want to leave her there alone. She might need someone after she had her conversation with her mother. If she didn't want him, at least she could have Bob.

"I'll see you later," he said and slammed the door on his way out.

Once on the porch, he looked back, wanting so badly to be inside with her. He wanted to kick the woman out and make sure she never hurt Joanie again. But maybe this was what Joanie needed. She had to face the past and try to get some answers. See that there was no curse. Merely a piece-of-shit mother.

Hopefully, then, she'd come out the other side in a positive place.

He put Cat in the truck, who found his spot on the dash, but instead of going straight home, he decided to make a pit stop first. He wasn't the only one in town who would be worried to know Joanie was at the house alone with her mother.

Joanie startled with the slamming of the door and briefly glanced that way, wanting to call Nick back. He would help her through this, she knew he would. He would do anything she asked of him. But that would be using him. She wouldn't be like that.

The instant Joanie had seen her mother and realized she was pawing through GiGi's possessions, she had a very good idea why she was there. GiGi had died and now Grace was looking for something. Money? Something of value she could pawn?

No doubt she was looking to score some cash, because Grace *was* the type who used people.

Memories had bombarded Joanie over the last few minutes. Arguments Grace had with GiGi, always making excuses to take money from her, calling her names. Hurting her. Grace Bigbee was not a nice person, and if people didn't give her what she wanted, she hurt them.

In a way, Joanie had done the same to GiGi after Grace had left. Both of them had been hurt. Both of them losing someone who was supposed to care. And what had Joanie done?

She'd acted just like her mother. Hurting her grandmother. Pushing her away. Staying out all hours of the night just to annoy her. She *had* been just like her mother.

No wonder hers and GiGi's relationship had plummeted.

She pushed the thoughts from her mind. "What are you doing here, Grace?"

"You're going to try to distance us by refusing to call me Mom?" Her mother's smile was a sneer. "I'll still be your mother. And Georgia's next-of-kin."

Yep, she wanted something. And then Joanie's brain replayed the snippet of conversation she'd heard before she'd come in.

It's worth plenty of money.

Then we'll go wherever you want.

Joanie's breathing became shallow as two things registered at once. Grace wanted the house, and she was still doing exactly what she'd always done. Anything to win over the man. Going wherever he wanted.

Just as Joanie had decided to do earlier tonight. She was willing to give up her life to move to Nashville with Nick?

A sour taste settled in her mouth that she couldn't seem to force down.

"How did you find out she'd passed away?" Joanie asked with caution, having no doubt that was why Grace was back.

Grace snorted, then laughed in a very unfunny manner. "I've kept tabs on you for years. It may not be much, but that house of hers is paid for."

"You're coming back to Sugar Springs?" Joanie knew she wasn't. She just thought she could grab the house out from under her.

"I wouldn't live in this flea-infested place again if it were the last place on earth. But I am her daughter. And there's been no mention of a will. The house belongs to me."

Why Joanie had never even considered that, she had no idea, but the fact that she was trying to sell a house that didn't belong to her, while having taken out two major loans to remodel it, made her stomach roll over. Her mother was going to sweep in and get the proceeds from the sale, and Joanie was going to be left holding the bills.

Because she hadn't heard anything about a will either. Hadn't even thought about one.

"Probably didn't intend to look me up and see that it got to its rightful owner, were you?" Grace asked. "Of course, I do appreciate you fixing it up. That'll bring in a pretty penny."

"Are you kidding me?" Anger suddenly fueled Joanie's words. "Why would I look you up? Ever? You left. You chose Bill."

A confused look passed over her mother's face. "Who?"

"Bill," Joanie snapped out. "The man you were dating when you left with him. Without me."

"Oh . . . Bill." The confusion cleared and her mother waved a hand in front of her face as if the memory were nothing more than a gnat. "I haven't thought of him in years."

The words were like a punch to Joanie's kidneys. He had meant no more to her than any of the others. "So you lost him, too?"

Of course she had. She couldn't keep a man.

No Bigbee could.

Nick's house came to mind, and her visions of the two of them living there together, as husband and wife.

No Bigbee could keep a man.

And she was about to do the exact same thing her mother was *still* doing.

Had she lost her mind?

The women in his neighborhood would run her out the instant they saw her cupcake van.

"You're despicable," Joanie spit out. Hating herself as much as Grace.

A hand swung out and slapped Joanie across the face so fast she didn't have time to keep it from happening. She jerked back, tripping and falling over a pillow on the floor, and stared up at her mother, shocked.

The woman had been gone for twenty years, and she came back thinking it was okay to hit her?

"Get out of my house, *Mom*."

"I will not leave until I get what I came for."

Joanie saw the police baton that Nick had left and picked it up. She rose to stand, facing her mother. "Get out, or I'll remove you."

Cold, dead eyes, so very much like her own, stared back at her. "That house is mine," she spit out.

"It very well may be, but you aren't going to come into *my* house and lay your hands on me. Get out and we'll deal with each other through a lawyer on Monday."

Grace stared at her a few seconds longer, then kicked at some papers on the floor. She slammed the door behind her as she left, leaving Joanie standing frozen in the middle of the room.

The woman had left on her thirteenth birthday, then returned twenty years later to the day. And all she'd had to say to her was "give me the house"? Not to mention the slap on the face.

The shock began to wear off and Joanie noticed her hands shaking. She dropped the baton and crumpled to the floor, unable to stop the flow of tears. A knock sounded at the door a second before it slowly began opening. Joanie grabbed the baton and jumped to her feet, assuming it was her mother.

"I swear I'll beat you to within an inch of your life if you step foot back in my house tonight." She hadn't known she'd had such anger toward her mother, but it felt pretty darn good letting it out.

The door swung wide and Lee Ann stood there, dark hair sticking out in all directions and a lightweight jacket thrown on over her pajamas. She peeked in, wide-eyed, and looked around.

"She's gone?" Lee Ann asked.

Joanie collapsed to the floor. "She's gone."

"Oh, honey." Lee Ann hurried into the house, closing and locking the door behind her, then lowered to her knees and wrapped Joanie in her arms. "Nick stopped by and told me."

Of course he had.

"What happened? Are you okay?"

"I—" Her words were cut off by loud, racking sobs. When had she become such a crier? Lee Ann held her tighter and they sat in the middle of Joanie's living room, both of them crying and hugging until all the tears were gone.

Finally, Joanie looked up, her face puffy, and confessed, "I had no idea I hated her so much."

Nick checked the display of his phone to make sure he hadn't missed a call or text. When he returned the phone to his belt, Cody chuckled from the driver's seat of his SUV.

"What's that make?" Cody asked. "Fifteen times since we hit the outskirts of Atlanta?"

"Fifteen times for what?"

"You sap." Cody shook his head. "Fifteen times you've checked your phone, you loser. What's the matter? You can't be away from her for one day without crying?"

Nick shot his brother a glare. They'd headed out early that morning, but Nick had yet to hear from Joanie about what had happened after he'd left her place last night.

"I don't cry, you asshole. I'm just worried about her. What did Lee Ann say after she went over there last night?" He hadn't wanted to ask Cody, preferring to hear it from Joanie instead, but he had to know.

Cody let go of the teasing and glanced Nick's way. "Said Joanie had a police baton in her hand when she got there, ready to smash her mother's skull in if she came back."

"Christ. Guess she handled herself just fine, then."

"Guess so. Lee Ann said she was a mess. Said she'd never seen her that riled up."

"I haven't either. Honestly, I didn't know what type of reaction she'd have to seeing her mother again. She was pretty ticked when I left, but the woman was being a hag. I was worried, though, that Joanie would calm down and end up letting Grace walk all over her."

"Apparently not." Cody motioned to the phone Nick had in his hand again. "She hasn't called you, then?"

"No. But she sleeps late."

"Her store opens at ten."

Nick was very well aware of that. Fifteen minutes before the store opened. He couldn't imagine she wasn't up and about. "Lee Ann say anything else?"

"That Grace intends to take the house."

"What?" Nick would have come off his seat if he wasn't strapped in. "She's been gone for twenty years. What right does she think she has?"

"She's the daughter. Next of kin." Cody caught his eye. "There was apparently no will."

"*Shit.*"

"Yeah," Cody agreed.

"She planning to move back to town, then?"

"No. She wants it sold. She just wants the proceeds."

Nick's teeth hurt where he was grinding them together so hard. "Likely has no plans to pay off the bank loan either, huh?"

"If I were to guess . . ." Cody let the sentence linger. They both knew the answer. The woman would take all the proceeds and walk.

Most likely, though, the house would have been put as collateral for the bank loan. That would slow things down, hopefully not leave Joanie in the lurch if they couldn't keep the house from going to Grace outright. He'd call his lawyer and see what he could do concerning getting Joanie some help. She may have booted him out of her house last night, but that didn't mean he would turn away from her now.

His cell rang and he had it off his belt in record time.

"Joanie?" He sounded too anxious.

There was a slight pause before she said, "Good morning, Nick."

"Why didn't you call last night?"

"I uh, went to bed, instead. She didn't come to the house, did she?"

"No," he said. "And if she shows up, I'll kick her out."

"It's her house, Nick. I'm not sure you can do that."

"It isn't her house until a judge rules it is. I'm calling my lawyer Monda—"

"Don't," she interrupted. "I can take care of it myself. Don't call anybody. I have a lawyer I'll use."

"My guy's good. We'll get it tied up so she can't just walk."

"Don't, Nick. I don't want you to."

Her tone had a strange finality to it that he didn't like. What had been said in that house after he'd left? "Don't want me to what, exactly? Are we only talking about calling the lawyer?"

There was silence and he could picture her on the other end, blinking as she tried to figure out how to let him down. Something her mother had said must have scared her, convinced her to back off. She was retreating behind the damn curse.

And she was about to dump him over the phone!

"Are you kidding me, Jo?" he asked, not waiting to hear what she had to say.

"I just think . . ." she started. He heard a little sigh and then she finished with, "Everything has moved so fast. Maybe we just need to slow down a bit."

"No," he said. "Slowing down is not what we need to be doing. Cody and I are in Atlanta already, but I'll be home tonight, tomorrow at the latest. I'll come over when I'm back and we'll talk."

"I don't think that's a good idea. I just need some time to think. You're heading back to Nashville soon."

"What you need is to get that woman out of your head. I'll come over."

"No." The word was not spoken hesitantly. "Don't. You're a good guy and all, but I—"

"Don't you fucking tell me I'm a good guy, but not the kind of guy you want. Don't *even* say it."

"That's not—"

"Save it," he snapped. "I don't want to hear your crap. Just like you didn't want to hear that I love you." He was yelling now. "Well, guess what, sweetheart? That's too damned bad. I do love you. Deal with it."

He hung up the phone and threw it in the floor before he could say any fool thing else to her. Sheesh, how big a mess could he make of things? He rubbed his temples with one hand. Joanie was going through a crisis, for crying out loud. And he had to go and push. Of course she would push back.

The vehicle turned off Peachtree and Cody lifted a brow. "That seemed to go well."

"I'm a blooming idiot."

"It wasn't me who said it."

"Shut the fuck up."

They drove in silence, Nick thinking about how he should have stuck to their original plan. Sex only. No emotions. Hell, he should have just screwed Gina when he'd had the chance, and never gotten involved with Joanie.

He dragged his hand through his hair, knowing that for the lie it was. He no more could have gone to bed with Gina than he could have not fallen in love with Joanie.

"What is it with women, anyway?" he asked. "Do they learn at an early age how to screw with a guy? Is there a class taught on it? Or are they just born that way?"

Cody laughed. "One often wonders what the reward is for putting up with them."

Nick eyed his brother. "So you're not sure about Lee Ann, then?"

"Oh, hell. I'm positive about Lee Ann. My life would be shit without her. But that doesn't mean she doesn't drive me insane most of the time."

"Yet it's worth it in the end?"

A wicked look covered his brother's face. "Oh, yeah." He pulled into a parking lot and shot Nick a lecherous grin. "Think about the best time you've had with Joanie, then compare that to every other woman you've ever met. Which do you want again?"

There was no question. Both in bed and out.

"How do I make it happen?" Nick asked.

"First, you don't go off half-cocked when the girl is working through some heavy stuff."

"I probably need to call her back and apologize."

"No," Cody stated. "Let her be, man. Whatever you say right now doesn't matter. She's messed up. She's scared. And she's seeing herself in everything her mother has done. She's trying to figure out if she can trust who she is, as well as you. Hopefully she'll see what she has and make a commitment for once."

"To me?"

"To you. Her store." He turned off the truck and pulled out his keys. "She's run scared her whole life. Pushing isn't what she needs right now."

Nick sat there silent. He knew that, he just couldn't seem to help himself. He could make her see that what they had was real.

"It's not what you need, either," Cody added.

Nick looked at him.

"You want it to be good, right?"

Nick nodded. "Of course."

"Then you need her full commitment. Not just because you're pushing so hard she has no time to think about it."

What his brother said made sense, though Nick found the idea hard to put into action.

"You and I worked because when you barged into my life, I'd just figured out I was looking for the same thing. She's different. She's not there yet. Give her time or you'll lose her for good."

This was a part of brotherhood he'd always wanted but had never expected to get. He nodded, knowing Cody was right. Joanie was on the cusp of walking and there wasn't a thing he could do to alter her decision. She had to work through what she wanted, and hopefully come to him at the end. He had to let her go to see what happened.

"Love is shit," he muttered.

Cody laughed and clapped him on the shoulder. "That it is, man. That it is."

They stepped from the truck and Nick eyed the high-rise across the street, taking in the many floors. They hadn't attempted to contact him before coming down, deciding instead to approach him cold to get a more honest reaction. It was how Nick had met Cody, and that had turned out okay.

"Looks like our brother is some sort of big shot." Nick spoke first.

Cody stood beside him. "I'm beginning to think we should have called. What are the chances he'll actually be here?"

"What are the chances we'll be able to get through security, much less up to his condo?"

They hurried across the busy side street and made their way to the building. The first entrance merely dumped them into a wide, circular driveway with a gazing pool and fountain in the center. Valets waited by the doors. It was a different world than Nick was used to.

Nick nodded at the attendant as the man whisked open the wood-framed door for them, and they entered the lobby. What they found inside confirmed what had only been hinted at from the street. Their brother was loaded.

Elegant, rich leather seats and bronzed side tables dotted the marble-floored lobby. Heavy molding covered the walls, framing muted light fixtures and abstract art. It was ten on a Saturday morning and people were coming and going, but everyone remained silent or spoke in hushed tones, the elegance of the space overshadowing everything else.

Nick and Cody headed to a curved desk where a concierge waited to help, and Nick whistled under his breath. "Never wanted to live in a condo like this but I've got to admit, it's impressive."

The investigator had revealed their brother's name to be Zachary Winston, adopted by Janet and Randolph Winston. The couple had been nearing forty, childless, and had paid a hefty sum to be parents. Late father a doctor, mother still alive. The mother lived in a suburb outside Atlanta where Zack paid her bills and provided for every imaginable need.

Zack had grown up to be a fast-talking, big-client, climbing-the-ladder defense attorney for one of Atlanta's largest firms. He seemed as far removed from Nick and Cody as Nick could imagine.

"May I help you, sir?"

Nick hung back, contemplating the differences in all their lives as Cody took the lead. One adopted by a well-to-do family, another bounced around from foster family to foster family, and the third growing up in a bug-laden apartment with a drunk for a mother.

Yet in the end, all of them—seemingly—had turned out okay. Funny how that worked.

Cody turned to Nick, a humorous look in his eyes. "He says Mr. Winston doesn't like being disturbed before two on Saturdays. For any reason."

Nick peered around his brother to take in the slight man behind the desk. He wasn't the type Nick would want guarding him or his property, but he imagined the cameras dotting the lobby hid much larger guys who could easily stop two crazed men making a run for the elevators. Nick stepped beside Cody. "Two, huh? Must have a heck of a Friday night regimen."

The man touched the brim of his hat. "He does, sir."

"Hmmm." Well hell, what did they do now? Nick took in the man's name tag. "Frank?" he said.

"Sir?"

"We have a little problem here. You see, we drove in from out of town, and it's very important that we see him."

Frank nodded as if understanding.

"We're his brothers." Cody added. "Brothers he doesn't know about."

"Wouldn't you think if Mr. Winston knew he had two long-lost brothers stop by, he'd be a bit upset you hadn't woken him?" Nick finished.

The nodding stopped as a puzzled expression covered the man's face. "He and his date were out very late last night, sir." He lowered his voice to a whisper. "I was told they didn't make it in until daylight."

Nick glanced at Cody. "Going to bed about the time we left? Definitely a different lifestyle."

"If he has a woman up there, they probably didn't get right to sleep." Cody grinned at both Nick and Frank. "If we're lucky, he hasn't even been to bed. Call him up, won't you, Frank? See if he's got a few minutes."

"Oh no." A firm shake of Frank's head followed up his words. "I value my job, sir."

Nick sighed and held up his cell phone. "Fine. We have his number. We'll call."

The man's eyes bulged. "You have his number? It's private."

"Yep." Nick was finished playing by the rules. They hadn't driven this far to be turned away at the door. He pulled up the number the detective had given them and placed the call. It went immediately to voice mail. Nick hung up. "Voice mail."

Frank shrugged as if he'd known that would be the case. Before any of them had time to speak again, a woman's voice yelled from near the elevators, shattering the peaceful morning. "Frank! Get me a cab!"

Frank hurried toward the woman. She wore an expensive cream-colored turtleneck and matching pants. Her jewelry was chunky but pricey, and her boots reminded Nick of something Joanie might wear. Sky-high heels. He tilted his head and took in her legs. Nice, but no match for Joanie.

"Frank!"

"Right here, ma'am." Frank reached her and relieved her of a heavy-looking bag. Nick didn't know if it was a purse or luggage, but it didn't seem to matter. "I have your cab waiting, ma'am."

"What do you mean 'waiting'? You didn't know I was leaving so soon." Her voice was half-slurred, and half an octave only dogs should hear. "Are you trying to imply something, Frank? I can have your job, you know?"

"No, ma'am." Frank hurried her toward the doors, seeming frantic to get her out of the building. "Not implying anything. We routinely have cabs waiting around the clock."

"Hmph." She calmed enough to shut up, but as she reached the door, she lasered her gaze on Nick and Cody. Her eyes widened a fraction and then narrowed to beady, black orbs. "Assholes!"

She marched outside and let Frank put her in a cab. When he returned, the man's shoulders slumped in exhaustion. He didn't immediately make eye contact.

"Should we know her, or does she call everyone that?" Cody asked.

Frank gave them a genuine smile. "You two look a lot like your brother."

"Ah, the infamous girlfriend."

Frank looked embarrassed, but nodded in acknowledgment. "I don't know how he puts up with her."

"Let me ask you something, Frank." Nick leaned on the granite slab of the high desk. "Do you keep cabs here around the clock?"

Frank's cheeks pinkened. "No, sir. Call for one about four hours after Ms. Claudia comes in."

"Does she come in often?"

"Often enough."

"Hmmm . . ." Nick considered their options. They could continue pushing the concierge—Nick was certain between the two of them they would get the man to help—or they could come back later. Given the fact Zack dated someone like *Ms. Claudia,* and fairly certain he hadn't had any sleep, Nick made a decision. He looked at Cody. "How about we check out the sights and come back around two?"

"Sounds like a plan."

A soft exhale sounded from Frank.

Chapter Twenty-Two

Joanie checked the time on the Barn's new kitchen stove as she paced. Ten minutes until five o'clock. The open house would be over soon. She grabbed a fresh-baked cookie off the platter Jane had kept continuously filled throughout the afternoon and turned, taking steady strides to the other side of the room, the heels of the boots she wore clicking on the floor. There were two couples still upstairs looking around.

It had seemed as if everyone she knew, and some she didn't, had shown up there today. Most just wanted to see what had been done to the place, but several, Joanie had noticed, were interested. Very interested.

Which had given her a headache.

Someone else was going to want her house and she would have to sell it to them.

Or worse, Grace would sell it to them.

Joanie clenched her free hand into a fist as she thought about the woman. Rumor was that she'd been traipsing about town earlier in the day, causing trouble any way she could, stooping so low as to stop in at the salon and mock Linda Sue's work. And to top it off, Grace had apparently not even bothered to visit GiGi's grave.

At least, the rumor was she hadn't been seen out there. Though Joanie had no idea who was keeping tabs on the Memorial Grounds just to see if Grace showed up.

Bert Wheeler and his wife, Betty, came down the stairs, smiling and nodding their heads. When Bert saw her, he turned in her direction.

"You weren't lying," he said, giving an appreciative whistle. "Nick did a bang-up job here. Me and Betty have been thinking about closing in our porch to make a nice den. We're thinking we might see if he can work us in."

Bert picked up one of Nick's business cards sitting out on the counter as Joanie nodded and smiled. She made the appropriate chitchat until they left, but honestly, she had no desire to talk up Nick's work today.

First, it could speak for itself. He was highly skilled and it showed.

Second, she was annoyed with him.

How dare he scream he loved her and then hang up? She just wanted a little break. They'd moved so fast, she had no clue what she wanted.

Then her mother had shown up.

Now Joanie was going to lose the house and owe a boatload of money.

Add to that, she'd started thinking she was the type to toss her life away and chase Nick back to Nashville.

It was all just too much.

She wanted to think about nothing until she met with her mother at the lawyer's office Monday. And she certainly didn't want to see Grace *or* Nick before then.

As for what she was going to do about Nick in the long run, she was backing off. They needed space. And he had to quit pushing. She wasn't the same person she'd been six weeks before, and honestly, she had no idea what she thought about that.

But she did know enough to know that she needed time to think.

If she went with her mother's experience, she should run from Nick. Push him as far away as she could. That way she wouldn't get hurt.

But she also wouldn't have Nick.

He'd been good for her. And she kind of liked the changes he'd inspired over the last few weeks. She had a cat she adored. She loved her job, loved that she'd created a business that represented both her and her grandmother. And she'd come closer than she'd ever imagined to reconciling with her grandmother before she'd passed.

Best of all, she wasn't going to sell Cakes.

Cakes made her happy. Life made her happy. And she hadn't even known she'd been unhappy.

She was also dating. Real dating. Which she kind of liked.

If they continued, she just had to make sure she didn't do things so wrong that it went from dating to stupid Bigbee behavior and everything would be fine.

She paced across the room again, anxious for the last couple to come down with Jane, and for all of them to get out of her house.

When they did finally make it down, Joanie was polite, smiling and speaking when necessary, but practically shoving them out of the house. The minute they set foot onto the porch, Cat zipped in from outside, and she threw the deadbolt, then turned to collapse against the heavy wood. Cat came over for some loving and she scratched him on the back of the neck.

She liked her life.

And she liked Nick.

She sighed, thinking about that. It was more than "like," and she knew it. But she wasn't supposed to be thinking about Nick right now. It was a Nick-free weekend.

Only, she had no idea how to spend the remainder of the evening.

Lee Ann had invited her over, letting her know that the boys wouldn't be back from Atlanta until tomorrow, but she wasn't in the mood for company. She thought about the boxes sitting on her living room floor.

She could go through those.

But what if she found something that made things even worse?

Or proved even more how unhappy GiGi had been?

Joanie didn't know what she expected to find, but that unknown had kept her from going through everything. She just didn't want to know that GiGi had been more miserable than Joanie already thought she had been. Today, however, seemed the time for facing it all. No one else was going to do it for her.

Making a decision, she nodded and grabbed her car keys. Nick wouldn't be around tonight, so she'd pack everything up and haul it back out here. It might be the last night she had the opportunity to spend the night in the house. It would also be the only time she'd ever spent there alone.

Other than that fateful weekend when she'd lost her virginity.

Stupid boys. She still couldn't believe she'd given in to him back then, but it had quit bothering her long ago. Life was all about lessons learned.

She hurried home, then dragged the boxes out to her car, muttering about the absurdity of wagging these same three boxes all over the place. Once she'd loaded them in her car, she grabbed Bob and an overnight bag, then locked her door and headed back out to GiGi's. Bob had learned from Cat that it was fun to sit on the dash, so that's where he immediately went. Joanie couldn't help but feel a lump in her throat as she looked at him. She missed Nick.

She got to the house and unloaded the boxes yet again, but only made it so far as the porch. The swing was inviting, and seeing it made her feel good. She'd dig through the boxes there.

When she went back to the car for her overnight bag, she noticed the handle of a canvas tote poking out from under her passenger seat. Pulling it out, she found the metal box she'd retrieved from the cabinets the first night she'd been here with Nick, its small lock still in place. She'd taken the box to her last visit with GiGi, but after the emotional exchange between the two of them, she hadn't asked her grandmother about the key.

If she didn't find it in everything stashed on the porch, she would figure out a way to cut the lock off. She had a feeling some of Pepaw's possessions that he hadn't taken when he'd left were stashed inside. Maybe things that had meant something to GiGi. Joanie wanted to know what they were.

She settled onto the swing and dragged the first box over to her.

Three hours later, more than tipsy and heading toward drunk on the bottle of whiskey she'd remembered was still in GiGi's kitchen, she moved to the final box. She'd turned the outside light on a while ago and felt like she was in the spotlight every time a car passed, but she couldn't say she cared. It was turning out to be one heck of a relaxing night, and she was enjoying it.

Most of what she'd worked through so far had been the owls that GiGi had kept in her room, or random paperwork Joanie hadn't run across at the house. Such as the deed to the house.

There was the original title to the car GiGi had owned thirty years ago. Joanie had sold it for junk two years before, just to get it out of the way. There had been a handful of other important documents located in the piles of paper as well, but most of it had just been junk: notes from nurses at the home, weekly menus, randomly scribbled notes in GiGi's unsteady handwriting.

The last box, from what she could tell, held GiGi's clothes and bathroom supplies. As Joanie dug through it, she found one lone box under all the clothes. It was about five inches deep, and bulging at the seams. She pulled it out and moved a rocker over in front of the swing to prop her feet as she went through it.

She poured herself more whiskey and wondered why she'd been so worried about going through this stuff. She hadn't found anything that had come close to upsetting her. It was just GiGi's small world that she'd had at the nursing home. Nothing whatsoever that showed anything Joanie hadn't already known about her.

Until she removed the lid of that last box.

She stared down at the newspaper clippings, seeing article after article of herself. Some were from her teenage years, or even before, but many were from the last fifteen years after Joanie had moved out. There was the ribbon cutting at the first business she'd opened. That had been a small gift shop that still thrived on the square today. There was even one from her inaugural trip with the cupcake van.

Where had GiGi gotten the later newspapers?

Joanie paid the bills every month, and there had never been a subscription to the weekly paper being sent to the nursing home.

She found an envelope mixed in with the clippings and pulled it out, spilling a few of the articles on the concrete porch. Inside the envelope were letters from Beatrice Grayson. The woman who had told Joanie about GiGi's attempts at having children had been sending GiGi the articles since she'd been in Knoxville.

At first glance, Joanie wondered if it was just Ms. Grayson butting in, spreading gossip—or maybe returning the favor she felt she owed GiGi from years before—but then Joanie read one of the letters and realized GiGi had requested her to do this.

Pressure built inside Joanie's chest at the thought of her grandmother wanting to know what was going on in her life, and caring enough to keep the evidence of it. She'd thought for so long that GiGi hadn't cared, but this box implied differently.

Pain weighted her down. They'd missed out on so much. All because of her.

She dug on down past the articles and found several old pictures of Pepaw, and the tears began. Almost all were pictures of GiGi and Pepaw together from their younger days. Pictures where they were smiling and hugging. Where they were happy.

There were also photos of the three of them. The pride showing in her grandparents' faces was unmistakable. The few pictures that Joanie uncovered that included her mother mostly showed her sullen, her arms crossed, and Joanie couldn't help but wonder what made someone so unhappy with their life. She couldn't imagine being like that. It made her feel sorry for her mother to know she'd been that unhappy her entire life.

How had that made GiGi feel? Surely it had broken her heart as it was doing to Joanie's now. You couldn't bear a child and then not ache for her every time you saw her unhappiness, could you?

Maybe Grace could. That woman didn't seem to have a nice bone in her body. Joanie supposed some people were just made like that.

Her hand landed on an envelope containing a single folded piece of notepaper. She pulled it out, flutters going through her stomach before she unfolded the creases. When she had it open, her hand began shaking as she saw it addressed to her and written in GiGi's shaky scrawl. It was dated the day after Joanie's last visit.

Tears dripped unheeded down her face as she read GiGi's good-bye to her. She spoke briefly about being sorry she hadn't done better over the years. She'd been scared she would lose Joanie as she already had Pepaw and Grace, but she'd also lived with the guilt of knowing Grace hadn't come back because of her.

GiGi also apologized for begging Joanie to bring her home. She asked Joanie not to worry about having to say no. According to her grandmother, Joanie had done the right thing. GiGi had been where it was best for her. Where she could best be taken care of.

Just as she'd once put Pepaw where it was best for him.

Joanie's gaze froze on the words before going back and rereading them. What was she talking about?

She blinked, trying to clear some of the whiskey from her eyesight, then plowed through the rest of the letter.

Your Pepaw had his pride, Joanie. Too much of it. And in the end, it hurt us all.

He never wanted you to be ashamed of him. He wanted no one to be ashamed of him. And he couldn't stand knowing what was happening to him.

I didn't agree with his decision, but I loved him enough to do what he asked. And as requested, I never told a soul. Until today.

I'm so sorry his leaving hurt you. I wanted to do better for you, but his leaving hurt me, too. I wasn't strong enough to be all you deserved, and for that I apologize.

I've included a key. There's a box in the house, Joanie. It was your grandfather's from when he was a little boy. It explains everything.

Please forgive both of us for not being there for you.

I love you.

Joanie jerked the envelope out of the box where she'd dropped it and shook it upside down. A small, dulled silver key dropped to her lap.

She gaped. GiGi had had the key to the box.

GiGi ended the letter by saying thank you. For Joanie being the granddaughter she was. She'd apparently given GiGi many proud years.

Tears landed on the bottom of the paper, smearing the ink, but Joanie got it out of the way before too much damage was done. She flattened the note out on the chair in front of her, then scooped up Bob when he padded onto the porch. It was as if he'd sensed and understood her pain. Cat followed not far behind, and soon she was sitting, legs stretched out on the swing, a cat snuggled into either side of her, and a small key in the palm of her hand.

She took a moment to close her eyes and simply listen to the night, enjoying the quiet of it. It was beautiful out there.

She dropped her head to the swing and let the pain wash over her. She missed her GiGi. She'd missed her for almost twenty years, but tonight was the worst. She wanted her back, if only for a few minutes. She wanted to make sure the woman knew how much she'd been loved. How much Joanie regretted how things had been.

She cut her eyes over to the tote she'd pulled from the car. It was tossed on the porch, up against one of the rocking chairs Nick had bought. There was something in that bag that would explain why Pepaw had left. Without looking, Joanie understood deep in her heart that the love she'd read in his letters to GiGi was real. They'd had something unique. They'd loved each other completely. Forever.

It had been so different than anything Joanie had ever witnessed between her mother and her selection of men.

Shoving papers out of the way, she suddenly couldn't get to the box fast enough. She didn't even take it back to the swing. Just sat on the porch beside the bag and pulled the box out.

The key fit smoothly and turned in her hand to make one small *click*.

Then she had the lid up and was peering down into a small collection of sentimental valuables.

The first thing she pulled out was a death certificate. She studied it, learning that her grandfather had died of pneumonia.

Beneath that was Pepaw's Purple Heart. He'd gotten it trying to save GiGi's brother. Joanie pressed it to her chest before laying it and the death certificate carefully on the concrete beside her.

Next was a folded birth certificate for Anthony William Bigbee. Their son.

If felt as if the wall of her chest was going to cave completely in on her heart as she read the details of her uncle's fleeting existence. She couldn't imagine all the hurt her grandparents had gone through together.

Closing her eyes, she said a silent prayer that if she was ever confronted with such obstacles in her life, she'd have the strength GiGi and Pepaw must have carried to overcome such tragedy. No doubt they'd leaned heavily on each other for support.

More tears rolled down her cheeks, but she didn't wipe them away. She reached for the small black-and-white photograph lying inside the box.

It was of her grandparents when they were very young. She'd seen old pictures of them before, and GiGi couldn't have been much more than eighteen in this one. They were standing in front of a wooden beam.

She scanned the details in the murky background, and if she wasn't mistaken, made out a bale of hay. Possibly another with a blanket thrown over it. And a small handful of flowers lying on the ground.

She then took in their clothes. It looked like they'd been wearing their Sunday best. But were they in a barn?

Joanie flipped the photograph over, trying to figure out what it meant, and a small piece of yellowed paper floated to the ground before her. It had been taped to the back of the photo, though the adhesive had long disappeared.

She picked it up, barely able to make out the thin scrawl under the piece of tape on top.

November 1, 1953

Which meant GiGi had been only seventeen.

And then she realized what this was. November first was the day her grandparents had gotten married. She squinted to make out the other words on the paper.

The old barn on the Bigbee farm. Our honeymoon.
We shared it with a pair of owls.

Joanie turned the picture back over and looked at her grandparents.

They hadn't had a lot of money, but they'd made a romantic spot for their honeymoon. And then they'd named the home they'd made in its honor. The Barn.

Wow.

She wished she'd known all this about her grandparents as she'd been growing up. Then again, she wished her grandfather hadn't left.

One more item remained in the box. It was a single piece of paper folded over on itself. When she opened it, she discovered a document GiGi had signed when she'd checked Pepaw into a veteran's hospital facility in 1988. That was the year he'd left. He'd been diagnosed with early-onset dementia.

GiGi's words came back to her. *He didn't leave me. He was a good man.* And then the note Joanie had read tonight. *He wanted no one to be ashamed of him.*

Pepaw had been an upstanding citizen and a good husband. He'd been honored by the town for his service. But he had been a hard man. And he'd apparently not wanted to be remembered as someone who went out by losing his mind.

So he'd made GiGi put him in a home?

It was hard to understand that kind of pride, but she supposed in his weakened state, he might not have realized what it would do to her and GiGi.

She couldn't imagine the town thinking that he'd walked out on his family was any better than knowing he'd lost control of his faculties, though. But she got that men were different. And especially men of that generation.

Joanie stood and went back to the swing, taking the document with her, her heart empty. She'd missed the last seven years of his life because he'd been too proud to let the world see the disease that had taken hold of his body. But also, if she were to guess, because he hadn't wanted Joanie to see him like that.

She grabbed the letter from GiGi and scanned it.

He never wanted you to be ashamed of him.

Yep. He hadn't wanted his only granddaughter to see him go crazy. Life was too damned complicated.

She stretched out on the swing, her feet dangling off the end, and put both pieces of paper on her stomach. Bob returned and jumped up to sit in the middle of the papers. Joanie merely chuckled. She loved her cat.

As they both lay there, she reached down and grabbed a handful of the newspaper clippings she'd pulled from GiGi's last box, going through them again. The articles spanned her entire life. GiGi had not only cared enough to save them—and get the later ones secretly sent to her—but she'd taken the earlier ones with her when she'd first moved to Elm Hill. Joanie could have never guessed she would have done that.

When she reached back for more, her fingers landed on something thicker. She pulled it out, squinting at the words on the front of the tri-folded document. It was several pages thick and looked to be a . . .

She bolted upright, causing Bob to flee from the porch. Oh my goodness. It was a will! Dated earlier this year.

Oh, crap. GiGi had a will.

Joanie flipped through the pages, noting it was written up by a lawyer out of Knoxville whom she didn't recognize, and witnessed by two of the nurses at the nursing home. It looked legit. Now it was just a matter of what it said.

Nerves had her fingers shaking as she flipped through the pages, knowing GiGi held very few possessions. Her house was pretty much it.

When she landed on the correct page, her heart stopped.

TO MY DAUGHTER, GRACE BIGBEE: THE BED THAT I BOUGHT HER FOR HER SIXTEENTH BIRTHDAY. IT'S THE CEDAR HEAD AND FOOTBOARD STORED IN THE GARAGE.

Joanie laughed out loud. It was the bed Nick had dragged up to the third-floor bedroom. That's all that was on the list for Grace.

To my granddaughter, Joanie Bigbee: I leave the Barn and the surrounding three acres, including every possession (other than the above-noted bed) found inside the home and on the property.

She dropped the papers. She was free. No more mother, no more worrying how long it would all get dragged out. She could put a stop to it right now.

Only, one thing bothered her. She turned to look at the glossy red shutters Nick had attached to the house, and took in everything she could see from her spot on the swing. She wanted the house.

She had to find a way to keep the house.

GiGi had wanted her to have it. And she loved it. She adored it, actually. Only, she still thought she might want to move to Nashville with Nick.

Also, she owed too much money.

Her shoulders sank.

The only way she could make the payments to the bank was to not have any other rental. She could move in here. But she still owed Nick at least that same amount.

Or she could move in with Nick and just make payments on this place. But then, it would sit here empty, and it needed a family to love it.

She sighed.

She had no idea what she wanted to do. Other than wave this piece of paper in her mother's face and tell her to take a hike. That, she was definitely going to do. But not tonight.

Tonight she was exhausted. She'd learned too much over the past hours, and had shed too many tears. Her heart was broken.

So tonight, she was going nowhere. She planned to sleep in her mother's bed up in the third-floor hideaway, pretend Nick was there with her, and imagine a life where she was able to keep all the people she loved.

Chapter Twenty-Three

Joanie stopped by the pharmacy to pick up aspirin for the hangover she was sporting—she'd ended up finishing the whiskey before she'd fallen asleep the night before—and to get the last of her pictures printed for her scrapbook. Next she was heading over to the diner. It would be crowded with the church crowd, but that was all right. She had nowhere in particular to be, and it was a nice day. She just wanted to enjoy it.

The only real thing she needed to accomplish today was to find her mother, and give her the will. She was almost giddy with the anticipation of it.

As she walked down the aisles of the store, she passed several people, who all greeted her.

"Enjoyed seeing you sit out on the swing last night, Joanie," said Sam Jenkins. He was in his seventies, and a fixture around town. His dog sat at his heels. "Used to see you and Georgia out there most nights as I headed home from work. It looked right, seeing you out there like that."

Joanie smiled at him. "Thanks, Sam. It was a nice way to end the evening."

"Saw your mother hanging around town yesterday, too," he added. "That didn't look right."

Joanie couldn't help it. She laughed at his droll tone. She petted his dog on the head and gave him a good scratching when his tail slapped against the floor. "She cause any trouble you know about?" she asked.

"Nah." Sam's dentures were loose and clacked as he spoke. "Just mouthing about how she's been getting the weekly paper for years and knows *everything* going on around here. I'll tell ya, for someone so bound and determined that we ain't nothing, she sure is awfully worried about us."

That had to be how she'd known GiGi had died.

"She say where she's been all this time?"

Bushy eyebrows popped high on his forehead. "Figured you might'a got that one out of her."

Joanie shook her head. "I didn't care so much to ask. Just curious."

"I'll sic Beatrice on it if you want to know. I'm sure she could find out."

Lee Ann's mother would never forgive her if Joanie went to Ms. Grayson before Reba for gossip. "No need, Sam." She patted his hand. "It's not a big deal. Grace will be gone soon, anyway."

"Oh yeah?" This came from Bert at the photo counter. "We got a bet going as to when, if you want in."

Joanie laughed. That was perfect. "Yes, Bert. In fact, I do want in. I'm feeling lucky with this one. I think I just might win."

She patted her purse where the will was tucked inside, knowing she had knowledge the others didn't, but there were no official rules saying she couldn't bet if she had insider information.

She put down her ten dollars, handed over her memory card, and paid for her aspirin and bottle of water. She then headed for the door, tossing Sam and Bert a wave. "See you later, boys. It's a good day to be in Sugar Springs, isn't it?"

"*Hmph*," she heard one of them mutter behind her.

Sam asked Bert, "Who has today?"

I have today, Joanie thought. She was running her mother back out of town just as soon as she could find her.

She stepped through the door and turned loose of it as Bert answered, "Probably not today. He didn't come back from Atlanta yet."

The door swung closed and she turned around to stare through it. Were they talking about Nick? What would he have to do with her mother leaving town? When she caught Bert's eye, both he and Sam ducked their heads, ignoring her.

Well, son of a gun. They were talking about the bet on her. They still thought she was going to fall victim to the curse?

Great. Way to squash a good mood.

She dumped three aspirin into her hand and headed across the street to get lunch, scowling as she went. As she stepped inside the diner, she couldn't miss her mother sitting in the center of the restaurant, yakking it up to whoever would listen. This was perfect.

Screw lunch, she had something else to do.

As she neared, she heard her mother putting down the fact that the town only had one stoplight, as well as the summer festival that had started to be advertised that week. It was more than a couple months away, but the town council liked to draw tourists back whenever they could, so they got the information out early.

Joanie couldn't believe someone would dis the Firefly Festival. No one else had synchronized fireflies like their area. Seeing the flashing light patterns match up over an entire hillside was an attraction that made the region unique.

What a heartless woman.

Marching up to her mother's table, she was taken aback by the flat look turned her way. How could someone dislike her own daughter so much? Joanie shook her head slightly. It made no sense, but the odder thing was, she didn't care. She felt free of her in a way she never had before, and she knew that once she showed her the will, she would likely never see her again.

Which was exactly what she wanted. Not because she hated her, but because she had no use for her. At all.

"I have something for you, Mother," she said.

"Did you get a buyer already? I heard it was a good open house." She smiled, the move unnatural-looking. "I'm counting on a top price, so we may not want to take the first offer."

The whole room had grown quiet. Every single person in the place seemed to be leaning toward them, not to miss a single word.

Joanie practically quivered with excitement. She reached into her bag and pulled out the copy of the will that she'd made. "Actually," she said. "You won't be getting any money."

Joanie slapped the will down on the table. "Unless you sell the bed that was left to you." She smiled, the expression containing as much love as her mother's. "That's all you got."

"What are you talking about?" Grace jumped from her seat.

The crowd closed in as Grace picked up the papers and started reading. When she got to the good part, she jerked her head up and shook the papers at Joanie. "This is fake," she shouted. "There was no will. You made this up yourself."

Joanie shook her head. "Not fake, mother. The house is mine. Should I help you pack your bags?"

"You ungrateful little—"

"Now, now, Ms. Bigbee." Brian had stepped out from the kitchen. He put an arm around Joanie's shoulders. "I'm not quite sure what you were about to say there, but I have the feeling it wasn't going to be too polite. I'm afraid I can't allow that."

Joanie tried to hide her smile.

"You need to back off, Brian Marshall."

"No, ma'am. You need to get your purse and get on out of here. I'm afraid you aren't welcome at this establishment."

Grace's cheeks flushed. "Does your mama know how you talk to your customers, boy?"

"My mama taught me everything I know." He picked up her purse and gripped her by the elbow. "Now let me show you the door."

The crowd quickly parted, leading a path to the door. When Grace and Brian got there, Grace looked back over her shoulder and spewed. "She always did love you more. That's why I left. She loved you so much I told her she could deal with you. Told her you were no better than me, though. You just pretend better. You don't even like these people who're protecting you."

The door closed on her as she continued to rant. Brian barred it so she couldn't come back in.

When he turned to face Joanie, the entire room turned with him.

"You okay?" Brian asked.

She nodded. She actually was. Her mother had it wrong, she was nothing like her. And thanks to GiGi, she hadn't had to spend the last twenty years of her life with Grace as an example.

Her mother was an idiot. Which explained her issues with men. Certainly not some lame curse Joanie had been teased with her whole life.

She smiled, looking around at all her friends and pulled in a deep, lung-filling breath. She had never been so good.

Now if only Nick would come home. She suddenly wanted to see him very much.

She'd just learned that she did know how to love.

And she wasn't going to lose her man without a fight.

"Not interested."

The blunt words caused Nick's fork to slip and clatter to the gold-trimmed plate in front of him. The intrusive noise echoed in the politely muted dining room, and he gave a tight smile to a frowning woman at a nearby table.

He and Cody had finally managed to catch up with Zack the previous afternoon on his way out of his building, but he'd looked at them both as if seeing two people who looked nearly identical to him—less polished, of course—meant nothing in the world.

Not completely discouraged, they'd left their cell numbers then hung around town for the night, hoping he'd change his mind. They'd been spot-on in waiting because the phone had rung at ten that morning.

"I can do dinner at eight if you want to meet."

The cryptic words had been most of the conversation, but here they were at the tail end of a meal at one of Atlanta's finest restaurants, working to convince Zack to visit Sugar Springs. The conversation throughout dinner had been more about the exquisite wine and the medium-rare elk tenderloins than about any of their pasts.

"I hope you'll reconsider," Cody said. As dinner had progressed, learning more about Zack's privileged upbringing, and realizing he had little interest in what had happened to either of them, Cody had shut down. Seeing him now reenter the conversation lightened Nick's mood. "We're not talking about moving there, of course," Cody pointed out. "Just visiting. It's small, but it's a good town."

"Cody spent a year there as a teenager, then came back a few months ago. That's where I found him." Nick sorted through a mental list of the town's highlights that might interest Zack, but crossed each of them off. Not because Nick thought they weren't good incentives, but because Nick found he had no desire to beg the man to give them a chance. They were all brothers, all equal. Even though Nick and Cody's upbringing hadn't been as prestigious, Zack was no better than them. The least they deserved was his respect.

Zack balanced his fork on the edge of his plate and settled his hands together in front of him. "Surely you two don't think there would be any reason I would want to visit. I'm not seeking long-lost family, and I don't need to see the backwoods of America to know that Atlanta is where I belong."

What an ass. Nick hid his irritation as Zack once again dismissed everything about them. "We thought you might enjoy spending some time with us." Nick shrugged. Nick had to return to Nashville, but he hoped to be back in Sugar Springs permanently soon. Assuming Joanie didn't thwart his plans. "Get to know us a little. We are your biological brothers, after all."

Zack peered at them both for two seconds before lifting his hand to a passing waiter. "Check please." He turned back to the table, his tone that of mild tolerance. "Forgive me if I don't have the same interest in jumping into some forced *brother bonding* that I can see you two have become quite good at."

Nick glanced at Cody and was taken aback at the anger he saw there. Cody had checked out. Nick couldn't blame him. If he wasn't so groomed to beg for love—

His thoughts came to a screeching halt. Groomed to beg for love? Did he really think that of himself?

He thought through all the times as a child he'd done whatever he thought would please his mother, trying to get her attention, hoping she'd do something that implied she loved him. In reality, she was a drunk and only cared if he cleaned up her vomit and brought her beer.

Suddenly, he didn't feel guilty about leaving her the way he had. He'd done nothing wrong. If he hadn't left, who knows how screwed up he'd be by now.

Then he thought about Joanie. She hadn't wanted to date him in the first place and yet, he'd done everything he could to force just that. Had that been him begging yet again? Close to it, probably, but that didn't mean he hadn't fallen in love with her along the way.

Dinner was over. He and Cody did not need this crap. He pulled his wallet out but Zack held up a hand. "Let me. It was, after all, my suggestion to dine here."

Zack pulled his own wallet from the inside pocket of his sports jacket, a gold crest pressed into the soft, black leather, and withdrew some bills. He threw down three hundreds and rose before either of them could say anything else.

"Gentlemen." Zack dipped his head but didn't offer to shake hands. "It was interesting meeting you. Now if you'll excuse me."

With that he walked away, leaving Nick and Cody sitting at the table, staring at the asshole's hundred dollar bills tossed carelessly on the table. Irritation threatened to erupt into what Nick was certain wouldn't be appropriate behavior in the trendy restaurant.

Cody picked up the bottle of wine and emptied it into Nick's glass. "I've got to drive, but no need letting this go to waste. It cost too damned much. Drink up, brother."

Nick picked up his glass and waved a silent toast, then chugged it as if it were a cheap bottle of beer. He managed to keep the belch inside, though. When finished, he looked at Cody. "Sorry I offered to buy you a kitchen." They were family without need of anything else. "You'll be getting a blender. If you ever want to upgrade, though, give me a call. I'll be glad to lend a helping hand."

A fast smile covered Cody's face. "Now that's what I'm talking about. *That's* what brothers do for each other."

Chapter Twenty-Four

J oanie sucked the thick chocolate shake through her straw, and enjoyed the feel of the warm water bubbling on her feet. She and Lee Ann had gotten shakes and come over to the salon for pedicures. She should probably be at the store preparing cupcakes for the coming week, but she'd been unable to focus since waking up that morning.

She'd stayed at the Barn again last night, wanting to surprise Nick when he returned, but he hadn't come home. Lee Ann had confirmed he and Cody had arrived back in town sometime after midnight. Their brother hadn't been interested in getting to know them, and Nick had stayed at Cody's instead of coming to her. Joanie didn't quite know what to make of that.

Worry had her chewing on her lip. Had she pushed him away too many times?

"Did you talk to Nick today?" she asked Lee Ann, who had her head leaned back and looked as if she was almost asleep. Her shake tilted at a dangerous angle. She'd admitted earlier that Cody had snuck over to the house for a while after the guys had gotten in last night.

"No." Lee Ann yawned. She lifted her cup and took a drink. "Cody said he said something about a job he had to take care of."

"Okay." Joanie let out a nervous little breath and caught Linda Sue smiling up at her from where she sat at her feet. The new girl, Katy, was taking care of Lee Ann, and gave her a sweet grin, too. Whatever was said there today would be out on the streets before she even left the building.

"Anyone know if Grace left yesterday?" she asked, not caring who answered, but certain at least one of them would know.

Lee Ann nodded, but didn't open her eyes.

Linda Sue spoke up, "Brian saw her drive away about thirty minutes after he kicked her out of the diner. I heard he went out the back when no one was looking so he could keep an eye on her. Wanted to make sure she left town." She sighed. "Isn't he the greatest?"

Joanie had to laugh. Brian had so many of the women twisted around his little finger. He was the greatest if you didn't get your heart involved. But he was the best kind of friend a person could ask for.

"Don't go there, Linda Sue," Joanie warned. "You don't want to try to tame that."

Linda Sue giggled and waved her hand. "Oh, honey. I'm aware of that. He went out with my sister once. But man, you should have heard her talk about him before he dumped her. Sweet Jesus, the things she said that man could do."

The door chimed. "The things who can do?" the newcomer asked.

Gina Gregory walked to the back of the salon and took in the four of them. Her eyes scanned over Lee Ann's comatose state, Katy working furiously to do a good job, Linda Sue fanning herself over thoughts of Brian, then stopped on Joanie.

Terrific. Gina had been pissed off at her for weeks. Wonder what she wanted now.

"We were talking about Brian," Linda Sue answered. "About the *things* he can do." She waggled her eyebrows.

Gina grinned. "I could probably add a few items to that list."

Sheesh. The guy had slept with everyone.

The five of them talked for several more minutes about Brian and a couple other men the ladies enjoyed looking at, then Gina turned to Joanie. "I heard there was a commotion at the diner yesterday that I missed."

"No commotion," Joanie said. "Just kicking my mother out of town."

"That's what I heard." She reached into her oversize purse and pulled out a small, but sizeable enough wad of cash. "Bert asked me to drop this off to you. It's your winnings. Apparently you were the only one who thought we'd get rid of her that soon."

Joanie leaned forward and took the cash. She would gladly accept the money.

"Course, I told him it seemed unfair to me. What with you having that will and all. Seems you had a leg up."

"Nothing says that's against the rules."

"*Hmph.*" Gina puckered her full lips. "Just don't seem fair, is all I'm saying."

She lowered herself into the remaining pedicure chair, looking for all the world as if she was going to stick around for a while, and Linda Sue returned to Joanie's toes. Conversation resumed about any and everything. When it turned to Joanie and Nick, they all seemed overly interested.

"So what exactly is going on with you two?" Gina asked.

"You still can't have him, Gina," Lee Ann good-naturedly warned the woman off.

"I never said I wanted him."

Everyone but Gina laughed.

"Like you didn't want Cody, either?" Lee Ann added, teasingly.

"Geez Louise," Gina finally admitted. "Who could blame me? Those boys are hot." Gina always called men who were younger than her "boys," even if it was only by a few years. "So what's the deal?" She leaned forward and stared pointedly at Joanie. "This gonna work out between you two, or what?"

Every head swung Joanie's way.

"I don't know. I haven't talked to him since he's been back in town."

"They had an argument," Lee Ann supplied. "He stayed with Cody last night."

"Oh, no." Linda Sue reached up and patted Joanie's knee.

"It wasn't an argument so much," Joanie began. Yes, it had been. She'd told him she needed time. He hadn't called her since.

She would tell him differently if she could just find him. She didn't want time. She just wanted Nick. She also wanted her house. Even if it meant she had to sell Cakes-a-GoGo to pay off a loan.

But she didn't want to tell these women all that before she told Nick.

"Also heard you had a breakthrough of sorts while at the diner yesterday," Gina tacked on. "Nick play into that?"

"What breakthrough?"

Everyone quietly watched except for Gina, who continued talking.

"Admit it. You're going to settle down with him, right? And you figured this out yesterday at the diner, didn't you?"

"She hasn't even talked to him yet, Gina," Linda Sue pointed out. "She can't know if they're going to stay together if he left on an argument and they haven't talked since."

"They didn't even talk on the phone all day yesterday," Lee Ann added.

"Wait," Joanie said. She held her hand up and looked from one pair of eyes to the next. "Why are you all so interested in what's going to happen with me and Nick? And why are you so worried about *when?*"

Every one of them shrugged and said, "Just curious."

"You all are so full of crap."

Silence.

Then she remembered the bet. The one where they were all betting on when she would fall victim to the curse.

"Do I mess everything up if I admit I don't believe in the Bigbee Curse?"

Linda Sue's eyes grew round while Lee Ann merely broke out in a happy little smile.

"Is there a particular reason why?" Gina asked.

"Nick, perhaps?" added Linda Sue.

Joanie looked from one lady to the other, still confused. "He might play into it." He had taught her how to love.

Gina squeaked. "And you figured it out yesterday?"

"What in the world does it matter?" Joanie asked. "The bet was for when I would fall victim to the curse. You all lost. There is no curse."

Lee Ann reached over and put her arm around Joanie's shoulders, giving her a tight hug. "It was for when you'd figure out you're insane about him, sweetie. And that you want him forever."

Well, hell. She slumped back in her seat, thinking about that one. They'd all figured out she was crazy about Nick before she did? She shook her head and looked at the women in the room.

"I can't believe you bet on that." Then again, it was Sugar Springs. "So you all think I should definitely be with Nick?"

Not that their opinions would change her mind. She had every intention of hunting that man down and making him hers. Permanently.

"Even I do," Gina said. "Though I would prefer if you told me you came to this decision yesterday."

Ah, Gina had yesterday.

Joanie looked around. "Who has today?"

"Brian." They all answered.

Hmmm. So, either her friend, or the woman who'd tried to seduce her man.

"What if Nick says no? Is the bet still good?"

They all eyed each other with confused expressions. Finally Katy, who had remained quiet throughout the whole exchange, spoke up. "That's not going to happen. Have you looked at that man when he's watching you? He's a goner."

Joanie couldn't stop the smile, and it seemed to spread to every one of the women. Now she just had to find her man.

Her cell phone rang and they all jumped.

"Maybe it's Nick," Linda Sue gushed.

Maybe. But no.

"It's Jane." Joanie answered, greeting the Realtor.

"So glad I caught you, sugar. We've got a deal."

The milkshake she'd been drinking grew heavy in her stomach. "Already?"

"Yes, aren't you excited? And it's a good one." The woman's voice was annoying.

Joanie frowned, then caught sight of all the women around her leaning a little closer. No doubt they could hear Jane's chirpy voice loud and clear. She swiveled in her seat, hoping they'd get the hint and back off. "How much?" she finally asked.

"Ten more than the asking price."

Joanie was stunned. She couldn't turn down an offer that was more than the asking price. Her eyes clouded over with tears.

"I'll bring the contract over today. The buyer wants to close soon."

They finished the call and Joanie hung up, once again facing the small crowd of women. She forced a shaky smile. "I got an offer on the Barn."

"That's a good thing, isn't it?" Linda Sue was the first to speak.

"No," Gina replied. "She wants to live in that house with Nick. Trust me, I saw her christening the place."

There were groans all around as Joanie sat there silent. It was a good deal. She'd be an idiot not to take it. And yes, she wanted to live there with Nick. But she'd take Nashville, as well. Wherever he was.

Only, she wouldn't sell her house.

"No," she said suddenly, pulling her feet away from Linda Sue so she could stand up. She had to go. "No, I don't want to sell the house."

"Your toes aren't done, Joanie," Linda Sue whispered as if reluctant to stop her.

Joanie looked down at her one painted foot, the polish glistening with a shine that could only mean they were still wet. "Then I'll just wear one shoe out, and come back for the other foot another time. I've got to go."

She had to find Nick. She had to stop this sale.

Nick heard a car door slam and looked out the window of the third-floor room. Joanie was home. Nerves began in his stomach as he reminded himself he would not push her for more than she was ready to give. He shoved the remainder of his clothes in his bag, and checked the room to make sure he wasn't missing anything.

The only personal items remaining in the house were the clothes that Joanie had brought over the last couple of days—he still wasn't sure what it meant that she'd stayed there while he'd been gone—and an old newspaper article he'd found about her out on the porch. He'd brought it in and laid it in the middle of the bed for her, along with the scrapbook he'd found on the bathroom counter. She'd apparently finished it. It, too, was lying in the middle of the bed.

"Nick?" she shouted from downstairs. Pounding feet followed the shout.

When the noise paused on the second floor, he yelled, "I'm up here."

He saw her peek her head around the base of the stairs, and he couldn't keep from grinning. The goofy grin he wore reminded him of the first time he'd spotted her in her go-go outfit. Christ, he'd missed her these last couple of days. She bounded up the steps, but came to a screeching halt, her gaze on the bag in his hand.

"You're leaving?" she asked.

"I . . ." He wanted to tell her he wasn't going anywhere without her, but that seemed like that pushing thing he was trying not to do. Finally, he nodded. "Thought I'd go on back to Nashville early. I signed a contract with the Marshalls today to build cabins on their property. I need to get a foreman lined up to get the work started."

Her chest rose with a deep breath. "Will you take me with you?"

The question stopped him cold. Moving away from Sugar Springs had to be the last thing she'd want to do. Plus, he'd learned from Cody that this house was hers, free and clear. Her mother only got the bed.

"No," he finally forced out. Her face fell with his word.

He would move to Sugar Spring to be with her, but he would never be the one to take her away. She belonged here. He belonged here, too. He just had to wait for her to figure that out.

"I'm getting out of your way," he told her. "You move in here. It's your house. Everything about it is you, sweetness."

Joanie took two steps forward, stopping within a foot of him. She smelled like warm maple syrup, and the tips of her hair were a light, golden brown. She also wore only one shoe. He couldn't imagine a world without her in it.

"I can't," she whispered. "I got an offer today."

He tried to show the right amount of surprise. "You could always reject it if you're not ready to sell. Take it off the market."

"What about all the money I owe? What do I do about that?"

He swallowed. He couldn't *not* offer, even if it was pushy. "I can loan you some more to cover the bank."

She took one more step, almost bumping him. "You'd do that for me? Even though I already owe you just as much?"

"I would do that for you," he stated.

"When would you want payment?'

He shook his head, intoxicated with the scent of her. "There's no hurry, babe. We can work out something."

"Because you love me?"

Ah, shit. What was he supposed to say to that? He needed Cody there for pointers.

"Do you love me or not, Nick?" Her voice trembled with her words and he dropped his bag to the ground to reach for her, but forced his hands to go no further than her upper arms.

"Of course I love you, sweetness. You know that. You've known that for a long time."

"Then why are you leaving me?"

He let out a shaky breath. "I'm giving you space. I'm not being pushy. I'm . . ." He shook his head. "Hell, Joanie. I'm giving you what you asked for. What else do you want from me?"

The woman drove him insane.

"I want you to marry me," she whispered. "If it's not too late."

When he gaped at her, she said, "Because I love you, too."

"Oh, babe." He closed the distance then, and put his mouth on hers.

Chapter Twenty-Five

Joanie stretched out in the bed her mother had apparently decided to leave behind, and smiled up at the ceiling. She and Nick had spent the afternoon making up for not seeing each other the last two days, and then they'd taken a nap. Now Bob and Cat were curled up in bed with them, with Nick stretched out on his stomach, one arm slung off the bed, looking to be out for the duration.

She rolled to her side, enjoying the view, and the fact that she got to wake him up for once.

She did it by leaning over and clamping down on his butt.

"What the . . ." Nick jerked away, but stopped when he saw where she was and what was going on. "You bit my butt."

"I did." She nodded. "I owed you one. Plus, you have a really nice butt."

It was a part of him she admired a lot.

He rubbed the spot on his rear where she'd tagged him and narrowed his eyes at her. "I'm pretty sure I didn't bite you that hard."

"You also didn't leave a hickey." She grinned. "But I did."

"You marked me?" He was wide awake now, and she could see that all of him was waking up. The man was ready to go at the drop of a hat.

"Only to make sure anyone looking knows you're mine."

He rolled to his back and pulled her over on top of him. "Sweetheart, anyone who's looking has known that for weeks."

"That's what Katy said."

"Who's Katy?" His hand swept up her back, making her purr like a cat. She stretched her neck out as he went to work nibbling at the base of it.

"She's the new girl at the salon. When we were talking about the bet today, she said that—"

"Wait. You know what the bet really was?"

She nodded. "You do, too?"

"Holly told me that day at the parade." He sucked a spot on her neck and made her wriggle against him. "That's why I kissed her. Though I'd do it again just to see your jealousy. That was hot."

"Sorry," she said. "I'm all out of jealousy. I know you're mine now."

He looked into her eyes, all joking gone. "And I know you're mine."

She caressed his cheek and gave him a light kiss.

"When did you find out about it?" he asked.

"Today. Given that they have to rely on my say-so as to when I decided that I want you forever, I basically get to choose the winner. I can either go with yesterday, which is *possibly* the correct answer. Or I can tell them it was today." She eyed him. "Given that everyone knows we argued and then didn't talk at all yesterday, they would believe me if I said today."

He slipped his hand down over her rear. "Who has yesterday?"

"Gina."

"Oh."

"Yeah. She tried to seduce you in front of me. I'm not sure I can give it to her."

He nodded in understanding. "Who has today?"

She gave him an evil grin. "Brian."

Nick growled at her and rolled them over so that she lay beneath him. "Gina wins."

"I don't know. I've got my money on Brian."

His mouth found hers and she moaned her approval. When he released her, she was out of breath, but ready for more.

"You do that really well," she said. "Even better, I think, than Brian."

At the expression on his face, she couldn't help the giggle that escaped.

"You wear jealousy well too, babe," she said. "And it makes *me* hot."

"I swear you're evil." It didn't sound as if he minded too much.

He started to kiss her again but she stopped him. "Let's talk about a few things first."

"Okay." He propped himself up on his elbows, but kept her underneath him. "Shoot."

"Your brother?" she asked. "The one in Atlanta. That's a no?"

"As of now, that's a no. He was a douche, so that's okay." He nuzzled the curve of her breast. "Next topic?"

"The house," she said. No way was she going to let someone take it away from her, but how bad was it going to look when she rejected an over-the-asking-price offer? "I don't want to sell it—though I'm going to feel like a heel telling the buyer no—"

"It was me," he said.

"You what?"

"Me. The one who put the offer on the house."

She pulled back from him so she could see him better. "Why?"

"So you didn't screw up and get rid of it before you came to your senses."

She sighed. "Okay, fine. But there's also the issue of the loans."

He rolled off her and scooted up to sit against the headboard. She followed him up.

"I owe both you and the bank a large amount," she continued once they were resituated. "I was thinking I could sell—"

"Not gonna happen," he said.

"What?"

He eyed her. "We're about to be married," he stated, his tone matter-of-fact. "You don't owe me anything."

"Nick, that doesn't feel right. You loaned it to me."

"And now I'm giving it to you. What's mine is yours, right?"

She studied him, still a bit overwhelmed at the changes in her life. She was going to share everything with this man. And she was going to love him forever. She supposed it only made sense that she let his loan to her be forgiven.

With a nip at her bottom lip, she gave him a small nod. "Okay, but I'll take care of the bank loan then. It seems only fair."

"And your solution is to sell Cakes?"

She gave a little shrug, hoping she didn't appear as helpless as she suddenly felt. "It's the only thing of value that I have."

"Do you actually want to sell the store?" he asked, his tone gentle and caring.

"No," she admitted. "I *actually* love it. But I can—"

He took her chin in his hand. "I'm going to be your husband, babe. I'll take care of the loan."

She let out a little sigh. "That just seems so wrong." She'd spent her life taking care of herself. It was hard to just turn so much of it over to someone else.

He got off the bed and went to the bag he'd dropped when she'd asked if he loved her. He rooted around in it while she enjoyed the view.

"Are you listening to me?" she asked, as he continued to dig. She had the feeling she was being ignored.

"I always listen to you, babe." When he stood up, he held a small box in his hand. It looked like a ring box.

"What is that?" her words were breathy.

"It's your engagement ring if you want it, but it comes with conditions."

"You got me a ring? We just decided to get married today."

He angled his head down at her. "Correction. You just decided today. Or actually yesterday, I guess. Gina wins. But I've known for weeks."

"When did you buy me a ring? And Gina isn't decided on."

"I got it this weekend." He sat on the bed beside her and linked his hand with hers. "I wasn't going to give it to you until you were ready. But I knew I was ready. So I bought it."

She eyed the box, finding herself giddy at the thought of seeing what was inside, but remembering what he'd said. "It comes with conditions?"

He lifted her left hand and kissed the center of her palm, and then the back of her ring finger, then he smoothed his thumb over the skin where the ring would go. "You have to let me take care of you." He lifted a shoulder. "Because that's what I do."

She nodded. "Okay." She kind of wanted him to take care of her. She liked it.

"That means I'll pay off the loan."

"Oh."

He smiled and waved the box back and forth in front of her face. "It's a really big ring," he teased.

"Nick, you're not being fair again." It seemed so wrong just to let him take care of it.

"I told you, sweetness, no one ever promised fair. I'm paying off this glorious house that the two of us are going to fill with babies, and you're not going to complain. You're not going to sell your cupcake business either. Or quit wearing the go-go outfits." He gave her a hard look. "Even though I'm going to continue being jealous of every man who looks at you in them."

Her heart filled with so much love, it felt it could burst. "We're going to live here?"

It had never occurred to her that he might move. She'd been too busy worrying about whether *she* could or not.

"There's no other place you belong," he told her.

She loved him so much. "I would move to Nashville with you," she said.

"I know you would." He stroked a finger down her cheek. "But we belong here."

She nodded. She wanted to stay there. In the Barn. With the love of her life. "Will you take the go-go outfits off of me when I get home?" she asked.

He lifted his brows. "The minute you walk through the door. But we're putting up curtains."

She laughed, the sound as happy as she was inside. "Okay, Pushy. If you insist, you can pay off the loan." She held out her hand. "Now give me my ring."

"There was actually one more condition."

She snatched her hand back and shot him a glare. "Do I get to make conditions, too?"

"No." He shook his head.

"Not fai—"

His pointed look stopped her. She supposed life wasn't fair. But she did have her man. "What's the condition?"

He leaned forward and kissed her, his tongue making promises she was ready to get to. When he ended it, he whispered against her mouth. "That you at least *try* to fight the urge to keep everything in the world like your grandmother did. Your mini-hoarding thing you've got going on is cute, babe, but you've got to keep it under control."

She smiled against his mouth. Not just because she was happy with him, but because she knew she was more her grandmother than she'd ever been her mother. Most of all, she was herself. A little odd, a big heart, and a slight tendency to hoard.

"You'll still love me if I fail?" she asked.

"I'll still love you if you fail." He opened the box and pulled out a huge emerald-cut diamond. As he put it on her finger, he said, "But I'll still throw your stuff away."

ACKNOWLEDGMENTS

Acknowledgments must go out to a couple people, without whom this book wouldn't be what it is today. To Lindsay, I very much appreciate all the scrupulous editing that caused me to bang my head against the wall in frustration. I know without a doubt that the book is far better from having you be a part of it.

And to Gretchen, thank you for our day of epiphanies. Everyone should have a friend who'll take a whole day to help them figure out just what is wrong with their characters, and how much more agony you can toss at them. Joanie, Nick, GiGi, and Pepaw *would not* be the same without you!

Also, a quick thanks to my cousin Janette for reminding me of the milk can that sat on Mema's and Pa's front porch for so many years.

And special thanks to those who make cupcakes. The world is a much better place with you in it!

ABOUT THE AUTHOR

© 2012 AMELIA MOORE

Award-winning author Kim Law wrote her first story, "The Gigantic Talking Raisin," in elementary school. Although it was never published, it was enough to whet her appetite for a career in writing. First, however, she would try her hand at a few other passions: baton twirling, softball, and music, to name a few. Voted "Bookworm" and "Most Likely to Succeed" in high school, she went on to earn a college degree in mathematics. Law spent years working as a computer programmer and raising her son, and she now devotes her time and energy to writing romance novels (none of which feature talking raisins). She is a Romance Writers of America's RITA finalist, a past winner of the RWA's Golden Heart Award, and currently serves as president for her local RWA chapter. Her books can best be described as a lighthearted mix taking her readers on a sexy, fun, and emotional ride. A native of Kentucky, she now lives with her husband and an assortment of animals in her Middle Tennessee home.